LEE BATTERSBY

THE MARCHING DEAD

WITHDRAWN

ANGRY
ROBOT

ANGRY ROBOT
A member of the Osprey Group

Lace Market House,
54-56 High Pavement,
Nottingham,
NG1 1HW, UK

www.angryrobotbooks.com
Rather be dead than cool.

An Angry Robot paperback original 2013
1

A catalogue record for this book is available
from the British Library.

ISBN: 978 0 85766 289 7
Ebook ISBN: 978 0 85766 291 0

Set in Meridien by Argh! Oxford

Printed and bound by CPI Group (UK) Ltd, Croydon, CR0 4YY

To my Bonus Boys, Aiden and Blake
as they prepare to set out across
their own adult landscapes.
Leap then look, boys.
What could possibly go wrong?

ONE

The day was perfect, as had been the day before, and the day before that. The sun rose early over the low-lying hills on the horizon, and the shutters on the cottage had been thrown open before breakfast to let the morning heat fill the white-painted rooms. Outside, bees buzzed happily through the waves of flowers that spilled out of the gardens and across the empty fields towards the hills, and migrating birds wheeled and floated in the updrafts above, painting the perfect blue sky with the sweep of their magnificent wings. The only sound that broke the serenity was the pitch-perfect singing of Keth, former dancing girl at the Hauled Keel Tavern as she ran out the kitchen door and into the perfect, perfect day, a wicker basket swinging below her arm as she waved and blew kisses towards the bedroom window. On the windowsill, a fat tortoise-shell tomcat named Alno yawned and stretched in the warmth, his sleek coat glowing in the sunlight. He swung a paw at an imaginary victim, enough so that it might have been mistaken for a wave goodbye, then settled back into sleep. Keth giggled and turned away from the perfect little cottage, running through the perfect fields of flowers towards the perfect line of the perfect hills, where she planned to spend the perfect morning picking perfect berries with which to make the perfect lunch. Everything was perfect. Just perfect.

Marius don Hellespont was so bored he could shit.

It had been three years, three interminable years since he had delivered on his promise and made things right with Keth. She had been living in a single room above the tavern in which she danced, and he had insulted it – insulted *her* – and everything she had fought and scratched and humiliated herself to acquire. It was a stupid moment, something he specialised in. She had responded by itemising every promise he ever made to her, and the one hundred per cent success rate in breaking them. It took losing her, not to mention losing his life for several months, before he realised what she meant to him, and how much he needed to win her back.

And he had done it. Not with empty apologies and facile gestures, but by doing what he had always promised to do some day: settle down, leave behind a life of petty larceny and confidence tricks, make some honest money and give her the life of peace and tranquillity she deserved. He did it for her.

And hated every bloody moment of it.

It hardly seemed fair that he should hate the payoff as well. But there it was: surrounded by everything that made the love of his life happy, he couldn't find a single damn thing to *do*. Marius was a creature of the city, or at least, of those parts of a city that represent the greatest thrill: the back streets; the illegal gaming rooms; the palace hallways. Anywhere a deal could be made, or a con was in play, or a margin for error could be exploited. That was his natural habitat. Even when he tried honest work – and for Keth's sake he had tried, oh, how he had *tried* – he somehow ended up in the darkest corner of the workshop, running a penny ante game between shifts. No matter how she might like to believe it, cottages in the country weren't bought by dockworkers. Not unless they were dockworkers like Marius, and could sniff out a game of Kingdom from a thousand yards, and a wide-eyed rube from even further.

But here, in these wide-open spaces, there were no shadows, no corners, and no angles. Just flowers and berries for lunch and big, fat, stupid cats grinning at him from the windowsill. Marius scowled at it. Oh, for just one street market vendor short of meat and willing not to ask too many questions. He sighed, staring out the window at Keth's perfect buttocks slowly disappearing through the flowers. When he couldn't see them any longer, and had them firmly fixed in his memory, he leaned back in his chair, yawned, and stood. Maybe it was time to get dressed, at least. There was only so long a man could lounge around the house in his undershirt before the love of his life began to suspect he wasn't quite as busy as he'd been making out. He ran a hand down Alno's back.

"Another day in fucking paradise," he said, and pushed the cat out of the window. It landed between the stickprickle bushes he'd planted there specially to catch it, hissed at him, and darted away beneath them before he could find a boot to throw. He watched it cut a purposeful swathe through the flowers, and sighed again. It would spend all day hunting mice, he supposed. Gods. Even the *cat* had something to do. Maybe the Blind Pig had opened its doors. He smiled. The cottage was a mile or so outside the nameless village for which the Blind Pig was combination post office, law court, and – most importantly – boozer. Keth would be gone all morning.

Marius held his hand in front of his face and concentrated. Slowly, his flesh lost its pink tones, drying out and shrivelling until it lay grey and tight across his bones. He glanced over at the brass mirror nailed next to the bed. His face, dead and pockmarked, stared back with blank white eyes. Dark skin faded to a dull grey, and teeth grinned at him through lips that lay black and peeling against them.

He had learned the trick four years ago, during that period he tried only to think of as "back then". Back then it had been forced upon him by the vengeful dead. They had mistaken him for their lost King, God's representative on Earth, the voice they needed to remind Him that they existed and were waiting to be harvested and carried aloft on shafts of gold to their eternal reward blah blah blah bullshit. Then their mistake became clear to them, and they inflicted this withering half death upon him as the weregild he had to pay for not being the monarch they needed. Now, it was a useful trick and nothing more. A mile between the cottage and the tavern, for example, might take him six minutes to run, but as a living man he'd spend over an hour catching his breath every hundred yards, pulling up lame with a stitch or a twinge in his calf, or just plain vomiting. But the dead did not need to catch their breath, and they never vomited. Without his ability to switch between normal human frailty and the untiring muscles of the dead, there was no way he'd be sinking his first pint of the morning within seven minutes, and he'd never be back in time to pretend he'd been digging that visitor's privy he'd been promising for two weeks. Leaning across, he took a final glance through the window, just to make sure Keth hadn't forgotten anything and come back. And frowned.

Cats don't normally run in straight lines. If forced to run at all, they do so in short bursts – enough to show that they could escape you any time at all, and that it would be far better for all concerned if you just gave up pursuit right now. Cats are bastards, and will never knowingly pass up an opportunity to taunt you. There is nothing more ludicrous than the sight of a fully grown human stumbling after an animal that saunters to a stop every six feet just to lick itself and make sure it's still being chased, and the furry little shits know it. That's why they do it. At least, Marius was pretty sure it was why Alno did it to *him*. Cats certainly never picked the shortest journey between A and anywhere else if they could help it.

But Alno was doing just that. Marius could see the flower heads waving as he raced through them. The cat had left the house behind and was tearing at top speed across the open field beyond, straight towards the spot where Marius had watched Keth's buttocks finally disappear, almost as if...

Before Marius was even conscious of doing so, he had placed his foot on the desk and propelled himself through the window. His heel caught the edge of the windowsill and sent him tumbling into the stickprickle bush below, but he barely noticed. He rolled forward, made his feet, and was off at full pace, through the little gate that bounded their yard and out across the field at a flat run. He caught up to Alno in half a minute, scooping him up without breaking stride. Alno twisted around in his grip, swung a paw at his chest in annoyance, then stopped. Slowly, he stared up at Marius' face, sheathed his claws, and curled back around so he lay more comfortably along the length of Marius' arm.

Marius cursed himself as he ran. Something was

wrong. He should have noticed, he should have *seen*. No matter that he had only the cat's behaviour to go on, or that outwardly the world remained as it had been all morning: shining sun, buzzing bees, gentle breeze. Something was wrong, and he should have known. He bent his head and put on a fresh burst of speed.

Alno jumped from his arm and shot into the bushes ahead half a second before Marius heard the scream. There was no doubt it was Keth. Marius knew every intonation of her voice, had experienced every aspect of its range from sex-soaked whisper to raging cry. The terror, so close to the edge of madness that Marius could sense it, was something he had never heard, and for a moment he felt his veins collapse in panic. The scream went on and on, straight ahead of him, a long, piercing shriek interrupted only by broken imprecations. A bank of lickleaf plants loomed in front of him, and Marius burst through them in time to register the sound of Alno yowling, and to duck as the cat flew past his head. He skidded to a halt at the sight beyond.

"Keth!"

"Marius!"

Something had dragged Keth across a dozen feet. Marius could see the path of broken flowers and scars where her fingers had gouged desperate runnels into the earth. He could see Keth, too; at least, her face was still visible, and one arm sticking up out of the ground. Of the rest of her there was no sign. As he watched, her head was jerked backwards. The ground rose to cover her eyes, leaving only her nose and mouth above. She screamed again. Marius dove forward, reaching for her free hand. He grabbed it, and winced as her nails dug deep into his flesh.

"Hold on!"

"I can't!"

"You can! You can! Hold on!"

"Marius!"

"No! Keth, no!"

Something belowground pulled on her, hard; harder than he could contend with. They yelled once, in unison. Then, with a dry slithering sound, the ground swallowed Keth up. Marius dove forward once more, plunging his head into the hole.

"Keth!"

He could see only darkness. He tensed, preparing to scramble after her. Then strong hands grabbed his ankles and pulled him backwards out of the hole. He writhed against them as the hole closed up behind him.

"You!"

A dead man was standing above him. Marius saw the uniform first, the tattered mantle and tunic bearing the burgundy pattern of the King of Scorby. But it was the face he remembered most strongly: the ruined eye socket, the flap of grey withered flesh hanging down over the shattered cheekbone where an axe had ploughed into it, releasing the nameless soldier's life. This was the man who had hauled Marius down to the underworld on that cursed day almost four years ago. He smiled, and dried soil dripped from between his jaws. His voice sounded inside Marius' head, and he winced. He had not talked with another dead man for almost four years. He had forgotten how loud it was.

"Surprise."

Marius scrambled to his feet and launched himself at the dead man. His adversary braced himself, rolled his shoulders, and clipped Marius across the temple with a rock-hard fist to send him crashing into the base of the lickleaf plants. Marius rolled away, clambered upright once more, and found the soldier standing six feet away.

"What's the matter?" the dead man asked, head tilted in amusement. "Lose something?"

Marius had no words with which to answer. All he had left in his lungs was a shriek of rage, so he let it loose and threw himself once more towards his assailant. The soldier braced himself, and raised his fists.

A tortoiseshell cannonball shot out of the bushes and struck the soldier flush in the groin. Dead or not, there are some instincts that *never* leave a man. The soldier cried out, plucking frantically at the growling, snarling mess of claws and teeth as it tore strips of fabric, and then flesh, from his most precious area. At that moment Marius drove a shoulder into the pit of his stomach. Momentum carried the three combatants backwards. They rolled several feet into the bushes in a confusion of fists, teeth, and curses, before their motion threw them apart.

The soldier finally managed to prise his fingers under Alno's chest. He peeled the maddened cat away and sent him flying into the undergrowth. Marius took advantage of his momentary distraction to close in once more. The soldier was off-balance – he swung an elbow at Marius' neck, but Marius easily evaded it by dropping to one knee. He lashed out, grabbing two hands full of flesh already dangling from Alno's assault.

"Fucker," he shouted, and reared back, pulling his arms down with every inch of his strength. The skin resisted for a moment, then, with a dry ripping sound, the soldier's groin came away from his body. Marius staggered back half a dozen steps. The two men stared at each other, and at the leathery band that hung between Marius' arms. Halfway along it, a small nub of flesh dangled, pointing accusingly at the ground.

"Is that my…"

"Eww." Marius dropped the flap of skin and ran his hands down his shirt in short, shaky wipes. The soldier smiled, the withered muscles of his jaw creaking open wider than a normal man's. He placed his palms together, hunched his shoulders, and began to draw his hands wide apart. As he did so, two feet in front of him, a hole in the ground slowly opened in time with the movement. "Keep it," he said, his words dry with spite. "I wasn't using it anyway." Still grinning, he sidled towards the hole.

"Oh, no you don't." Marius hooked his foot under the edge of the discarded flesh and kicked forward. In his youth he'd spent a dozen years running with street gangs, where any stray gravel that crept up between the cobbles was a weapon. His kick was true. The giant skin flap wrapped around the dead man's face with a vicious snap. He staggered back a step, and Marius leaped towards him.

And stopped short, impaled upon the sword the soldier drew and thrust before him. Marius stared down at the rusted metal that had entered his chest just below the breastbone. He could feel the blade's point pressing against his spine, feel every red hot inch of it drawing a line through his body, bisecting him into two distinct parts – that below, through which his strength was draining into the ground, and that above, where he could see the reason for his sudden weakness but could not quite comprehend what had happened. He tried to grab the blade, to pull it back out and make his body one whole, uninterrupted unit again, but his arms were too heavy and he couldn't quite control them the way he wanted. It took all his concentration to rest his hands along the top of the rusting metal. He stared curiously at the tiny red flakes that peeled off as his hands slid away from the blade. He could see them pricking his flesh but there was no sense of feeling, no understanding. They may as well have been the stars, turning red at the end of the sky. Marius watched them from a million miles away.

The soldier removed the flap of skin from his face with his free hand, and waggled the sword to get Marius' attention. Marius gasped as the line of heat inside him expanded with the sideways movement of the blade. Slowly, with infinite weariness, he raised his eyes to meet his assailant's gaze. The soldier held up the strip of flesh and then, with great ceremony, he draped it over Marius' unprotesting head, patting it down so that his former genitals hung down his victim's forehead, just above the eyes. He patted Marius on the cheek: the insolent slap of the victor.

"That's twice I've killed you now," he said. "It's getting to be fun."

He pulled the sword out in one swift movement. Marius fell to his knees, hands still curled up against his chest. The soldier raised a foot against his shoulder, and gently pushed him over so he lay on his back. Marius watched through a descending wall of black as the dead man stepped over to the hole, and dropped through it without a backward glance. Then the blackness finished its descent, and he saw nothing else.

TWO

Something heavy was sitting on his chest. Marius couldn't breathe. Was this what it was to be dead, then? Properly dead? This never-ending burden, dragging your life down, filling your insides with the weight of the universe, so that bodily functions were no more than memories, and all that remained was the pressure, making absolute the impossibility of breath?

The weight meowed, and licked his chin.

"I wouldn't let him do that," said a familiar voice. "You wouldn't *believe* what we just caught him eating."

Marius peeled open eyelids encrusted with grit. A concerned face loomed over him, a florid, open, pig farmer face Marius had thought he'd seen the last of four years previously.

"Gerd?"

"Hi."

"What was he... Never mind." Memory flooded back, and Marius recalled the humiliation of his last moments. Please, he thought, let it have fallen off before Gerd saw it.

"Oh, I wouldn't worry," said a second voice just off to the left. "It was barely a snack. I've raised chickens with bigger ones than that."

"Granny!" said Gerd, sharply.

17

Marius rolled his head towards the new voice. He couldn't quite understand what it was he saw. Someone appeared to have played a cruel trick upon a rotten apple. They'd given it a body, and taught it how to speak. Marius frowned, bringing all his current mental powers to bear. Slowly the apple resolved itself into a rough approximation of a human face. A face like an unsolved jigsaw puzzle, perhaps, but all the bits were there and they moved in roughly the correct order. It was attached to a thatch of brittle grey frosting that he tentatively identified as hair, and the whole ensemble perched approximately at the top of what might be a bundle of random sticks thrown together in the dark and covered with a sheet the local pigs had decided was no longer good enough for a bed but was probably, on balance, her body.

"I know you."

"Oh, you've stayed sharp." The face leaned closer. Marius smelled cabbage soup, and death.

"Granny."

"Top marks for the genius." The old woman leaned back out of view. "And you're certain this is the man who's going to solve our little problem, are you?"

"What problem?" Marius decided to experiment with life in three dimensions. He sat up, then immediately decided to go back to life in a prone position. It didn't stop the sky rotating like a Catherine wheel, but the patterns were prettier. "Wait..."

"Here it comes."

"You're..."

"Almost there."

"I'm...!"

"So close he can taste it."

Marius sat up again. This time, the world stayed

where it was.

"But I'm…" He clawed at his chest, tearing at the rip in his undershirt. A raw, red wound sat just below his breastbone. Marius touched it experimentally. It opened up under his touch like sucking lips. He slipped a finger into it, then another, then slid four fingers inside himself to the third knuckle. "I'm dead."

"Well, yes."

"Really dead."

"Duh."

Gerd coughed. "Granny, I think that's enough." He extended a hand. Marius took it, and hauled himself to his feet, his other hand still embedded within his wound.

"Could you… not do that?"

"What? Sorry." Marius removed the hand and wiped the blood on his trouser leg. Gerd wrinkled his nose. "What… oh, gods." He stared at the field around him. "Is this what it feels like?"

The world was leaking colour. Marius turned in a circle as the flowers around him grew pale and empty. Alno sneezed, and he stared down at the cat in fascination, watching him turn from a multi-coloured ball into a lint-coloured lump. "Is this… is this how you see it?"

"You've been dead before."

"I know, but…" Marius stopped. He *had* been dead before. Four years ago, in the aftermath of a battle, he had been mistaken for the King of the Dead and dragged down to the underworld. Once they realised their mistake the underworlders had killed him, right before they sent him out into the world to find them a *real* king. But those feelings of death had never been like this, and he'd always been able to go back to his living senses when needed. "I'm dead. I'm really, properly dead." He stared down at his hand, as grey and toneless as the rest of him. "I'm dead."

"You're not the only one, pallie." Granny poked him in the chest. Her finger slipped inside the wound for a moment and they both jerked back.

"What?"

"You're not the only one."

"Well, no, I mean obviously… Wait." He squeezed his eyes shut, gathered himself, took a deep breath. "All right, one at a time. What do you mean?"

"Granny's dead."

"Congratulations."

"No, really." Gerd stepped behind his grandmother and laid a protective hand on her shoulder. "You remember."

Marius did. He and Gerd had parted ways in Scorby, three weeks after they had delivered Scorbus the Great, first King of Scorby and, not entirely coincidentally, thousand year-old skeleton, to the underworld. Gerd had wanted to return to his village in the mountains, to be there for his aged grandmother when she died, and to guide her through her adjustment to life underground; the same adjustment he'd been forced to make some months previously. Marius had not seen Gerd since.

"So… why are you not, you know…?" Marius pointed to the earth below them.

"We tried, but…"

"But?"

"It was closed."

"*What?*"

"Listen, sonny." Granny stalked forward, and poked Marius again with a stick-like finger.

"Don't do that!"

"Listen, you. I get all gussied up, say all my fare-thee-wells and the like, all prepared to be sent to my final reward for a life of hard labour and looking after young Gerd there…"

"That's the same thing. Ow. Don't *do* that!"

"And what do you think happens?"

"I don't know. Your reputation preceded you?" Marius flinched away from Granny's raised digit. "Okay, okay. What?"

"Nothing, that's what. Not a blessed thing."

"We buried Granny in the village graveyard," Gerd said before things could go any further. "After a week, she dug herself out and came to me for answers."

"But weren't you waiting for her?"

"I had. I'd gone down to the underworld to meet her, show her around, you know? Help ease the transition from up here to down there. But she never came. After a few days, I went back to the farmhouse to think."

"And sure enough, she came back."

Gerd shrugged. "We've been in the mountains for thirty generations. We always come back."

"The nut never falls far from the tree, eh? Will you stop that!" Marius rubbed at his pectoral and took two very deliberate steps away from Granny. "So why didn't you just, you know…" Marius opened and closed his hands in imitation of the soldier, "Do that openy-uppy thing and go down there yourselves?" Marius had never mastered the trick of opening holes in the earth where a corpse had lain. The dead used them as gateways between the upper and lower worlds, and he had never wanted to identify himself so closely with the non-living that he wished to use them. It was a skill that Gerd could manage easily.

"I did. It was empty."

"What do you mean, empty?"

"Empty. Gone. No one there. We wandered about for days and never saw anyone. We went to the throne room, all the corridors, every inch of the underworld I'd ever been to, everything. In the end, the only thing I could think of was to come and see you."

"What on earth for?"

"That's what *I* said," croaked the old woman.

"Granny."

"Well, it's true. Look at him." Granny favoured Marius with a sneer it had taken fifty years to perfect. "He's about as useful as a porridge enema."

"Thanks for that image. And you're an old, dead, blind woman who can't even die properly."

"Marius!" Gerd looked genuinely affronted.

"Well, it's true." Marius looked from one to the other, and finally to Alno, who stared back at him with the blank expression perfected by all cats who wish to declare: "Fuck you, buddy, I've just eaten so you're on your own."

"Look," he said, "I'd like to help, really I would…"

"Liar," snapped the old woman.

"Granny."

Marius matched gazes with Gerd.

"Keth's gone."

Gerd sighed. "I knew it couldn't last. What did you do?"

"I didn't do… No! Taken." Marius pointed at his feet. "Below."

"What? Why didn't you say? What happened?"

"Someone's taken her. She came out here… The soldier, you know the one, the one who killed me… last time he killed me. He was here. He was the one who…" Marius flapped a hand at his chest.

"Again? That's twice!"

"Yes, thank you. Anyway, he took her. Took her down. I've got to get her back."

"Wait a minute." Gerd held up a hand. "Took her down, you say? As in…"

"Yeah. Down there."

The two men glared at the ground beneath their feet.

"Something's not right."

"Keth's gone. That's what's not right. I've got to go."

"No, I mean…" Gerd pinched the bridge of his nose. "The underworld is empty. Nobody came to help Granny."

"Maybe they knew she was coming."

"Ha bloody ha. But really – think about it. What if nobody helped because nobody was there? What if nobody is helping anybody?"

"It's not my fault she's… What? Nobody at all?"

"I don't know. If there's nobody underneath, then there are no paths being opened." He gestured to the horizons around them. "What if it's all over?"

"Somebody was here to take Keth."

"Yeah. Funny that. I mean, right here, and nowhere else. And if Drenthe is involved…"

"Drenthe?"

"The soldier who killed you."

"Is that his name? I never got around to finding out."

"Yes, well, he's worked his way up since you last crossed paths. I've been back below. He's always there, whispering in ears, *advising*." Gerd made the word sound little better than punching babies. "He's Scorbus' man, now, through and through."

Marius groaned at the mention of Scorbus. If not for them, he'd still be lying in his crypt at the top of the Radican, the mountain at the heart of Scorby City upon which the royal palace sat.

"What would he want with Keth?"

"I don't know. But if Drenthe is involved, nothing good is going to come from it."

"That decides it then. I've got to go. Now."

"We're coming with you."

"What?" Both men turned towards Granny. She stared at them in defiance, her blind eyes nailing them in turn.

"Don't be so bleeding obtuse. It's obvious, isn't it? You're going to the land of the dead to find this poor girl, who's probably far better off and happier without a conniving lump of shifty like you anyway, and I need to get someone to show me around the place so's I can have my final rest that I've worked all my life for. I've earned it! So we're coming with you."

"But..." Marius looked at Gerd. Gerd looked at Marius. Two sets of shoulders sagged.

"Right," Marius said to nobody in particular. "Right. Why not? Off in pursuit of a homicidal groinless madman, armed with nothing more than an old blind woman, a boy who still can't tell the difference between a wooden penny and a gold riner..." Alno meowed. Marius picked him up. "And a cat."

"Got a problem?"

A wry smile contorted Marius' face for a fraction of a second.

"I've worked with worse."

They gathered round the spot where Drenthe had made his exit and stared down at it. The ground now looked distinctly undisturbed and non-gravelike under its blanket of flowers.

"Can you open it?" Marius asked. Gerd shrugged.

"Don't see why not. Doesn't look much like a grave, though."

Granny snorted. "That don't mean nothing. Whole world's a resting place for somebody or other." She lifted her head and took in the broad, flat plain around them. "Nice open expanse like this. Bound to be more than one battle here over time. Could probably throw a stick and hit some poor bugger's last breath."

Marius and Gerd exchanged glances.

"And how, exactly," Marius asked, "do you know what this place looks like? Last time we met you were as blind as justice." He leaned forward to stare into her milky eyes. "They don't look very functional to me."

Granny snorted. "Dead people don't need eyes to see, boy. Gods' sake. We talk without breath, we move around without a heartbeat. Seeing without eyes is easy. Been dead six weeks, long enough to learn."

"Right."

"Try it yourself." She reached up and poked a finger at his eyes. Marius reared back. "Go on. Close them, see what difference it makes."

Slowly, Marius did as he was told. He stayed very still for long seconds, then raised his eyebrows in surprise.

"Good gods." The world was there in front of him. Slightly blurry, as if seen through, well, a pair of translucent eyelids; slightly out of focus and a strange shade of washed out grey he couldn't quite identify, but most definitely there.

"Dead sight." Granny said. "Stays the same whether it's night or rain or snow. It's a nice view, after so long without one at all."

"I'll be beggared." Marius turned on Gerd. "How come you never told me any of this?"

"Because he's thick, that's why." Granny laid an affectionate hand upon Gerd's forearm. "He's beautiful, and loyal, and ever so good with pigs. But being dead doesn't really suit him. Not like me. I had years to prepare for it."

"Bloody hell." Marius swung his gaze to the ground around them. Everywhere he looked, faint grey lines criss-crossed beneath the wavering flower stems, like a spider web of scars spreading out across the landscape.

"Told you," Granny said.

"Are they…?"

"Seams, I reckon. Places the ground can be opened up by the likes of us." They glanced down at Drenthe's exit point. Sure enough, a grey line ran directly across it.

"What? What is it?" Gerd closed his eyes and swung his head from side to side in confusion. Granny and Marius met gazes.

"I told you," she whispered.

Marius watched his young friend. "You see it because you were ready for death," he whispered back. "What does that say about me?"

Granny said nothing, simply patted him on the arm and snapped her fingers for Gerd's attention.

"Here," she said, pointing down. "Do it here, love."

Gerd nodded, and pressed his hands together before his chest. He exhaled once, then slowly drew them apart, in unconscious imitation of Drenthe. Soundlessly, the ground opened up before them.

"What I don't understand," Marius said, gazing down at the thirty or so feet of dark hole, "is that the first time I went underground, it felt like I was dragged through every bloody square inch of dirt between the tunnels and the surface. Now, it's all holes and climbing."

Gerd shrugged. "Does *any* of this make sense?"

There didn't seem anything worth adding to that. Alno stepped lightly between Marius' feet and crouched at the edge of the hollow. Without looking back he leaped, disappearing into the blackness below. Marius sighed.

"Follow that cat, I suppose."

They spent the next twenty minutes scrabbling for handholds, faces pressed to the dank earth walls. It wasn't until the group was once more gathered together, on the cold earth floor of the underworld, that Marius was able to look around and gather his thoughts.

They stood in a tunnel. A dozen feet across, it swung away and downwards, as if whoever had carved it had created a loop that rose from some deeper cavern with the express purpose of reaching a high point where they stood, before falling back to its starting point. The walls were rough, as Marius had come to expect from the underworld, but the floor was smooth, as if trampled into place by the passage of countless feet. The ceiling was high enough that they could all stand comfortably, and

where he might have expected the fresh, loamy smell of unfiltered earth there was something musty and spoiled to the air. He wrinkled his nose.

"Not exactly homey, is it?"

The others were sniffing, too.

"It smells rank."

"It smells dead," Granny replied. "Dead and left."

"Like a pig that's been carried off."

"Thanks for that image." Marius walked away a few steps, then returned and moved away up the other arm of the tunnel. "It's coming from down here." He returned to the group. "So. Do we go towards or away from the nasty dead smell?"

The others glanced at each other but said nothing. Marius sighed.

"Why do I always have to be the grown-up?" He nudged Alno with a toe. "Go on. You decide."

Alno favoured him with a look of high dudgeon, then streaked away towards the smell. Marius cursed silently and followed.

Once round the corner, the tunnel descended for another dozen metres or so before meeting a cross channel. The three travellers stopped next to a bundle of sticks leaning up against the wall. Alno was curled up in the centre of the pile, gnawing upon what at first glance appeared to be a round stone the size of a skull. Nobody wanted to be the first to admit that it was most definitely not a stone.

"He has a bad habit of doing that," Marius said, as he gently prised cat and skull apart. "I must speak to Keth..." At the thought of Keth, he dropped Alno and settled down onto his haunches, staring at the bone in his hand.

"It's okay," Gerd said. "That isn't her."

"I know that," Marius snapped, turning it over in his hands. "Just... why is this here?" He indicated the jumbled pile. "And what..." He stopped. "Look at this."

Every bone in the pile had been broken, from the femur right down to each individual finger bone. They laid them out, just to be sure. Even the skull had a small, irregular hole punched into its rear. When the skeleton was as assembled as best they could manage they stood away from it, and pondered its destruction.

"It's an execution," Marius said slowly. "They've executed him."

"How do you know?"

"I'm not sure." Marius backed away. "It just... It's the only reason I can think of to do... that. Come on." He moved further down the corridor. "Let's get out of here."

"But why would someone want to execute a dead person?"

"I don't know!" Marius made the corner and stopped, sniffing in each direction down the cross tunnel. "The smell's coming from this way," he said, pointing towards the right. "Are you coming or not?"

Gerd and Granny joined him. Marius set off with quick steps, forcing the others to jog after him.

"I don't understand," Gerd said as they walked. "Why do something like that? It doesn't make any sense."

"No." Marius rounded on him, pushing him against the rough earth wall. "It doesn't. And I don't care. I don't have time for mysteries. I'm trying to get my lover back."

"I know." Gerd took hold of Marius' fists and peeled them away from his shirt. "I know. But that was disturbing. And if Drenthe took her this way…"

"I'm trying not to think about that, all right?" Marius stepped back, and dropped his hands. "Sorry about the…" He indicated Gerd's shirtfront.

"It's all right. Let's push on, shall we?"

Marius nodded. Gerd clapped him on the shoulder, and they continued their journey. They hadn't walked for more than a minute when Gerd puffed out his cheeks.

"Gods, it's absolutely feral now. I can barely breathe."

"You don't need to," Granny replied from half a dozen feet in front of him.

"You know what I mean. The smell. It's overpowering."

"I know." Granny was standing still, staring further down the corridor at something the others couldn't see. The two men came up on either side of her, and followed her gaze.

"Oh, good gods."

"No," Granny replied. "I don't think so."

Someone had dug a trench the width of the corridor, and perhaps three or four feet long. It was impossible to tell just how far down it went. The bodies obscured the view. They rested in messy abandon, discarded toys thrown away by a petulant god. Not one of them was complete: arms were piled up in one corner, heads in another, legs lay intertwined with each other like fossilised branches. There were no torsos amongst the victims, just extremity upon extremity, a patchwork of perhaps a hundred or more dismembered corpses with no hope of restitution. The three companions stared at it in growing horror.

"Broken," Marius finally croaked. "All of them. Look." He pointed at the nearby legs. Each one was bent at several places. Some clearly showed the ragged ends of bones poking through the flesh. "They've all been smashed."

"This isn't just an execution." Gerd stepped back, hands over the bottom of his face. "This is…"

"Genocide." Granny was staring from face to smashed face. "This is genocide." She looked up at Marius, confusion plain upon her features. "Is that what happens? Is this what you do when people arrive?"

Marius shook his head. "No. This is… this is something else. Something wrong." He tore his gaze from the devastation in the pit. "We were meant to see this. *I* was meant to see this."

"How do you know that?"

Marius strode away from the pit, back up the tunnel towards their entry point. Gerd and Granny scrambled to keep up. "Drenthe knew I'd come for Keth. He kept her above ground just long enough so I would know where she'd been dragged and could find it. He killed me to get me to get me down here. He knew I'd pass this spot. We've been led here for a reason. Alno!" The cat came slinking out of the shadows and jumped up into his arms. "First we make this right, then I'm going to find Keth. Then I'm going to cut that fucker into little pieces while he tells me what his game is."

"How are we going to do all that?"

They reached their entry point. Marius jerked his head at the roof above them. Gerd drew the earth open, so that they found themselves staring into the burning sun.

"Fire," Marius said. "We start with a fire."

THREE

"I have wood piled up for the winter," he explained as they crossed the field. "Gerd, you grab a decent armful or two. Granny, there's tinder and kindling in the kitchen, and lucifers above the oven. Bring them all."

"What are we going to do?"

"We're going to set fire to the pit." Marius stopped, facing his companions. "Those poor bastards deserve not to rot in pieces in that hole. And we can send a message to Drenthe at the same time."

"What message?"

"We're coming."

"Coming where?"

"I don't know." He wheeled away and continued walking. "Do you have to ruin all my really good prophetic statements?"

"Sorry." Gerd looked shamefaced for a moment, then gazed past Marius and pointed. "What's that?"

A plume of black smoke rose a few hundred yards in front of them. Marius stared at it for a second, then began running.

"No. No!"

"What is it?"

"The cottage. It's the fucking cottage!"

Marius was there in under a minute. He stood and

stared at the devastation while Granny shuffled her way behind him, Gerd holding her arm. The fire had almost done its work. The cottage was little more than a few blackened uprights, mounds of ash, and a pall of smoke that began to thin out and dissipate even as they watched. A neat circle of burned ground spread twenty feet around the remains of the walls. It was obvious the fire had been deliberately lit. It was too neat, too final to be anything else. Marius walked through the shin-deep cinders, disconsolately pushing them apart, hoping to find at least one small memento or memory still partially intact. Nothing remained. Everything had been destroyed down to its component dust.

"Someone took their time over this," Marius said as he shuffled through the destruction. "Someone took things out and put them back again to make sure they were all burned up." He eyed the neat circle where the burning stopped. "Someone made sure it didn't spread."

"Drenthe."

"Of course Drenthe." He stood in the middle of his burned-out life and turned in a slow circle. "He's leading me about like a dog on a chain. Rubbing my nose in my messes."

"But why?" Gerd stared at him over the blackened ground. Neither he nor Granny had set foot upon it. "It's been four years since you've had anything to do with the dead. Why attack you now?"

"You said it yourself." Marius began to kick his way out of the circle, then stopped as his foot struck something solid. He crouched and began to dig into the hot ashes. "He's cunning, ruthless, and he's just about in charge. Whatever's going on down there, he wants me out of it."

"Or wants you to know all about it." Granny was

staring at the ground outside the circle, her eyes firmly closed.

"Yes, that's a…" Marius pulled out the unharmed object and brushed residue away from it. It was a small picture frame, perhaps four inches by two, woven from dried reeds and painted in a simple blue that matched the colour of the distant hills. Someone had glued a pressed flower inside its border, a brittle and faded cousin to the countless yellow blooms that waved outside the circle of devastation. Marius stared at it for several long seconds, then held it up so the others could see it. "Keth made this for me in the first couple of days after we moved in. That's the first flower we picked from the garden. There's no way this could have survived the fire." He tucked it inside his shirt; then thought again, and laid it gently on top of the nearest pile of ashes. "I was meant to find this. I was meant to understand why." Standing, he wiped soot from his trouser legs. "We've been watched since the day we arrived, probably longer. They've been planning all of this for years." He moved over to the other two and stood with his back to the burned cottage, staring out over the unharmed landscape. "You were right, Granny. They want me to know," he said. "And now I do."

"Close your eyes," Granny said. Marius did. He turned in a slow circle, stopping when he faced the same direction as the old woman.

The ground was a mess of grey stripes, marks of deaths from battles long past. On the far side of the burned circle, five lines stood out from the rest. They glowed, a sign they had been recently used as entrance points for residents of the underworld. Three of them formed a straight line at ninety degrees to the blackened circle's edge. Two more intersected the line's farthest point at opposing, acute angles. An arrow, visible only to someone with eyes accustomed to being dead, pointing towards something at the edge of vision.

"The village," Marius said. He glanced at the others.

"Go."

Gerd had been looking from one to the other in confusion. Now, he stepped forward into the circle. "Wait." Picking up the flower frame, he held it out to Marius. "Don't you want this?"

Marius eyed it. "That's over," he said in a dead, flat voice. "I'm never coming back."

"But Keth…"

"Keth's dead," Marius called over his shoulder as he began to run.

"That doesn't mean she doesn't need you," Gerd called back. He held the frame out uselessly to Marius' retreating back, then placed it inside his jerkin as Granny called out to him.

"Come on," she said as he took her hand. "Let's get after him."

It took Marius exactly five minutes to reach the village, but he could see what had happened much earlier. The buildings were surrounded by a ring of light grey lines at varying distances: the sites of farming accidents, a roadside robbery or two, and one spot where old Ratek had had a heart attack one night on the way home from the tavern but everybody had just thought he was pissed and mucking about. Inside that ring of old deaths, there was nothing but rubble. Nobody had set any fires this time. Nobody had needed to. There were perhaps twenty buildings in the village. Homes, mostly; modest dwellings cobbled together from any material available within walking distance, but kept clean and decorated in whatever meagre way the villagers could manage. It was one of the things that had attracted Keth to the place. It had reminded her of her room above the Hauled Keel, reminded her of her own attempts to create some sort of haven, and the order and sense of belonging she had carved out of the ugliest parts of her life. If Marius was honest, which he was careful to be only on very rare occasions, he saw just another set of lopsided and obsessively-swept dwellings, no better than any of a thousand other villages scattered about the unwanted fringes of the country. Just over a dozen or so homes, alongside the tavern, a communal stables, a smithy that was more tinker's repair shop than anything else, and a watering station.

But now it was gone. An angry giant had swung a scythe, felling the entire village with a sweep of his arm. Not a single stone remained whole. Not a single stick was unbroken. Twenty buildings lay in cruel disarray, architectural skeletons in a mass grave. Marius walked into what had been, for want of a better word, the town square and picked his way through the rubble, turning over the occasional piece of detritus with his toe. The entire square was a puddle of broken edges, dusted with the powdered remains of the dried grasses that had served the villagers as thatching, firestarters, and food when times grew tough. The simple well had caved in, and pots lay smashed around it. All that was missing were the battered faces of familiar corpses. Not a single body lay in sight.

He knelt down amongst a spray of old cobbles that Missus Belcher had brought with her from a trip to the big city thirty years ago, when she was young and had a nice set of hips and caught the right worker's eye when they were breaking up old Pudding Alley. Marius picked up a jagged shard and pieced it together with another.

He worked quickly, scrabbling amongst the dirt for the right pieces, discarding the wrong ones, concentrating on putting together one stone, on making just one thing right again. Underneath his concentration, thoughts were turned over and assembled in the same way, drawing him closer to one conclusion, one perfectly rounded course of action.

"Executed," he said as Gerd and Granny arrived and picked their way across the rubble. "Just like our friends in the tunnel." He held up the finished cobblestone. Gerd took it from him and gently cleared a space to place it. "The entire village."

"The villagers?"

"Close your eyes."

Granny did as she was commanded. After a while she opened them again. "They're not here."

"How do you do that?" Gerd watched them both. "Seriously, I've been dead longer than both of you–"

"Sound." Marius placed his index finger against his lip. "Stop yapping and actually listen."

Gerd fell silent. "It's quiet."

Granny nodded, and Marius indicated the air around them. "Even on a battlefield, the dead make a noise. The wind flaps their clothing, birds call to each other as they peck out the soft bits, metal scratches against rock, there's always *something*. Close your eyes and listen."

Gerd did so. "Nothing. There's no sound at all."

"Finally. Dead for four years and you actually manage to show me something."

Gerd sneered."So where are they?"

Marius watched his fingers scrabble through the dirt, searching out the beginnings of another cobblestone. "Taken. And no, I don't know where. Just not here, obviously."

"Why?"

Marius said nothing until a second stone lay next to the first. "These people were my neighbours." He pulled a stick from the rubble, tied it to another with some shredded thatch. "*My* neighbours." He pieced together a second branch, and a third, letting the anger flow now, giving everything he'd suppressed until this moment full rein. "They didn't do a damn thing to anybody. This was all they had, all they fucking had." He swung around, his outflung arms encompassing the whole site. "Shitty lives in a shitty little middle-of-nowhere toilet bowl of a town with sixteen hours a day in the fields just so they could spend a couple of hours once a week sitting in a tavern drinking pissy scrumpy and throwing darts at a board in the corner." He picked up a jagged rock and threw it across the square. "There were seven children in this village, you bastard!"

Then, just as soon as it was released, the anger left him. He stood, shoulders slumped, and let his fists clench and unclench of their own accord. The echo of his voice died away, and the world was silent again.

"You've changed," Gerd said, when it seemed safe to speak. Marius closed his eyes, and tilted his head back to face the sky.

"I'm dead now."

"That's not what I meant."

"I know." He spun back towards his handiwork and picked up the repaired branches. "I've been stuck in this shitty little backwater for three years. Keth loved it. All the nature and fresh air and good honest toil and all that utter bollocks." He snapped a branch, glanced down at it, then bent to repair it once more. "Three years. I haven't been in one place for that long since I got shot of my parents."

"It was your home."

"Keth was my home." He inhaled, and placed the sticks down on the restored cobbles. "But these people were *her* home. And I'm going to destroy whoever did this to them."

"We know who did this to them," Gerd said. "Don't we?"

Marius stood up, staring across the ruins to the single track that exited the village. Behind them it meandered past his former cottage and onwards up into the hills. Somewhere there it might intersect a valley, split into a thousand different possibilities, adventures, and lands he had never seen. Ahead it fetched up against Mish, the nearest thing to civilisation that existed on this part of the plains. Beyond that lay the roads to the great cities, and the past he had given up for Keth.

"It takes an army to destroy a village," he said. "Even this one."

Gerd looked around them. "Wouldn't there be some evidence? Like some signs that an army had been here?"

Marius brandished a stone, threw it hard into the ruins around them.

"Is this not enough of a fucking clue for you?"

"Well, I kind of meant... footprints or something." Gerd shuffled from foot to foot, avoiding Marius' gaze. Marius stared at him, his temper suddenly cooling towards ice.

"If I say an army destroyed the homes of the only friends and neighbours I've allowed myself to get to know in the last twenty years, then it was an army. Is that clear?"

Gerd nodded at his feet. They stood in silence for several moments, then Gerd found the courage to squint up at his friend.

"So what do we do?"

Marius looked down at his handiwork. Two round cobble stones, with two bent and patched sticks jammed between them. Two circular shields, bisected by paired sword and quill or, at least, as close as he could manage. The crest of the family don Hellespont: merchants; King's Men; and, the last time he bothered to check, seventh-richest family in Scorby City. He smiled, a thin disfigurement of his mouth that, just for a moment, revealed something nasty lurking behind his eyes. "First, I think it's time I regained my heritage. Then I'm going to buy the cruellest, most brutal mercenaries the docks have to offer. Then I'm going to find these villagers, get Keth back, and see how many pieces I can cut Drenthe into before he dies for good. Want to come?"

"I thought you said Keth was dead."

Marius shot Gerd a look of stunning anger. "Has that stopped us?"

"No, I just… I thought you meant, you know." Gerd shuffled uncomfortably. "*Dead* dead."

Marius spoke carefully, enunciating his words in single bites. "Then I'll recover her bones. Is that all right with you?"

"Fuck it." Granny hauled herself to her feet and nodded at him. "I've got nothing planned."

Gerd looked between them. "Me neither," he said. "I thought that went without saying."

FOUR

Philosophers will tell you that money cannot buy happiness. Philosophers often live in discarded wine barrels and have trouble distinguishing between a timeless aphorism and a load of bollocks. They also rarely spend time in a town like Mish.

If money is the root of all evil, then towns like Mish were the truffles of evil: pungent and hard to find, but if you'd acquired the taste for them then very nearly an addiction. Mish was built upon one very simple philosophy: people end up in soil-poor floodplains because they are either stupid, powerless, or hiding a secret – preferably all three. Humanity had made an art form of sending its least worthy out into the wilderness to die. Mish made an art form of feeding from the carcasses. Part trading post, part street party; part gambling den, whorehouse, and fighting pit; the owners of Mish created it to fill one side of a timeless equation: other people had money, and they wanted it.

Marius sat in the scrub overlooking the town entrance and watched as Gerd and Granny approached the single steward who guarded the entrance. Stewards were different to guards, in his experience. Less heavily armed, and more likely to be draped in felt jerkins and brightly-coloured tassels than beaten and rusting armour; but that only represented another kind of danger. Anybody can swing a mace and hope their chest plate holds out longer than the other guy's. It takes intelligence, and a form of ambition, to demand tribute from strangers while armed with little more than a shiny shirt and a ceremonial dagger. Even so, the guardian of this particular entrance was doing a roaring trade, judging by the constant stream of up-country types pouring through over the last three hours. Down by the gate, the negotiation with Gerd and Granny reached a crescendo, and they were turned away with a few pushes to Gerd's chest and a clip across Granny's shoulder that sent her staggering. Marius stroked Alno with renewed intensity until they clambered up to his vantage point and sat down.

"Half a dozen riner," Gerd reported, kicking at the ground with suppressed fury. "And he called Granny an old... old... thingy."

Granny cackled. "Used to be dating talk, where I come from." Gerd fidgeted again, and she laughed even louder. "Oh, my poor sheltered boy. It's such a pity you can't blush."

Gerd did his best. "Why can't we just go around?" he asked. "Why do we even have to go through this town?"

Marius contemplated the gate as he talked. "Firstly, we're at least a six-week walk from Borgho City. I don't want to wait that long. I want horses, and maybe a cart. And I don't want to turn up to my family home in a torn undershirt and bare feet and no hat. Call me vain, but I want breeches, I want a coat, and I want a knife at my hip. I want money in my pocket."

"So we can buy what we need on the way."

"Sure. Let's say that." Both men ignored Granny's snigger. "Besides, look at it. How many people do you reckon are in that town? Two thousand? More?"

"I guess. Maybe."

"So how many people do you think die in a town that big in, say…" he glanced at Granny, "seven weeks? And what do you think has happened to them?"

Gerd and Granny stared at the wooden wall of the town for a long minute.

"I want to find out," Marius said. "I want to know as much as possible before I go after Drenthe. I know how soldiers think, how they strategise. Take the cities, and leave the towns to starve. Whatever he's up to, I'm willing to bet he's bypassed this one while he goes after a bigger prize further on. Which means he won't be paying attention to them, but I can guarantee they'll have paid attention to any army that went marching by. Which means I might just learn something useful."

"So what do we do?"

Marius stroked Alno. "If he hadn't hit Granny, I'd say we get ourselves eighteen riner and walk in. As it is, though…" He dropped the purring bundle and stood. "Come on, cat." He strolled out from behind the bush and down the path to the gate, Alno padding silently after him.

The steward eyed him as he approached, and Marius had an opportunity to size him up properly. Up close he was shorter than Marius had thought, not small so much as compact. He was dressed in a rich red tunic and leggings, a short black cape hanging down his back. Tightly-wound muscles shifted under his shirt as he changed his stance, and the dagger at his hip hung loose, not tied down as it would be if there purely for show. This steward expected to use it at some stage of his day, and looked like he knew how to do so. He waited until Marius was almost abreast before he held up a hand.

"Stay right there, pal."

Marius stopped, the very picture of innocence. "Yes, officer?"

"Don't get smart with me. You know what this emblem means." He pointed to an insignia sewn into the breast of his tunic, a splash of dark black against the blood-red fabric. Marius peered at it with a bemused expression, and recognised it immediately. The personal seal of Mistress Fellipan, owner of the largest pleasuring house in Mish. By Marius' reckoning it shouldn't have been her turn to take responsibility for town security for another three months. Either something had afflicted Benlut, the breeder of fighting dogs, or there had been a silent coup some time in the year since Marius had been in town. He squinted at the crest, and made a great show of considering it.

"I don't quite... Is it a dog buggering a soldier?" he asked, his voice as innocent as a stage comedian.

"Very funny." The steward dropped a hand towards his dagger. "You can fuck right off, jester man. There's no place for lepers in this town."

It had taken three days to walk to Mish. Marius knew he looked little worse than a man climbing from his deathbed. Granny was significantly more decayed, even if the full extent of her seven weeks of death had yet to really play itself out upon her features. The underworld had ceased to come for its denizens, and so death had ceased to act upon those who lived there. He smiled, and held out his hands.

"Leprosy? Are you talking about my sense of humour?"

"Off you fuck. Now." The steward had his fingers wrapped around the hilt now. His arm tensed, and in that moment, Marius moved. He had been working his toes underneath Alno as he spoke, and now he swung his foot upward, flinging the tom forward. Alno, angered by the sudden absence of warm ground against his paws, reacted as Marius had expected. His claws sunk deep into the steward's forearm. His teeth ripped through the thin shirt to lodge themselves into the delicate skin on the inside of the steward's elbow. Before the other man could scream or grab the heavy burden that had his weapon arm impaled, Marius had stepped forward and rammed a fist into his mouth. His other hand came round and gripped the hair at the back of the man's neck. He pushed the steward backwards so his knees buckled. In one quick moment the only thing holding him on balance was the strength in Marius' arms.

"You know, I normally don't mind a bit of graft and corruption." Marius shook the steward's head just enough to emphasise his point. "But I've had a thoroughly shitty week, and watching you punch an old woman has really given me an opportunity to work it out of my system." He tightened his grip, and was rewarded with a bulging of the shorter man's eyes. "Now, I'm going to make a few guesses, and you're going to tell me whether I'm correct or not, okay?" He moved his hands up and down, making the steward nod in agreement. "Good. Guess one. Mistress Fellipan has moved against the council and taken control of the town." A shake of the head. "No? Then she's working behind the scenes." A shrug. "I'll take that as a nod. Guess two. You've got at least sixty riner in that little bag I feel hanging round your neck." Nod. "More?" Pause. Squeeze. Hurried nod. "Guess three. You're going to give me that bag and let my friends and I walk into town, and you're going to suffer an immediate and permanent case of amnesia about us." Pause. Squeeze. Raise of the eyebrows and an amused stare over Marius' shoulder. Marius frowned. And felt the prick of something razor sharp against the back of his neck.

"Bugger."

Very carefully, making sure his hands could be seen at all times, he straightened the steward up and took a step back. Alno dropped from his victim's arm and ran between his legs before a kick could connect, streaking into the nearby brush in an instant. The steward flexed his bleeding arm, looked at Marius, and smiled. Then he drove his fist into Marius' unprotected stomach, doubling him over.

"Enjoy yourselves," he said. Someone grabbed the back of Marius' shirt and hauled him upright. He was spun round so that he faced the three guards who stood behind him, smiles like predators spread across their flat peasants' faces.

Guards are different to stewards. Firstly, they often have swords and a lot of metal covering their bodies. Metal on their heads, and over their fists, and very often over their knees and feet as well. Secondly, it's a steward's job to police the region in which they work, whereas guards usually just beat up whomever they're pointed at. And they'd just been pointed at Marius.

In all fairness, it wasn't the worst beating he'd ever received. Guards are often the poorest paid members of a town's security, drawn from those sons considered a bit too dim to take over the family farm, or smithy, or pick-pocketing ring. And all that metal can make a man clumsy. The three assailants crowded each other out in their eagerness to get their lumps in. For each blow that landed, another two were interrupted by an errant arm or leg. It set up a mighty clamour, all that metal hitting metal, but Marius knew how to survive a guard beating. He crumpled at the first blow, curled up as soon as he hit the ground, and let his shoulders and back take the majority of the punishment. He had plenty of time to reflect on another advantage to being dead: there's no need to protect your kidneys if you have no intention of using them. The same might go for nose, ribs and genitals, but Marius was quite fond of those.

In the end, the guards quickly tired of thumping an inanimate lump that neither begged for mercy, attempted to fight back, nor tried to escape. It was over in less than two minutes, and then he could relax and let himself be dragged through the gates and along the cobbled street towards the town's gaol.

And it was, Marius reflected – once he'd received another beating from those guards who had missed out on the first one because they were guarding it – a rather nice gaol indeed. Prisons in gambling towns, or well-run gambling towns at least, are not like those in big cities. The object of imprisonment in a big city is to punish the inmate until such time as a magistrate can be persuaded that there is a monetary value to be gained from giving you a damn good hanging or exiling you on the nearest ship to the Forgotten Continent. Cities are presided over by people who crave power, and power can only be truly expressed by holding it over someone else.

The owners of gambling towns, however, have no interest in nebulous concepts like power. They prefer money. And the best way to get a lot of money is to persuade punters to come back a second time and spend more. In gambling towns, repeat business is God. There is no value in exiling someone for the crime of running out of cash. Far better to allow them a short rest away

from the excitement of the town's attractions, the better
to help them remember where they might have a bank
account they haven't accessed yet, or a favour they can
call in, or best of all, the name of that nice fellow who
struck up a conversation last night and mentioned very
reasonable loans at half the going rate of your average
bank in Scorby. It can be difficult to have those sort of
internal dialogues while a rat is nibbling at your toes.

So the gaol in Mish was relatively well-appointed.
Marius had a bench raised off the floor, with both a
pillow and sheet to lie upon. The guards provided him
with a ticket he could redeem to get his boots back,
with only a two riner administration fee to be paid
upon receipt. The fact he had no boots was a simple
administrative inconvenience. This was Mish. Boots
could be purchased at the gift store. Even the bowl of
gruel he was given that evening had hardly been pissed
in at all. Marius still had the sense to sniff at it carefully.

"Arjen!" Another small difference between gaols:
here, the guards wanted prisoners to remember their
names. It helped a confused punter – and they were,
to some extent, *all* confused – to remember who to pay
back for all the little kindnesses they were told had been
done them while they were sleeping. "What's in this?"

Arjen paused in his journey to the next cell, and
returned to the window of Marius' door. Every
guardhouse had an Arjen. There had to be *someone*
willing to scrub the floors, and unblock the privy, and
feed the prisoners while the other guards got ready to
go out of an evening and start calling in all those favours
they did for the town's prostitutes earlier in the week.
In a city guardhouse such a duty often fell to the oldest
member of the watch, the guy who crapped away all his
graft when he found out that it was the uniform, not

the man, which spent the last forty years getting booze and snuff and hand-relief for free. But in gambling towns, there were no guards of retirement age. Either they got smart, and retired as soon as their hidden nest egg became too large to keep in the nest, or they stayed stupid, and found themselves marching next to a thousand other slightly bamboozled "volunteers" the next time the King's army came through the area looking for recruits to fight whatever war was being fought that season. Even so, there was always one who got left behind, who zigged when he should have zagged, raised when he should have folded, or stayed loyal to Tallian Rosie when even the town rats knew she'd contracted the pox. Somebody had to shut the gate after the horse had bolted. He pressed his face up against the door, and viewed Marius with gentle, trusting eyes.

"Don't you like it?"

"I don't know." Marius sniffed again. "I don't want to taste it until I know whether I've worked up an immunity to whatever's in it."

"It's cinnamon," Arjen said in a hurt tone. "It won't poison you."

"Cinnamon?" Marius was genuinely wonderstruck. "Who puts cinnamon in prison gruel?"

"I do." Arjen had his pride. It wasn't big, and it wasn't worth anything, but it was *his* pride, and he was quite proud of it. It may have been a shitty job, but if it was worth doing, it was worth doing with a modicum of something, and pride was all he had left. Arjen was in the wrong job. He should have been a teacher of small children, or the proprietor of a petting zoo; some occupation where small kindnesses were noticed and a caring attitude wasn't considered a weakness. But then, every guardhouse has an Arjen, and the world does not need another petting zoo. "I thought it might make the gruel seem a little nicer."

"It does." Marius took a spoonful – they had even allowed him a spoon, and only added five pennies to his bill – then finished the bowl off in a flurry. "It really does. Thank you." He wiped the bowl clean with his fingers, and held it up to the window for Arjen to retrieve. "Thank you, Arjen. That was delicious."

Arjen smiled. His was not a job that attracted gratitude. "You're most welcome."

Marius returned his smile. "You'd best be getting on," he said. "The other prisoners will be wanting theirs, and I think they'll be most pleased when they get it."

"Oh, there's only one other prisoner." Arjen pointed off to his left. "And he's probably still drunk. He won't appreciate it."

"Only one?" Marius was puzzled. "In a gaol this size? You must run a very orderly town, my friend."

"Not us." Evening had fallen. The day guards had gone off-shift, dispersing to whatever bordello or back alley they'd been saving up in their imaginations over the last week. The night watch were slowly filtering through the city streets towards the gaol. Arjen was always lonely at this time. All he had to look forward to was the long climb to his room in the attic, to count out his weekly pay and put the coins in envelopes to be collected by the series of loan sharks who kept him working and glad he still had a roof over his head, even if it only cleared him by an inch and a half. Leaning a shoulder against the door, he shook his head. "It's been a lot quieter since Master Benlut was elected mayor."

"Has it, now? Why is that, do you think?"

"Well, he's been clever, hasn't he?"

"What's he done?"

Arjen stretched, and yawned. "Used to be that whoever was mayor had to supply all the stewards and pay for the entire guard. But Master Benlut, well, he's changed all that. He's doled it out through the entire council, so's all six of them have to contribute a quota. Master Fellux covers all the gambling houses..." Which he already owns, thought Marius. "Master A'alk covers the merchant's quarter..." Ditto. "Mistress Uill covers the taverns..." Marius was pretty sure he could see a pattern forming. "And so on."

"And poor Mistress Fellipan has to cover her, ah, houses of convenience and all the town entrances and exits, am I right?"

Arjen harrumphed. "Yah, well. Serves her right, it does."

"Why is that?"

"A slattern like her on the council." Arjen was quite moral, in his own way. Naïve, and possibly deluded, but moral. "They may be necessary, but a woman who charges for providing God's own special gift should make up for it somehow, I say."

"Ah." Marius was a past master at hiding a smile. He did so now. "Would I be correct in thinking you are a member of the Ascetic Temple?"

Arjen bowed his head. "Sadly lapsed, but I do still believe."

Marius made the sign of the Seven Austerities. "Thank you for the gruel, brother."

Arjen quickly returned the sign. "And you, brother."

"Thank you also for the conversation, but if I may, I might attempt to sleep now." Marius indicated his surroundings. "A tiring day, as you can imagine."

"Yes, yes, of course." Arjen glanced around the cell. "A better tomorrow, brother."

"And you."

Marius waited until he was sure Arjen had moved through the door at the end of the cellblock. Only then did he smile, and lie down on his shelf. He loved the religious. He really did. A stranger was just a friend they hadn't met yet, and friendship was a coin Marius could flip any way he wanted. He listened to the sounds of the night watch coming in to the floors above him. Dinner had been acceptable. The cinnamon was a nice touch. But he had no desire to sample breakfast. Still, the night was long, and the dead don't sleep. Gerd and Granny might be gods-knew-where, running around in panic without him. He might be trapped, and further away from discovering Keth's resting place than he had been since he started his journey. And he might have no hope that she had survived, even in such a state as his, but he still *very much* wanted to find her resting place before he tore the marrow from Drenthe's bones. Still, he had learned important information, and more importantly, he had made a friend. All he had to do now was decide how to flip him.

There were hours in which to decide. Just as the day has a rhythm, a flow of spirit that determines mood, alertness, and most importantly for a conman, reaction speed, so does the night. It holds its own versions of the late-for-work rush, the slow morning dissolution of dedication, and the torpor that comes from a particularly boozy lunch full of sausage rolls and pastries. Marius listened to the night watch settle into its long-held routines. There was plenty of time for the first burst of energy to dissipate as the evening stretched. Details might differ, but guardhouses all over the continent ran to the same general tempo, especially at night. A quick check of the paperwork, the assignation of patrols, dealing with the grumbling from whomever struck unlucky and wouldn't be patrolling anywhere near a decent pie shop, bar, or whorehouse. Then settle in, light the fire, do the midnight rounds, get comfy, and try to wait out the long, quiet hours until the day watch arrives and you can go home.

Marius listened to the sounds filter dully through the door at the end of the cellblock, marking off each event in its turn. He had plenty of time to wait, and in waiting, to ponder his own situation, and just what the hell had led him here. Marius had been in plenty of gaols before. He knew the dangers of too much contemplation: how it could lead to inaction, and from inaction to despair. But sometimes it was better to smooth out the past, to make a better platform from which to jump. He lay with one hand beneath his head, raised the other one up and stared at it as he turned it this way and that.

Marius had been dead before. Compared to then, this time didn't look so bad. After a week of non-life his skin showed no signs of decay and, when he raised it to his nose and sniffed, there was no smell of putrefaction. Marius had robbed more than his share of corpses. He knew the smell of death intimately, and could identify a time of demise by how bloated and spongy a body had become. He felt well; better, he felt as fit and healthy as he ever had. Rarely had he lain in bed without some sort of twinge or bruise or physical complaint. But death seemed to suit him. He felt strong, vibrant, his body free from complaint despite the beating it had received only hours earlier. Marius knew something was wrong. Wasn't there always? Decay should be crawling along his veins by now, eating his flesh from the inside. But there were no signs of damage. If not for the hole in his chest and the sallow greying of his skin he'd be in the best shape of his life. It might have given him hope for Keth, if not for the identity of the corpse who had abducted her. Drenthe was not the type to leave loose ends. Keth was dead, final and absolute, of that he had no doubt. Drenthe would see to it. Dead and *dead* were two separate things. As long as Death stayed absent, if any other man had been involved... there might have been a chance that Marius could find her, if not alive, then, certainly not quite so *dead*. He bit his lip. And then what? Two dead lovers, with no home and no *living* future together. What could they have but a long, slow decline into putrefaction?

Marius poked the skin on his hand. Would that have been so bad? Other couples died separately, for the most part, parted by time or geography, or class. Did they find each other afterwards? Did they haunt the corridors of the underworld, calling out each other's names? Or was there a forgetting, a slow numbness of thought as the things that were once important faded and were discarded along with the flesh that fell from their bones? Marius had no real idea what went on in the halls of the dead. He'd tried not to think about them for the last four years.

But Gerd's reappearance... now that was something. Marius considered his friend. The young swineherd had been dead for four years. What did a corpse that old look like? Not like Gerd, of that he was sure. So many years of rot would do things to a body. Yet he showed nothing of it. He was a little sunken around the edges, and his eyes were slightly filmed over, but nothing so much that it couldn't be explained away as the result of a debilitating disease – something tropical, from one of those jungle countries explorers were always coming back from with fevers and strange outbursts of fear at dinner parties. Marius remembered meeting Sir Folmer Duckett at a reception to honour his return from the Hidden Territories. He'd looked worse than Gerd, and smelled like a crocodile's privy to boot.

Marius wasn't a doctor. He'd pretended to be one on several occasions, usually when a foreign potentate's daughter needed something explained away. But this was too different, too *medical*. He needed knowledge he couldn't hope to understand, and he couldn't think of anyone who might have it. Placing his hand behind his head with its twin, he stared at the rough ceiling of his cell. Get outfitted, get to Borgho City, and get himself an army. Get Keth. Get revenge. Get answers. In that order.

He lay that way, barely thinking, letting his eyes wander the cracks and bumps of the ceiling, until the sounds of the watch house diminished. The minute groans that indicated a fire warming the stone walls settled into stillness. The night deepened and widened, in a way that only someone used to being awake long after sensible people have gone to bed can recognise. When he was sure the torpid post-midnight hours were at their nadir, Marius swung himself off his bench and examined the door to his cell.

Holding cells are a curious hybrid of imprisonment and ease of access. Dungeon doors are designed to open twice in a prisoner's life: once to let him in, and once so the guards can collect his body for burial. A true gaol cell is designed to open once a day: in the morning, so the prisoner can be removed to whatever work gang, exercise yard, or beating they've been assigned to, and then be closed again behind them when they return for the night. But holding cells may only contain an occupant for an hour or two whilst an appropriately large bribe is delivered to the sergeant in charge. In a city big enough, or corrupt enough, such a cell might see a dozen different occupants a day. Nobody wants to haul on a heavy steel door twelve times a day, not when the guardhouse might have twenty doors or more. Much as the holding cell itself is designed to give only the appearance of long-term despair, so the door gives only the *impression* of weight, the *essence* of impenetrability. Such a door, in such a cell, in a town where the occupants are treated as no more than temporary debtors having a quiet moment to rediscover their wealth… such doors presented no impediment to a professional like Marius.

There is a reason why real cell doors have small, flap-like windows: to prevent prisoners from reaching through and identifying the lock hanging from the hasp as, for example, a Tightlok Number Five, one of the cheapest and most widely available in Scorby. It is widely available because it is produced to a single design, and cheap because it is made from inferior materials. It is almost never used to contain hardened criminals inside a cell because it only has one combination of tumblers, and if a person happens to be carrying a key that fits one, it will fit them all. An experienced lockpick with a piece of wire can open a Tightlok Number Five in under thirty seconds. Or, if they lack a wire, a suitably long sliver of hard wood will do the job. Which is why most *real* cells have a bundle of rags on the floor on which to sleep, and not a wooden shelf.

Marius was out in under three minutes.

He immediately sank into the shadows at the other side of the corridor. One of the first things he had learned as a street thief on the Borgho streets was how to make use of the darkness, how to fall so still that a mark would walk within fingers' reach and never see the dip that removed his wallet. Marius had stayed small enough to retain this skill into his adulthood. If his exertions caused anyone to come into the corridor, his childhood training might give him the extra second or two he needed to get past. He waited a full minute, letting his breathing slow, then remembered he wasn't breathing to begin with, and suppressed a smile. Being dead had too many advantages. He was going to have to avoid the temptation to go back to his old ways.

When he was sure nobody was coming, he slunk towards the door and examined it. A lightweight internal door, it even bore a handle just waiting to be turned. Marius shook his head. They really weren't expecting proper criminals in this part of town. Slowly, in tiny increments, Marius turned the handle, waiting between each minute movement for any sound from the room beyond. None came. He placed his hand flat against the wood and leaned the smallest measure of his weight against it. The door shifted. Unlocked. Marius stifled a giggle, and let it slide shut again. This was too easy, even for Mish. Even a gambling town had the occasional thief, or the odd mugger. There was no such thing as a murder-free town, especially when money and whores were involved. Where were they kept? And what was on the other side of the door that gave the guards confidence enough to keep them in such pitiful security?

Marius stepped back. There was no way to find out, short of walking through. He closed his eyes, and ignored the grey line that appeared on the floor at his feet to show that at least one prisoner had done more than leave peacefully under their own power in recent days. He took one unnecessary breath, and prepared to sneak through. To his immediate right, someone snored. Marius froze, then relaxed as he realised who it was. Arjen had mentioned another prisoner. Curiosity took hold. Marius tiptoed to the cell door through which the snore had erupted, and peeked through the window.

An idiot lay on the floor. Flat on his back, arms and legs thrown akimbo, for all the world like a child sleeping the unselfconscious sleep of innocence. Marius knew him for an idiot immediately. Firstly, he hadn't managed to stay on the sleeping shelf. More importantly, his expensive-looking jerkin bore the crest of the House of Tesnuk, the most powerful family of merchants in the south of the continent. A simple foot soldier would not have a shirt so fine, nor trousers and belt so obviously handmade. No soldier would think to remove their high leather boots and stand them neatly at the end of the bed before he succumbed to his drunken stupor. All of which marked out this particular occupant as a Tesnukian merchant-son, a member of the family itself; and therefore, very rich indeed. And if he hadn't the sense to pay off the guards to take his inebriated arse back to his hotel to see off his drunk there, he was plainly an idiot. Marius eyed the clothes, the boots, the strap of the moneybag he spied peeking out above the collar of the drunkard's shirt. And smiled.

"Psst."

The prisoner stirred.

"Psst. Mate."

The prisoner, oblivious to his newly acquired friend, snorted and delivered a fully rounded fart. Marius sighed, and fingered the sliver of wood with which he had opened the lock on his cell door. Marius had won the Keeled Haul's annual darts tournament seven years in a row, mainly because most of his opponents were too pissed to hold the darts the right way round. Even so… He took aim, and sent the sliver arrowing straight at the sleeper's cheek.

"Wha…? Ow! Lady fuck!" The drunk jerked upright, slapping the dart away from his face. "Fucking hell!"

"Psst. Mate." Marius tapped on the window bars. "Here."

"What? What?" The drunk looked about himself blearily. "Oh, fuck me. Not again."

"Oi. Are you thick or something?"

It took some time, but eventually the idiot managed to point his head and both his eyes in the right direction. "I told you I don't want any gruel."

Marius sighed again. "Do I look like the gaoler?"

"Actually…" The prisoner focussed. "No. Who are you?"

"A fellow prisoner."

"But you're outside."

"Not yet." Marius leaned in closer. "What's your name?"

The drunk puffed out his chest. The change in his centre of gravity made him wobble. "Toshy. Toshy Tesnuk."

"Really?"

"You don't believe me?"

"No, no. It's just–"

"I'm an important man, I am. I'm Assistant Special Envoy to the… the…" He waved a hand in the vague direction of "out there", and continued, "We're selling stuff to all the towns and shit."

"Ah." Assistant Special Envoy. A merchant title, afforded to all useless sons and idiots, the better to send them on long journeys and keep them the hell away from any important goings-on.

"I've got duties, I have. Special duties."

"Really? What are they, then?" Despite himself, Marius' interest was piqued. Rumours circled the Tesnuk merchants like wary scavengers. They were assassins, spies for the Scorban king, slave traders, terrorists dedicated to the overthrow of the establishment by creating financial instability, anything but simply a powerful merchant family who knew a thing or two about business. All Marius knew was that wherever he went, and whatever discord he found, there was a Tesnuk lurking nearby. It would be nice to know if it was merely coincidence.

But he wasn't going to get anywhere this time. Toshy was already making a clumsy attempt to tap his nose with his finger. Nose, eye, cheek, wince. "Special," he said. "Secret and shit. Need to know and all that."

"Ah, well. Fair enough, your special envoyness."

"Anyway..." Toshy had taken the long way round, but he'd arrived at a thought of his own. "What you doing out there?"

"Helping you."

"Helping me do what?"

"Return to your special duties."

"I don't get it."

Marius tried not to roll his eyes. "I've come to get you out. But I need your help."

"I don't get it."

Gods help me, Marius thought. "You want to get out of here, yes?"

"Suppose."

"You want to get back to your delegation?"

"Will Kitty be there?" Toshy made kissy-kissy sounds. "Here, Kitty, Kitty. Come here, darling. Got a hunnert riner. You know what I like..."

"Yes, yes." The dead have no gag reflex. Marius was

grateful. "Kitty's waiting. But I need your help."

"What?" Toshy stopped fondling his imaginary whore. "You said you were helping me."

"I am. But the guards..." Marius rubbed his thumb and forefinger together in the universal motion for "money, baby". Toshy t'ched.

"Fine, fine." He fumbled the moneybag from around his neck. Marius avoided chortling like a crazed banker. That was one *hell* of a large moneybag. Toshy found his feet at the third attempt, and staggered over to the door. Marius took the bag, and pocketed it.

"Excellent. Now..." Marius glanced past Toshy. He shouldn't try this, he really shouldn't. He should just take the money and scarper. But here he was, standing in the corridor in nothing but his torn and filthy undershirt, with the cold seeping up through his bare feet and even the slightest breeze playing havoc with his gonads. And there was the idiot son, kitted out like a minor princeling with not a thought in his empty head for the needs of others. Besides, he thought, glancing at the end of the bed, they are *such* nice boots.

"I need your boots."

"What? What you want my boots for?"

"Ssh." Marius waved his voice down. "Watch the volume."

"But what... what you want my boots for?" Toshy asked again in a stage whisper.

Good question. Marius thought furiously. "Disguise, isn't it?"

"Huh?"

"Think about it." He beckoned Toshy closer, so they stood mouth to ear with only the inch of wood between them. "Nobody's going to believe that someone like me has the money to free an important person like you."

There was no way he was getting away with this. There really wasn't. "But if I disguise myself…"

Toshy got the idea. "They'll think you're me."

"Exactly."

A dark thought crossed the drunkard's brow. "Wait a minute."

Shit. "Yes?"

"Wait." Toshy was grasping at something. Marius could see it coming. He braced himself to run. He should have been satisfied with the money. He shouldn't have been greedy. Perhaps he could get through the door and out the exit before anyone reacted. Perhaps…

Toshy's thought found its way to the front of his brain. "Boots won't do it." Marius relaxed. The Assistant Special Envoy was earning his title.

"Sorry?"

"You need all my close." He leaned right in, breathed seven kinds of alcohol across Marius. "Perfick disguise, see? Look jus' like me."

Marius could have laughed. He could have kissed the little idiot, but then he might have been mistaken for Kitty, and that would be all *kinds* of ugly. So instead, he settled for nodding in agreement. "You're absolutely right."

"Right." Toshy began to strip, giggling like a clever princess. Marius shook his head in wonderment. Far too much inbreeding in the Tesnuk clan, he thought. There's a fine line between protecting your assets and creating an army of Assistant Special Envoys. The booze-stained jerkin came through the window, then his shirt, trousers and belt, then his underpants. Marius picked them up between thumb and finger and dropped them back in the cell.

"You keep those," he whispered. "You don't want to ruin your own disguise."

"I get a disguise?"

"Oh yes." Marius quickly stripped, and slipped on Toshy's clothes. A little on the large side, and a little… he sniffed… boozy, but they'd more than do. He shoved his dirty, torn clothes through the window. "You get to be me."

"Magic!" The young Tesnuk frowned as another moment of clarity threatened to upset his mental equilibrium. "Who are you, again?"

"Your rescuer."

"I know that. Whass your name?"

"Oh, didn't I tell you? Boots, please."

He handed the boots through. Marius slipped them on. Oh, they *were* nice. He could walk to Borgho in boots like these, no problem.

"Well?"

Marius looked up, the soul of innocence. "Drenthe. Drenthe McScorbus the Third. At your service."

For the first time, doubt managed to get its fingertips into Toshy's attention span.

"You're taking the piss. That's a made-up name."

"Oh, is it, Toshy Tesnuk?"

Toshy considered. "Yeah, fair do's."

"Thank you. Now," Marius indicated his undershirt. "Get yourself in that, and lie on the bed. Turn your face to the wall and pretend to be asleep. I'll be back for you as soon as I've sorted everything out, okay?"

"Okay."

"Not a sound now."

"Okay."

"Got me?"

"Got you." Doubts banished, Toshy gave Marius two thumbs up. Marius tried to return the gesture, gave up, and settled for a little wave.

"Not a sound," he warned again, and turned his attention back to the door. Behind him he heard a short scuffle, then a thud, as if something large and stupid had fallen over trying to get its trousers on.

"I'm all right."

Marius hung his head. "That's nice." Before he could bear witness to any other acts of Assistant Special Envoyness he braced himself against the door, turned the handle with minute slowness, and slid it open far enough to press an eye against the gap.

The room beyond was dark, almost consumed by shadows. To his right, a pair of entrance doors shone dully against the darkness, their edges illuminated by a light shining through the gaps from behind. The exit to the outside world, Marius guessed, which meant the main desk would be somewhere off to the left. He shifted his weight, squeezing hard against the wall to get a glimpse in the other direction. Behind him, Toshy scrambled onto the bed shelf, cursing as he slipped and cracked something then *shhh*ing himself only slightly less noisily than an invading army. Marius winced. He could see the edge of the desk, bathed in a soft, flickering glow. He pushed his face harder into the gap. There. A wall sconce, its light falling down upon a fat guardsman with a moustache like a privet hedge. He sat with his back against the wall, a large hat tilted down over his eyes and massive, booted feet perched on the desk. Obviously the duty sergeant: everybody else would be patrolling the streets. The edge of the hat fluttered in a regular rhythm. Marius counted to three between ripples. Asleep. Perfect. He slid the door open another inch, paused, then another. Slowly, it opened enough that he could slide his head and upper body through. A quick check of the surroundings and he slipped through the door completely, stepping to the side so he was lost within the deep shadow by the wall. Nobody moved.

Marius took a moment to centre himself, to think shadowy thoughts. The room remained still. Unbelievably still. If not for the sleeping sergeant, Marius might almost believe the guardhouse had been abandoned. There was none of the constant activity that marked a gaol at even the most sluggish of times. No passage of guardsmen in and out; no protests from prisoners hauled off to the waiting cells; no dull thuds or muffled cries from the miscellaneous staff and hangers-on that any establishment of this size attracted – clerks, cooks, cleaners, whores, dips, low-lifes, fathers, mothers, blackbirders, street vendors, kids, dogs, you name it. Even the ghosts had given up and shot off for the night. Marius had never seen a guardhouse so utterly serene. It was unnatural. He was almost set on breaking cover and approaching the desk out of sheer curiosity when the front door banged back on its hinges. Two guards barrelled through, deep in argument. Marius released a silent sigh of satisfaction, and settled deeper into the shadow to watch.

"...not right!" the taller of the two was saying. His shorter, more heavy-set companion waved both his hands in a gesture of frustration.

"What does it matter?" He stopped in the middle of the empty room and gestured at the silence around them. "You don't like this? No little bastards underfoot. No whining women – 'Wah, wah, he's a good man officer, he don't mean no harm...'" His voice took on the shrill, nasal tone of a backwoods wife.

"It's not that. You know it isn't." The tall one leaned over as if shielding his words from the door behind them. "It gives me the creeps, that's all. And it should you."

"What creeps?" snapped the shorter one. "What *creeps*?"

Behind the guards, the sergeant's feet were quietly being drawn back behind the desk. A hand came off his chest and tilted his hat back, revealing a face that had learned the hard way the difference between boot and stick and fist and wall. As silent as death, he leaned forward, placed his elbows on the desk, rested his massive cliff of a head on his fists and waited to be noticed. Marius could have laughed himself sick, but his desire to see what came next kept him silent.

"How can you mean, what creeps?" The taller guard pointed back towards the outside. "You know there's something not right about those blood-robed…"

"Ssh, ssh." His companion glanced uneasily at the door. "You want them to hear you."

"See? You know what I'm talking about."

"I…" The little man stiffened. "I'm sure I don't know what you mean."

"Yes you do. You know exactly what I mean."

"And exactly what," the sergeant said gently, "*do* you mean?"

It was as if someone had dropped a little bomb under the guards' feet. They leapt in separate directions, quivering to attention, eyes pinned to a spot a perfect three inches below the juncture of wall and ceiling. The sergeant smiled, like a snake deciding which mouse to eat first, and repeated his question. The taller guard, obviously finding the prospect of verbal evisceration less creepy than whatever it was he had experienced on the street, found his voice. It was an octave higher than the one he had been using, but at least he found it.

"The Central Gaol, sir."

"Don't 'sir' me, Pyoc. I work for a living."

Marius couldn't help thinking "Oh, really?" at this, but kept his own counsel. Something interesting was unfolding. He had the feeling he was about to learn something of great value.

"Yes, sir. Sorry, uh, Sergeant."

"Now, am I to understand that you, despite long-standing orders to the contrary, are not performing your duties to the standard I expect from the lovely lads I've taken under my wing?"

"No, si– Sergeant. It's just…" Pyoc glanced over to his fellow guardsman for some sign of brotherhood. His brother guard, knowing exactly where the gravy for his bread came from, remained traitorously uninvolved. Pyoc decided to jump and save the hangman the trouble of tightening the noose around his neck. "I just… I still don't like it, sir. We drop 'em off, and then we never sees 'em again, you know? It's like…"

"Like what, guardsman?"

Animals in the wild can sense an oncoming storm. Their highly developed survival instinct prompts them to run away, to find logs to hide under and burrows to slither down, all the better to wait out the ensuing hail of destruction and danger. Pyoc seemed to have left his survival instinct in his other uniform. "It's like they just disappear, innit? I mean, it's okay for the bad ones, I mean, like, fair enough and all, but Missus Tumbletee went in three weeks ago, sir, and we only nicked her coz she didn't make payment for her best girl, and we normally let 'em out after a clip and a reminder, and…" he faltered, momentum dissipating in the face of the Sergeant's unruffled calm, "and, and, it don't seem right. Somehow. Sir. Sergeant. Sir."

He wound down and shuffled his feet, not daring to look at the immobile figure behind the desk. Animals in the wild would already be under a fallen log three forests away, counting their offspring and hoping the lightning didn't come too close.

"I see." The sergeant turned his attention to the statue at Pyoc's side. "And what about you, Mister Figmin? Do you have any revolutionary thoughts on the nature of our assigned duties? Anything you'd like to share with your dear old sergeant?"

"Sergeant, no Sergeant!" Figmin's stance, delivery, and obedience were parade-ground perfect. Figmin, Marius decided, was a crawler.

"I see." The sergeant inhaled deeply through his nose. Wild animals would have been praying to wild animal gods, and promising utter obeisance if only they survived the coming onslaught. Marius allowed himself a small smile.

"Mister Figmin."

"Sergeant, yes Sergeant!"

"Be a good lad." The sergeant indicated the door. "Fuck off and leave me and young Pyoc alone for half an hour, would you?"

"Sergeant, ye– What?"

"You heard me, Figmin."

"I..." Figmin looked from Pyoc to the sergeant and back again. "Uh, yep. Sure, Sarge." He hit the door at a flat scurry and was swallowed up by the night. The sergeant leaned back in his chair and swung his boots back onto the desk.

"Stupid boy," he said softly. "Get over here."

"Sergeant?"

"Do you want the whole bloody city to hear? Get over here. Now." He beckoned Pyoc closer. The young guard shuffled over. Marius closed both eyes, then opened one in a squint. As Pyoc reached the desk the sergeant slammed his feet on the floor, loud enough to make even Marius jump.

"What the fucking hell do you think you're doing, discussing my orders in the middle of the fucking street?"

"But…"

"Don't you 'but' me, boy!" The sergeant's fist hit the desk like a cannonball. "Who do you think you are to talk about my orders where the public can hear you? Are you fucking stupid or just *completely* fucking stupid?"

"But…" Pyoc was on the verge of tears. This wasn't going to take long at all.

"Do you think you get a breastplate and boots because you're smart enough to *think*, boy? You don't think when I give you orders. You follow my fucking orders and do what you're fucking told!"

Pyoc was taking huge gulps of air now. Even "But…" was escaping him. He flapped his mouth a couple of times, his whole body quivering. Marius hadn't seen a guard turn to custard this quickly since his days in the Tallian Brigades. He might even have enjoyed it, if not for the memory of what else he'd seen in the Tallian days. He was contemplating ways to make it to the door unobserved, when the sergeant's tone changed, and things suddenly became very interesting indeed.

"All right," the sergeant said. "That should see him off."

"Are you sure?" Pyoc was all business, fear and custard banished in an instant. The sergeant raised a hand, and they both listened.

"Yep, no doubt. The door's not so muted in the wind. He's gone."

"Okay."

"So. What have you found out?"

Pyoc shook his head. "Nothing new. The place is tied up tighter than my grandmother's arse. Nobody outside a Fellipan uniform gets past the front desk, and nobody in a Fellipan uniform is talking. I'm not convinced the foot soldiers know anything, anyway. It's the others we need to get to, the ones at the back of the house. But…" He shrugged.

"Fuck's sake. It's been three months."

"I know, boss. I'm trying. But all I've got is what I'm getting from the street patrols. Anyone who goes in doesn't seem to be coming out. And not just strangers. They took Durlie Haver in last week on a drunk and disorderly, and nobody's seen him since."

"Haver! But he's the only thing between us and the Rat Gangs! The streets'll be running with blood!"

"That's the funny thing. Nobody's seen half the Rat Gangs, either. I'm sorry, boss. Unless I can get someone past the front desks, I don't know what else I can do."

If there was one thing Marius had come to recognise after thirty years in the con game, it was an entrance line. He stepped from the shadows as if on cue, clomping his expensive new boots on the wooden floor.

"Gentlemen," he said in his best Master of Ceremonies voice. "Let's talk!"

FIVE

"Who the holy roaring fuck are you?"

Pyoc and the sergeant were quicker than Marius had expected. He had barely swept his arms back in an entrance gesture before they were on him, swords held at his throat and gut. He smiled and reached out to push the blades away, but the points held firm. Strong wrists, Marius thought, and quickly gave them his friendliest grin.

"Me? I'm the answer to your problem, Sergeant."

"It's not me with the problem, laddie." The old guard's sword slid forward a half inch. Marius felt it pin back the skin of his throat. He raised an eyebrow, and met the sergeant's eyes.

"Do you always kill your prisoners? Or do you let Mistress Fellipan do it for you?"

The Sergeant said nothing, but he and Pyoc exchanged a lightning-quick glance. The pressure at Marius' throat and stomach eased slightly.

"What have you heard?"

"Enough to know you don't like what's going on in your town." Marius stepped back and to the side, away from the swords. "Enough to know that you and I might just be wanting answers to the same question."

"Oh? And what might they be, Tesnuk?"

"Huh?" Marius looked down at his jerkin. "Ah, yes." He shrugged, and smiled. "Where do you bury your dead?"

"In the graveyard, of course."

"And where is that?"

Pyoc tilted his chin towards the door. "Out past the Southern Quarter, back of the Debtor's Gate."

"Close to the main gaol house?"

"Middling."

"But closer to the main gaol than any of the other guardhouses."

The two guards considered for a moment. "Yes," the sergeant admitted. "Closer. What's that got to do with anything?"

"Maybe nothing." He turned to Pyoc. "Why don't you tell me what your problem is, and let's see if ours match, eh?"

"Sergeant?"

"Go on, son." The older man eyed Marius. "I've heard rumours about Tesnuk traders. Maybe there's a reason why this delegation stopped here just when we were investigating something."

Not for the first time, Marius was glad to hitch his agenda to somebody else's reputation. He turned to the young guardsman, avoiding the sergeant's speculative gaze.

"How about it?"

"Well, sir–"

"Call me Marius."

"Well, Marius," Pyoc's thin face grew even more grave. "It's like this…"

Much of Pyoc's story was as Marius had suspected. Mayor Benlut had been elected three months ago and had all but retired from public life, only appearing at the odd public ceremony and never for more than a few moments. Edicts were issued via his deputy, the suddenly-promoted Mistress Fellipan. Within a month, stewards of House Fellipan had infiltrated all levels of the town's government, firstly in concert with those who occupied the role and then, increasingly, in place of the incumbents. Much of the town's infrastructure now hinged on the Deputy Mayor's voice. Nobody seemed to notice; or at least, nobody very much objected. Mish was a town built for pleasure, and as long as that pleasure was still liberally applied, nobody cared very much who provided it. But the changes raised concerns amongst some of the older and more cynical of the city's servants. A number of high-ranking guardsmen had retired suddenly, and been replaced by red-shirted stewards. More and more crimes became punishable by incarceration at the Central Gaol. Once, only the higher-level crimes merited internment in their dungeons and punishment chambers. Now any infraction, no matter how minor, was reason to fear the men in red. The smaller guardhouses, which functioned as a means of keeping minor criminals and drunken idiots off the streets for a few days, became emptier. Crime was the sole province of Mistress Fellipan's troops.

Then it was noticed that certain low-level known figures were being picked up and weren't returning to their usual haunts. Street girls, mainly, and leaders of the smaller youth gangs. Nobody important. Just the local faces that the local guards might bother checking in on if it was a slow night. The gaol houses grew quieter, and the back alleys less populated. More and more people were delivered to the Central Gaol and never seen again. Then the crimes themselves became more inconsequential. A disorderly drunk might have expected to spend a night in the warm and welcoming confines of the local cells. Now they were hauled off to the foreboding edifice of the Central Gaol, delivered into perdition alongside stabbers and fondlers and the beaters of courtesans. For the last six weeks, orders had come down on a daily basis, detailing the ever more pitiable crimes that resulted in transportation across town. The local cells were left empty and clean and those in charge of them had an ever-increasing list of questions. Questions that nobody in House Fellipan was answering. Even attempting to question orders was beginning to result in officers of the watch leaving their posts at the end of their shift and never coming back.

"So you decided to find some answers for yourself?"

"We've tried," Pyoc replied. "Trouble is there's been such a turnover in guardsmen in the last couple of weeks, men moving between watch houses and new ones turning up. It's impossible to tell who you can and can't trust anymore. Nobody's talking to anyone else because nobody wants to walk out one night and find themselves – well, we don't know what. A man might be honest as his mother's life, but if he's come into your station in the last three weeks…"

"Like Figmin."

"Like Figmin." The sergeant nodded. "Says he came in from Shivel a month ago looking for work. Had his own sword with him and got lucky at the Rubble Street watch house just as they were looking to replace a leaver. Could be he's on the line, but…" He shrugged.

"But he isn't from Shivel, I can tell you that."

Both men eyed Marius warily. "And how do you know that?"

Marius pointed to the scabbards hanging at their hips. "Shivel men tie their blades backwards on the same side

as their sword hand, so they can draw like this..." He
swept his hand from front to back, slipping an imaginary
sword from its sheath. "Point's facing you soon as it's
drawn, see? But your friend has his tied in the same
cross-body way as you. So..."

"So he's one of them."

Marius shrugged. "Or he just doesn't need anyone
finding out about his past. There are a lot of reasons
for some men to lie, and they're not always what you
think." He kept his gaze from his rich clothes, but the
thought reminded him. "So there's no crime that brings
a man to your door at all, then?"

"Ach, not many." The sergeant shook his head in
frustration. "We try to keep a few back, if we can, and
we still give the rich ones the comfort of our facilities..."
Marius breathed an inner sigh of relief. There was no
mistake, then. Toshy would wake up sober, angry,
and hoodwinked, but at least he'd wake up. "But we
only manage a few a night at best. Fellipan's men are
everywhere. We can't risk too much."

"Well," Marius smiled, and clapped him on the
shoulder. "Risks are what I do best." Liar, said a voice
inside his head. Rotten, cowardly, lying liar. And it
was right, of course, but Marius had a slimy, slithering
suspicion wriggling through his mind, and there was
only one place to go to step on that suspicion's neck.
Risks might not be what he did best, but perhaps it was
time to find a new best thing to do. "Why don't you tell
me what happens when you deliver a prisoner?"

SIX

"And you're absolutely sure you want to do this?" Pyoc muttered for the umpteenth time. And for the umpteenth time, the little voice in Marius' head answered no.

"For the umpteenth time, yes."

"It's your funeral."

"Again."

"What?"

"Nothing."

They strode through the darkened streets of Mish, past taverns that had closed hours before normal, and bordellos with shuttered doors. It was unnatural. Mish was a money town. The streets should be packed with fools just begging to be parted from their bankrolls. Doors should be thrown open, light spilling into the street in a warm, welcoming haze of professional innocence and bonhomie. The air should ring with the sounds of song, cries of welcome, laughter, shouting, fighting, fucking, fighting *while* fucking... and there was nothing. The night was black and silent. Marius' footsteps kicked up minute puffs of dust where the dirt street should have been compacted flat by the never-ending passage of feet. Where he expected the air to be thick with the odours of sweat, cooking, incense, and cum, he smelled only fear. The few travellers they came upon scurried onwards as if they had no errand more urgent than getting back to their hotel and hiding under their beds.

"How long has it been like this?"

"About a week or so," said Pyoc, keeping his gaze smartly down the centre of the street and speaking from the side of his mouth. "But it's been coming for a while. First we didn't notice, then we didn't understand. Now we don't know how to stop it."

"And you still don't understand."

"No, we don't." Pyoc grabbed his arm and stopped their progress. "Act drunk."

"What?"

"Now."

Two red-robed figures emerged from a side street. They slid from the shadows with silent grace, faces hidden by bright red hoods pulled down low so the robes seemed to float disembodied above the dirt. Marius smothered a grin. An old trick, employed by secret policemen and inquisitors across the continent, designed to create unease in those they approached. He felt Pyoc stiffen. It still worked. Marius was more cynical, and was able to watch them as they approached rather than worry about what the approach meant. Something about them was familiar. They made no sound as they moved closer: no rustle of clothing, no rasp of breath in the cold night air. The long knives hanging from their belts hung loose and didn't so much as slap against thighs that barely moved beneath them. Marius closed his eyes and viewed the approaching figures with dead sight. Very gently, a piece of the puzzle he was pursuing clicked into place.

"You have a miscreant?" one of the Fellipani stewards asked. Marius kept his face still. Someone who wasn't looking for it might not notice the lack of movement from the robe's hood as the steward spoke. They might also not observe that it was impossible to tell who actually spoke. The voice came from the general direction of the approaching Fellipanis, but not directly from beneath either robe. Marius was now certain of what he would find if those hoods were thrown back, and the faces beneath revealed. He bent from the waist, turned his head so that he looked up into the bowed hoods, and focussed on piercing the blackness beneath. He saw their faces, and experienced a surge of satisfaction. He was right. Pyoc took firmer hold of his arm, and shook him fully upright.

"Just a drunk," he replied. "Out a bit too late for polite society."

"We will take him."

"He's my collar."

"We will take him." The voice was more insistent, the arm that was raised to take hold of Marius came out rigid and demanding. Pyoc tightened his grip.

"I need a receipt from the desk," he insisted. "I have to show my sergeant."

"There is no need. We will inform your masters."

Pyoc took a step forward but found his path blocked. "And how do you know who my masters are, then?"

"You are Guardsman Emil Pyoc, of the Ludd Street Guardhouse. Your sergeant is Quincy Lukaku."

"Quincy?" slurred Marius, giggling a little.

"Shut up, you." Pyoc gave Marius a shake. He shut up.

"You reside on the top floor rear room of Missus Fiffitt's boarding house on Rolling Penny Street. You take your dinner at the Brown Carvery, and eat your breakfast in your rooms. You take an extra slice of toast and an egg for your midshift meal, which you eat at the guardhouse unless you eat it at the empty lot between the Cattery and Rollo's Hi-Lo Card House. You visit Luscious Lyn at the Cattery three nights a week for a bath and three-riner special. Your father is deceased. Your mother lies in Mockenham. You have no siblings. You have been asking questions about the operation of the Central Gaol." The steward let the information sink in. "We have been asking about you."

Marius felt Pyoc swallow, and the muscles in the guard's arm clench in sudden fear. "That's as may be. This man is still my collar."

"You will be suitably rewarded for your efforts." Marius was under no illusion as to which efforts were being discussed. He decided it was time to turn the Fellipani's attentions away from Pyoc.

"Hey!" he yelled and suddenly lurched forward, out of the young guard's grasp. Before Pyoc could react, Marius swung round and embraced him in a clumsy hug. "You, you shtay boodiful, okay buddy?" He planted a sloppy kiss on Pyoc's cheek and whispered, "This is us. Be back soon as I can."

The guardsman, to his credit, played along and pushed Marius off. "Get off me, you lush."

"Hey, hey, don' be like tha'." Marius weaved between the three men. "Thish guy…" He slung an arm around one steward's shoulder and leaned into him. "Thish guy… Boodiful guy." He leaned against the man, arms hanging loosely at his side. One quick twist of the wrist, and the steward's knife was off his waist and up one of Marius' sleeves. "I love thish guy." He reared back and waved at Pyoc.

"I shee you lader, boodiful guy," he shouted. "I'ma gon' go with theshe guysh, 'kay?" He gave his new best friend a loving shake of the shoulders. "Love thish red shit." The steward ignored him, his attention remaining fixed upon the guard. Pyoc slowly acquiesced, letting his gaze slip away and nodding.

"As you wish," said Pyoc. "A good evening to you."

"Guardsman Pyoc."

"She you lader, boodiful guy!"

Pyoc turned and strode back up the street as quickly as possible. Marius and his new gaolers watched him go. Once he had turned the corner, Marius straightened and faced them.

"So," he said, smiling. "Now we've dealt with that, let's cut the shit and talk business. How long have you two been dead?"

The stewards stared at him and said nothing. Marius maintained his smile but the joy left his eyes, replaced by a coldness that changed the nature of his face entirely.

"Come on," he said. "Look at me. Really look at me." The dead men grew even more still. After a moment, one of them tilted his head in surprise. "Ah," Marius said. "Got it now."

"How long?"

Marius raised his hands in a "ta-da" motion. "About three weeks. Had a bit too much to drink, missed the wrong step on the stairs…" He let his hands tumble over each other in a falling motion. "Woke up the next morning in a back alley, naked and not breathing. Dog had nibbled one of my toes off. Couldn't even feel it. What about you?"

"That is not your concern."

"Oh, come now." Marius clapped his companions on their shoulders. "We're all friends here, surely? No need to keep secrets." Quick as a snake, he reached up and flipped the front of their hoods backwards, revealing the dead men's faces. "There," he said, while their white eyes bulged in surprise. "Isn't that better?" They looked as dead as him, he noticed: like corpses freshly dug up and brushed free of dirt, no real decay or putrefaction. Just a lack of animus, and the unrelenting reek of otherness.

"Fool." The stewards reached for their hoods, but Marius had a fistful of their robes and he dragged them closer while they were still off balance.

"Let's not fuck about," he said. "We're obviously going to the same place. I just like to know what I'm getting myself into. Don't you think you can spare a little bonhomie for a fellow corpse, brother?"

His new friends were both larger men than Marius. They may have been caught out, but now they gathered themselves, disengaging their clothes from Marius' grip with a minimum of effort. He let them go with a smile. They reached up and replaced their hoods.

"I'm Loncelno. This is P'Shet." Neither one indicated the other. Marius decided not to ask which was which.

"Toshy."

"We have orders to deliver all miscreants to the Central Gaol, brother Toshy."

"Does that include a fellow deceased?"

The stewards paused, but only for a moment. "Our Lady does not distinguish."

"Ah, fair enough." Interesting phrasing. It certainly brought one or two questions to the front of Marius' thinking. "Best proceed, then."

They turned as one towards the end of the street, Marius in the middle of the two red-robed figures. "Tell me," he asked as they began to walk, "Does it worry you, walking around dead like this?"

"We do our duty," Loncelno, or perhaps P'Shet, replied. "We are loyal to our Lady."

"Your lady? You mean..." He indicated the crest on their chests.

"The Mistress Fellipan. We are her bondsmen."

"Does she know about your… little infirmity?"

"She knows."

"Ah. And that doesn't bother her?"

"We serve her loyally."

"Oh, of course." Another piece gently clicked into place. "Does she provide a lot of opportunity for persons of our… disposition?"

P'Shet, or Loncelno, shrugged. "We do our duty. We don't question our mistress' plans."

"Well, no. Why would you? Glad to have the work, I expect."

The stewards stayed silent. Slowly, the gloomy grey edifice of the Central Gaol emerged from the shadows of the surrounding houses. It sat at the end of the street, brooding and sullen, and let its coldness seep out along the cobbles, leaching all the colour and noise and liveliness away like a cranky great-grandmother. The younger buildings around it shrank away, as if forced into a form of respectful silence. No sound interrupted the frigid silence, no movement other than the bent-over, shameful scuttling of quiet figures in and out of its entrance. This was not a place for joy, or emotion, or basic human courtesy. That sort of behaviour may be all right for other, less well-raised neighbourhoods, but the buildings around the gaol house were brought up right, and knew how to behave around their elders.

"Cheery," Marius observed, staring at its bowed front steps and unlit lanterns.

"We shall escort you inside."

"Of course." They ascended the steps, pausing before the massive oak doors. "One thought," Marius said. "Just out of interest."

"Yes?"

He laid a hand on the wood. "Why *does* everyone end up here, anyway?"

The stewards pushed the door open.

"Mistress Fellipan orders it," one of them said. Marius snorted.

"Of course, she does," he said, and stepped inside.

Bustle and noise and protest and violence. Orders, shouting, threats, feet thumping on floors, drunken singing, doors crashing against walls, the thud of coshes against backs, wailing, crying, fear, objections, the screaming protests of whores and drunks and mothers and wives. Chaos, pandemonium, violence, brutality, indifference, anger, and hate.

This was more like it. This was a *real* gaol house.

Marius hung back in the doorway for a moment and watched the multitude of tiny passion plays being enacted in front of him. There was an order to the chaos, as there is in any properly functioning gaol house, a pattern to the seemingly random assortment of beatings and draggings and fights that constitute the processing of a night watch miscreant. And, he had to admit as he watched the rhythm of the Central Gaol dance, the Fellipani stewards were beautifully efficient.

Sullen guards from the other watch houses were stripped of their charges at a desk set just inside either of the entry doors, and a receipt was issued before the guard could launch into well-rehearsed and well-worn litanies of complaint. Then they were simply ignored as a steward appeared from out of the swirling crowd to rap the prisoners on the back of the legs with a weighted nightstick before dragging them over to another table, where they were stripped of their outer clothing with efficient grace. The guard, with nothing left to say and the next prisoner already being herded past them to the table, had no option but to get out of the way, and nowhere left to go but outside again. They were quickly and subtly bustled in that direction by the Fellipani stewards who passed, seeming to bump them only on the side necessary to move them the right way. The prisoner, meanwhile, still too busy trying to regain control of their legs and process their sudden near-nakedness, was pushed up against a wall by two gorilla-sized gaolers, where they were held still while a third patted them down and removed any objects still hidden about their person. Then they were lifted clean off their feet and frogmarched through swinging doors at the far end of the room, where they disappeared from sight. The gorillas were back within fifteen seconds, and already throwing the next prisoner against the wall before the door had finished swinging. Marius noticed that all the Fellipani servants in the room were dressed as the steward at the city gate had been: in felt jerkin and simple hat, their faces clearly in view, and also very much alive.

Anybody who had the misfortune to be accompanying a prisoner, be it wife or loved one or pimp, was simply squeezed out by the press of red-shirted bodies until a passing steward could grip their arm and push them back out into the night.

It was a perfect, functional, and brutal system. As Marius watched, half a dozen collars were processed, not one taking more than a minute to go from one end of the chain to the other. Despite himself, he couldn't help but be impressed. Only one problem presented itself. The knife he had stolen from Loncelno, or P'Tesh, weighed heavily against his forearm. There was no way it would remain undiscovered if he was thrown into the jaws of that inexorable human machine.

"I'm not going through that," he said, more in hope than certainty.

"No need," one of them replied. Marius sighed in relief, then frowned.

"Actually, why not?"

"There is no need."

"Right."

He allowed himself to be marched between the two robed figures, past the processing tables towards the door at the rear of the room. The milling chaos opened up before them as they moved, swirling behind them as if the disturbance had never existed. The other stewards made a point of avoiding the two robed figures at Marius' side. No one so much as glanced towards them as they passed.

"Do they know?" Marius asked.

"They have no need. They are told not to acknowledge those dressed as we are."

"And they're all loyal."

"They do their duty."

"She must be something to inspire this kind of loyalty, your mistress."

They shrugged in unison. "She is our Lady."

Marius had never understood the notion of blind loyalty. He had served everyone from kings and caliphs to head dishwasher at the local brothel, and only ever with one objective: to relieve someone of the cruel burden of their money. As far as loyalty went, it began and ended with himself. It was a necessary trait in his kind of work. Loyalty to another made people stay in the path of danger long after running away became sensible. It stopped a man from knowing when to cut his losses, when to leave comfort and go back to relying on one's wit, when to recognise a losing game and get

out of it. A loyal man forgot when to scarper. Marius'
complete lack of it had kept him alive for so long.

Except, of course, that he was dead. And it was loyalty
to Keth that had set him on that path to begin with.
Which, he reflected, pretty much proved his point.

Their little group reached the rear door and stepped
through. And everything Pyoc had been working so
hard to discover was laid out before Marius in a single,
awful moment.

Directly behind the door, a corridor stretched past a
dozen cells to an open entrance leading directly outside
the building. The walls of the corridor were rough
stone, unfinished and cold, as if the builders had got
this far and given up in disgust. The floor was uneven,
with large runnels between flagstones, and was sticky
under Marius' boots. Looking down he saw thick, dark
stains across the stones and into the grouting, pools of
black tarnish that refused to reflect the light from the
few smoking braziers on the wall. The only real light
came from a sliver of night sky that slipped through
the entrance, and most of that was blocked off by what
appeared to be a high stone wall outside. As the stewards
herded him rearwards the view became clearer: a
marshalling yard at least twenty feet long, cleared of
anything but a number of half-naked prisoners who
milled about in stunned, silent confusion. But it was the
cells that captured his initial attention, and answered
every question Pyoc and the sergeant might have had.

As Marius watched, a prisoner was bundled through
the door to the main hall. Two hooded stewards waited
inside. They took possession of him and rushed him
down to a waiting cell. The prisoner made one attempt
to protest, but it fell into the void: the stewards simply
swung him sideways as they ran, crashing his head

against the wall and pushing him inside the cell door before Marius was even sure what had happened. By the time he had blinked they had taken up position again and were already grabbing the next entrant. Marius scurried over to the cell door. Another pair of hooded figures had the prisoner by the arms, whilst a third watched. They pulled his arms outwards, and the gaolers bent him backwards so that the only balance he had came from the two men at his side. Marius turned to his companions.

"What the hell...?"

The waiting steward grabbed the prisoner's hair and tilted his head backwards in one swift movement. Then, just as swiftly, they cut his throat.

He was turned so that the jet of blood struck the far wall. Marius leaped forward, but his own gaolers held him fast in unconscious imitation of those inside the cell. When he struggled they simply lifted him from the ground and stepped in opposite directions until his leverage disappeared, and all he could do was watch as the flow of blood slowed, and stopped, and it was clear the prisoner was dead. Only then did they let him go. He sagged, and watched the gaolers haul their victim upright and slap him until his eyes opened. Then he was bundled out of the cell, bundled down the corridor past Marius and his captors, and shoved out into the moonlit yard to stand with all the others who had been harvested before him.

Marius slumped against the wall and watched as a dozen prisoners were deposited in the yard in just over three minutes. Every time he thought he had the new rules of death worked out, somebody came out of the fog of misunderstanding to deliver a mighty slap to his equilibrium. It was Scorbus' fault. It had to be. Death simply didn't work anymore. Not when a man could pour out his blood onto a stone floor and then simply get up and walk away. The natural order had not simply been overturned. It had been bent over a barrel and sodomised. Scorbus had to be responsible. The King made the rules. The King always made the rules. Somewhere, deep inside him, a voice tried to remind Marius that he had been the King, even if it was only for a few minutes. He put mental hands around the voice's throat, and choked it into silence.

"I can see," he managed to say to his guardians, "why it wasn't necessary for me to be processed."

"Our lady requires it."

"But this is…" He waved a hand at all of the goings-on. "This is slaughter. This is… It's barbarism."

"It is necessary."

"Necessary? Necessary for what?"

And then it struck him. He turned slowly, watching the milling, confused crowd in the yard. It was at least thirty feet to a side, running the length of the entire building and taking up a full plot next to it. High stone walls leaned slightly outwards to discourage climbing, and the expanse was hidden from view of the surrounding buildings by a thin roof of fabric stretched across retractable poles. They were extended now, almost all the way across the space, leaving only a square in the middle no more than two feet across, through which Marius could see the thin shaft of night he had spied from the doorway. He took a few steps outside, the red-robed figures silent by his side, and glanced around. Directly behind him, above the door, a short balcony jutted out from the wall. More than three hundred dead men and women stood half-naked, the fresh cuts across their throats like some sort of macabre uniform, marking them out forever as the possessions of the house that had created them. Their blood-stained chests and undershirts stood in obscene parody of the red and black shirts of the Fellipani stewards who continued to push stunned corpses out into the yard.

Marius had seen this sort of thing before. Crowds of confused, silent civilians, stumbling about marshalling yards with no idea where they were or how they had got there, but knowing with dreadful certainty that the life they had been ripped from was one they would never see again. Waiting to be told why. Waiting to be told *anything*.

Press-ganged sailors. Dragooned soldiers. Blackbirded slaves. Conscripts.

"An army," he whispered. "A fucking army."

"Our Lady demands it," Loncelno, or P'Tesh, replied, and pushed him through the door. "Now she is your Lady too."

Marius stumbled forward. By the time he had turned to protest, the stewards were gone. Marius frowned. Back to wandering the streets, no doubt, waiting to snag more unsuspecting volunteers for the throng behind Marius. Besides, what was he going to protest about? This was exactly where he wanted to be, wasn't it? At the heart of the mystery, with ample opportunity to explore his surroundings without interruption, and maximum potential for discord and chaos. He sidled away from the door, and slid along the wall until he came to the corner, where he could step into the deepest shadows and view as much of the courtyard as possible. The knife slid easily from his sleeve. He tied it to his waist, high enough that the sheath sat inside his trouser leg and the hilt was hidden by the folds of his jerkin. He straightened up and, for the first time, began to examine his surroundings.

Not that there was a great deal to see. Marius' initial observations had proven accurate, but now that he was at a different angle he could see the great wooden doors leading out to the street. They were painted black and, as far as he could tell, were held shut only by a thin rope looped between the handles, as if whoever had been put in charge of securing them had knocked off early on a Friday afternoon in the hope that everybody would take their inaccessibility on trust. What was more, it seemed to work. The inmates shuffled past them without a glance, and Marius gaped in astonishment as he watched corpse after corpse *not* stop to test them. He was about to sidle over and do just that when something more important caught his attention.

Not all of the dead were as aimless as he had supposed. Now that he was becoming accustomed to the pattern of movement in the yard he could see small knots of men standing stationary in the corners. Conversations were taking place. He fixed his gaze upon the nearest group. They stood with an air of purpose, their bodies angled to shield something, or someone, from general view. Marius shifted position until he was no more than two feet away, close enough to overhear the murmured exchanges taking place.

"...advantages, in the long run," a familiar voice was saying. "There's no fatigue, and you never need to sleep. And hunger. Do you know what it's like to never be hungry?"

There was a murmur of assent. Marius listened to the figure in the centre of the group spruiking the advantages of being dead for perhaps another minute, then leaned past the protective circle of bodies, grabbed the talker's ear, and pulled him sharply out of the group.

"Ow! What the hell... Oh. Hi!"

"What the hell," Marius shook the ear, "are you doing here?"

The other members of the group turned towards Marius. He shook his victim again.

"He's with me," Gerd said, holding his hands up to placate them. The men looked at Marius again, then drifted off, glancing at him over their shoulders as they went. Marius stared them down, then went back to his assaulting his young friend.

"Let me ask you again..."

"Let go." Gerd wriggled free. "I've been here all day," he said, looking Marius up and down. "Nice boots."

"Thank you. And *why* have you been here all day?"

"We saw you getting thumped up and dragged inside the walls, and I thought you might need some help. So I went scouting around the city walls to see if there was some sort of hidden entrance or a grave or something I could go down and come back up inside the city, so I could find you and give you some assistance."

"I see. And..."

Gerd looked sheepish. "I didn't get very far."

"What an amazing and unsuspected surprise."

"Well it's not like you were an overwhelming success."

Marius gazed at his young friend for long moments. He couldn't decide whether a witty retort or a simple clip upside the head would get his point across better. Finally, he settled for a simple question.

"What about Granny?"

This time Gerd really did look embarrassed. "She said she wasn't an idiot, and that she'd catch up with us once we'd managed to dig ourselves out of whatever stupid holes we got ourselves into."

"She's smarter than she looks."

"She always has been." Gerd straightened up, rubbing his ear. "That's what makes her so frightening."

As they spoke, two more newly dead came through the door. Blood-soaked stewards stood inside the courtyard for a moment, then stepped back and swung the door shut, letting it fall into place with an echoing thud. The sound of bolts being rammed home scraped across the air. Gerd nudged Marius and pointed to the balcony.

"Here we go."

"What?"

"Watch."

There was a burst of flickering light from the rear of the balcony as a door opened and shut. A figure appeared, dark against the stone. A hooded steward lit two braziers at either side of the railing, and once they were alight, removed a robe from the figure. She stepped forward to stand between the two cones of flames.

Marius had no heartbeat, which left him at a loss to explain why so much blood suddenly rushed towards his trousers.

"Holy snapping duck shit."

"Impressive, isn't she?"

"Impressive" wasn't the first thought that occurred to Marius. "Yes, please," was probably closer to the mark, although Marius couldn't concentrate on forming words right at that minute. The woman under the torchlight was like every naughty schoolboy fantasy he'd ever had, made flesh. She was stunningly tall, with legs that went all the way up and forgot to stop. Her narrow waist had somehow been encased in a corset whales must have fought for the honour of dying to be part of, and her dress and bustier were so black they seemed to swallow the night, providing blinding contrast to the white, white flesh above. Her long arms disappeared into elbow-high gloves of equal black, and everything tapered up to a swan-like neck that was topped by a pointed, elfin face and hair pulled back tight against her skull. Dark eyebrows stood out above large, cruelly smiling eyes, and the red of her lips was like a thick slash of blood on ceramic, holding back all the nasty truths every truly dirty little boy like Marius longed to hear. Marius could have described the whole effect as severe. He could have also described it as every secret thought he'd had between the ages of thirteen and twenty. He didn't know whether he wanted to have sex with her or beg her forgiveness. Both, probably. Simultaneously.

Mistress Fellipan. Head of the House of Fellipan. Recently anointed Deputy Mayor of Mish, owner of all the whores and bordellos and courtesans and knocking shops and – especially – houses of discipline in town. And didn't she just *know* it. Marius understood with absolute certainty that he could never, in a lifetime of honesty, afford a woman like her. Nobody could. And every man who ever met her would try. He wished for a moment he had breath in his body, just so he could hold it.

"Yes," he finally managed. "Impressive."

"She's come out every three hours," Gerd whispered. "Wait until you see what comes next."

"How do you know?"

Gerd shrugged. "I learned a few things from you about hiding, you know."

"Hmm."

"Just watch."

Mistress Fellipan had removed a riding crop from somewhere. Marius spent precious seconds trying to work out from where, and several more cursing himself for having missed it. Now she brought it down hard on the railing, three times in quick succession. The few dead below her who had not yet noticed her entrance swung round towards the sound. She waited until she had their full attention, then placed her hands on the railing, leaning forward to view her captives. Marius gulped.

"Ladies and gentlemen," she announced. "Welcome to your new life. You have–"

"Wait a minute! Wait a minute!" A figure pushed its way through the crowd to stand before the balcony. "Who the fuck are you, and what the fuck is your fucking game?" One of the men from Gerd's little group. Marius glared at his young friend.

"I didn't tell him to," Gerd muttered. "No way would I tell him to."

The crowd slowly edged backwards until a space of perhaps three feet surrounded the man. The dead aren't stupid. They recognise suicide when they see it. Mistress Fellipan didn't even twitch, or look at the interloper. She didn't move at all. Instead, the two massive stewards whose job it had been to rush the prisoners from the foyer of the building into the slaughtering cells materialised from the dark as if by magic, and grabbed the protestor by throat and groin. Within seconds he was pinned to the ground, the strongmen holding his wrists and ankles as far apart as possible. Still, neither Mistress Fellipan or the crowd stirred. She stared over their heads at the rear wall, as if far more interested in the interplay of brick and torchlight than in anything below.

The door to the building opened, and a third steward entered the yard. In his arms he carried a post maul of the type used by carnival roustabouts to drive stakes deep into the ground. The thick wooden head was dark with something crusted and dried. He stepped up to the struggling prisoner. Then, without a pause, he swung the maul overhead and brought it down onto the man's right knee.

The prisoner screamed. He continued to scream as the hammer-wielder moved slowly around his body, bringing the maul down again, and again, first on his legs, then his arms. The stewards stepped away, exposing his hands and arms, but the crippled protestor could no longer pull them back or make any move to protect himself. All he could do was scream. His hips were next, and his ribcage. Then, finally, the hammer came down on his skull, twice, three times, until the jaw was broken and the round dome of his skull was flattened like a broken plate. Even then, the scream continued for long seconds, until it slowly drained away and died. The stewards exited in silence. Marius was rigid, every muscle locked into place by the sudden terror the act had caused. Gerd touched his arm and he flinched, then recovered himself enough to look at his partner.

"Twice now," Gerd whispered. "It's been the same thing. At least we know what happened in the tunnels now."

Marius tried to make his jaw work, but found himself bereft of words. Gerd waited until he had composed himself, then directed his gaze back to the balcony. Around them the rest of the crowd was doing the same. Mistress Fellipan had still not moved. She waited until every eye was upon her, then continued as if nothing had happened, as if there had been no break in her moment of revelation.

"You have been chosen to receive the protection of the House of Fellipan, and to share in a most glorious adventure."

Typical, thought Marius. There's always glory involved when someone embarks on large-scale murder.

"You have entered service as armed soldiers of the Fellipani Cadres, in service of a cause so great, so all-encompassing, that you will thank me for bringing you to my side now, before the decision was taken out of your hands."

"Ah, well, at least she saved everyone that worry."

"Shh." Marius was concentrating. There was something wrong, something more than had already been revealed. It wasn't so much Mistress Fellipan's words as what lay behind them, hidden behind the smoke of her thoughts. He leaned forward, staring at her as if he could pierce the gloom and see the heart behind the oratory.

"I may have the body of a weak and feeble woman…"

"Body of a demon's favourite dominatrix."

"Shut. Up." He hoped his voice was aloud in Gerd's head as it was in his.

"But I have given my body to service of a King…"

"I bet."

Marius reached out and jammed his thumb into Gerd's ear. Gerd took the hint and stopped whispering.

"A King who will deliver foul scorn on those who have sought to defile his realm, and who has called upon me to take up arms, to be your general. And I shall join you at the side of your King, to whom you shall show your obedience and valour, and to whom you shall deliver victory!"

Marius had heard it all before. Every tuppenny prince with a chance to carve away a piece of somebody else's unearned lands, and with enough money to hire an army and invent a reason, had delivered a speech like it. Marius had marched with enough of them to know that every single word she spoke rang like gold-plated tin. The crowd around him stared at each other as realisation of their enforced servitude filtered into their bones. He stayed still, focussing on the black-clad figure preening above them. And saw beyond her words, and realised.

"Her chest."

"What?"

He grabbed Gerd's arm and slowly, inch by inch, drew him back into the deepest shadows against the wall.

"Look at her chest."

Gerd laughed. "If you insist."

"I'm not joking." He pinched Gerd's arm. "Look."

Gerd stared. "Wow."

"You see?"

"They're magnificent!"

Marius rolled his eyes.

"Look at them properly."

"I am, don't worry."

"No, not... look *at* them."

"I can't take my eyes off them!"

"They're not moving."

"God, it's like she's smuggling two bald men in there."

Marius cuffed Gerd on the shoulder. "I said look, not gawp like an adolescent farm boy. Look closely."

"I *am* looking closely. Any closer and she could charge me rent."

"They're not moving."

"They're moving just fine to... oh." Gerd pulled up short. "They're not moving."

"Not once since she came out here."

"But that means..."

"How did you not notice?"

Gerd shrugged. "I didn't really look."

"Didn't really... What's wrong with you?"

"I'm dead?"

Marius blinked. For once in his life he had absolutely no retort to make. Gerd tilted his head towards the balcony.

"So when do you think…?"

Marius snapped out of his reverie. "Some time in the last couple of months, is my guess."

They pondered the dead woman together.

"Why, do you think?"

Marius bit his lip. "I don't know. An overdose, maybe? Choked on a chicken bone? I'm not sure that's the real question."

"Then what is?"

"The real question is…" He broke away from his contemplation long enough to glance at Gerd. "Did it happen before or after she took power? And what's happened to the mayor?"

"And which king is she talking about?"

They both turned back to the balcony. Mistress Fellipan was waiting, staring out across the crowd while the shocked murmuring died down.

"A dead woman in charge of dead stewards, creating an army of the dead."

"Oh, no."

Marius nodded. "I think we know what king."

"But… why?"

"I don't know." The door to the gaol house was opening. Red-hooded figures stepped out and lined up along the wall. "But I think we need to find out." He took Gerd by the sleeve and slowly stilled himself, letting the shadows close over them deeper and deeper. Gerd followed suit, until only the most determined searcher could have picked them out against the patterns of darkness across the brick. Ahead of them,

Mistress Fellipan had straightened up, and was holding her hands out in front of her.

"Go now," she cried, "Take your place amongst my troops, and fulfil my destiny!"

She closed her hands, and drew them outwards again. A hole opened up beneath the executed prisoner, wider and wider until three men could have climbed down without bumping shoulders. The broken corpse tumbled into the darkness. Marius heard it strike bottom, and winced. The holes varied wildly in depth, depending upon the corridors the dead burrowed beneath them, and the proximity of each hole to the caverns below. Marius might have preferred not to hear the impact of the body so near to the surface. For a moment he contemplated listening to it fall, and fall, without reaching bottom. On further consideration, he decided he would not.

The stewards moved forward, herding the crowd to the hole's edge and beyond: silent, inexorable, brooking no dissent. The new recruits had none to offer. Still stunned by the manner of their deaths, bludgeoned into submission by the shock of their fellow inmate's execution and the news of their dragooning, they allowed themselves to be herded into the hole until the yard was emptied, fifty or more souls climbing down towards their eternal servitude. In short order, only the stewards remained, their Mistress overlooking them. And Marius and Gerd, still burrowed into the corner of the yard. The hole closed over, and Fellipan's servants went back into the gaol house in silence.

"We have to get out of here," Marius projected.

"How?"

"I..." Marius glanced up at the balcony. "Oh, bugger."

"Mistress Fellipan was staring down at them, her face a frozen mask.

"Oh, bugger."

As they watched, she raised her crop and brought it down onto the railing. The crack of impact had barely stopped echoing when two enormous bloodstained stewards stepped into the yard.

"I think," said Marius, as the stewards strode across the yard towards them, "that we are about to be very seriously fucked up."

Gerd stepped forward.

"Stop!"

"What are you doing?"

"Trust me."

"Trust *you*?" Marius hissed. "Trusting you is what got us here."

"Trusting you is what got me killed."

Marius paused to consider the fact. "All right," he conceded. "This once."

"Thank you." Gerd raised his hand in a gesture of command. "Stop in the name of King Scorbus," he said aloud.

Marius stared at the back of his head. "*This* is your plan?"

"Trusting me now."

"I didn't know *this* was going to be your plan!"

Mistress Fellipan raised a hand. The stewards stopped.

"See?" Gerd whispered. Above them, Fellipan creased her brow in thought, then crooked her finger in a "come here" motion. Gerd paced forward half a dozen steps, Marius behind him. Fellipan gazed down at them from a million miles of higher breeding.

"This," she said lazily, "had better be *spectacularly* good."

"My lady," Gerd bowed, with all the gentlemanly grace of the swineherd he was.

"Forget the cheap flattery." She lowered one eyebrow in a gesture of rapidly diminishing patience. "Just tell me what possible reason you could have for expecting me to do anything in our King's name."

"Because we know him." Marius pushed past Gerd's bent frame and into her full gaze.

"Oi!"

"My turn." He slapped Gerd on the forehead without turning. "This is my area of expertise."

Fellipan stared coolly down at him. "And you are?"

"Marius don Hellespont, lady, from the don Hellesponts of Borgho City."

"Ah, yes." She smirked, a tiny, cruel flicker of her lips. "I know your family."

Marius frowned, but did not press the matter. "This rough fellow is Gerd, a breeder of pigs I seem to be permanently saddled with."

"Fascinating."

"For him, perhaps." He risked a further step forward, so that he stood directly under the opening in the canvas above, illuminated by the few stars shining through the gap. "We know Scorbus, milady. We assisted his ascension to the throne."

"First time or second?"

"Uh, most recent."

They matched stares for long enough that Marius was able to make another mental scan for potential exit points from the yard, and confirm once again that there really weren't any. Then the woman above slowly lowered her hand and leaned forward.

"The cathedral," she said.

"We tricked soldiers into removing the lid of the crypt."

"The palace."

"We escaped into the royal apartments. Then out through the window and jumped into the midden below."

"The crown."

"Once belonged to mad King Nandus until I rescued him from the sunken ship *Mary Tulip*. He was killed by a shark." Marius felt his face turn to stone. "I liked him."

"Well, well, well." Fellipan smiled the first actual smile Marius had seen since she had first appeared. It didn't suit her. Rather, it floated just above her features, as if *from* her face without actually being *of* it. Marius stared at her large, white teeth, and took pains not to shudder. "I think that perhaps you may actually be who you say you are. What providence." She tilted her head to the side and slightly backwards: half challenge, half come-fuck-me. "Would you like to join me?"

Right at that moment, Marius would have joined with her in any number of lewd and unnatural fashions, but he settled for a short nod of the head. "Certainly."

"Excellent." She stood back from the railing, and swung in a smooth arc, sliding gracefully back through the door. Marius and Gerd watched her leave, but the stewards barely noticed, their eyes remaining fixed on the two of them. Marius shook his head.

"You're not just dead," he said to them. "You're unconscious."

The door into the gaol house opened. Marius gestured to his friend.

"Come on," he said. "Her ladyship awaits." They stepped past their silent guards and into the darkness within. "Try not to drool all over her."

SEVEN

The House of Fellipan began life as a bordello like any other, catering to any passing traveller with a pocket full of winnings and the need for some soft and pliant company. Soon, however, the mistress of the house came to realise that such fellows had very simple needs, and simple needs can be satisfied by anybody willing to ignore their shame long enough to get the job done. Such a living might suit an average merchant, but Mistress Fellipan had little desire to be an average merchant, and even less tolerance for the average customer. She had ambition, and a merchant with ambition soon learns that the favour of powerful people can only be won by providing services of the highest and rarest quality. Slowly, with an exquisite eye for detail, she transformed her simple bordello into an exclusive retreat for the rich, wherein highly personal and specialised services were offered. Men of a certain quality, of a certain stratum, availed themselves of whatever peccadillo was necessary to relieve the frustrations of a life of power. No judgement was passed. Not a single perfectly-curved eyebrow was so much as raised. No condemnation was proffered, no damnation, no disgust. At least, not unless specifically requested, and then only once a fee was negotiated.

Within a year, Mistress Fellipan was the richest woman in Mish. Within three, she had purchased a seat on the City Council. Within five years, her exquisitely long fingers were cupping the balls of every man of power in the city. Whatever Mistress Fellipan wanted, she got. All she had to do was squeeze.

Furs, tapestries, mahogany furniture, slaves, exotic fruits, gold, power, decisions. The Deputy Mayorship. Control of the Central Gaol. Freedom. And the boudoir at the top of the Central Gaol's clock tower, the highest point in the city, where she could lie across a four-poster bed large enough for half a dozen bodies to writhe in complete comfort, and stare out through any window in any direction, and know that she owned – in fact, if not in name – everything she could see.

Marius and Gerd stopped just inside the door and took in the sweep of roofs below.

"Nice view."

"It certainly is." Gerd stared at Mistress Fellipan stretched out on the bed. Marius sighed.

"Eyes front, soldier."

"I am."

"Not *her* front."

Fellipan watched Gerd with a look of bored amusement.

"How old are you, young man?"

"He's not. He's dead." Marius perched on a bench in front of the nearest window.

"Of course. I meant, how old were you when you died?"

Gerd stared at his feet. "Nineteen. Almost twenty."

"And had you ever been with a woman?"

"A human woman," Marius interjected. He couldn't help himself. He liked Gerd, he really did, but something about his young friend's discomfort was eternally amusing. Gerd shot him a look that would have blown holes in his chest if it could have, and then resumed contemplation of his feet.

"No," he mumbled. "There wasn't much... No, not really."

Marius felt a momentary pang of guilt. If Gerd's life had gone as scripted he'd be nearly twenty-three years old. He'd have inherited his grandmother's hovel and her filthy sty full of pigs, had three rocky and weed-infested fields to cultivate, and been rich enough by the standards of the inbred mountain people he came from to have married some tubby distant cousin from the next village. By now they'd be well on their way to spitting out gods knew how many children, and he'd be as happy as an ignorant peasant could be, cold-washing the pig shit off his arms before he climbed into bed and wriggled in between his wife's squishy thighs. Instead, thanks to Marius, he was a dead virgin with not a single idea about how to act in front of a woman, and no chance of learning what to do with one. He caught Mistress Fellipan's glance, and let the guilt fall away from his face. A corner of her lip twitched, and she reached out to ring a small bell on a table next to her pillow. A steward appeared in the doorway.

"Take... What is your name again, young man?"

"Gerd."

"Take Gerd to the House, and tell Vonyvve that he is to be accorded every method of hospitality available to her." The steward nodded. "And B'Sone?" He looked up. "*Every* method, is that clear?"

He nodded again, and gestured to Gerd to follow him. Gerd looked from Fellipan to Marius in confusion.

"Go on, boy." Marius nodded at the door. "Make sure you keep your liquid intake up."

Gerd frowned, and followed the steward. Fellipan laughed, a disturbingly girlish sound for someone dressed as she was.

"A virgin," she tittered. "Poor Vonyvve won't know where to start."

"He's a good boy," Marius said, settling himself back on the lounge. "He'll probably fall in love with her. And with you, for making it happen."

She inclined her head in acknowledgement. "A professional risk."

"More like a professional skill," Marius countered. "No offence."

"None taken." She nestled back on a mound of pillows and regarded Marius like a well-fed panther. "I'm proud of my business acumen."

Marius turned to stare across the expanse of Mish. "And you've used it well, I see. Question is, to what end?"

"What other end is there? Power. Control. To be in charge of my own destiny."

Marius thought back to his little cottage, and Keth. She had used almost the same words to defend the little sanctuary she had carved out for herself, despite a lifetime of dancing in the grubbiest taverns in Scorby. "No," he said. "It's more than that." He glanced up, and rested his gaze upon the long gloves on Fellipan's arms. "I think you're already very much in charge of your own destiny, Madame. I think you've taken it very firmly by the throat, and put a collar there." He pointed at the glove on her right hand. "I'm willing to bet you have your destiny on a very short leash."

She laughed again, and with deliberate burlesque charm stripped the glove from her arm, then extended it for him to see more clearly. Marius saw, just where he expected to see it, a clean, three-inch cut along the inside of her wrist.

"Clever boy," she said, amusement clear in her voice.

"So, again. To what end?"

She rose from the bed with feline grace and stalked across the room, slipping down onto the bench next to him with only the merest rustle of her skirt. Together, they looked across the city to the land outside the walls.

"How many people in Mish, do you think?" she asked.

Marius kept his eyes firmly on the vista. "Two thousand, perhaps, a town this size. Maybe three."

"Such a small place. So far away."

"I've known smaller."

She shrugged. "Have you known easier? More pathetic?" Her voice hardened, and just for a moment Marius fancied he heard the woman behind the conqueror. "Every step I've taken in the last five years I've done so without a moment's opposition. There's not a man in this city I can't control with a tickle of the crop or a purse of my lips. I want to be great, Marius. Is that a bad thing for a woman to want?"

"No."

"I have a brain, and ambition, and I know how to make things work, how to make *people* work." She turned towards him, and he saw the hurt and sense of powerlessness she carried. "Would it be so bad," she asked, "for a woman with brains to ascend as far as she could?"

"No." The room was closing in on Marius, growing hotter, and smaller. Fellipan's eyes were growing, taking up more of his vision, drawing him in against his will. He tried to breathe, and couldn't, and then struggled to remember why he couldn't.

"I just want…" Her voice caught. "The world is so big, Marius, and so badly run. I just want to make it run better." They were so close now, so very close. Her lips were barely an inch from his. "I just want to make things the way they should be. I want…"

And then she was upon him, and he was responding, and her hair was in his hands, and her fingers were tearing the shirt from his chest, and for the longest while there was nothing else in the world worth thinking about.

EIGHT

The best thing about the human body is the almost innumerable ways in which it can be bent, positioned, and folded around itself. More than anything else, it is a superb piece of athletic engineering. There were monks in the mountains, so Marius had been told, who spent their entire lives honing their bodies to a point of pure elasticity, training each and every muscle until it could bend and stretch and twist to its fullest capacity, giving the monks a flexibility and physical capacity beyond the understanding of ordinary mortals.

Marius was pretty sure he knew exactly how they felt. It had taken the better part of a day, but there wasn't a single inch of his body that hadn't been enlarged, flexed, bent, bound, pinched, bitten, licked, pummelled, soothed, pounded, and otherwise pleasured within an inch of his... well, life, if he'd had one. He lay somewhere in the middle of the bed, his sense of direction utterly askew, aware only of the tingling of his flesh and the cold, white body perfectly intertwined with his. There were fingers in all sorts of places he'd never imagined fingers could fit so well, and he possessed not the slightest inclination to move them, or, if he were perfectly honest with himself, anything else. There would be repercussions, he knew: bruising, hopefully, and an overwhelming sense of guilt and shame at his betrayal of Keth's loyalty. But right now, for this moment, he just wanted to relax in the glow of the most extensive internal and external exercise he'd ever given himself. Parts of this night were going to pop up in his memory for eternity. Even his eyelashes felt tender.

"You want me to take you to Scorbus, don't you?" His tongue and lips felt like they belonged to someone else. They'd grown used to completely different movements. It took all his will to get them to work in the proper order. Speech sounded wrong. He felt Fellipan stiffen momentarily – which, given the position they were in, wasn't at all bad – then relax as she responded.

"Do you think that makes me bad?"

"No." He shifted slightly. Things rubbed against other things. "*That* makes you bad. The rest of it… just business, right?"

Fellipan turned her head towards him and matched his gaze. She flexed her fingers, and he gasped. "Does that feel like business?" she asked innocently.

"No?"

She smiled, and disengaged herself from him. It took more than a few moments, especially as they kept stopping to experiment when a movement brought an unexpected sensation.

"Not all business," she eventually admitted, and gave him a long, deep kiss. "I might even like you."

"I… I have someone. Had someone. It's complicated." Or it wasn't a small voice inside his head said. But it probably was. Fellipan straightened away from him, leaving a hand across his chest.

"I have several someones. It's not a problem."

"It is if you feel guilty."

"Guilty?" She laughed. "What for? There's nothing wrong in it." He arched an eyebrow at him in a perfectly lascivious way. "It's not necrophilia if we're both dead."

"No, I mean…" Fellipan slid from the bed and began to recover clothing. Marius took a few moments to admire the view. "Guilty because she's… was… *is* someone special."

"Darling." She flung his trousers towards him. "They're *all* special." She raised a hand before he could object. "Don't worry, I know what you mean." For a moment she looked almost sad, then recovered herself and began to fold herself into her outfit. "Someone you've promised yourself to, and who makes you view this as a lapse in good judgement instead of anything else."

"I—"

"Don't worry." She busied herself in making a million minor adjustments to clothes that clung to her frame as if sprayed on, while Marius watched and felt as if his innards were twisting and writhing in response to emotions he tried very hard to ignore. "You can tell yourself you were forced to do this to discover just what nefarious plans I'm brewing. That I cunningly trapped you as part of my plan to get closer to Scorbus and grasp the nettle of power in my wicked fingers."

Marius attempted a smile. "Well, you do have wicked fingers."

Fellipan stared straight at him, her face an open statement. "Remember that."

Marius didn't dare reply to the statement her body language was making. He turned away and began to dress.

"Okay," he said. "Okay."

NINE

The road north from Mish was deserted. This close to the middle of the day, any creature outside in the heat that layered the surrounding landscape in several layers of shimmer was either an animal too stupid to burrow beneath the nearest available source of shade, an animal already dead or a recent resident of Mish regretting the decision to bet their citizenship papers on that sure thing they'd been told about by that nice fellow at the bar last night. Or already dead. There was nothing to be had for almost ninety miles in any direction: no comfort, no relief, no water. The plains were at their plainest here, a featureless grassland with scrub so hard and unpalatable that even the herds of wisent that wandered disconsolately across the landscape couldn't be bothered trying to chew any nourishment out of it. Millennia of human occupation had produced not a single monument until Mish had risen like a wooden boil.

The track that had been scoured out of the grasslands by the passage of thousands of feet soon turned towards the coast out of sheer boredom and started to throw up boulders and the occasional tree just to relieve the monotony. Even the wind couldn't be bothered, and was waiting until the day got a bit cooler. A hawk –

obviously, at this time of day, a rather stupid hawk who hadn't worked out why he was so damn hot and there was nothing around to hunt – could launch himself from the city wall and fly the length of the spear-straight road without seeing a single thing move the entire way.

The black carriage that sat by the side of the road a dozen miles outside the city gate was as still as the unbreathing horses that had pulled it through the morning. They now stood before the carriage without a ripple of sweat, waiting for the next bite of the whip on their flanks.

Four figures sat inside the carriage, alone in the gloom afforded by the thick black curtains drawn across the windows. Gerd, freshly washed free of goose grease, stared at Marius, a dreamy little half-smile plastered onto his features. Vonyvve gazed at Gerd and shifted from one bruised buttock to the other. Marius and Fellipan sat across from them, staring at anything but each other. Eventually, as the sun reached its apex and began the slow slide towards the horizon, Gerd finally regained the power of speech. "So…" he said, looking across at them.

Marius and Fellipan exchanged glances, and looked away. Marius sighed and rubbed his eyes.

"Scorbus is gathering an army."

Gerd frowned. "Has he got Keth?"

Fellipan found something on the nearest curtain-hem of life-altering interest. Marius rubbed his eyes harder, and replied: "No. Maybe. I'm not sure." Letting his hands fall into his lap, he blinked. "It doesn't matter."

"Doesn't matter? But how…"

Marius glanced at Fellipan. She was staring at the fascinating curtain, her face utterly neutral. He examined her eyes for a flicker, and found nothing.

"If he's gathering an army it means he's going to war. And there's only one place he can be thinking of going to war with."

"Scorby?"

Marius shook his head. "The upper world." Now Fellipan noticed his existence. They stared at each other, giving nothing away, making no acknowledgement.

"Why?"

Marius sucked at his upper lip. "Heaven," he said slowly. The others looked at him expectantly, waiting for him to work through all the angles, to clue them in. Marius stared past them, at the velvet lining of the coach's rear wall. "He's promised them Heaven," he said eventually. "He's promised them…" And suddenly, there it was. The explanation, clear and simple, and oh, so understandable. "He's promised them Heaven."

"So you said."

"Yes, but don't you see?" he turned wide eyes on them all. "If he wants to remain King, and gods knows he'll want to, he's lain in a box not being King for a thousand years, he has to give them what he promises. He needs a Heaven to give them."

"But where?" Gerd was frowning now, as realisation slowly tiptoed towards him with an innocent smile and a large cosh hidden behind its back.

"How many worlds have you experienced, boy?"

Gerd stared at Marius, then down at the ground beneath the floor of the coach, then out the window at the world outside. Then back at Marius, as realisation whipped the cosh from its hiding place and fetched him a good one upside his head.

"Two," he said. "Just two."

"Yep." Marius pointed to their feet. "Underworld." Out the window. "Heaven."

"You mean he's…"

"He's going to invade. He's going to invade the world."

"But… they won't believe that, will they? I mean… they've *been* here."

"And what seems more like Heaven to you? Down there, or up here, where you used to be happy?"

"But…" Gerd twitched from side to side, his lips fluttering as he tried to work it out, to calculate a million imponderables he was incapable of considering. Finally, he fell back upon the one thing he could know with utter certainty. "We've got to stop him."

Marius nodded, and saw Fellipan do the same. "Yeah," he said, although whether it was to Gerd or the silent understanding he was reaching with Fellipan he wasn't sure. "We have to."

Gerd glanced between the two of them for several seconds as his own understanding dawned. "But what about Keth, then?" he asked, hesitantly.

"Keth will have to wait."

"Ah."

Marius turned his gaze upon Gerd, just for a second, but long enough to shut the younger man up. Gerd sat back and held Vonyvve's hand, while Marius returned his attention to Fellipan.

"We're going to leave now," he said. "There's someone I need to visit." Fellipan was watching him as if from a great distance as he spoke clearly, with great care. "Mistress Fellipan has kindly offered to bring us here to enable us to continue our journey. She herself will be taking her recruits to the hills overlooking the ruins of the old Post-Necrotic Monastery at Cistrion. Scorbus will muster there to drill his troops before he approaches Scorby City."

"How do you know?"

Marius smiled a tight, humourless smile. "I've been in three armies that tried to invade Scorby. They all did it."

"Ah."

Marius held Fellipan's gaze. "Tell him that I request he changes his mind. Tell him that I say to remember the portrait in the hallway." They had stood beneath it, during their rescue of the King four years ago – a single portrait of Scorbus in his prime, hanging alone in the hallway outside the royal balcony – the last thing any monarch saw before they addressed their subjects, a reminder of what a king should be to his people. "Tell him it still hangs. He won't change his mind, but he'll know I know. And it will make you his friend."

Fellipan tilted her head – the merest nod of thanks. Marius nodded back, and leaned forward to open the door. He jumped out, and stuck his head back through to glare at Gerd.

"Come on."

Gerd gained his feet, and bowed awkwardly to Vonyvve and Fellipan in the cramped space.

"I... um..." He looked at Vonyvve, bowed again, convulsively, and tried to back out of the door at the same time.

"Gerd."

Gerd looked up at Fellipan and immediately banged his head. Vonyvve giggled, and he bit his lip.

"Gerd," Fellipan repeated.

"Yes?"

"Tell Marius thank you. And tell him..." She paused, and stared straight at Marius, glowering up at her from under his brow. "Tell him to be careful."

"Yes, ma'am."

"And you be careful, too."

"Yes, ma'am."

She smiled at him, a gentle, knowing tilt of her lips. "Best be going."

"Yes, ma'am."

Marius stepped back and let Gerd negotiated the door successfully this time. The door closed. They watched as the coach wheeled around and headed back towards the town.

"She said–"

"I heard."

"Oh." They coach become a plume of dust, and then disappeared. Gerd looked sidelong at his companion.

"So. The Post-Necrotic Monastery at Cistrion, eh?"

"Yes."

"That would be the Cistrion at the westernmost tip of the Spinal Ranges, would it?"

"Maybe."

"Thirty days march away from all the major cities of the plains. A thousand feet up a mountain, perched on an isolated outcrop, room for maybe forty or fifty monks as long as they walk in single file and don't all jump up and down at once."

Marius shrugged.

"That the monastery you mean?"

Finally, Marius hung his head and allowed himself a wry smile.

"Yes, that's the one."

They stared in the direction of the invisible coach.

"Scorbus is amassing an army," Marius said. "Now there's at least one brigade who'll be moved off the board before the fighting begins."

"Uh huh." Gerd kept his gaze fixed upon on the horizon. "So you like her, then."

Marius said nothing. Gerd absolutely did not smile in the slightest.

"So," he said. "What now?"

Marius inhaled, held the breath, and released it in a deep sigh. Not needing to breathe was one thing, he found. Needing to sigh was quite another.

"Now we wait."

"What for?"

As if in answer, a tiny drift of dust appeared several hundred metres down the road. They watched it approach, painfully slowly, as a figure resolved out of the heat haze. Something small detached itself and ran towards them – a fat tortoise-shelled cannonball that sped past Marius and launched itself into Gerd's arms. While they renewed their acquaintance, Marius kept his eyes on the blind, shuffling figure that walked towards them.

"Granny," he said, as she finally reached them.

"You bastard." She aimed a kick at him that he evaded with ease. "You saw us standing there, don't tell me you didn't."

"What?" Gerd looked up from Alno and frowned at them in turn.

"Don't you lie. I saw you looking out the window." She turned to her grandson. "He looked right at me. Three miles in this heat."

Marius said nothing. Gerd rolled his eyes.

"Marius?"

"I have no idea what you're talking about. The only thing I saw on the way out here was a withered-up old snapping turtle. I thought it best to park out of its reach. For safety's sake."

"I'll give *you* safety." She aimed another kick at his legs, and again he sidestepped it. Gerd and Alno shared a glance.

"If I might intrude," Gerd said in a tone of voice that made it clear intruding was all he would do until the others grew up and behaved. "Do we have a plan now, or was this little side trip just for the fun of it?"

Marius turned towards him. Granny took her chance, and landed a full-blooded kick on the edge of his shin.

"Ow! For fuck's–"

"Granny!"

"What?" She backed away, holding her hands up in innocence. "Must have been a snapping turtle. Don't look at me."

Marius did look at her, a look with a million unpleasant murders within it. She smiled back, promising a million and one in return.

"Vicious old crone."

"Whoremonger."

"Granny!"

The old woman swung sightless eyes towards her offended grandson.

"I'm not lying, though, am I? Him with a recently dead wife and all–"

"Lover. Not wife"

"You didn't object to the dead bit, though, did you?" She eyed them both balefully. "I saw that pair of tits with a mouth attached sitting next to you. Don't tell *me* you didn't give in and bounce around on her like a bad donkey ride the moment she had her back turned, or her front, or whatever angle you come at it from, you dick-thinking miscreant–"

"Granny, please."

"And as for you," She pinned Gerd to the desert floor with a glare. "I hope you had better sense than to follow his example. I didn't raise you to…" She stopped, leaned in closer, her grey-filmed eyes growing wide. "You *did*, didn't you? You had one."

"Granny–"

"You filthy, disgusting…" She began to beat Gerd around the shoulders with an open palm, her skinny arm rising and falling in rhythm to her words. "Horrible little reprobate, disgusting, awful, to think of all the years I spent… raising you… disgusting…"

"Granny. Stop it." Gerd flinched away from every blow. "Stop it."

"Consorting with hoors and trulls–"

"Granny."

"Lying with strumpets–"

Marius coughed.

"What?"

"You forgot 'rutting with disease-ridden witches'."

"Right. Thank you. Rutting with… Don't you get smart, whoremonger. I'm blaming you for this."

"Don't look at me." Marius placed his hand over his useless heart. "I didn't oil him up and play hide-the-piglet all night."

The dead can't blush. Nevertheless, the only thing Gerd didn't do at that point was turn beet-red from hair to foot. He certainly managed to give every indication of a man who was trying his best to curl up and die on the spot. Again. Granny stalked over to Marius like a bird and stretched her neck out, standing on tiptoes to get as near his ear as she could.

"If you weren't already a dead man," she muttered, "you would be for that."

"Death is full of little disappointments." Marius winked. "I can be yours." He swung his attention away from her, and back to his friend. "Can we get back to business now?"

Gerd looked up from his intense examination of his toes.

"Gods, please, yes."

"Right." Marius bit his lip in concentration, then stopped when he realised he could taste no salt, no sweat, despite standing out in the heat of the sun. "If Scorbus is recruiting an army it's because he means to invade, yes?"

"Sure."

"But why does he need to?"

"Sorry?"

"Why does he need to?" Marius spread his arms. "Think about it. If all he wants is control of the living world then surely there are simpler ways?"

"Like Mistress Fellipan."

"Exactly."

"Whore."

Marius rolled his eyes. "Maybe, but an ambitious whore, as we've discovered. And she didn't start killing people until *after* she'd assumed power, and then only to provide herself with a specific type of troops."

"That's your apology for her, is it?"

"Shut up. I'm serious. If Scorbus thought like her then all he'd need to do is insinuate himself into the right meeting rooms in the right capitals, and start putting words in the mouths of the right people. He wouldn't need to create a dead army. He could just wait until they came to him. No." He shook his head. "He doesn't think like that."

"Who does he think like, then?"

Marius saw the portrait in the royal apartments in Scorby: a monster of a man, heavy as a mountain, brooding, covered in furs. "Scorbus the Great. Conqueror. He thinks like himself." He nodded to himself, then set off up the road away from Mish. "Come on."

Gerd and Granny scurried to catch up.

"Where are we going?"

"To the library. Specifically, my father's library."

"What for?"

"Scorbus is thinking like Scorbus, the man who invaded and subjugated his kingdom a thousand years ago. Five gets you ten he'll use the same tactics now as he did then. And my father has a history of the Scorban campaign in his library. So that's where we're going." He laughed. "We're going to read about our war before it even happens."

"So where does your father live, then?" Granny sneered from half a dozen steps behind him. "A gutter near a college?"

"V'Ellos." Marius smirked at her over his shoulder. "We're going to V'Ellos."

"V'Ellos doesn't exist."

Marius turned away from her, and set his face towards the invisible coast behind the mountains.

"It does if you're rich enough."

TEN

Marius led them out of the valley and across the edge of the plains towards the coast. They travelled without resting, across land that soon flattened out into farming communities where ramshackle fences provided opportunity for Alno to trip the travellers up while they struggled to climb through tangles of hedgerows and rough-carved gates. Marius managed to liberate a clutch of horses from the cruel imprisonment of a warm barn and mounds of hay, and they kept to the back roads for the final three days of their journey. Marius gave the horses their head, luxuriating in the feel of something alive and breathing under his hand after so long in the presence of cold flesh. They rode past a dozen hamlets, each one a mirror to the last: outlying farmlets that quickly gave way to a beaten-up main road where wooden huts pressed up close around a well, a store, and perhaps a smithy and drinking hole if the villagers thought they were doing well enough.

Alno streaked along beside them, feline muscles refusing to tire, streaking off into the long grass at a moment's whim to torture some small animal or another for a while, returning when he felt like it to playfully swat at the horses hind legs. Each time he successfully spooked one, causing the rider to curse and spit down at him in an attempt to get him the hell away, he simply smiled his bastard cat smile and took off once more.

The horses began to tire towards the end of the day, and Marius took care to feed them from outlying fields, where they had plenty of time to escape should an errant farmer spy them and give the alarm. He had to remind himself these were living animals that occasionally needed to stop and rest. It was too easy to fall into the rhythms of the dead, to hold that single unmodulated tone of existence that droned onwards without end. It felt good to work with something that snorted and sweated, and transmitted the warmth of its body up through his thighs into the pit of his groin.

After three days they left the last tiny outlet of what passed for civilisation in farming country, and rode through increasingly thick groves to a wind-ravaged strip of shale beach.

"This looks lovely," Granny shouted over the gale, gazing around at the blasted landscape. "I can see why all the really rich people want to live here."

Marius ignored her and pushed his horse forward. They cantered along the beach, dull water slopping up against the shore to one side, thick lines of stunted black-barked thorn bushes to the other. After half a day's ride he pulled them over into the lee of a sandbank and dismounted. Gerd and Granny followed his example. Marius took their reins from them, while Granny scooped Alno up into her arms and surveyed their surroundings.

"I've always wanted to spend my holidays in a desolate shithole," she said. "Now I know what I was missing."

"You're supposed to spend holidays somewhere different from home," Marius replied. He walked the horses up the slight rise into the nearest stand of bushes and let go of their reins. They stood, blinking stupidly at him until he sighed and slapped one on the rump. It skittered away from him, then turned and began to slowly pick its way through the bushes. Its companions gave Marius an "Are you sure?" stare before following. Gerd and Granny were giving him the same look. Alno was too busy licking himself.

"What the hell did you do that for?"

"We don't need them anymore." Marius walked past him and sat down on the rocks. "We're here."

Gerd turned in a circle. There was nothing to indicate the presence of even a particularly desperate hermit, never mind the fabled secret hideaway of the rich. The beach was a depressing grey slice of fuck-all, with added depressing fuck-all to one side and only slightly wetter depressing fuck-all to the other. If the middle of nowhere ever got lost, it would be on this beach. It sloped along the edge of the water like a truculent child forced onto a walk by a health-obsessed aunt, terminating in a spur that rose a dozen feet above the surrounding countryside, overgrown with wild spearthorn bushes that formed a hedge thick enough to destroy any hope of light getting between them, as if to make the thought of clambering over the rise deeply off-putting. Outside of the rise, and the hedge, the three travellers looked like the most interesting thing to have happened to the beach since the dawn of time.

"Excuse me?"

Marius jerked a thumb towards the spur. "Have a look."

Gerd and Granny clambered up the spur's sheer wall. Marius watched them go. They cleared a gap through the spearthorn bushes amidst much swearing and blaming of each other, and slowly disappeared into the hedge's depths. Marius waited, staring out over the grey water, losing himself in contemplation of its greasy motion. After half an hour, he heard a commotion behind him. He turned, and saw Gerd fighting his way back through the viciously barbed plants. He stood at the edge of the rise, and gazed into the distance for several minutes, absentmindedly pulling three-inch thorns from his arms and chest. Eventually he nodded slowly, and slid back down to hunker next to his older companion.

"Ah," he said.

"Yep."

"So this whole beach…"

"Designed to demoralise and weaken the resolve. Nobody ever bothers to push past that lot up there."

"Designed?"

"Yep."

"Manmade?"

"By the finest and most depressed landscape designers money can corrupt."

They stared back along the stretch of inhospitable rock, a thin line of black that switched back a dozen times before disappearing into the horizon. No animal moved within their sight. No bird wheeled through the sky, no fins broke the surface of the sludgy grey water. It looked for all the world like the bank of a river the dead might travel across to the underworld in some of the more imaginative afterlife cults.

"So…"

"This is the only approach, yes." He waved a lazy hand at the forest to one side of them, around to the becalmed water. All this, in a thirty mile radius, designed solely to keep the riff-raff out. And by riff-raff, I mean the rest of the world. Impenetrable forests, stinking dead water, soul-destroying, filthy beach. Bereft of wildlife, edible plants, drinkable water, company, sunlight, fresh air, happy fluffy bunnies and blowjobs. Would you want to walk more than an hour past any of it, if you had a choice?"

"Wow." Gerd settled back onto the rocks, shifted about to make himself more comfortable. "Wow."

"Yep." He called out to Granny. "May as well come down now. We'll head over in the morning, when they can see us coming."

"In a minute." Something had softened in Granny's voice, as if her soul had awakened in a way she was completely unused to. Marius leaned back and placed his hands beneath his head. Slowly, the sun descended towards the edge of the world. After it had disappeared there was a repeat of the sounds Gerd had made clambering out of the bushes, a short slithering sound, and Granny slipped down next to the two men.

"It's..." she began, then: "I never expected..."

"Apology accepted."

"No, but, you don't understand—"

Marius sighed. "Two miles down the perfect golden sand beyond the rise is V'Ellos. It's the most beautiful sight you've ever seen. Like something that exists only in the mind of the most talented landscape painter in the world, and the thought of it brings him to tears because he knows he can never truly capture it on canvas so it can only live inside his mind, but there it is, right before you, in shining white stone and terracotta tile, shining under a sun you never believed could be so bright, so soft, so warming all at the same time. You never realised a town could be so perfect, so magnificent. Every town, every village you've ever set foot in is like a child's poorly remembered imagination in comparison. How could mere buildings and streets shine so perfectly, achieve such grace and beauty? It's like buildings have souls, like they can sing and dance and paint and they've dressed themselves in their most beautiful outfits to present themselves at a dance of the gods. How am I going?"

"You're mocking me."

Marius glanced over at her: a tiny, bedraggled old woman who had never gone further than the limits of her backwoods hovel in life, and never had more than one meal ahead of her in all her days; suddenly understanding what could be done with time, money, and an overabundant sense of entitlement. He sighed again and admonished himself silently.

"No," he said. "No, I'm not. It hit me the same way the first time I saw it, and I thought I lived in a pretty nice house up until then." He remembered standing on the same rise, a short trail of caravans behind him, until his father barged past and he twisted his ankle on the shifting rocks. He recalled having the same feeling that Granny was struggling with – that no matter what he achieved in the rest of his life, he would not be worthy enough to own even a perfectly-proportioned outhouse in the meanest angelically-manicured garden below.

"Just remember," he said, staring up at the splash of stars beginning to emerge from the dark. "When people want to poison you, they hide it in something sweet."

They sat and watched the stars in silence, waiting for the morning.

ELEVEN

There was no town in the world quite like V'Ellos. For one thing, nobody quite knew where it was, if they even believed in its existence at all. It was always somewhere over there, or back down towards that way somewhere; or someone knew someone who met a guy at a bar one night who said he'd sailed past it in a storm and swore it roamed the world on a floating island made up of the ragged corpses of paupers.

For another, in a world where almost every town large enough to afford one was ringed by defensive walls for the protection of its populace from marauding bandits, opposing armies, or just *you*, V'Ellos had not a single physical barrier to separate it from the rest of the world besides the beach on which Marius and his companions had sat. It had no need. V'Ellos was *not* an ordinary hamlet.

It only contained somewhere in the region of two hundred citizens, although if eighty percent of the world's wealth was owned by twenty percent of its people then those two hundred citizens could use the wealth of *that* twenty percent as toilet paper. And it really was a town without a sense of place. Only those few who earned themselves an invitation by dint of sheer wealth could find it, and they weren't sharing.

It was situated in a valley of such perfect dimensions that believing a god or gods of your choice had created it would belittle the efforts of the town elders who had actually designed it, and the armies of vassals who had dug, cut, paved, sculpted, and been buried beneath the reimagined earth to construct it. The valley lay somewhere between a settlement of merely enormous wealth and a region that considered itself the political powerhouse of the continent because seven kings of Scorby had happened to be whelped there. The rulers of the region had no idea how hilarious their belief was to the people of V'Ellos, who sat on their barques as they floated in their perfect bay and lit their imported cigars with flaming wads of money worth more than the surrounding region had ever produced.

V'Ellos was founded on one very simple maxim: only people who are good enough can live there, and you're not it.

It was a haven for the über-rich, the kind of people who could afford to give interest-free loans to kings but wouldn't on the basis that they didn't deal with such riffraff.

"I don't get it," Gerd said as they left the golden beach behind and approached the nominal entrance to the town, a point in the road a dozen metres or so before the first set of gardens, where the simple sand became a line of granite cobbles. To either side of them towered trees of such soaring beauty that it was difficult to remember that they existed purely to shield V'Ellos from the outside world. "Who does all the cooking? The cleaning? I mean, do they have servants? Where do they live?"

"I don't know." Marius stepped up to the line of cobbles and stopped, the toes of his boots resting against the outer edge. "I left years ago. I've only been back twice. Once when we thought Mum was dying and wanted to see me before she went, and once later on, when she was leaving him again and I was expected to come between them again."

"Again?"

He shrugged. "She was always leaving him, or coming back, or leaving him again. Especially the last couple of years."

"What happened?"

Marius winced as he remembered the drawing room of the house on the hill, and a scene he'd managed to suppress for almost twenty years. His mother, curled up in her high-backed chair in the corner, a blanket pulled to her chin, her eyes wide and red where she had been crying for days, thin hair at all angles. His father, fists raised, blocking the path between his wife and young son, Marius' glass of thirty year-old Ribellian whiskey down the front of his smoking jacket, his cheek already beginning to puff and redden where Marius had struck him. The threats that passed between them, the hatred that had finally boiled up in his father's eyes and out into the room, poisoning whatever hope of reconciliation they might have had. Marius wheeling about and stalking out of the house, smashing every ten-thousand-riner vase he passed on the way. Then later, standing at his bedroom window, watching his mother climb into her carriage, seeing her hand raised towards him before someone else reached past her and closed the door.

"It didn't work."

"Oh." They eyed the short road ahead. "So what do we do now?"

Marius reached into his coat and pulled out a small square of stiff card. "Now we grease the guard and make our entrance."

Gerd and Granny frowned at him. They had stopped at a small village at a fork in the road a day previously, waiting until nightfall so that Marius could break into the miniscule staging post and rummage around in the mailbags. Their happiness when he had emerged, waving his piece of card, had been noticeably nonexistent.

"Watch."

With deliberate care Marius stepped forward onto the cobbles. A head appeared over the fence line of the nearest house.

"Ho, yuss!"

A figure stepped from behind the fence. A bear of a man, his frame encased in a billowing grey kaftan, his bald head skirted by a beard of heroic proportions. He marched towards them at a military clip, hobnails clanging off the stones, a sword pointed directly at Marius' chest.

"Identify yourself!"

"Who the hell is that?" Gerd hissed in alarm.

Marius grinned. "*That* is Mad Arnobew. Relax." He raised a hand in greeting. "It's me, Arnobew. Marius don Hellespont."

"Master Marius?" Arnobew dropped his sword and rushed forward to smother Marius in a hug. The sword hit the road without a sound. Gerd picked it up and held it out to Granny.

"Card."

Granny raised her eyebrows. Arnobew released Marius.

"Let me see you, lad." He settled his gaze on Marius' face, and his look of joy fell away.

"Oh no," he said. "Not you as well."

"What do you mean?"

"Nothing." He straightened up, and resumed his soldier's stance. "It's good to see you again, young Master don Hellespont."

"Oh, cut the Master crap, you old bugger." Marius held up his square of card. "I come bearing gifts."

"Ohhhhh." Arnobew leaned forward, and grasped the edges reverentially. "Oh, Marius, she's a beauty. Wherever did you... no, don't tell me. I've got just the place for her, just the place." He turned away, square held at arm's length, and ran back to his post. The three travellers watched him go

"So," Granny said as he rounded the edge of the fence. "Can't imagine why you call him mad."

"Nothing to do with that." Marius nodded them forward, and they wandered over to wait at the fence's edge. "I've seen saner men than Arnobew with fetishes that would make you blush until your head exploded."

"Really."

"Really. Anyway, Arnobew's not really mad. He's got a bit of a delusion, that's all. He's just picked the wrong place to have it."

"And what is that, then?"

"He's actually the fourth or fifth richest man in V'Ellos. Trouble is, he got bored with the endless cocktail parties and cordon bleu breakfasts and began to wonder how the other half lived. Now, well..."

He pointed around the fence. Granny and Gerd followed his finger. Halfway up the beautifully manicured lawn, between the goldfish pool and the thirty-room house with the genuine Gsenkish marble frontage, someone had built a hovel. And a midden. And a guard box. As they watched, Arnobew emerged, and patted himself down.

"Poor, mad Arnobew," Marius said. "Lives in V'Ellos and thinks he's working class."

"Mad," Gerd agreed, eyeing the house behind him.

"As a porridge enema."

Arnobew made his way across to them. Gerd held out his cardboard sword, and he accepted it with a muttered "Thank'ee."

"So," he said, clapping Marius on the shoulder, "You'll be wanting to see your Da, me old mucker."

"I'm afraid so."

"I'll escort you."

They wheeled away. Gerd and Granny took one last, longing look at the house, and then followed him as he strode down the street towards the hill at the far end of the little town.

"Arnobew, what did you mean when you said 'Not you as well'?"

"Nothing, nothing." The shambling guard led them around a corner and up a slight incline. "I can't say."

"Can't?"

"Can't, certainly can't. Not allowed."

Gerd and Granny remained silent behind them. Marius could feel their eyes rolling.

"Why are we headed this way?" he asked. "Father's house was down by the marina, last time I was here."

"He's gone up in the world, your Da," Arnobew said as they walked. "He's gone places."

"Oh, yes?"

"Oh, yes," he replied, and pointed toward the top of the hill.

There, crouched a full dozen feet higher than its neighbours, sat a townhouse of understated and elegant simplicity that couldn't have been in poorer taste had there been a thirty foot-high sign screaming "Caravanserai Trash" jammed into its perfectly manicured front lawn. Sloping, elegant retaining walls of white stone girdled a slim, neutral frontage without so much as a single stone lion to announce its owner's wealth. Simple doric columns supported a wide, airy second story patio, and unadorned front walls just *existed*. Not a single swooping gable or leering gargoyle drew the viewer's eye upwards in appreciation of just how fucking tall the damn thing was, and just how little right a person had to even look at it, never mind think about ruining the walkway with their grubby little commoner feet. It was as if the owner hadn't made any effort to spend any of their vast hidden wealth upon the place *at all*. It was gauche, it was insulting; it stood out from its neighbours like a hard-on in a nunnery. Whoever lived here was obviously a complete bastard. Marius looked up at it and felt something small inside of him keel over and die.

"Yes," he said. "Gone places is one way to put it."

TWELVE

Marius' father had been the fifth richest man in Borgho City when he arrived, which as far as the elite of V'Ellos were concerned – and they were *all* elite – was equivalent to being the fifth largest turd in the alleyway. But Ygram don Hellespont had a simple yet stunningly effective plan for climbing the social ladder: he lied. Being out of touch with the world around them wasn't so much a fault for V'Ellosians as a badge of honour. Who, after all, would admit to knowing what the little people were doing? So Ygram simply lied, and took advantage of their ignorance of the world. His aim was simple: to sit at the biggest window in the drawing room of the largest townhouse on the highest hill of the richest city in the world, and look down upon everyone and everything and satisfy his hatred of them all.

And he'd done it.

V'Ellos was the place where the richest people in the world retired. They turned their backs on the constant rounds of balls and parties where the real politics of rulership were carried out, and instead settled back to enjoy the rounds of balls and parties that served for idle entertainment while, outside, the bally world could jolly well burn to the ground as long as the supply of Tallian truffles and '67 Chateau du Clarioux remained uninterrupted. Marius' father had also retired here to engage in his own form of entertainment: namely, gipping his neighbours out of as much dosh as he could while they were too busy swigging their stinky fungi and overpriced bubbly vinegar to notice. It was a hobby at which he was stunningly successful. He may have been only the fifth biggest turd in the alleyway when he arrived, but there was no bigger turd in the world than Ygram don Hellespont these days. Thief to thief, Marius could have loved his father for it, except that he already loved his mother. In Marius' family, caring for one person meant no room for any other.

Ygram loved money, which left no room for anybody, and he was obviously less than pleased to see his only son standing in the foyer of his domain. "What do you want?" he asked, standing on the top step of a marble staircase as he looked down at the motley crew of travellers. In truth, he would have looked down at them even had he been standing in their midst, but at least this way he had the physical advantage as well as the monetary. Marius rolled his shoulders backwards to relieve the tension that automatically clenched them upon entering the house, and stared back.

"Twenty years, Father. Are they really going to be your first words to me in all that time?"

Ygram raised an eyebrow, tilting his head back so he could view the assembled company from even further down his nose.

"And in the company of dirt farmers. How appropriate."

"Excuse me! *Pig* farmer." Gerd stepped forward. Marius laid a restraining hand on his arm.

"Gerd, why don't you take Granny down that hallway to the servants' quarters, and freshen up?"

"Excuse me? Is *that* what we are now? Did we step into some strange, alternative world when we came through that door, where you're all of a sudden–"

"Gerd." *What is the first rule?*

"Wha... oh."

There had been three months of instruction, when Marius first plucked Gerd from his pig farm high in the Spinal Ranges, on the rules and responsibilities of thievery. A long list, longer than Gerd was able to absorb, of the ways and means to easy prosperity, and if you can't manage that, then at least how not to get spitted like a pig the first time you try to run a whoopsy-doodle scam on somebody with a sword and more muscles than you. At the end of which, Gerd had been spitted like a pig by a soldier as he looted a battlefield, so that was that as far as education went.

Still, he could at least remember the first rule: never steal what you can't swallow. It had been his efforts to remind Marius of it that had led to him being spitted in the first place. He stared at his mentor for perhaps half a minute, his hand idly running up and down the front of his jacket, just above the scar left by the soldier's sword.

"Ah." Two and two were put together. Pennies dropped. The obvious stopped bleeding. He glanced down the hallway to the left of the staircase, and saw at least three richly appointed doors between him and the end of the corridor. "Right you are."

"Take Granny. Show her the way."

"Okey dokey."

"Father and I have to have a little talk." He placed his foot on the first step of the staircase. His father glanced over at his companions.

"Tell them to keep their hands off the fittings," he said. "And bring tea when I call."

"You heard the man." Marius stared hard at Gerd. "Don't touch the fittings."

"Gotcha." Gerd took Granny by the arm. "This way, Granny." The old lady had said nothing. Now she glanced down at the cat in her arms, then the stairway, as if calculating how hard a throw it would take to land Alno on the rich man's face. Gerd tugged gently. "Please."

Reluctantly, she allowed herself to be dragged to the side of the stairwell. They passed a portrait of Ygram, a delicate rendering in oils that was clearly the mark of a master artist. Reaching out, she ran her thumbnail across the surface, leaving a deep tear in the paintwork.

"Whoops," she said with complete lack of sincerity. Ygram and Marius watched them disappear behind the staircase.

"You'll pay for that," Ygram said. "And anything that goes missing. That was a Dellotas."

"You can get him to do another one." Marius made the top step. "And they're poor people, not dishonest ones."

"Obviously." Ygram sniffed, as if testing the air for the unwelcome smell of poverty. "In the library, if you will."

"Perfect." Marius climbed past him and made his way to the golden-gilded door. "Just where I wanted to be."

THIRTEEN

Marius had just turned eighteen. There was no celebration: there was no time for it, and besides, they were in V'Ellos now. In V'Ellos, you weren't worth a thing unless you were worth everything. There wasn't an eighteen year-old in the world with enough money to be worth celebrating. There had been an argument at dinner – something trivial, a small matter of etiquette or a money-making opportunity that slipped sideways at an inopportune moment, he really couldn't remember – which had led to the drinking, which had led to more argument, which had led to his father drawing his hand across his chest in anticipation of marking his mother's cheek with it. Marius had drawn his dinner knife like a dagger from the table and driven it into the priceless Barbantine wood table an inch from his father's other wrist. Now Mother was packing, and Marius had retreated to the library, where he could recover some measure of safe emotion surrounded by the conflicts and mistakes of history.

He could hear her, slamming doors and dragging her valise from under her bed. Separate bedrooms. The young Marius shook his head. There was his family, accounted for in a single image. Ten minutes from now she would appear in the doorway, announce her inability to stay, and be off with a kiss on the cheek, an exhortation not to let his father do to him what he had done to her, and the smell of *eau de parfum*. It was a smell that would cause him to break down until he was well into his thirties. Until she appeared, he knew from long experience, they would stick to their separate tiny empires, a world war contained in twenty rooms. Give it a week, maybe two, and she'd be back. A truce would be declared. Battlegrounds would be left to grow fertile and would be spread with new loam of hurt and mistrust until ready for harvest. Give it a month, maybe two. Marius was used to the cycle. It had been a decade in the making. It had an infrastructure now, a validity. He traced the spines of books as he passed them, letting the feel of cold leather against his fingertips provide a focus. There, the bang of the bedroom door. Feet on the stairwell, the *thump, thump, thump* of the valise dragging behind. Comforting sounds, almost, the familiar rhythms of his family carrying out their appointed duties: self-judgement, self-sentencing, self-execution. He leant his head against a copy of Yintus's *Histories*, let the objectivity flow from the pages into his brow, then turned towards the door.

There. His father, on schedule. The library door would crash open. The front door would crash closed. His father would be an outline in the doorway, bottle hanging loosely from his hand, hair askew, the reek of fifty year-old Tallian brandy rolling towards Marius in waves.

Except: not this time. There was the bang of the front door, as it should be. But the library door swung open on oiled hinges, kissed the wall with the faintest of knocks. And there was his father, but not the raging drunkard that family tradition demanded. He stood a moment in the doorway, calm as a hunting cat, and pinned Marius against the bookcase with steel-sober eyes. He wore his best suit, pressed and cleaned for the occasion. His hair was pomaded back into a slick, grey skullcap. While his wife was racing towards her temporary freedom he was shaving, splashing spiced oil across his jaw line, trimming his moustache with military precision. Man as predator, man as knife: sharp, clean, gleaming and deadly. He let his son absorb the sacrilege for a long moment. Marius stepped away from the bookcase. Ygram stalked into the room, sat in the vast leather easy chair that was his personal throne, and raised his eyes to his young son. Marius stared back, suddenly bereft of certainty.

"Get out," he said, and there was no misunderstanding between them. His father did not mean just the library, just his presence. Marius had been banished, perfectly and forever. He would spend twenty years telling the world he ran away, sick of his father's corruption and the stink of rotten money. But in that moment, alone without the cushion of familial civility, father and son forged a moment of perfect clarity.

Marius ran.

Now, twenty years later, Marius stood in a different library in a different house and sought out the Yintus on the crowded shelves. He found it, and let his fingers rest against the cracked spine as his father entered behind him. Ygram crossed to an armchair next to a small table, and sat. A brandy snifter sat aside a crystal decanter. He poured himself a generous measure, then raised the glass to view the amber liquid rolling around inside, ignoring Marius' presence. Marius took the opportunity to give the room a proper viewing, and shook his head. Row after row of leather-bound books circled the room, housed in rare, white-wooded shelves. Deep burgundy rugs hid the floorboards. The fittings were newer, the accoutrements of a better quality, the chair a more luxurious leather, the panelling an altogether deeper shade of wood. But in its layout and number of appointments it was an exact copy of the library of his late youth, which had been an exact copy of the library of his childhood, back in the days of the Borgho docks and business conducted at midnight. He shook his head again. He could walk around this house with his eyes closed. The kitchen would be as it had always been, the dining room, the bedrooms, all would be exact copies of exact copies of exact copies. He caught his father's eye for a moment. *Except for my bedroom,* he amended himself. *I bet my bedroom no longer exists.*

"Nice place you've got here," he said, running a finger along a shelf. "Mindwood shelving and everything. I was part of the crew that cut down the last mindwood grove in Flemg, did you know that?"

"What do you want?"

Marius crossed the floor and picked up the brandy decanter.

"No second glass?"

"No."

He smiled. Raising it to his lips, he took a deep draught, and coughed.

"Fuck me, that's good stuff."

His father sighed and lowered his glass.

"What do you *want*?"

Marius looked down at him. "I've been away for twenty years, Father. Don't you at least want to know what I've done in all that time, where I've been?"

Ygram was the very essence of stillness. He kept his head averted from his son's gaze, staring at the partially parted curtains across the room and the vista of V'Ellos beyond.

"Your mother used to open the packages you had delivered, the posters that said you were an actor." He might have been saying *child molester*. "Even a fool could see they were fakes."

"Did she like them?"

"She was a fool."

Marius nodded. She had chosen to believe. He tilted his head, noticing for the first time the utter silence that surrounded them.

"Where is Mother?"

Now his father turned his head, and stared directly into his son's eyes. A smile distorted his lower face, the type you see on alley thugs' faces just before the knife in their hands becomes the blade between your ribs. He took time to sip his brandy, then held it up so that his eyes peered at Marius over the lip of the glass.

"Why do you think I used past tense?" he asked, with all the mocking pleasure in his soul.

Marius didn't scream. He didn't break down in tears, or stagger back, hand clutched to his heart in sudden tragedy. Instead, he matched his father's stare for several seconds, then very carefully lowered the decanter so it sat safe and neat in the centre of the little table. He retrieved the volume of Yintus from its shelf and stood with his back to Ygram as he slowly and methodically ripped every page out, letting each individual sheet fall to the floor. Whilst his father watched, he made a slow circuit of the library, head tilted to the side, reading titles as he went. It took him half an hour to scour every shelf, Ygram sipping from his brandy all the while.

Marius finished his destruction and walked to the door, exiting without a backward glance. His father said nothing, did nothing to stop him. He climbed the stairs to his father's bedroom, situated upon the top floor at the front of the house as it always had been, and examined the bookshelves there, ignoring the opulence of the fittings, ignoring the way it mirrored the bedroom he remembered from earlier days. When his search came up empty he descended to the ground floor, to the space behind the reception room his mother had sequestered for her sleeping quarters thirty years before in a different city. He slipped inside in respectful silence, closing the door behind him before he could remember the way she looked first thing in the morning, when the child Marius could still run in and snuggle under her blankets before the day really started. He stood with his back against the door and surveyed the room for near on three full minutes. It was exactly as he recalled; a confectionery of creams and lace, with tiny bottles crowding every available surface, each glittering with a quarter inch of perfumed liquid. An oval mirror sat above a dressing table adorned with countless arcane female implements. He crossed over to it. The table bore a thin layer of dust. Marius ran a finger through it, then turned, eyeing the bed for long moments. Slowly, he knelt down and looked under it, nodding to himself. The valise was missing. Silently, he left the room and returned to the library. Ygram sat where Marius had left him, the decanter a full two inches emptier than when he had departed. The remains of Yintus's *Histories* were gone.

"You said she was dead."

"You may have thought that."

"You bastard!" This time Marius did rage. He threw himself about the room, hurling books from their shelves, bouncing volume after volume onto the floor near the armchair. The decanter was an early casualty. Ygram's glass survived only until the next volume. Books rebounded from the arms of the chair, the back, the overstuffed head. The table was overturned, the top smashed. Ygram sat perfectly still. Not a single page struck him. Finally, Marius' fury ran down. He stood over Ygram, one hand on either arm of the chair, and leaned into his father's impassive gaze.

"Where is she?"

"One hundred and eighteen thousand riner, eight tenpenny, sixpence."

"What?"

"The value of your destruction. Not counting the Dellotas your dirt farmer woman destroyed. Someone like you could never afford that."

"She's a pig farmer, you arrogant fuck."

His father shrugged.

"Where is she?" Marius leaned in further, slid his hands up the arm of the chair until his hands circled Ygram's biceps, pinning him.

"Where do you think?"

Of course. The sound of slamming bedroom doors. The sound of suitcases being dragged towards the front door. Memories twenty years old, twenty-five, thirty. Marius blinked, staring at his father in sudden shock. Ygram stared back, disdain clear upon his face.

"You stupid, worthless, bastard child."

Then there was no option but violence. Marius' hand was under Ygram's jaw before he could formalise a thought. He lifted his father up the back of the chair so the older man was bent over, the back of the chair digging into his spine and all of Marius' weight pressing down upon his upper body. Marius pushed his face into Ygram's, squeezing his fingers together so the older man choked and struggled for breath.

"You call *me* stupid?" Marius hissed. "Take a good gander at me, did you? You notice I'm not breathing?

You notice what I look like?" He shook his father from side to side. "You think I have the patience for your fucking games anymore?"

He dragged Ygram over to the nearest book shelf, slammed his face into the leather spines, hauled him along the shelf then on to the next one, face *thump thump thump*ing across the spines faster and faster while Marius growled.

"*The Campaigns of Scorbus*. Green spine. Bronze lettering. Two inches thick. Where is it?" *Thump, thump.* "Where is it?" *Thump, thump.* "Where is it?"

Until, finally, Ygram sputtered and grabbed weakly at Marius' arm and begged him to stop. And Marius did, dropping the old man in a heap in the corner, where he scrabbled himself into a sitting position, gasping for breath that did not want to come. Marius squatted in front of him, no breath, no sweat, no sign of a single exertion. He tilted his head, like a lizard predator staring down at sweating mammalian prey. Ygram found some measure of air, wiped snot away with the back of his hand.

"Storehouse," he managed. "Down at the docks. Taupe frontage. Business name. On plaque. Across from yacht."

"Which yacht?"

"You'll know it." Ygram slumped down, coughing. "All there. It's there."

And Marius was gone, down the marble staircase to the front door, calling out for his companions as he went, leaving the crumpled husk of his father behind for the final time.

They convened in the foyer. Gerd nodded back up the steps.

"So that's your dad, then?"

"Yeah."

"Wow. No wonder you never argue when people call you a bastard."

"Yeah, well, I… Wait. Who calls me a bastard?"

Granny and Gerd didn't hesitate. "Everyone!"

Marius glanced towards the library door. He saw it twitch open half an inch, then stop.

"That's not as funny as you might think."

His friends exchanged glances, but said nothing.

"Come on," he said, and opened the front door.

Arnobew was waiting for them when they emerged.

"Oh, gods," he said when he saw Marius' face. "He's sent you to the marina, hasn't he? Wait here. Just…" He moved off, held up his hands in a "stay" motion. "Just wait. I'll be back in a minute."

He ran off down the street. The threesome watched him go. As he turned the corner, Marius glanced at Gerd.

"What did you get?"

"Sorry?"

"What did you lift?"

"Oh, right." Gerd rummaged around in his pockets, and eventually presented Marius with a small pile of glittering gewgaws. "I found a dressing room on the top floor, at the back. It looked like it hadn't been touched in years."

They knelt down and examined the pile. Three necklaces, a scattering of rings, all adorned with jewels that twinkled genuine in the afternoon sunlight. Two coins from the reign of Grejjiq, back in the days of the old Dynasties three thousand years ago. Alno meowed, stretching out a paw to play with the shining pile. Marius batted it away, and held a coin up to Gerd.

"At least a thousand riner just for that. Swallow it."

Gerd did as he was told, jerking his throat back and forward like a bird to make up for his dead man's inability to create spit. When it was down, Marius held up the second.

"What you expecting him to do?" Granny asked as she watched him force the second coin down. "Shit tenpennies?"

"First rule of thieving," Gerd replied, wincing as the coin finished its journey. "Never steal anything you can't swallow."

"When this is over," Marius said, running his fingers through the rest of the booty, "there's enough in those two coins to set you both up for the rest of your lives. Deaths. Whatever." He shook his head. "Contingency fund. Whatever."

"Hmmph." She eyed him speculatively. "That's probably what you take for being nice. Thank you."

"You're welcome."

"What about the rest of it?"

Marius looked down at the meagre collection of jewellery. "My mother's." He scooped them up and placed them in an inner pocket of his jacket. "I'll give them back to her when I see her."

"Will you see her?"

Marius glanced up towards the darkened windows of his father's townhouse. "Oh, yes. How long do you think the room was unoccupied?"

"Dunno." Gerd shrugged. "Long enough for a lot of dust."

"Hmm." Marius turned his attention to Granny. "And what about you? Did you get anything?"

"Just this." She reached under her skirts and withdrew a long, slim sword in a leather scabbard, its hilt glittering with inlaid jewels. "Want me to swallow it?"

"Father's rapier." Marius' smile was nasty. "I'll have that."

He removed his belt and slid the scabbard onto it, buckling back up just as Arnobew raced back up to them.

"Ready!" he announced, skidding to a halt three feet from the group. They eyed him up and down as one, various levels of disbelief on their faces.

Arnobew was wearing armour. A full suit, from the pointed toes of his boots through greaves, gauntlets, skirt, chest plate, right up to the plumed top of his helm, every inch bedecked with curlicues and fleur de lis, vine leaves and regalia. The suits of armour displayed in Scorby City's Museum of Kings would hide their faces in shame at being so shabbily decorated in comparison. A coat of arms emerged from the centre of his breastplate by a full three inches, the motto "Humility before honour" picked out in script across the curve of his belly. It was a work of art of the most baroque extravagance, all the more impressive because the entire ensemble was so clearly made of cardboard. From his left hand dangled the twin chains of a cardboard flail, and in his right he held that most fearsome of melee weapons, a cardboard mace.

"Arnobew!"

"Arnobew no more!" he roared back. "I am Warbone!"

Alno stalked over and sniffed at the cardboard warrior's leg, then rubbed against him, a furred figure-eight going in and out and around his legs like a Moebius strip.

"Right." Marius bit his lip. "Right. Warbone."

"Yes, *sir*!"

"Got you."

"Sir!"

The three travellers avoided each other's gazes. Marius stared over the rooftops of the nearby, lower houses.

"So…" he began, stopped, and tried again. "The marina…"

"Yes, sir! This way, sir!"

Warbone marched back down the road. A cross street slid down the hill towards the bay that Marius could see twinkling between the surrounding houses. Alno skipped along next to him, one mad warrior in synch with another.

"Come on," Marius said, and the little group set off after them. They walked slowly through the streets, boots echoing on the perfectly aligned cobbles. Around them, the cleanest houses in the world sneered down at them in perfect symmetry.

"Weird," Marius said, eyeing shuttered windows as they passed. "I don't remember V'Ellos being a hive of activity, but this…"

"Deserted."

"Feels like it, doesn't it?"

"Maybe there's a festival or something?"

Marius sucked at his teeth. "The rich don't do festivals. That sort of stuff is to keep the peasants distracted while they raise taxes."

"Cynic."

"I'm my father's son."

Gerd cast him a sidelong glance but kept his own counsel. Up forward, Arnobew began to sing a jaunty marching song that Marius recognised from his time in the Tallian mercenaries.

"Joined cause I was out of luck–"

"Arnobew?"

"Tell me who I have to fuck–"

"Arnobew!"

"To get my chest free of this badge–"

"Damn it, Arnobew!"

Granny chuckled and took up the refrain: "I'll even eat the queen's old vadge."

"Warbone!"

"Granny!"

Two fiercely smiling faces turned towards Marius and Gerd.

"Yes, sir?"

"Lot of soldiers come through the mountains, boy. Wasn't born in a nunnery."

Marius did his best to ignore Gerd's embarrassed splutter, never mind Granny's chuckle, like the sound of a young farm girl's skirts being hiked over her hips. He pointed down the hill towards the marina, clinging artfully to the sweep of the town's small harbour below them.

"My father's warehouse is down there somewhere," he said. "Do you know it?"

Warbone stared down at the profusion of brightly coloured buildings. "Aye," he ventured cautiously. "I know the one he means."

"Why would he need a warehouse, Warbone? He stopped being a merchant when we moved here. Didn't he?"

"Oh," the big man ran cardboard-gauntleted fingers through the hedgerow of his beard. "I reckon as how he did some running, here and there. Likes to keep his hand in, your Da. Likes to deal."

Marius eyed him. "There something you're not telling me, Warbone?"

"No, no." Arnobew shook his head, fooling nobody. "There'd be no secrets he'd be trusting to a working man like me, now would there?"

"No." Marius loosened the scabbard's hold on his sword a fraction. "I expect not." They continued to walk forward, false cheer dispensed with as the grim set of Marius' face affected the others' mood.

"Where is everyone, Warbone?"

"I'm not sure I understand, sir?"

"I'm asking you where everyone is, soldier." Marius saw him stiffen. "That's a direct request."

"Sir, yes, sir."

"Well?"

The townhouse stopped at the bottom of the hill, and the smooth stones of the street widened out into a long boulevard that rang along the edge of a sparkling marina. To their right, the bunched masts of small pleasure craft dipped and swayed in the gentle swell of the harbour, their massed ranks moving in synch like drunken fence posts. Hulls of shining wood sat in quiet order, one to a berth, gleaming in the afternoon sun. Brass accessories added a million reflections. The names on the nearest boats reflected the general view that here, on the water where the poor could not reach them, the super-rich could find freedom from the irritating press of lesser humans. There were perhaps three hundred boats docked here, not one more than thirty feet long, all single-masted, with little more than a couple of seats and a set of oar brackets behind the tiny cabins. The big yachts, the ones with a crew and hot-and-cold-running virgins, would be reached via these little skiffs. Those boats were berthed around an island further out in the bay that had been constructed purely for the purpose. These smaller boats were for when a man wanted to be alone, with only the sea for company, where he could enjoy his champagne and cigars without interruption from anyone but the gods of wind and water. They were used a lot more often that the big ones.

To the left rose a line of warehouses, blank facades thirty feet high with great wooden gates, distinguishable only by the change in colour from one frontage to the next. Small brass plaques were set into the front wall, next to modest entrance doors. In the daylight they presented a profusion of colours, rainbow splashes like tropical birds, announcing "Here is my money, here is my endeavour, here is where I keep my stock and nobody else gains entry unless I wish it." To Marius' deadened senses they blended into one another. He brought the little party to a halt, and turned to face Arnobew directly.

"I'm waiting for an answer, Warbone," he said, hand hovering a half-inch from the handle of his sword. Arnobew slammed to attention, his gaze pinned to an invisible horizon.

"They're here, sir."

"Where?"

"Here." He glanced down at Marius, then back up again. "Every last one of them, sir."

"Why?"

"I'm not the one to ask, sir."

Marius frowned. His fingertips brushed the sword handle. "Who is?"

"Who is what, sir?"

Behind him, Marius and Granny had bunched together, heads turning from side to side, drawn quiet by the feeling that something had suddenly gone very wrong. Alno dragged a paw down the leg of Gerd's pants. After a moment Gerd bent down and scooped the cat up into his arms, where Alno lay still, large eyes staring down the dock.

"Who is the one to ask, Warbone?"

"I think, sir, that it might be him."

He pointed beyond Marius, along the dock. Marius heard Gerd mutter "Bloody hell," before he turned and saw the object of Arnobew's attention.

Halfway down the dock stood a taupe-coloured warehouse significantly larger than those around it, fully eighty feet to a side, with a gently angled roof that threw slab-like shadows across the fascias of its neighbours. The massive sliding doors on its frontage appeared to be drawn back. At this angle Marius could see a thin band of light against the base of the cavernous entrance, the edge of the door a full dozen feet above his own, but nothing beyond. It didn't matter, because three feet out from the open entrance stood a figure they all recognised.

"Drenthe."

Marius had drawn his sword and was already a dozen steps away from the group and running before he was aware of his actions. Behind him he heard Granny curse, and Gerd yell at him to stop, but they were dull sounds on the edge of hearing, barely discernible over the drum of hatred in his skull. Then even that was drowned by the war scream rising ragged from his throat. The point of his sword was aimed unerringly at his enemy's one good eye. And his enemy was laughing now, raising a hand towards the cavern beyond the warehouse doors. The vast overhang above the doors plunged the depths of the building into shadow, but even so, he could see a platoon of the dead standing motionless inside, two hundred or more silent corpses lined up and waiting for the signal Drenthe now gave them.

They stepped forward as one. The rich of V'Ellos, wearing liveries that had coloured Marius' teen years, and which he had taken special delight in stealing from as an adult: Garl Skeni, the textile merchant, who had parlayed a thousand tonnes of wobbly tartan into a craze for lopsided fezzes that had lasted a dozen years and as many different shades; Sond man Sip, the northern arms merchant who introduced hundred-folded steel to the King's armies; Ghag man Rep, his second in command – embezzler, fraudster, multi-millionaire, forgiven friend; and all the rest – two hundred splashes of colour stepping out into the sun in perfect unison, standing behind their master, dead eyes staring at Marius and his friends in pure, undistilled contempt, the matching white scars at their jugulars filling his vision.

"Where is she?"

Drenthe parried Marius' first blow almost without looking, his sword flickering past the first lunge to nick at his shoulder. Marius parried wildly, swung his fist at Drenthe's face and caught him a glancing blow on the chin. The sheer momentum of Marius' lunge rocked his opponent a step backwards. He recovered his balance. His sword flicked out again, steel against steel, blocking Marius' charge.

"Where is who?" He smiled, and Marius doubled his assault.

"Tell me, you son of a bitch. Tell me where she is!"

"Which one?" Drenthe pushed Marius off for half a moment, using the space to step away and face his enemy. "The long-legged, lithe and lovely, lascivious whore you seem to like so much? Or the whore you started with?"

"I'll kill you!"

"Really?" Drenthe laughed. "Won't *that* be something different?"

Marius' reply was little more than an incoherent scream. He threw himself forward, sword crashing down against Drenthe's blocking blade, no more technique or style now, just vicious, battering overhead blow after overhead blow. Drenthe skipped backwards, raising his arm so that Marius' assault careened off metal, slowly dancing out of reach as Marius continued his advance.

"You do know," he said as he led him towards the open doors of the warehouse, "that we can keep this up all day, don't you? I mean, I'm not getting tired. Are you?"

Marius said nothing, simply maintained his unthinking rain of blows. Drenthe retreated before him, sword across his body, blocking everything that rained down upon him. Somewhere behind Marius, Gerd was screaming his name. Marius no longer cared. All that remained within him was the need to smash through Drenthe's defence, to see his blade cave in that smug, smiling face, to stand above his fallen foe and smash his sword down again and again until Drenthe's skull was nothing more than a broken pot leaking mush onto the floor and his mocking voice faded forever from the inside of his mind.

"You should listen to them," Drenthe said, as if on cue, clear and mocking. "They can see what's happening."

Marius slowed.

"That's right," Drenthe said. "Look around you, boy. Look at what you've walked into."

He lunged forward as Marius' arm lost its energy, and gave him a hard shove to the chest. Marius stumbled backwards, thrown off balance. His arm swung down onto thin air, and fell to his side. Marius realised where he was, finally, and looked around.

The dead had closed in behind him as he had raced forward after Drenthe, blocking him off from his companions. Now they ringed him, a solid wall of dead faces. But he barely saw them. It was what he saw beyond them that made Marius cease his furious assault.

A thousand dead stood in ranks inside his father's warehouse, shoulder to shoulder, pressed into the space like logs waiting to be carried outside and burned. The servants of V'Ellos, each one wore the livery of his father's house. Each dead body was clothed in the colours of the don Hellespont merchant firm with the family crest borne over their unbeating hearts. They stared at Marius with blank dispassion. Even in the dark he could see the clear white scars that bisected their throats. He faltered, then. His arm lost its strength. His father's sword fell to the floor.

"Oh," Drenthe said. "You understand now."

"He…"

"He? He?" Drenthe turned the question into a laugh. "Your father, sonny. Your very own Master of V'Ellos. Supplier of arms, recruiter of troops." Drenthe stepped close, thrust his face into Marius'. "Chooser of sides."

Marius stared past him, at the army of sacrifices his father had created.

"What did he… what did he give them… for… for this?"

"Oh, little Helles." Drenthe's jaw creaked open. Marius could see into the desiccated mouth, see the ridges of his spinal column as the sound of his laughter echoed off all the dark places in his mind. "He promised them service forever, Helles. And he promised them that they could deliver you!"

A thousand faces turned towards him. Recognition spread across them like a lit match catching flame. Marius backed away from it, bumped into the wall of bodies behind. And something brown and roaring came barrelling into the bodies behind him, crashing through their ranks, into the space between Marius and Drenthe.

"Marius!" Arnobew lashed out. His flail caught Drenthe on the shoulder, and crumpled. He flung it away, destroyed his mace on the dead man's ribs and threw that away too. Finally, a bear-like swat of his arm caught Drenthe across the side of his neck and clubbed him to the ground. "Run, boy!"

Marius wasted precious seconds gaping at his saviour. Arnobew struck out with a leg, catching the nearest corpse in the groin and doubling him over with the strength of his kick.

"Go!"

The crowd was beginning to re-form, recovering from its initial shock and moving to close the gap that Arnobew had created. Marius shook himself back to his senses. He swept up his sword and bludgeoned an attacker in the side of the head.

"Arnobew! Come on!"

Now Gerd arrived, and grabbed two dead at the back of the gap, smashing them against their compatriots, keeping the gap open. Marius plunged into it, kicking and elbowing to widen it, swiping his sword from shoulder to waist in long, slashing movements as he struggled against grasping hands. Arnobew turned towards him, and as he did so, Drenthe rose up from the floor behind him.

"Arnobew!" Marius shouted, but his warning was too late. Drenthe whipped his sword forward and back in a lightning-quick stroke across the side of his throat. Arnobew's hand flew up to the wound. He swung his shoulders, knocked Drenthe backwards, took another step towards Marius as the crowd closed in around him. Marius saw him stumble, saw him lift one blood-soaked hand over the sudden swell of heads, and then it was gone, and the crowd was surging once more. Gerd grabbed at Marius' shoulder, got a handful of fabric, and pulled him past the final body, into the space beyond.

"Arnobew!" Marius threw himself back at the throng. Faces were turning towards him, bodies drawing together to close off his escape. He battered at the nearest body, forced it to its knees. Gerd was pulling at him.

"He's gone, Marius. He's gone."

"No! Let me go. Fuck you, let me go!"

And then Drenthe appeared before him, popping out of the small break between bodies like a snake between broken bricks. He dove, and caught Marius' shirt-front in fists still wet with Arnobew's blood.

"Run, mummy's boy," he shouted, laughter filling Marius' mind. "Run now!"

Marius ran.

Granny had already begun to back away. Marius and Gerd swept her up by the arms and ran with her suspended between them, back down the dock towards the road that climbed the hill towards escape. They almost made it. They almost reached the last building in the row. But then its giant doors swung back, and a torrent of dead flowed out, blocking their escape.

"Back, back!" They turned again. The first group was still advancing. Marius looked about wildly.

"There!"

The nearest jetty jutted out into the water a dozen feet away. Marius and Gerd made for it at a flat run. The mob closed in behind them. The jetty was narrow, the three of them barely fitting onto it side by side, the regular stanchions along its edge and the profusion of ropes across it making for a treacherous passage. Marius let go of Granny's arm and ran ahead, scanning the boats to either side. All were tied fast, masts empty, sails firmly furled and tied down. The troops of the dead were crowding about the far end of the jetty, bunching up as the wide stone harbour gave way to the slim wooden extrusion. Marius risked a quick glance over his shoulder, saw Drenthe push his way to the front and start organising a platoon to step onto forward. They matched gazes, two enemies with nothing between them but thirty feet of walkway. Drenthe smiled, and Marius heard his voice inside his head, clear as panic.

"Keep running, don Hellespont. Make me work for it."

Marius bared his teeth, and returned his attention to the boats ahead. Drenthe sent him an image of the massed troops under his command stepping slowly, casually, onto the jetty. Thirty dead men, three abreast, taking their time, making sure of their footing. He closed it out. A few boats ahead, he saw a flash of white, and heard the snap of stiffened fabric against the breeze.

"There! There!" He turned towards Gerd to point it out.

And slipped.

Gerd was too close, right on his heels. There was no chance to stop, to jump over Marius' flailing heap of a body. He went full-length over him, letting go of Granny's arm as he fell. She stopped running as the two companions rolled away from her, kicking at each other's legs to disentangle themselves. Their motion took them a half dozen steps away from where she stood. It was Marius who looked up, saw Drenthe's troops break into a run behind her. He raised a hand to point.

"Granny! Get moving!"

She turned to see what he was pointing at, took one step backwards in shock as the front row of minions reached her. Gerd wasted half a second rolling onto his front to push himself up. His ankle collided with Marius' outstretched leg, and he slipped onto his face.

And just like that, Granny was lost. Drenthe's men reached her and dragged her into their ranks: half a dozen arms wrapped around her, and the fallen friends watched in horror as she was whipped past the front row into the depths of the mob in a silent second. Then Gerd found his feet and launched himself at them.

"Granny!"

He drove his shoulder into the first row of attackers, and for half a second it looked as if he would share Granny's fate. But the wall of bodies held, and he resorted to swinging his ham hock fists at them. His attackers crumpled, then held, their bodies propped up by the unmoving screen of corpses behind them half an inch beyond his despairing grasp. And slowly, the front row began to reach forward, to grab at his clothing and pinion him against their bodies. Marius scrambled upwards, and grabbed at his arm.

"Gerd! Come on! Gerd!"

"Get off!" Gerd swung backwards. He caught Marius across the shoulder and knocked him backwards. Marius fell to his knee, then righted himself.

"Granny!"

Gerd was clearing a space. The weight of his blows were finally driving those nearest to him back a few steps. But the task was hopeless. The wall of bodies was still standing firm, and the narrow jetty gave him no room to push beyond them. All Gerd was doing was ensnaring himself in a pincer movement of his own making. Soon he'd push himself past the centre of the first row, and they would close in behind him, cutting him off. If that happened, Marius could not reach him. There was no way he could fight his way past the first line of three assailants, never mind the one behind it, or the one behind that. Gerd would simply disappear, sucked backwards towards the waiting army at the far end of the jetty, as Granny had been. Drenthe's troops could simply evade Gerd's blows, waiting until he was completely absorbed within their embrace before overwhelming him with sheer weight of numbers.

"Granny! Granny!"

Gerd was blind to it, blind to anything beyond his simple-minded assault. Marius gathered himself and, as the big man reared back to deliver another blow, he lashed out with his foot. He caught Gerd just behind the knee, and his young friend staggered. Marius leaped upwards, grabbed the raised fist, and pulled. Gerd tottered backwards. Marius swung him round, grabbed two fistfuls of shirt in his hands, and shook him.

"She's gone, boy!"

"No!"

Gerd tried to return to the attack, but Marius had spent the happiest six months of his life teaching wrestling techniques to the all-female Supreme Cohort of the Empress of Thylenia. He dug his knee into the bend at the top of Gerd's leg, shifted his weight forward, then back, and spun him away from the mob.

"We have to go," he shouted, pushing him again. "Now!"

The corpses pushed forward again, grabbing at Marius. He yelped, and shook Gerd one last time. "Go, go!"

Gerd glanced at their attackers, saw the wall of bodies pressing down towards them. Marius yanked his arm, and the big man turned reluctantly away. They scurried down the jetty, Drenthe's troops hard at their heels.

"There!" Marius pointed out the boat he had seen: a small, single-masted skiff, large enough to seat four at the most, tied up with mast open and sail already rigged. He shoved Gerd into it and threw the rope off its stanchion. The boat immediately began to slide out of its docking. A hand grabbed Marius, and he wasted precious seconds peeling it off, finger by grasping finger. Gerd was lying in the bottom of the boat, unmoving. Marius' feet found the edge of the jetty, and he launched himself in a desperate lunge for the receding stern.

There is a law, as immutable as all the laws of nature: if a jump is undertaken in a life or death situation, the distance to be jumped shall always be tantalisingly out of reach. The more desperate the leap, the closer, yet ultimately more unsuccessful, it shall be. The boat had travelled several feet since Marius had loosed it from its mooring. He wasn't even close.

The last time Marius was in the water he'd been thrown out of a canoe in the middle of the ocean and had sunk to the bottom. Then he had simply walked home. This was an advantage of being dead. Unfortunately, the memory of his underwater journey was a logical, conscious one. There was no time for his body to access it. The water hit him in his face, grabbed his clothes with slippery fingers, and pulled on his sword with desperate urgency. It slipped up his sleeves, stole his knife and sent it spinning to the sands below, invaded his nose and mouth, and pushed into his boots. Marius did what any normal person would do. He panicked, thrashing about like an octopus having a tantrum. The rope had slid from its position on the stern and now trailed through the water. Marius lunged for it, missed, lunged again. His fingers caught the loop at the end. Slowly, with abundant glubbing and coughing, he dragged himself up the side of the hull and onto the deck.

Gerd was already there, curled up in a foetal ball. Marius flopped down next to him, spraying him with water.

"Gerd." He leaned over, shook his companion's shoulder. "Gerd!"

The boat was still slowly moving forward. Marius lurched to his knees, grabbed the tiller and threw it over. The boat began to describe a slow arc away from the jetty and out towards the middle of the bay. The wind caught the sail with a gust and pushed the little skiff forward in a sudden burst of speed. Marius flopped onto the short bench at the stern, grabbed the rudder with a firmer hand, and stared back towards the quay.

The jetty was full of dead people. They stood in their silent ranks, filling the little wooden walkway, staring po-faced towards the boat as it slid away from them. Marius slumped in his seat, and glared at them with a frown. They could follow him, he realised. They could climb down and drop into the water, and begin striding across the flat bed of the harbour after him. If they really wanted to take him...

He wiped water from his eyes. A slight figure pushed through the front of the line and waved.

"Run away, Helles," Drenthe's voice was as clear as a bell within his mind, thick with amusement. "Fly your little boat away."

Marius said nothing, simply sent an image of red-hot hatred back towards his tormenter. Drenthe's laugh overwhelmed it. "No, no," he said. "Thank *you*. Thank you for the recruits. Thank you for the old lady."

The wind strained the sail. Marius pushed the tiller over savagely, catching it hard, driving the boat towards the headlands in futile anger. The jetty diminished behind them, the figures reduced to a single, uneven black line. As it dropped out of view, Drenthe called one last time.

"Granny says bye-bye, young Gerd. Such a shame, when a mother figure is torn away from her son." He laughed a final, mocking laugh. "Bye-bye…"

The boat rocked. Marius looked forward. Gerd had found his feet, was standing over Marius, his fists clenched by his sides. Marius glanced up at his reddened, furious face.

"Gerd…"

Without a word, Gerd swung away and perched in the prow. He crammed his beefy frame as deeply as possible into the angle of timbers, turned his head away from Marius, into the breeze that blew his hair back from his face and forced him to close his eyes. Marius stared at him for a few moments, then slowly steered the boat out into the bay, gazing back over his shoulder at the disappearing docks. Marius wished he could summon a mouthful of spit so that he could launch it at his tormentor. Instead, he settled for projecting a last image of Drenthe being pulled apart, one limb at a time. He received a laugh in return, and a mocking voice that echoed across the space between their minds.

"Soon, Helles," it said, "sooner than you think. And Helles? Look under your hand."

Marius turned his back on the sight, and willed the little boat to cut through the swell faster. His hand rested on the wooden handle of the tiller. He glanced at it. The wood was highly polished, gleaming in the sunlight. He frowned. There appeared to be nothing special about it. It was a piece of white wood, oiled and polished, attached to the rudder stock in the traditional way. He stared at it again. White wood.

Mindwood. The same wood as in his father's study.

Very slowly, Marius lifted his hand. Underneath, below the thick layer of varnish, someone had painted a short phrase. Seven words, in a hand Marius knew intimately: *Bring it back when you've finished, boy.* And underneath, his father's signature.

And next to it, in perfect script, freshly carved into the wood as if the man who engraved them would rather have been driving the point of the chisel into Marius' flesh, four simple words. A final message, from father to son.

Marius stared at the single line of writing as the boat swirled across the bay in a wide loop, driving past the sandy headlands that marked the bay's entrance and out into the ocean proper. He drew to starboard, set the prow parallel with the forested beach, and fell back into a contemplative stupor. The boat could steer itself, he decided, and what would he care should it drift out to sea, or smash itself to pieces on the sands that passed by? There was no ocean he could not walk back from, and right now he really couldn't care whether or not he might be battered into smithereens by hidden rocks. His whole life was hidden rocks, with everyone he knew simply waiting to push him onto them. Let them. He had nowhere left to walk back from, and no reason to wish to escape destruction. Sunlight thudded down on the unprotected boat. Marius squinted up at the sun. He didn't feel the heat, didn't even recognise the tightness that came with the advent of sunburn. Wind sprayed salt into his eyes, and he had not the slightest inclination to blink. In a final indignity, a lone gull shrieked overhead and dropped something wet onto the side of his head. Marius sighed and wiped at it, barely offering the smear of white crap a glance before letting his hand dangle backwards into the wash behind the stern. He watched the water sweep around his fingers, before pulling them free and turning his attention back to the sail above him as it made a loud crack in the sudden change of breeze.

Gerd had shifted around on his perch, and sat staring at him. Marius raised an eyebrow. Gerd spoke, and Marius frowned.

"What?"

Gerd repeated himself. Marius shook his head.

"What?" He pointed to the sail. "Speak louder. Project."

Gerd rolled his eyes and gestured impatiently, a "come here" snap of the wrist. Marius levered himself up, ducking under the boom and scuttling forward. He stopped a foot in front of the younger man, swaying with the roll of the boat.

"Now, what?" He leaned forward, and placed a hand on either side of the prow to steady himself. Gerd glanced at Marius' hands, then shot a fist upwards, catching him perfectly on the chin. Marius' legs deserted him. He crumpled backwards cracking his head against the mast footing. Then Gerd was upon him, one knee pressed into his chest, the big pig-herd's weight crushing him into the bottom of the boat.

"I said," he projected with perfect clarity, "you killed my Granny, you son of a bitch!"

Very carefully, Marius raised a single finger.

"First," he said in his most reasonable and not at all argumentative voice, "your Granny was already dead. And secondly…" He turned the finger so that it pointed directly at Gerd's rage-crumpled face, then drove it straight into his eye. Gerd reared back, instinct conquering rational thought, and clapped both hands to his abused eyeball. Marius drew his hand back, and jammed the point of his elbow into the younger man's groin. Gerd slid from his chest, and curled up around himself. Marius sat up, and looked down upon him with exasperated pity. "Secondly, why do you even do that when you know you're dead, too? And third, we didn't even see…" He paused, staring at the ocean beyond the boat. Gerd squinted up at him and, seeing the look upon his face, sat upright.

"We didn't even see what?"

"We didn't see it." Marius said in a wondering tone. "We didn't see any of it."

"What? What do you mean?"

Marius slowly focussed upon him. "How do you know they killed your Granny?"

"Are you joking? I saw it. *You* saw it."

"What did you see?"

Gerd threw his hands up in frustration. "You were right there!"

"Indulge me."

"Right. Fine. I saw them swallow her up. I saw them grab her. I saw them…" He stopped.

"Yes?"

"Well, I saw them…"

Marius nodded. "But we didn't, did we? We didn't actually *see* them destroy her."

"I… no." He looked at his older companion in shock. "I just…"

"Just *knew*."

"Yes." He nodded. "I did."

Marius was nodding, too. "Exactly like Keth. I just knew, too. But I didn't actually see. I saw…" He waved his hands in little circles. "Oh, gods." He looked up at Gerd in sudden torment. "I didn't *see*."

"Just enough."

"Yes." The two friends stared at each other. "Just enough to draw the wrong conclusions."

Gerd held his hands in front of his face. His fists clenched spasmodically. "The conclusions we were supposed to come to."

"Exactly."

They looked at each other, seeing their anger in the other's features.

"Drenthe."

"Drenthe."

"But…" Gerd frowned, suddenly uncertain. "He killed Arnobew. We saw that."

"Yes." Marius nodded, "We saw that." He squinted. Suddenly, the sun was hot. "But…" He rubbed his face. Lines of thought were warring, suppositions fighting for dominance. He closed his eyes. "Arnobew was… unexpected, maybe. Random. He's only been following us for, what, three years? He wouldn't have known about…" He pinched the bridge of his nose. "I don't know. I'm just piecing it together."

"But if you're right…" Gerd struggled with unaccustomed thoughts. Marius could see him turning possibilities over, trying to come to terms with deviousness outside his experience. "Then… why?"

"Why indeed?"

They lapsed into silence. Marius clambered to his feet and scuttled back to the tiller, patting Gerd on his shoulder as he passed. He regained his place, sunk onto his haunches, and let his gaze fall onto the thin stretch of ocean between them and the shore. After a while, Gerd clambered sternward and joined him. Marius nodded towards the line of text on the tiller handle. Gerd frowned down at it.

"What does it say?"

"'You're fucked, love Dad.'"

"Oh." Gerd settled down next to him and draped an arm over the side of the boat. "Still, nice of him to write it on a boat. Think of how useless a piece of paper would be right about now."

Marius snorted and lay back, letting the boat find its own way, coaxing it along with a gentle tug on the tiller every now and again as the wind dipped or swirled, cutting the boat across the line of breeze to keep the single sail full. Gerd watched the water swooshing by underneath the hull. The sun reached its apex and began the long, slow descent towards the land. Fins cut the water ahead. Marius banked around them and watched them fall behind.

"Ah."

"What?"

Marius nodded to himself, his eyes fixed upon the receding fins.

"He's a slutfish."

"What?"

"A slutfish." Marius leaned forward, and pointed to the water. "Have you ever gone deep sea fishing?"

"I live a hundred feet up the side of a mountain."

Marius snorted. "You don't *live* anywhere."

"Okay, fine. I death halfway up a mountain, does that make you happy?"

"Nothing halfway up a mountain would make me happy."

"You know, if I was trapped in a small boat with someone much larger than me who I'd just made angry by acting like an utter twat and getting his Granny murdered in front of his eyes, I'd probably be careful about goading him, But I guess you're made of stronger stuff, aren't you?"

Marius eyed him warily. The boy showed no external signs of anger, and he was sure they'd followed the line of logic surrounding Granny's disappearance to a moderately satisfying end. But last time he'd actually come to blows with Gerd, he'd ended up face down in a pile of pig shit with a razor sharp hoe pressed against the back of his neck. He seriously doubted it was possible to find a pile of pig shit on a tiny boat in the middle of the ocean, but Marius would lay odds that Gerd could do it. Gerd probably had some weird bumpkin pig shit location organ that normal people didn't possess.

"So. The slutfish."

"What about it?"

"I spent a couple of summers working the Perench fishing boats when I was younger–"

"Stealing from fishermen? Do you ever reach bottom?"

"No, actually. I wasn't." Marius had been working his way through several of the fleet's daughters. Technically it wasn't actually stealing, so much as it was keeping warm in a place known for winds that could turn a man's gonads into ice shavings. "I was working as a freezer man on one of the larger boats, making sure the ice in the boat's hold stayed up to level." And making sure the booze stayed accessible once the fish started to come in. "We used to see a lot of slutfish out around the coral beds at the north end of the Barrier Line. They're little fish, see, about this size." He held his hands ten inches or so apart. "Not really worth the net space, and they taste like a granny's backside."

"Hey!"

"Oh, I'm sorry. Not your granny's backside, obviously. I'm sure that tastes much better."

"Fuck off."

"If I could. Anyway, the point is, they're only little fish, but they're the most colourful fish you've ever seen in your life. They look like they've been painted by blind children, colours everywhere, no one pattern matching the next. You can see them from miles away. And the way they swim – uneven, flapping about making a hell of a stir. You watch them and it's like they *want* to get eaten. Then you watch them for a bit longer and you realise just what a clever bastard of a fish it really is."

"Why?"

"Because it's usually in a relationship with a teether."

Gerd looked at him blankly. "And?"

"Picture an explosion of teeth with a gut attached, big as your torso, never stops being hungry, got a personality about as pleasant as having a pitchfork shoved up your arse. It's the nastiest, most vicious fish in the Barrier Sea, and even better for the slutfish, it's got the table manners of a miner."

"What's all this got to do with Drenthe?"

"Because he's a slutfish. See, the slutfish has a tiny mouth. It can't eat fish in its own right. Can't get its mouth round a body to take a decent bite. But it's worked out a system with the teether, right? The slutfish swims around, all colourful and lopsided and just begging to be eaten. And a fish comes along, thinks 'I'll have a piece of that', and sets off in pursuit."

"Right into the Teether."

"Right into the Teether. Who eats like a spastic child in a porridge factory. Bits of fish going every which way in the water, all chewed up and bitten through and just the right size for a fish with a small mouth to swallow."

"Symbiotic."

"Sym*what* now?"

Gerd sneered. "You think we don't have books halfway up our bumpkin mountain?"

"No."

"Well… we've got one, okay. It's an old farming manual. Uncle Merkus bought it when he was in Hoolash one year. Talks about companion planting and how certain animals and plants get on better together. I read all about it."

"You read."

"Fine," he admitted after a moment. "Uncle Merkus read it to us."

"And people wonder why there are so few farmers in the universities."

"Yeah, well, at least I knew the word."

Marius sighed. "Yes, so you did. I guess we'll call it a draw."

"Okay. So, Drenthe." Gerd screwed up his face. "You think he's a decoy, then?"

"I'm beginning to, yes."

"But why?"

"Think about it. Every step we've taken, he's ahead of us. He started us on the road–"

"He started *you* on the road. Me and Granny, we were just visiting."

"And do you think he didn't know that? Do you think it's a coincidence that all this started at the exact moment you and I saw each other for the first time in four years? Really?"

"No. No, I guess not."

"No. That's what I mean. Whenever he needs us to be somewhere, he jumps up and down and waves his arms and makes sure we notice him. And whenever we make a decision and head somewhere on our own accord, he's been there before us, laying the ground, pushing us in the right direction, making sure we keep moving."

"Like Granny?" asked Gerd. "We think he killed her…"

"When he didn't."

"Why?"

"Why didn't he kill her?"

"No, why does he want us to think he did?"

"I'm not sure. To push us a certain way? To keep us from stopping and thinking about this stuff, keep us off balance, so he can move us about where he wants us to go?" He shrugged. "I don't know. But he's got something in mind, and it's us that's going to do it for him. And you know what? It's not just Granny." Marius stared out over the water, seeing the fields around his home, the earth reaching up, Keth screaming and clawing at the ground... "The same goes for Keth. Both of us, we saw the one we love being taken away–"

"And we filled in the gaps."

"Exactly as he knew we would."

"Gods." Gerd ran his hands down his face. "We're idiots, aren't we?"

Marius smiled, small and nasty. "Well, you are. Me, I'm an old fisherman from years back."

"What's that supposed to mean?"

Marius leaned back and stared over his shoulder at the wake spreading out behind them. He concentrated, and let his sight pierce the water, down to the dim outline of the ocean bottom a dozen feet below them.

"He let us escape. He wanted us to. He could have sent his troops after us. They could have walked under there, no problems. I've done it. But he didn't, so why? He doesn't really want to capture us. And he knows where we're going. He's told us that."

"How?"

"Something he said to me when we were fighting. Called me a mummy's boy, like he was planting the seed, like he already knew we were being herded towards my mother, and he was just making sure the thought had well and truly taken. Father first, mother next."

"So what do we do?"

The wake spread out behind them, a liquid arrowhead with the boat's bow for a hardened point, strong enough to pierce any potential future. Marius watched the water churn, the edges folding over themselves in constant motion, chaotic movement reigned in and directed towards a common purpose.

"We do exactly what he wants us to do."

"But why? I mean…" Gerd spread his hands to indicate the horizon. "We've got a boat, we've got a good wind. We can go anywhere. He's not watching us, is he? We can find a beach, and double back, and sneak into the warehouse–"

"He'll be gone, and so will any chance of tracking him. Besides, don't you want to know why he's sending us this way?"

"Not particularly. I just want my Granny back."

"And to stop Scorbus invading the kingdom and bringing death to every living thing in Scorby."

"S'pose."

"Don't worry. The two things are the same. I know why we're going to see my mother."

"And?"

"She's got the book. The history of Scorbus' campaigns."

"But why would Drenthe want us to have that?"

"Because I don't think he's playing for Scorbus' team anymore. I think he's got something deeper going on. And I think he's using us to put it together. Besides…" He stretched, and looked up at the sun. "I want to see my mum."

"But if Drenthe is one step ahead of us–"

"Then he needs to be careful."

"Why?"

Marius grabbed the tiller, swinging the boat around so that it pointed away from the sun, back towards the shore and the distant cliffs that housed his mother.

"Because there's a fine line between following someone because they're leading you about, and following them because you're stalking prey. And I've just crossed it."

FOURTEEN

Fifteen hundred years ago, during the time of the Countless Fiefdoms, the Dorision Emperor Callusian looked upon the cliffs of Tylytene and pronounced them so sheer, so inhospitable, so completely fuck-ugly that no civilised man would entertain the thought of living near them.

Within a year they were home to six nunneries, thirteen self-defence classes, and a secret college dedicated to teaching all those bits of common sense that get you hanged for being a witch (since the idea of a woman with common sense scares the living shit out of ninety percent of men, who generally have none to speak of). It had evolved over the centuries, responding to the mood of the times and the women who flocked there – sometimes in secret; and sometimes, as with the Witch Races in the late Bookless Ages, in numbers so vast that the tents across the cliff tops added two dozen feet to their height.

Tylytene was sacred space, the home of secret women's business, an oasis untroubled by men and their ridiculous ideas of war and booze and the search for the perfect bacon sandwich. Generations of nuns had carved great images into the stone, friezes a hundred feet high that heralded a simple message for those who saw them: We are the kind of people who use entire cliffs as our canvas. Do not fuck with us.

The cliffs shone white in the western sun, a beacon of purity at the edge of a land stained by blood, a lighthouse of femininity and contemplation. They were a symbol, a paradise, an unrealised ideal.

They were also, as Gerd pointed out, really, *really* high.

The little boat bobbed in the swell a hundred metres off the cliff face, far enough away that the top could be seen as a thin line of green between the blue sky and the white chalk, but close enough to see the broken rocks that littered the water below, shattering the waves as they came in and promising destruction and ruin to any boat that attempted an approach. Marius knelt on the boat's prow and scanned the rocks while Gerd sat securely in the stern, gripping tight to the nearest rail with fingers that would have been white even if they hadn't already been leached of all colour.

"What now?" Gerd shouted over the thunder of the water.

"There's supposed to be a path up the cliff. There!" Marius pointed to a tiny seam, almost indistinguishable from the scattered lines of the precipice above. He traced it in the air, steadily rising at an extreme angle, switching back on itself until it disappeared from view a hundred feet or so above them. "There's a safe channel through the rocks and a mooring at the base of the steps. I've just got to..." He sputtered as a wave thudded against the boat's side and drenched his face in spray. "Just got to find it and work out how to follow it in."

"I've got a better idea."

"What?"

"You go to hell."

"What?"

Gerd risked unpeeling a hand from the railing long enough to wave it at the chaos before them. "You can go to hell if you think I'm going to do all that."

"It's fine. It'll be–"

"I. Don't. Like. Heights!"

"Ah." Marius stared towards the top of the cliff, then back at Gerd, curled against the rear seat and most deliberately not looking up from the boat floor in front of him. "That could prove somewhat of a problem."

"Not if you like hell."

"I spend time with you, don't I?"

Gerd's raspberry was lost as waves crashed onto both sides of the boat simultaneously. Marius slid across the prow on his knees, grabbed the railing to stop himself going over the side, and crabbed his way back into the relative safety of the stern. He plunked down next to Gerd and watched his young friend fail to cope with the sudden sideways movement of the boat. After half a minute of desperate retching over the side, Gerd regained his seat and looked at Marius in misery.

"I hate not being able to vomit."

"Whoever thought we'd get to say that, eh?"

"I hate you, 'n'all."

"I know." He clapped Gerd on the shoulder. "Let's get away from here, shall we? Would that help?"

"Yes." Gerd burped up nothing, looked as green as he could without actually changing colour, and swallowed. "Yes it would."

"Okay. Give me a hand."

Together they hauled the anchor in and stowed it, before Marius took the wheel and laboriously hauled the skiff around so that it tacked away at right angles to the cliff. Once they were out of the immediate vicinity of the rocks he gave the little boat its head and let it run across the swell with the wind that whipped across the sheer rock face, driving them a mile or more away from the now-invisible stairs and back out into deeper water. The wind died down once the giant funnel of rocks and chalk was removed, and Marius took up the slack, turning the boat so that it once again pointed towards land, bobbing gently in calmer water a couple of miles offshore.

"So what do we do now?" Gerd had recovered some of his equilibrium. He sat straighter, exposing his neck to the breeze behind them. He tilted his head, closed his eyes, let the wind wash across him. Marius loosed the anchor again, and came to sit next to him. They sat that way for several minutes, finding their individual centres, thinking their separate thoughts. Then Marius blew out his cheeks and stared at the cliffs again, their size more manageable with distance.

"If we can't go up, then we need to make landfall and go across the top."

"Where?"

"I'm not sure." He stared at the distant line at the top, watching it undulate across the sky. "It looks as if it begins to tail away to the right there. We can follow it around, maybe find a beach. But we'd best get a move on. It's nightfall in a couple of hours and I'd hoped to be at the nunnery by then. I don't want to be on the water at night."

"Afraid of the dark, sweetheart?"

"Afraid of driving the boat against the rocks and smashing us into jelly."

"Ah. Best be getting on then, hadn't you?"

Marius wiggled his eyebrows and went forward to the wheel. Gerd hauled up the anchor, and they were on their way.

•••

Night caught up with them three miles down the coast. It came earlier here than they had hoped, the sun cut off prematurely by the cliffs, their massive shadow – almost an entity in itself – pushing out from the shore to engulf them in gloom a full hour earlier than expected. Even their dead vision, allowing them a fuzzy, detail-poor glimpse of the world in the pitch-black of midnight, struggled with the crisscross of curling water, distant shore, and darkening sky. Marius furled the sails early, leaving only the little triangular headsail up to help them jink across the swell towards a tiny curve that looked as if it might be a sheltered cove with some sort of small beach upon which they could ground.

"Keep your eyes on it," he called to Gerd, holding his arm out like a signpost until Gerd joined him at the wheel and turned his head in the right direction. "Don't let it disappear. We should be all right as long as the approach is clear and you keep guiding me."

"And if it's not?"

"Then hope it's a sandbar or something we can walk into shore from."

"You just flood me with confidence, you do."

"Let's not say 'flood' for the moment, shall we?" He made sure Gerd's attention was pinned to the right spot, and bent back to the helm. The boat swung around, and they began the long, slow approach to shore.

With the fall in light came a fall in mood. The two companions sat silent, concentrating on their tasks and their internal thoughts, allowing the rhythm of the waves to lull them into dull contemplation. The shore slowly bobbed closer, only the slap of water against the hull breaking the empty silence. Then, off to port, something wooden slid through something metal with a clunk, drawing each man out of his mental space.

"Did you do that?" they said simultaneously, then: "Don't look at me."

Gerd turned to stare at Marius.

"Shit!"

"What?"

"The cove! I've lost it."

"I told you not to turn around."

"I'm sorry. I just–"

"Ssh."

"What?"

"Shut up."

The sound came again.

"There." Marius stared into the gloom off port.

"What–"

"Shush."

Gerd shushed. More sounds manifested in the dark: the creak of wood, the splash of water against moving objects, the occasional muffled slap as a paddle missed its mark and skated across the top of a wave instead of biting into it. Marius swivelled from side to side at each sound, gauging distance, straining to discern movement through the darkness. Gerd gave up trying to relocate the curve of shoreline and turned to his mentor, questions deep in his eyes.

"Five," Marius mouthed, pointing to various spots in the dark to either side of them. "At least."

"Who?" Gerd's voice was loud inside his head, and he winced.

"I don't know. Soldiers, maybe?"

Troops had attempted to destroy the nunnery before, back when men fought by rules of chivalry and misogyny. They had learned the hard way that warfare-trained women with no thick-headed assumptions about the inequality of the sexes will gouge your heart out of your chest before you've finished reading the list of your lord's demands out to them in a clear, patronising tone of voice. Easier just to let them be. Easier to control the women you already have, and persuade them that living in the cliffs represents a form of punishment. It had been a good couple of centuries since anybody was stupid enough to try an armed takeover. Armies fight with honour, and respect for the rules of warfare. Nuns fight dirty.

"What do we do?"

Good question. Marius considered the unseen boats to either side, the feel of the hull bumping gently across the rolling swell. The boats were tightly packed, pointed towards the same invisible curve of beach. They moved slowly under the command of oars and minimal sail, as if waiting for the right moment to unfurl and sweep down upon the land in a sudden rush. There was no room to manoeuvre sideways without running the risk of collision, no chance to drop anchor and wait out the other boats' progress. Besides, the swell was rising, and the wind that had dropped during the late day was increasing as the cold night began to cool the surface of the water. Conditions would get rougher, and he had no idea whether the boat could ride out the night without seeking some sort of shelter.

"I don't know. Wait and see."

Gerd's reply had no words, but Marius could sense it anyway: a confusion of fear, exasperation, and impatience. He felt it too. Marius had few rules, but central to his way of life was the notion that any movement was better than none. To sit still, to let the world dictate his actions to him, to let fate have even the smallest grip upon his progress, was alien and uncomfortable. He strained to see forward, to discern some tiny escape route between them and the cove that even now was beginning to make itself clearer to his dead eyes.

Nothing came. His view was too fuzzy. Clearer than those around him, certainly, but not so much that he could make out any but the most general details. A shallow curve of shingle, lighter than the water in front of it and perhaps thirty feet wide, with blank white cliff walls to either side, narrowing to a defile that was undoubtedly riddled with paths leading upwards to the moors above. Marius could just about make out puddles of dark at the base of the cliffs – caves, maybe, or overhangs worn into the soft chalk surface by millennia of waves scraping along their side. But only one cove, only one beach, and not even the benefit of a decent-sized boulder to hide behind. The whole thing was as featureless as a Post-Necrotist's cathedral: one stripe of grey against different stripes of grey, with nothing to draw the eye away.

Except… Marius frowned. Something to the side, near the black patches of the maybe-caves. There. And again. A tiny pop of yellow light against the darkness, momentary and quickly muffled. It happened again as he watched: a pinpoint of illumination, then another, a sequence of flashes that disappeared as quickly as they happened.

"Marius!"

He saw it at the same time as Gerd hissed his name. An answering flash of light to his left. The sequence from the beach repeated, quick as a snakebite, before the dark reasserted its dominance. Marius almost laughed aloud, then bit down on it.

"What?"

He projected the image of a grin. "Smugglers."

"And that's good?"

"You bet it is!"

"How?"

Marius shifted his hands until they were comfortable, and gauged his position within the mini-fleet. Six boats, now that he could distinguish their positions more closely. Yawls or ketches, most likely – large enough to carry a decent load from nearby kingdoms but small and fast enough to evade pursuit and still come to shore under the command of oars if need be. His own boat would be amongst the smaller of them, but it was at least a coast-hugger, able to be beached without disrupting too deep a keel.

"Marius. How is this a good thing?"

Marius sighed. It was easy to forget just how much of a farm boy Gerd was. He would know of smugglers only through word of mouth, if at all: horror stories from news sheets and penny presses, believed wholesale because they had the magic effect of being written down by someone who professed expertise in the matter.

"Smugglers means secrecy," he projected. "If they're landing here then they're probably bringing in applejack or cock ale from the Northern Reaches."

"Why?"

"To make money, of course. Why else?"

Gerd's face crumpled in confusion.

"But why are they sneaking it in? I've drunk applejack all over the place. It's not against the law."

"Yes, but what did you pay for it?"

"Huh?"

"Scorban taxes, boy. That's what smuggling is for. Whoever's bringing it in is paying Reaches prices and avoiding the duties. If they serve it at Scorban prices…"

"More profit."

"In one." Marius frowned. "Mind you, it's a three day ride to the nearest city from here, and there are beaches further down the coast that would do just as well. Doesn't seem... Oops, wait a minute."

"The lights were flashing again: a burst of three in rapid succession, then a gap, then another three. Boats creaked around them. Marius responded by sliding a quarter to starboard, in tune with the rest of the fleet now. He found the swell and rode it past a short sandbar that crunched against a hull somewhere to their rear.

"Smugglers are better than soldiers, believe me." The tiller twitched, and he righted it. "Soldiers would have one task in mind, and they wouldn't welcome finding strangers in their midst. Smugglers have a code."

"But I thought you said they want secrecy. Won't they be afraid we'll blab or something?"

"Yes, well, that's possible. Still, they have a code." A code of silent knives, he added to himself, hoping Gerd could not pick up on his inner worries. At the least, it was a code that respected other people's secrets. He just needed to persuade them that he and Gerd had no interest in their work, and everything should be fine. Perfectly fine.

The lights shone again, closer now. The beach reached out to them, shining grey in Marius eyes, filling up the world until cropped off at either side by the cliffs. They glided to the far end of the cove in silence. Then their hull ground against the shingle, and stuck, and he and Gerd were over the side and dragging their little vessel up the beach and as far to the side of the others as they possibly could.

FIFTEEN

The night was loud with the crunch of footsteps, as sailors hauled barrels up the rocky beach and dumped them in a pile in front of the nearest cave. Marius and Gerd loitered around the phalanx of hulls at the water's edge until everyone around them was focussed upon the task, then stepped away from their boat as quietly as they could. They matched their footsteps to those of the smugglers, heading at an angle away from them towards the path at the far side of the beach, angling upwards through the messy scrub that formed the beach's boundary. They had successfully traversed almost eight feet when all sound behind them ceased. They froze.

"What—"

"Ssh." Despite the quietness of their conversation, Marius had never learned to concentrate on external matters while also listening to someone's voice inside his head. He frowned, trying to locate the hidden sailors.

"What's happening?"

"Someone's coming. From up there." Marius pointed towards the path. Behind them, careful footsteps resumed. Marius heard movement back towards the boats and the almost silent hiss of weapons being retrieved and unsheathed.

188

"What do we do?"

"Stay still and keep quiet."

Something pointed and extremely sharp pressed coldly into the back of his neck.

"Well now," said a voice in his ear. "What do we have here?"

Marius discovered new depths of stillness.

"How the hell did you do that?" he asked quietly.

"I think," the point dug slightly deeper, "that I might ask the questions first, don't you?"

"You know, I think you might."

"Mighty civilised of you." The sword in his neck urged him around, pointing him back towards the beach.

"My pleasure."

A poke had him moving back down.

"Don't speak too soon."

They trooped in silence: Marius, Gerd, and the two unseen bearers of the swords. They reached the overhang at the base of the cliff, where their legs were kicked out from underneath them, depositing them onto the shingles.

"Ow."

The sword pricked him on the chin.

"Shush, now."

Marius shushed.

"What now?" Gerd in his mind.

"Just wait."

"What for?"

A shape appeared before them, dark upon dark, blocking out the grey cliffs at the other end of the beach.

"Oh," Gerd projected. "That."

"Yep."

The shape stepped into the overhang.

"And what the fuck," it said, with a female voice that wouldn't have been out of place in a classroom of naughty children, "have we brought in with us tonight?"

Marius peered at the figure. "Brys? Brys Kenim?"

"Keep your bloody voice down!" The reaction was automatic, quickly followed by: "Marius?"

A short scrape of metal on metal as the cover of a lantern was swung open. A flash of light momentarily blinded both men.

"Bloody hell! Marius! What the bloody hell are you doing here?"

"Hello, Brys."

"Bloody Marius bloody Helles. Give us a hug, you lovely bugger." The shape leaned down and scooped Marius to his feet, enveloping him in a blanket of arms, boobs, and long black hair.

"Brys, this is my pal, Gerd. Gerd, Brys Kenim, smuggler, pirate and all-round cove," Marius mumbled in the few moments he was able to peel his face away from Brys' embrace. "Brys and I ran weapons together for a while."

Gerd groaned, and rolled his eyes. "Is there anyone in this country you haven't shagged?"

"I never…" Marius was swallowed by the embrace once more. His hand waved behind Brys' back: never, then, one finger. Two. Five. More or less. Finally, she let him go, and held him at arm's length.

"Marius bloody Helles. Let me look at you." She scanned him up and down. "Bloody hell. You as well, eh?"

"What do you mean?"

She jerked a finger behind her. "Half my crew are dead men. Work cheap, and carry twice as much as a live one. Figured you had a few more years in you before you copped your whack, though."

Marius shrugged. "I've not let it get to me." He looked at her appreciatively: a tall woman, broad in the hips and bust, strong face dominated by a nose just the right side of conk and long, expressive eyebrows that were currently raised most of the way towards the hair that flowed past her shoulders and over a red jacket. Velvet trousers, long boots, two swords hanging from a wide leather belt. If Brys Kenim wasn't already a smuggler queen, she could have played one. "You're looking good. The eye patch is a nice touch."

She laughed. "Earned it in a hamlet further north. Didn't like what we were taking from them."

"What was it?"

"Don't know." She laughed. "I only grabbed it on a whim."

Marius nodded. "So what are you doing *here*?"

"What comes naturally." She crouched down, and drew the two men into a rough sitting circle. "Nunnery up the cliff needs supplies it can't acquire by ordinary means. I'm supplying." She eyed them both. "But what about you? How did you come to be in the middle of my little fleet?"

"Similar story. We need something they have, and picked the same approach."

"Why not climb the cliff stairs?"

"That'd be him." Marius pointed to Gerd. "He likes a flatter type of land."

Brys' face went empty. "Big coincidence."

"Overcast night, low swell, one beach along the entire cliff line." Marius stared into her good eye. "Similar purposes. Sounds to me like the equations throw up the same answer."

"Hmm." Brys sniffed, then smiled. "You always were a calculating sod, Helles." She clapped her hands on her knees, and it was only then that Marius noticed they had been resting on the hilts of her swords. "Sounds like we have a common destination, then."

"Just like old times."

"Hmm." She looked him up and down for a moment, performing her own calculations. "I doubt it. Come and meet the crew."

They clambered to their feet and ducked out onto the beach. Brys' crew stood in a rough semicircle around the pile of barrels. Marius saw a dozen men of varying sizes, all with the rock-hard leanness of the professional sailor, all with the same long-distance stare that came from a life of mistrust and fear of capture. Marius and Gerd stared at them, then at each other. Every last one of the sailors was dead.

"Why?"

Brys laughed. "Do you know how strong a man becomes when he's dead? Of course you do. What am I saying?" She stalked over and ran an appreciative hand down the arm of the nearest sailor. "I recruited from docks all up the northern coast. Men who died in fights, or back alleys, slung into the harbours for a quick disappearance. Had Cheggmar here for just over two years. The rest have followed."

Marius frowned. "And it's never bothered you? Dead men walking? Working? Not being dead?"

"Should it?" She slapped Cheggmar on the arm. "I've seen it all over. Men ain't dying the way they used to. They work cheap, last longer…" She slapped the arm again and smiled at him. "Much longer. Don't have to be too smart a woman to see where there's profit."

"Right." Marius stared at the dead man. "You ever ask him what he thinks about it?"

"The captain gives me work," he said. At the same

time his voice sounded clear inside Marius' mind: "Don't push it, brother. Let it drop."

Marius resisted the temptation to shake the twin voices out of his head. He flicked his gaze across to Brys. "Your loyal crew," he said.

"Don't you know it." She stepped back to him and poked him in the chest with a pointed finger, letting the nail run three inches down his shirtfront. "I value loyalty."

"So I recall." He nodded towards the pile of barrels. "So what are you carting?"

"The usual," Brys said.

Cheggmar's voice whispered once more in his mind. "She won't tell us," the dead smuggler said. "But tobacco don't rattle, and neither does gin."

Brys pointed. "Forty eight tubs, twelve tubmen. Half the time it would take a living crew. But now you're here, we'll go even quicker."

"I'm sorry?"

She clapped him on the back. "There's only one destination out here, boyo."

"So?"

"So. We're going to the same bloody place, Helles. We may as well help each other out."

"Really."

"You carry tubs for me," She nodded at her crew, "and I won't get them to tear your limbs off."

Gerd groaned. "Do you ever leave a woman on good terms?"

Marius eyed the dozen sailors, a dozen pillars of dead strength standing silent in the dark. "It's a family failing," he muttered. "Wait until you meet my mother."

It wasn't that bad, really, Marius was forced to admit.

The barrels – *tubs*, he reminded himself, smugglers called them tubs – were only two foot long or so, and tied together in pairs by wide leather straps that fitted over the shoulders so that they hung one on either side of the body, front and back. A normal man could have carried one pair without needing to rest for a mile or so. The dead men managed two pairs with ease. He quickly fell into line in the middle of the column as it climbed up off the beach and onto the scrubby moor beyond. The nunnery was invisible from here, but Brys turned them along the cliff edge without hesitation. They trooped along in silence, a column of stiff-backed corpses led by the swaying hips of their captain, silent but for the swish of her velvet-draped thighs and the occasional creak of leather or clunk of wood as the tubs shifted with the movement of the journey.

Marius kept his eyes pinned to the tubs on Gerd's back.

"What did you mean," he projected as they walked, "about rattling?"

The tubman's voice came back to him, whispered and fearful despite being entirely a projection of will. "Just what I says. The tubs rattle sometimes, and that ain't what I'm used to hauling." He paused. "Cheggmar Pan, brother. Been running tubs from up north a dozen years till I fell asleep in the wrong whorehouse."

"Marius Helles."

"I know you, brother."

"What? How?"

An invisible chuckle. "Word gets round. Heard you put the King on his throne."

"Well, I–"

"You needs be careful, brother. You gets to kingmaking, you can't help but make enemies."

Marius felt the wound in his chest itch. "So I've noticed. How many times have you made this run?"

"Eight times this last two years. Every quarter, just before the festival days."

"And you've never seen what you're hauling?"

"Never once. We goes down into the lower halls after we've delivered our load, and waits while the captain makes merry with the white-clad bitches–"

"My mother lives in that nunnery."

"Apologies, brother. We waits while the captain meets with her customers…" A pause to make sure Marius had no other objection. "She comes gets us when it's time to leave. And we do."

"Do what?"

"Leave."

Marius thought for a moment. "But not all of you."

"Now why would you be saying that?"

He shrugged, slipping for a moment as the tubs rearranged themselves. "Because you wouldn't feel the need to tell me you did, if it was that simple."

A longer pause. "There's usually one of us doesn't come back. We always figures that's what they're dealing for upstairs. Which one of us they needs for their tasks or whatever it is."

"And what would nuns be wanting with a dead man?"

"Guess even nuns got needs, brother. Meaning no offence, like."

Marius ignored the implication. "And you've never been tempted to find out?"

"And do what, brother? Escape?" A laugh flittered around the edges of Marius' concentration. "Dead or alive, brother kingmaker, we're still our captin's bondsmen. We does what she tell sus, and if she wants to sell us on, well that's her privilege."

They trudged on in silence for another half hour, until the low rise they were climbing levelled out. Two skeletal shapes formed out of the darkness ahead. Brys whispered a halt. They slung their tubs into a pile on the grass and stood in a circle, waiting for her next order. Gerd sidled up to Marius.

"What's happening?"

"We're here."

"Where?"

"The nunnery." Marius nodded towards the shapes looming a dozen feet ahead: two giant beams, embedded deep into the rock, rising at an angle over the edge of the cliffs until they ended six feet above their heads, and three feet out into the empty air. Two baskets dangled there in midair, suspended from ropes that ran the length of the giant beams to terminate at a wheel assembly where the massive logs ploughed into the ground. The baskets were big enough, he calculated, to hold a person and a weight of goods as well. Marius felt Gerd take in the sight.

"How very interesting," Gerd projected. "I expected the nunnery to be on top of the cliff."

"I thought you might."

"It's what – halfway down?"

"A bit less."

"A hundred feet?"

"Say eighty."

"Hmm." Marius' mind was filled with a vision of Gerd nodding. "That *is* interesting. Very, very interesting." Much nodding. "Well," he said. The sound of hands clapping together decisively. "See you later."

"What? Wait on!" Marius surreptitiously grabbed the hem of Gerd's shirt as the younger man tried to swing about on his heel. "What the hell are you doing?"

"I'm getting out of here." Gerd pointed towards the beams. "What did you think? That I was going to get a head start on jumping off a cliff in a coal basket? Do you even know what happens to a farm boy if you drop him umpty hundred feet into a roaring ocean?"

"Nobody's going to drop you."

"You're not wrong!" Gerd tugged at his shirt. Marius tightened his grip.

"Stay still."

"Let go!"

"Stay still, for the gods' sake!"

"Fuck off!" This time, aloud.

For one awful second the cliffs rang with Gerd's shouted command. Marius winced, then turned towards the sound of rapidly approaching Brys.

"And what," she hissed, "is the subject of conversation here?"

"Nothing, nothing." Marius made a conciliatory gesture with open palms. "It's just my boy, here–"

"Oi."

"My boy here, he's just realised…. Well, he's a bit nervous about heights."

"Oh, is that right?" Brys twitched. Before Marius could react, her cutlass had left its holder and was pressed tight up against the side of Gerd's neck. "How nervous does he get about having his head severed from his stupid, shouting neck?"

"Um," Gerd choked out a response. "Quite nervous, actually."

"Good. Then we're all in agreement." She gestured, and two tubmen appeared out of the gloom on either side of the young swineherd. "You can be first."

"What? No."

As one, the tubmen grabbed him by the arms and began

dragging him towards the cliff's edge. Gerd struggled, but as large and beefy as he was, the tubmen were larger. Their dead arms had strength honed by years of manual work hauling ropes and cargo. Within seconds he was pinned to the ground, a slab-like hand placed over his mouth, his head hanging over the edge of the cliff.

"Brys. Brys!" Marius caught up to the tubmen and put himself between them and her approach. "Give him a break, Brys. He's a stupid farm boy, that's all." Gerd broke off his mental scream long enough to tell Marius to fuck himself, then continued. Marius raised his hands to Brys, palms outwards. "He's new to this, Brys. He doesn't understand the silence, the secrecy."

"Well, then." She wheeled about in one easy motion. Marius felt the prick of her sword tip against his chest. "He'll be glad of the bloody education, won't he?"

Marius pursed his lips. He reached down and grasped the rear of the blade, drawing it up so that they stood chest to chest, with the cutting edge pressed tight between them.

"Let me do it."

They matched stares for long seconds. Brys snorted once and smiled, then stood back, running the blade gently down Marius' torso before she sheathed it.

"Proceed," she said, stepping back and motioning Marius forward with an exaggerated sweep of the arm. Marius eyed her for a moment, then turned to the two tubmen.

"Let him up."

The tubmen glanced at their mistress for confirmation, then rose as one, moving behind and to either side of her. They watched as Marius bent down and offered Gerd his hand.

"Come on."

Gerd scrambled to his knees and crawled away from the edge as fast as he dared, stopping only when confronted by the wall of tubmen legs. Oblivious to their quiet, sneering laughter, he shook his head at Marius.

"You can't make me. I won't."

"No." Marius sat down next to him and gestured up at the dead sailors. "I'm not going to make you."

Gerd followed his glance, saw a dozen eyes staring down at him. "They can't make me."

"I don't believe they intend to."

"Fine."

"I believe they intend to throw you over the edge and make me carry your tubs."

Marius kept his expression as open and honest as he could without straining something. Gerd stared at him for a very long time.

"What?"

Marius nodded. Gerd peeked upwards. Brys smiled back at him.

"See, the thing is," Marius said, surreptitiously manoeuvring himself so that he sat between Gerd and any attempt at escape, "now that we've carried the tubs up here, she only needs one person at this end to load them in the basket and one at the bottom to take them off. And she already has plenty of people she trusts to do that. We're only here on sufferance, which means she doesn't actually need us."

"But–"

"She doesn't care about our plans, or any mission we might be on. Brys is a mercenary. She's not a nice person."

Gerd looked at him in defeated terror.

"I can't–"

"I think the general argument is that you have to."

"My legs won't work."

"I don't think that's considered an issue." He stood. The two tubmen leaned forward and pulled Gerd to his feet. Marius saw him dangling there, and sighed in pity.

"Do it yourself, lad. Be a man."

"I'm not a man. I'm nineteen."

"You've been nineteen for four years. You're always going to *be* nineteen."

"Yeah, well, it's worked until now."

Marius smiled, and nodded to Gerd's captors. "Let him go."

They did so. Gerd wobbled slightly but kept his feet.

"Good lad. Come on."

They threaded their way between the waiting tubmen until they stood beneath the nearest beam, staring out at the basket at the end of its rope.

"I'm going to be sick."

"Just look at the basket."

"I mean it. I'm going to be sick."

"Dead men don't vomit."

"Don't care."

"Just look at the basket. Nothing else exists. No cliff, no sky. You're standing on a nice, flat piece of land, and there's only it and you, nice and close and easy."

"You're a lying bastard and I'm going to be sick."

"Just close your eyes. Go on, close them."

Slowly, reluctantly, Gerd did so.

"You have no idea just how many things I blame you for."

"Yes, I'm a terrible person. Now, here you are, on a flat piece of land. You feel it beneath your feet?"

"Of course I do."

"That's good. Now, can you see a cliff?"

"Of course I can't see the sodding cliff!"

"It's not there."

"I've got my eyes closed, you git."

Marius poked him in the ribs. "It's not there," he said through gritted teeth. "And there's no sky. Just you and the basket. That's all. Open your eyes and all you'll see is the basket."

"How will–"

Marius took a step back. "Open your eyes."

Gerd opened his eyes.

"Do you see the basket?"

"Yes, I–"

"Good. Don't forget to grab it."

He pushed Gerd in the centre of his back as hard as he could. Gerd teetered for a moment then, with a scream, toppled away from the cliff's edge and into the basket, which swung out from the cliff, then back to crash into the white stone. Slowly, in diminishing arcs, the basket returned to its original position, twisting this way then that around the taut line of the rope.

"Gerd?"

"You're a bastard."

"Are you all right?"

"I'm going to be sick."

Marius turned to Brys.

"He's all right."

"Oh, good gracious. I'm so relieved. Can we get the hell on with it, now?"

"Gerd?"

"What?"

"You need to stand up."

"No thank you."

Marius sighed. "If you don't stand up, they're going to throw tubs on you until your face breaks and then they're going to let the rope go. Is that what you want?"

In answer, a hand appeared over the top of the basket. It gave Marius a short single-digit salute, then gripped the edge. Another hand joined it; then slowly, Gerd rose like a violently ill frog out of a swamp.

"I'm going to be so sick you'll have to empty this thing with a bucket."

"Look alive."

"Is that a joke?"

The first tub was already on its way. It hit Gerd in the upper chest and knocked him backwards. Marius glanced across at the other rope. A tubman stood in the hanging basket, patiently waiting.

"One more, and then you go down. There'll be someone with you all the way."

"Good. Then *he* can clean up all the sick."

"Heads up."

Gerd wasn't quick enough.

"Ouch."

"I warned you."

"Now I *am* going to be sick."

"Can we please get a bloody move on?" Brys was at Marius' elbow, her impatience like a hot blast of steam in his ear.

"Yes, let's go." He stepped back. "Gerd."

"Being sick now."

"When the bucket stops you need to throw the tubs onto the platform."

"Here it comes."

"Gerd!"

"Hope you've got a big sponge."

Marius sighed.

"Fuck it." He turned to the tubman standing at the wheel behind him, and made a circular motion with his hand. "He'll work it out."

The tubman stood to one side of the toothed wheel. A short length of wood protruded from the ground near his feet, hinged at the bottom and sticking up between the teeth of the wheel, holding it in check. A large wooden handle extended from the centre of the wheel at waist height. He put both hands on the handle and braced himself. A quick kick of one foot against the chock, and the wheel began to spin. The tubman brought the wheel under his control, though not before the whole cliff heard Gerd scream and emptily retch. The sailor shook his head at the sound, then slowly and calmly began lowering the basket out of sight below the cliff.

Twenty minutes later it returned, empty. Marius stepped forward to take his turn. Brys put a hand on his chest.

"Not yet." She signalled to the tubman behind the wheel. "Rexal, you're next. Cheggmar, take the wheel." Cheggmar took up position. Rexal swept up the next two sets of tubs, walked past Marius with a derisory glance, and jumped straight into the centre of the basket. Marius raised an eyebrow towards Brys.

"Internal matters," she muttered. "Got some straightening out to do."

Marius said nothing, simply watched as the tubman disappeared. One by one, the remaining tubmen picked up their barrels and made the journey down to the nunnery entrance, only Brys, Marius and Cheggmar remaining up top.

"Your turn." Brys pointed at the wheel. Marius took over while Cheggmar hopped into the basket. Brys strode over to the base of the beam and leant against it, her back to Marius, blocking the tubman from his view. Marius leant against the handle, and fixed his gaze onto her backside. It was some consolation for the work.

"Cheggmar." Brys waited until she had his full attention, then slipped her cutlass from its sheath.

"Brys?"

"Shut up, Marius."

"What are you doing?"

"Shut *up*, Helles. Cheggmar." While both men watched she drew the sword across the rope in a single, sharp slice, cutting through nearly a quarter of its thickness. The wheel lurched in Marius' hands as the rope juddered.

"Woah!" Marius pulled against the handle, as if that might somehow make up for the sudden weakening. "Brys, what the hell are you doing?"

"I said shut the fuck up, don Hellespont."

"As she says, brother." Cheggmar's quiet voice intruded on Marius' thoughts. He fell silent as Brys spoke again.

"When are they coming?"

"Who are coming?" yelled Marius.

Brys slid the blade across the top of the rope so that the point swung an inch past his throat. All he could see was her back, and the tip of the sabre at the end of her rigid arm. All it would take was for her to lean back, twist her hips and transfer her weight onto the knee closest to him, and she would spit Marius like a roast. He daren't take his hands from the wheel for fear of sending the basket plummeting downwards. She had him trapped. Which, he realised, was exactly what she had planned. "Don Hellespont, I swear to all the fucking gods in the sky, if you don't shut the fuck up…"

"Nobody is coming, mistress." At the same time, in Marius' mind: *Step carefully, brother. She's fishing for enemies, is all.*

"You're lying to me, Pan."

"No lies, mistress. No lies."

Marius moved not a muscle. *Are you lying to her?*

"You're lying to me, Pan."

"No lies, Mistress." *Perhaps a small one, brother.*

"I know you're lying." She swung the sabre overhand again. Another slice of the rope, another quarter of its width destroyed. "You ratted us out to someone, Cheggmar. I want to know who it was."

"What have you done, Cheggmar?" Marius, again.

"Nobody, mistress. I swear." *You know what's in those tubs, brother? You know what they're worth?*

"Last chance, traitor."

"For fuck's sake, Cheggmar. Tell her!"

"I'm not your traitor, mistress." *Absolution, brother. They're carting absolution. You know what that's worth on the open market? A bloody fortune, and she's wasting it on a bunch of–*

"Chance over." Brys stepped away from the beam and swung her sword backhanded at the rope. It bit deep, splitting the final cords and hitting wood. The severed line whipped up the beam and over the far end before Marius could yell. He had one final look at Cheggmar's blank face, before the bucket dropped below the level of the cliff.

"Kenim! What the fuck have you–" And Marius stopped his furious turn towards Brys, because Cheggmar was still talking.

"A bunch of bloody nuns, brother, and she's giving them the keys to absolution. There's bones in those tubs, bones of martyrs, and every one worth a fortune to the right priest. One tub, that's all they're wanting. One tub, and we'd be rich."

"Who? Who, Cheggmar?"

"Scorby City, you fool. They're all going to die. They'll pay–"

"Cheggmar? Cheggmar!"

But there was no reply, only the sound of Brys tugging her sword free of the wooden beam and cursing at the state of her blade. Marius stared past her at the edge of the cliff.

"What a waste."

"What?" Brys looked up from her work. "Him?" She snorted. "I can find five more like him the next time I stop for a drink." She slipped her sword back into its sheath. "I don't tolerate disloyalty, Helles. You know that."

"You don't tolerate denial much either, do you?"

"Not when it's bullshit."

"And how do you know it was? How do you know he wasn't telling the truth?" Brys was already striding towards the second basket, and Marius trailed in her wake.

"Because," she flung over her shoulder, "he was the only one who deliberately chose a tub when we left the shore. Why would he need to pick and choose if all he's doing is delivering them, hey?"

"Maybe he wanted an even load. You can't kill a man for that!"

She reached the wheel and kicked out the chock, sending the second basket spiralling down out of sight. "First of all, he was already dead. Second of all, it's not the first time someone's tried to stiff me on a load; and third, I paid fifty riner to a carnie for that useless fuck so I can do to him whatever I want. That okay by you?"

"I..." Marius stared at her for half a second, then dropped his gaze. "What are you carrying in those tubs anyway?"

"Wigwams for a goose's bridle."

"Very funny."

"I'm carrying the same thing I always carry, Marius. Goods, that's all. I don't ask and I don't count my money until I'm far enough away not to be robbed straight back. You know how it works."

Marius did. He also knew that you never carried anything unless you knew exactly how dangerous it was to be caught with it, and who to bribe to get the hell away. For the first time he began to wonder just what was waiting for him at the bottom of the rope, and what he might have already sent Gerd into. He eyed the rope at the far end of the beam.

"How do we get down, anyway?"

"Well," Brys smiled, and made herself comfortable on the grass. "As soon as you start turning that handle, you'll find out, won't you?"

Marius pursed his lips, and bent to the task. Ten minutes later the basket crested the edge of the cliff. The tubman inside jumped lightly off and took Marius' place at the wheel. Marius and Brys leaped into either side of the basket and grabbed the rope. The tubman took hold of the handle, and they began their descent.

There are any number of perfectly innocent trains of thought that can be followed if you're crushed into a confined space with a big-breasted woman in a pirate's uniform. Unless you're male. After five feet of the descent, Marius was focussing desperately on counting the number of strands that made up the rope in front of him.

"It never ceases to amaze me," Brys said, smirking, "how even being dead doesn't stop a man rising to any occasion."

Marius decided not to answer. He also decided to stare past Brys at the cliff wall, and perhaps to try to do his twelve times tables backwards. Brys snickered and stretched, pressing her chest against him and pushing her left thigh forward.

"Still," she said, flexing her legs so that she slid slowly up and down the rope, and against Marius. "It must be frustrating, knowing that nobody can see us, and all you'd have to do is work out how to make Darrjy stop working his handle."

Marius forgot what came after seventy-two and had to start again. Brys leaned her face into his ear.

"I like a man who knows how to work his handle," she whispered, her breath hot and moist. Marius went from one hundred and thirty-two to one hundred and twenty-three, and silently swore.

Brys chuckled and leaned back. "Stand fast, soldier." She glanced down over the edge of the basket. "The top of the carving's coming up. Not even you would be fast enough to finish before we hit the first windows."

"Thank you so much," Marius managed to grumble between gritted teeth. Then he fell quiet as the rough cliff face gave way to carved and polished stone.

The nuns of Tylytene had been in residence for nearly fifteen hundred years, and in that time had mastered innumerable arts. Their ropes were prized across the continent. Their wines were cellared in palaces and country estates. Several vintages formed the cornerstones of the most valuable cellars. Over the centuries they had become expert at farming, medicine, archery, calligraphy, distilling poisons, tantric sex, woodturning, and countless other skills vital to the preservation of their community in a hostile and money-driven world. Somewhere along the line, it became apparent that the best defence against the kind of people who view conclaves of peace-loving women as easy targets was a good defence. They moved their entire operation from the top of the cliff to inside it, learned stonemasonry, and conquered that, too.

Many of the rocks that the water below crashed into were the detritus of their efforts, jagged-edged discards from the process of creating windows, hallways and stairs. Much of the silt that muddied that water was the result of work done by those nuns who put their newfound skills to use, roping themselves outwards to carve and smooth and polish designs of such beauty and magnificence that, even after half a dozen visits over twenty years, Marius was still brought to silence by coming face to cliff-face with them.

Swirling scrolls flowed over the white stone, proclaiming, in dead languages, dominion over the earth of the hundred or more gods the nuns had aligned themselves to over the centuries. The existence of God or of gods might be a concept the nuns needed to ensure their sanctity, but not so much that they couldn't be flexible when necessary. Birds light as gossamer flittered between them, carrying vines and ropes and laurels so real that Marius had to control the impulse to try and pluck a leaf from them as he passed. Gargoyles loomed out of crevices, vomiting water across sprites and mermaids and tentacles that writhed and wrapped themselves around famous saints and politicians, whose faces offered a parade of self-importance forgotten by time and the skilful hands of mocking artists. Windows appeared, disguised as eyes, open mouths, or the gaps between trees that arched and provided a canopy for Green Men and satyrs to couple in ways nuns shouldn't even have known about, never mind recreate so accurately. Balistraria dotted the monumental frieze, disguised as the strings of a lute here, the folds of tree bark there. Marius caught occasional glimpses of wooden machinery through the gaps, waiting to hurl rocks, or oil, or captured attackers, down upon anyone attempting to climb the rock face without permission. A trail of nymphs, staggered in a rough V-formation like sea birds across a granite sky, heralded the basket's descent to a balcony finished in an ornately formal manner. The remaining tubmen waited there, with Gerd at their centre.

"Did you see?" he began as soon as the basket had touched down. "The trees, and the wood nymphs, and… and…" Gerd waved his hands at the stonework disappearing above them, pointing out features distorted beyond recognition by the angle. "There was a bull over there, did you see it, and a boy jumping… he was upside down, between the horns… And flowers… And there was such a rude section, just above a dolphin and I think it was a kraken, they're the ones with the tentacles on their faces, right?"

Marius grinned. "Overcome your fear of heights, then?"

"Well, I mean, I couldn't stop looking. I just, I was looking, and I couldn't stop. There were so many things, and then, well…" He shrugged. "Then I was here, and a lady was helping me out." He smiled guiltily. "I think I missed some stuff."

Marius laughed. "Ready to go again, then?"

"Maybe."

"Don't worry. It strikes me the same way, every time." He patted his friend on the shoulder. "Last time I was here one of the nuns was working on an illuminated parchment, showing the whole thing with annotations. Maybe you can see if she's finished and ask her to talk you through it."

"You think?"

"Oh, yes. I've always had a great fondness for nuns."

"And pirates," a sardonic voice muttered behind him. Marius scowled.

"Oh, yes. Brys is with me."

"Ah." Gerd glanced the smuggler. "Did you, um. Were you the one who..." He mimicked a basket falling with his hands. Marius nodded.

"Caught with his fingers in the tub." At the same time, he projected: *Figured out a secret too many.*

"Ah, not smart." *Too smart for his own good?*

"You know it." *You know it.*

Marius caught a fleeting image of Gerd nodding. "So what secret?"

"I'll tell you later. Let's get inside and get away from observation, first."

A stronger nod: agreement.

The tubs were in a pile in the middle of the balcony. Brys swished past them and whistled three short, sharp blasts into the arched entrance. In less than a minute a white-clad figure emerged from the gloom.

"You didn't need to do that," the nun said. "We were waiting until you were all assembled."

"I'm a busy woman."

The nun glanced past Brys at Marius. "I'm sure you have a lot of things need doing. Please tell your men to deposit their goods in the usual place. Marius don Hellespont?"

"Helles."

"Come with me, please."

She spun on her heel and disappeared back into the darkness. Marius and Gerd exchanged glances.

"Okay, then." He nodded to Brys.

"I'd love to say it's been fun..."

"Oh, don't worry yourself, lover." She slapped the nearest tubman on the arm and started directing the collection of the barrels. "I'll be around for a little while. We can still have some fun." She glanced down at his groin and winked. "There's bound to be a replacement basket or two in a storeroom somewhere."

Gerd groaned. "I never, ever, want to be you when I grow up."

"Who said he's a grown-up?"

"Can we go, please?" Marius stalked to the archway and beyond, leaving Gerd to scurry after him. Brys' laughter followed them down the corridor.

SIXTEEN

There is a small but significant philosophical gap between a vow of poverty and living on the bones of your arse. For one thing, the first is voluntary, whilst poverty is usually the result of bad luck, bad parentage, or trusting the guy with the loud jerkin and a red-hot tip for tonight's dogfight. You don't have to be an idiot to live on the bones of your arse.

If, however, you decide to remove yourself from the comforts of society in order to follow a set of rules laid down by some guy hallucinating in a desert halfway across the world a thousand years before you were even born, and who claims to have received these rules from a god or gods who expect you to follow them without question – well, good luck to you. And if the god or gods of your choice never once pop in just to make sure you're actually doing what you're told, and you haven't nipped around the back of a metaphorical garden shed to have a quick drag of a philosophical pipe when the god of your choice wasn't looking – well, you're already a moron so why compound it by turning your back on a few creature comforts along the way?

The nuns of Tylytene had been many things: suppliants, farmers, educators of young princes, whores, warriors, and occasionally even religious devotees. They had never been morons. They may have believed in a god, but it was always the god most likely to bring in the maximum number of offerings. There was nothing in their statutes that ordered them to bunk up in tiny cells without the comfort of a nice cosy bearskin over the floor. Marius had walked palace halls that were less handsomely appointed. Tapestries lined the walls at regular intervals, and thick rugs were spaced out between them so that very little of the cold rock was allowed to touch the feet of those who travelled the corridors. Fresh air wafted gently across their faces. Everything was bright and clean. Gerd stared around him in wonder.

"Mirrors," Marius muttered in answer to his unspoken question. "They dug shafts up to the surface and mounted mirrors down the inside. The sunlight is reflected and magnified down here." He pointed to a hole above them, the size of a man's head. "I wouldn't recommend staring straight up."

Gerd did exactly that, and staggered.

"Told you."

"What do they do when it rains?" Gerd rubbed his eyes and blinked.

"Light torches, same as everyone else."

The nun stayed silent ahead of them, but Marius saw her shake her head.

"And what about the air?"

"Fans, mounted on the shafts. Last time I was here they were all linked to a set of wheels in the lower casements."

The nun bowed her head. "We take an hour's constitutional each day, turning the wheel as a service to our sisters."

"But…" Gerd waved his hands ineffectually. "What if a shaft breaks down, or gets clogged up with something?

Or an animal steps into one by accident? What if… what if someone pours something down one?"

The nun glanced back over her shoulders, a look of wry superiority in her eyes. "We fix them."

Gerd sank back into silence.

They reached a set of stairs and began to climb. Marius watched Gerd marvel at the paintings that hung on the rock walls, and the urns and vases that stood on plinths within smooth-hewn alcoves. He had forgotten, in the time they had been apart, that Gerd was still a simple country farmer at heart. Marius had shown him some sights four years ago, before they had gone their separate ways: the great Bone Cathedral at the heart of Scorby City; the docks of Borgho City; the gambling houses of the Merchant Kings. But once they had separated, with all the world and time immemorial at his behest, Gerd had retreated to his mountain farm and his dying Granny. Marius had trod roads high and low across the continent since turning his back on his family, had seen sights that most men would not believe, never mind experience. It was easy to forget that for most people, the world ended less than a day's walk from their own hearth. An art gallery in a cave thirty feet below the surface of the earth was nothing new to Marius. In fact, it wasn't even the best he'd seen. To Gerd, though, it would be some sort of miracle. Marius was gratified. He wasn't sure what was coming, but he was pretty certain none of it was good. Let the boy lift his heart while he could.

They climbed six flights until Marius guessed they were near the very top of the nunnery, perhaps no more than twenty or thirty feet below the surface of the world. The light seemed brighter here, less diffuse, as if coming more directly from the sun without quite so much assistance from mirrors. Marius was sure it was a trick of perception, but nevertheless he sensed the change in atmosphere and suddenly felt more exposed because of it. He was becoming too used to being underground, he thought with a shiver. He was coming to think that having earth above him was a type of protection, and he didn't like that realisation.

They reached an antechamber and the nun stopped.

"Please wait here," she said, and turned away. Gerd looked at Marius in sudden panic.

"Wait," he said. "You've not told us why we're here."

"The young master knows," she replied, and nodded to Marius. Gerd looked between them.

"Young master?" he said. "He's twice your age!"

"I wouldn't say *that*." Marius straightened his back, and winked at the nun as lasciviously as he could manage. She gave him a blank look and left. Gerd turned on him as soon as she was through the door.

"What did she mean, 'young master'? And what are we here for anyway?"

Marius ignored him and looked about the room. It was small, with little more than two chairs and a side table to the right of a door across from the entrance corridor. A balistraria dominated the wall to their left, its top point higher than a man, its bottom disappearing past the floor to the level below, and with a cross-slit wide enough that Marius could have stretched his arms out and fitted comfortably inside its reach. Someone, long ago, had carved around it in the shape of a tree, so that the window formed the bole and main cross branch. Corpses hung from the branches: soldiers wearing a hundred different coats of arms, some so old their lines were almost worn smooth. Through the window Marius could make out nothing but clear blue sky, giving the tree a glowing aspect at odds with its gruesome countenance.

"Gods, that's cheery," Gerd said, taking a step back towards the safety of the interior wall.

Marius shrugged. "As warnings go, it's all very unsubtle. Wages of sin surrounding a nice open sky. I'm guessing they send very junior nuns up here to be lectured by very crusty old ones. Anyone with any sense in them isn't going to be scared off by that."

"It's the sky I was talking about." Gerd fumbled for the chair behind him and sank into it. "We're rather high here, aren't we?"

Marius smirked. "Depends on your point of view. We're below ground, so we're actually very low." He leaned over and whispered, "Can't you just feel all that rock and earth pressing down on you? Doesn't it make you feel all *claustrophobic*?"

"Nobody likes you, you know."

Disappointed, Marius slumped into the remaining chair and glanced at the table. A stoneware jug and two tumblers sat upon it. He peered inside.

"Water," he muttered in disgust.

They stared at the death scene across the room in silence.

"So why are we here?"

Marius' attention had been captured by a vignette partway up the bole. Fresher than the others, it looked to have been carved only a few years ago. A merchant, in familiar livery: two circular shields, bisected by paired sword and quill. The crest of the family don Hellespont. The merchant was hanged most fiercely, his neck bent at an angle that would have resulted in decapitation in real life. His head was turned towards the room with a tilt that oozed superiority and an inborn arrogance.

His face had been carefully carved, and then just as carefully scratched out. But it was the figure next to him that caught Marius' attention: a young man, perhaps seventeen or eighteen years old: short compared to many of the others, with hair pulled back into a queue, wearing a distinctive jacket that Marius had not seen since he traded it for a meal and a thrupenny-upright at a southern alehouse almost twenty years ago. The space above the figure's head was empty. There was still room for a noose, or a laurel, as if the artist was waiting to be told which one to sculpt. The face on that figure was outlined with infinite precision, and it was staring directly at the seat in which Marius sat.

"Did you enjoy meeting my father?" he asked, gazing into the image's empty eyes.

"Ummm, no. Let's say not."

"Well," Marius smiled grimly as the door next to them began to open. "You're probably going to want to keep that in mind."

A tall, ascetic-looking woman in starched white robes glided into the room. She paused, and turned to look at the two men down the length of a long nose. Her arched eyebrows framed dark eyes that offered no welcome or recognition. Marius tilted his head so that she could not escape the full measure of his face. She stared at his ravaged features for several seconds until, ever so delicately, small white teeth bit down onto her lower lip.

"Oh, Marius," Halla don Hellespont said in a cracking voice, "whatever have you done?"

Marius watched as her self-control deserted her, and quiet sobs began to shiver the length of her body. He leaned back and grinned.

"Hello, Mother."

SEVENTEEN

The room behind the door was small but richly furnished. Marius stepped past his mother and checked out the wooden bookshelves and overstuffed chairs, depositing himself on a couch by the wall and stretching his legs across it.

"You're doing very well for yourself."

His mother shuffled in, wiping wet cheeks, and slid behind a desk, leaning forward to rest her head on her hands and look at him.

"Mother Superior loaned me this room in which to meet you. This is her office. My room is a little more humble."

"Only a little, I suspect."

Halla said nothing, and simply continued to observe him with such sadness in her eyes that Marius found himself unable to match gazes, contenting himself with leaning back into the couch and turning to look about the room. It was, he was forced to admit, not that well-appointed on second glance. The furniture was clean and old, but now that he was staring at it he could see it was handmade, probably by some past acolyte of the nunnery. Everything was the tiniest bit lopsided, as if the skills to produce it had been learned on the job. Marius was sure that most of the drawers would stick, were he to try them, and the desk probably wobbled if any weight was put on the far corner. Even the couch was unevenly stuffed, and he wriggled to find the most comfortable configuration of lumps for his backside.

"So," he said.

"So."

"You wanted to see me, did you?" He leaned back, squirmed his hip between two errant springs. "Like what you see?"

"Marius–"

"Let's not 'Marius' me, mother." He stared up at the rough-hewn ceiling, finding designs in the unfinished scrapings of long-dead chisels.

"Marius." This time Halla was firm, more in control of her emotions. "You came to me. Do you really know why you are here?"

"Is that it?" He swung his face towards her. "Is that all you have to ask? Not 'How could this happen?' or 'Who did this awful thing to you?'"

"I know who did this to you."

He sat up. "You do?"

She nodded. "It was your father, wasn't it? He finally did it. He finally… You went to see him, didn't you, and he did this."

Marius closed his eyes, and slumped back. "Oh, for…" He tilted his head back, stared through his eyelids at the grey, dead world around him. "You can't let each other go, can you? Can't just decide it was a terrible marriage and leave each other to rot in peace in your separate little holes."

"But you did go there."

Suddenly, he was sitting forward, staring at her – his mother, upright and regal in her liar's uniform, daring to look at him as if visiting his father was some sort of crime. Never mind how it had ended. Never mind how great the hatred between his parents has been. What irritated her was nothing more or less than the proximity. It had always been this way. If the three of them had been in a room he could have picked a favourite, and it would have been her every time. But they were alone, just the two of them, and even as he knew it for the conditioned response it was, and hated himself for it, the old don Hellespont traditions took hold. If two were together, they would sting each other to death like scorpions in the sun. The poison couldn't sit in his throat any longer: he had to spit it out, and she was right in front of him, an unmoving target.

"It wasn't him that brought me to this," he hissed. "Not alone." He stood and leaned over the desk, a pointed finger aimed at her eye like a dart. "All he ever did was hate me. It was you." A jab of the finger. "You, and this imaginary bullshit, running out any time it all got too much for your delicate sensibilities–"

"I did what I had to."

"But you never took *me*!" Marius almost stopped, surprised by the hurt in his voice, by the need. "Only when it suited you. If it was that bad, how could you justify it to yourself, leaving me behind when it was so bad?"

She lowered her gaze for a moment. "It was never you he wanted to hurt."

"He still did!" The finger became a fist, banging against the desk with each word like a judge's gavel, pronouncing sentence. "Did you ever stop to think, did you ever take a moment to work it out? Hurting me hurt you. Basic fucking logic, mother."

The world fell silent. Marius could feel his words being soaked up by the stone walls, reflecting back only the essence of his hurt and anger, absorbing the meaning.

He pushed away from the table in disgust.

"I'm here for as long as it takes to get what I need, and then I'm going."

"The book."

He stared at her for long moments. "What?"

"You want the book."

"How did you know?"

She raised her head to look at him, and he saw in her eyes a flash of the mother he once knew, the quiet pride he had watched slowly erode and fall away. "You went to see him."

"Yes."

"First."

"What?"

"You went to see him before me." She reached into a desk drawer, tugging at it as it stuck. She pulled a book out and laid in on the table between them. "Whatever you say, Marius, whatever you feel, just remember that." She pushed it across, and watched as he picked it up. "When you needed something, you went to him first."

Marius took the book and stood without a further word. Without looking at his mother he slid the chair back against the table with exaggerated courtesy, exited the room, and closed the door quietly behind him. Gerd was sitting on the couch, lost in contemplation of the carved walls. As Marius entered he looked up.

"Hey, have you seen that guy?" Gerd pointed at the carvings. "He looks just like… What's wrong?"

Marius ignored him. He crossed the room to the chair at the far side of the foyer and settled into it. Drawing his legs up under him, as he had done when he was a child and had snuck into his father's study to read forbidden books while Ygram was away, he began to read.

EIGHTEEN

So it was that the usurper Scorbus of Kefundy led his forces from their encampments under the hills of Tinmer and arrayed them at the northern edge of the fields that bordered the City of Jollis, wherein sat Mellik, rightful king of the plains peoples. Twenty thousand Kefundian invaders stood at Scorbus' back, alongside Tallian mercenaries and flesh-eating Northerners who he paid in the bodies of villagers they slaughtered as they made their ruinous way across the plains.

Thus they came upon the walls of Jollis and made their camp beneath them. But Scorbus, having come so far and caused such misery as if it were his right, was gripped by fear, and neither attacked the walls nor attempted a siege. Instead, he sat indolent and fearful, and lit fires by day as well as night, and sought parlay with the rightful king. And King Mellik made reply that Scorbus had no claim to any throne of man, as was known by all who had no favour of his purse, and that only a sharpened blade would sit upon his brow unless he made recompense with sorrow and withdrew beyond the plains.

And Scorbus sent no emissary, but sat silent, so that N'Nosi, who led the Northerners, was disgusted, and took a force of Kefundians to the city gates to beat upon them and force shame and action upon him.

Thus the King came upon the Kefundians by surprise, catching them hard against the wooden walls of the city with the majority of their forces unprepared, and there was a deathly fight for possession of the ground. There was killed the Princes Sonnig and Knert; and the Kefundians who remained were put to flight and variously killed, so that what survivors crawled back to their leader were condemned to death for being too weak to fight further. And thus did Mellik claim possession of the place of death.

But the usurper was not found wanting of tricks, and so he devised an attack by traitors amongst the King's own kind, who had been promised lands to either side of the city itself where fields were lush and much desired. And they came upon the King as two rivers of men from within his own city on the ground he had won so hard-fought and recent, and they came upon him before he had call to marshal his own soldiery.

But the King, being well-supported and righteous in his claim, made hard battle against his traitors, and there was great slaughter done to both armies. His men he drew into a ring around his standard. As the traitors charged, his brother Prince Vaddcoldamadi, who bore the name of the old King in the speech of his ancestors, and who led the traitors in defence of his own unfounded claim to the throne, was thrown from his horse at his master's feet. And Mellik, being so noble of spirit and owning of the righteousness of battle, raised him to his feet, saying "I will not fight a brother that has fallen. Rather he slays me than I take such a victory over him." Whereupon Vaddcoldamadi rose with words of thanks upon his lips, and did kill the King by means of a knife hidden upon his person.

At this, those troops loyal to the city were overwhelmed, and the mangled bodies of the most noble and virtuous troops were broken open by the hooves of the traitor's horses, while the usurper waited with his invaders and let the city's men fall upon each other. And the traitor Vaddcoldamadi was possessed of the crown, and did cross the field before his remaining victorious troops, whereupon he presented it to the usurper and proclaimed Scorbus King of Jollis, in return for the lands to the west of the city walls and the promise of succession over the dead King's sons, who had been put to the sword.

And all the traitors around him shouted their assent without hesitation, and were joined by the heathen Northerners and the money-fed Tallians, so that all within the walls heard a multitude of demon's voices and knew that the old, honoured ways were lost and that the time of usurpation was upon them.

And Scorbus rode into the City as if it were his by right of conquest, and the men of Jollis were rounded up, aye, and slaughtered, along with those traitors who had fought for Vaddcoldamadi, and the traitor prince himself. With nobody left to oppose him, Scorbus was anointed first King of the place now called Scorby after him, and set about to make himself the master of the world. And all sons of the city were fathered by the bastards he brought with him, and the woman subjugated and afeared, and all who opposed him were fed to the dungeons and forgotten.

NINETEEN

Marius closed the book slowly and sat staring at the sky through the balistraria for a very long time, his hands folded across the book's dry leather cover. Finally, with deliberate care, he placed it gently on the side table and stood. He took one deep, unnecessary breath, nodded to himself, and walked to the door.

His mother was waiting in her room. Marius stood in the doorway and matched her stare for several seconds.

"So," he said. "Where did you get that book?"

"It's been in the family for years," she replied. "You know how your father likes to collect valuable things."

"I've read that book a dozen times. I've never read *that* book."

Halla smiled. "Everybody has read the book in your father's library. That book is *authorised*. The one you've just read..." She shrugged. "There were only thirty made, hand-copied by monks in an obscure monastery at the base of Mount Terrun. After Scorbus found out about it, there were no copies. Or a monastery, or monks to remember it."

"No copies, and yet..."

"That is not a copy."

"The original."

"Written by the Venerable Gifgy in the year of the Long Fire, and sent to the nuns of this nunnery a year before Scorbus learned of its existence. Once Scorbus found out, he had Gifgy tortured and broken until he revealed the location of all of them. He told him where they all were, except his original. It's been here ever since, hidden, secret, safe. Until today there seemed little need to bring it back into the light."

"But…" Marius frowned. "The version at Father's house… he said you took it with you."

"I did. It's in my library." She pointed to a small bookshelf against the far wall of the room.

"Then this one?"

"He wanted you to find it. He said you had to read it for yourself, that you had to understand."

"Father said that?"

"No. Not your father." Halla looked sideways, towards the door. "Someone else."

"Oh, no." Realisation took Marius, just as he heard the handle lower. He swung as the door opened, his fist raised, ready to launch himself at the ruined visage he knew was about to enter…

"Keth!"

She stood in the doorway like a sudden beam of light in a dark room, her long hair pulled back into a simple ponytail, her slim figure hidden beneath the folds of a simple white dress that was too broad across the shoulder, too big in the bust, so that it hung off her like a shroud. She held her long, thin hands across her chest, fingers knitted together as she stared at him in complete shock for long seconds, her white face seeming more white than Marius remembered. Then he was upon her. He buried his face in her shoulder, breathed deep, drowning himself in her smell. His arms enveloped her, pulling her into him so that every hair on his body reached out to touch her.

"Marius. Marius."

He pulled her back, stared at her, then threw his arms around her again.

"I thought you were lost. I thought… I thought you were…"

"Dead?" Slowly, she disentangled herself from him and placed hands on either side of his face. "Would that have been so bad?"

"I…" He placed his hands over hers. "I thought I'd lost you. I thought he'd…"

"Kept her safe." A figure stepped out of the shadows behind Keth: a familiar broken shape. "While you travelled dangerous roads."

"You!" This time Marius did launch himself forward. His forearms struck Drenthe in the upper chest, knocking him back against the wall. His hands slid upwards and dug deep into the loose skin of his throat. Drenthe raised his eyebrows at the fury on Marius' face.

"If you're trying to choke me," he said with perfect clarity, so the whole room could hear. "we could be here for quite some time."

"Marius, please." Keth was tugging at his arm, trying to pull him away. "You have to listen to him. Please."

"What?" Marius glanced at her, then back at his nemesis. "What have you done to her?"

"Nothing. He didn't do anything."

"Marius." Halla stood in the doorway. "Mr Drenthe delivered Keth here ten days ago, and asked me to look after her while you embarked on your journey. She's been here ever since, Marius."

"You've got a fucking funny way of keeping people safe."

"Would you have let me take her if I'd knocked on your door and politely asked?"

Marius held his stare for long seconds, then slowly eased backwards. "How are you doing that?"

"Doing what?"

"Speaking. Out loud." He pointed at Drenthe's unmoving jaw. "You've never done that before."

"I do it all the time." The jaw stayed still. The voice came from somewhere just behind it. "Just not with you."

Marius bunched his fists. "You took Keth."

"And brought her back."

"And what about Granny? And you killed Arnobew."

"If you mean that somewhat spiteful and rather hilarious old lady your farm boy friend cares so much about, they're currently getting reacquainted in the mother superior's lavish bedroom, which I believe she commandeered the moment we set foot on the premises. After all, could you imagine her climbing a thousand steps unaided, or jumping into one of those delightful baskets?"

Marius snorted. "I can imagine her scaring the nuns into carrying her. But what about Arnobew?"

"Is that the fellow all dressed in cardboard?" Marius' mother asked.

"He's here?"

Drenthe sighed theatrically. "Killed, yes, Helles. But not just killed." He pushed Marius away, and ran his hands over the remaining straggles of his hair, patting them into place across his skull. "Recruited. We face a war, Marius. And how surprising that a man calling himself 'Warbone' would turn out to be a willing conscript?"

"You killed me!"

"I removed the final impediment between you and your rightful claim to the throne."

"What, the seven foot-tall maniac with an unconquerable army and an actual track record of being king?"

"I removed the second-last impediment between you and your rightful claim to the throne."

"You don't think you might have fucking *asked* first?"

"Oh. I didn't realise there was a chance you would say yes."

Marius clenched and unclenched his fists. Drenthe raised an eyebrow.

"There will be plenty to hit soon. For now, try listening." He inclined his head towards Marius' mother. "May we use your quarters, good lady?"

"Don't you be nice to her," Marius muttered, just as his mother replied: "Of course."

"Thank you, my lady." Drenthe walked past her into the room. "Come on, Helles."

Keth took Marius' hand, peeling the fist apart to wrap her fingers in his. "Please, Marius."

Reluctantly, Marius re-entered his mother's room. Drenthe was leaning nonchalantly against the bookcase, the irreplaceable account of Scorbus' war campaign in one hand.

"So," he said, as Marius faced him across the room. "What have we learned?"

"You know," Marius replied. "You've read it."

"I have. And I know what I learned." He tossed the book to Marius. "I want to know what *you* learned."

Marius stared down at the cover.

"It's not his, is it?" He looked up at them all. "The crown. The throne. He had no legitimate claim." He raised the book as if to dash it to the ground, held it for a moment, then lowered it and gave it back to his mother. "He didn't even fight for it, just waited until someone else got it and then paid them off. He's a usurper."

"That's right. And what else does that mean, Helles?"

Marius closed his eyes. "It means I've got to find another damn king."

"Not quite."

Marius opened his eyes and saw his mother, Keth and Drenthe standing in a group, all staring back at him with the same patient expression. He glanced from one to the other as understanding dawned.

"No."

"You were crowned."

"You took it off me."

"You weren't dead. Now you are."

"But you took it off me."

"You were never deposed, nor did you abdicate."

"I abdicate now."

"No you don't, Marius."

"Well… it's not mine any longer, is it?"

"You are the rightful King of the Dead, Helles. You were crowned. You accepted the coronation. You know the path Scorbus takes your people on is not that which leads them to Heaven."

"But…" Marius seized on Drenthe's last utterance. "I don't even believe in God. Or gods."

"You will. Once you wear the crown, you will."

"But…" Marius turned towards his mother. His mother the nun. Then he tried Keth, but no joy there. She had always believed, Marius knew that, had always made allowance for his lack of faith, his nihilism. "But…"

She came towards him now, taking him gently by the hands. "Marius. My love. If you don't do something then nobody will. Nobody can. You are the only one who has a claim against Scorbus. You could turn your people against him. They believe in the crown he wears, your crown. But if you don't..." She took her hands away, raised them towards the world outside. "Then who?"

"I don't know. Somebody. The King of Scorby! If he marshals his troops well, if he stays close to the city walls... he can call on the Tallian Amir for aid! I mean, if Scorbus takes Scorby he'll look there next–"

"Marius. The King is ten years old."

"His regent, then."

"Who is eighty-two years old and will likely be advising Scorbus within three weeks, given the amount he drinks," added Drenthe.

Marius stared at Keth. "I don't want to."

"I know, my love. But what would you do, if you could?"

"Run away. Hide. Pretend none of this was happening. With you. Somewhere safe and far away."

She ran a hand down the side of his face. "You know there is no far away, not this time. If Scorbus takes the living world then there will be nowhere safe for us to hide."

"And what will happen when he takes over the whole world in the name of God, and the thousands he commands, and the millions he will come to command, discover that it is not Heaven after all?" Drenthe asked softly. "What do you think will happen then?"

Marius turned on the dead man. "You. You did this to me."

"You did this to all of us."

"If you hadn't pulled me under..."

"And what were you doing when I mistook you for the King, Helles? What were you holding?"

Marius glanced at Keth and his mother. Drenthe had first taken him to the underworld when he was looting the King's corpse in the aftermath of a battle. It was the crown he prised from the dead man's helmet that persuaded the Dead of his nobility. There are some things you don't want your mum and girlfriend finding out about. The fact that you steal jewellery from dead people is probably one of them. He stalked over to Drenthe and leaned in close enough to stare directly into the corpse's single eye. With his dead sight he could see beyond the shattered orb, to the life that stared back at him from behind.

"I don't like you."

"You don't have to." Drenthe leaned back. "You just have to believe me."

Marius examined a moment longer, searching for a reason to doubt, to start their fight once more. Finally, he nodded.

"That means yes, Helles?"

"That means: what fucking option do I have?"

"Hey!"

"Sorry, mother."

"I should think so. Just because you're dead doesn't mean you should forget your manners."

"Yes, mother."

Keth hid a smile. "I *like* her."

"You be quiet, or I'll tell her what you do for a living."

"You wouldn't dare."

"Why? What does she do?"

Marius squinted like a vaudeville pamphleteer. "She cooks babies and feeds them to temperance advocates."

"Oh, well." His mother blew a raspberry. "We've *all* done that."

Marius turned to Drenthe.

"I can't believe I'm going to say this."

"What?"

"I want to hear Gerd's opinion."

He found him in the lower dining hall, seated at one of the long tables used by the nuns at mealtimes, with Granny seated opposite. Other than that, the room was empty. They each had a bowl before them, and a small loaf of bread had been torn open. As steam rose from their meals, Marius watched them as they dunked lumps of bread and chewed on the resulting sopping mess.

"What the hell are you doing?"

"You should try this." Gerd held up a sodden ball of bready goo. "Turnip soup. It's good."

"We don't eat." Marius plonked himself down next to them. "We don't have to eat."

"I know. But it's really good."

Marius glanced at Granny as she slurped up another spoonful. "It's not turnip," he said. "You see any turnip fields on your way here?"

"What is it, then?"

He leaned towards her. "We're sixty feet underground," he muttered. "What do you think they do with all the worms?"

She threw him an evil little smile, and sucked on her fingers. "Then it's good worm soup," she said, taking care to flap her lips and spray his face with droplets of it.

"Oh, gods." Marius wiped his face. "When are you two going to get it? When are you going to stop thinking like..." He fell silent.

"Thinking like what?"

"A living person." Marius pulled at his hair. "Bloody hell. We're all doing it. *I'm* doing it." He glanced at them both. "I am such an idiot."

"No argument there." Granny slurped up the last of the bread and began attacking the inside of her bowl with three fingers. "I mean, you see me turning down free food just because I don't have to eat? No, sir. It's warm and it's filling, and I don't have to do the washing up. You'd *have* to be an idiot to turn that down."

"Granny."

"What?"

"Be a love." Gerd pushed his bowl over. "Take these down to the kitchen, would you?"

Granny peered at the empty crockery, then at the two men. She pursed her lips.

"All right," she said. "Long as I don't have to wash them."

"Thank you." Gerd sat back and raised his face as she passed. She leaned down and grudgingly accepted a kiss on the cheek. "Don't be long."

"Aye, well." She squinted at Marius. "You *are* an idiot. You both are. Telling you to look after him has been a load of bollocks all along, so…" She pinned her gaze to Gerd, and her voice immediately softened. "Give him good advice, boy. Look after you both."

"I will."

"Hmmph. Be seeing you do."

She scuttled out the door, leaving the two companions alone.

"Well, then." Gerd said as soon as she was gone. "What's happened, then?"

"You've got Granny back."

"Yep.

"I've got Keth."

"Oh, good."

"We could let it go at that, couldn't we? We could go now. We've done what we set out to do."

"Yep." Gerd looked at Marius, then at the door through which they'd come. "But the job's only part done, isn't it?"

Marius stared at him. "How much do you know?"

"Not much. But you wouldn't be coming in here asking my permission to run off if it was something you wanted to do, would you?"

Marius sighed. "No, I guess not."

"What is it, then?"

Marius rubbed his face once more, then told his friend what had transpired in his mother's room. Gerd listened in silence, waiting until Marius ran out of words before he placed his elbows on the table and rested his chin on his clenched fists.

"Well," he said. "If you want my permission to run away from that, you can have it. That's a hell of a job to be handed and no mistake."

"What? Really?"

"Oh, yes. I wouldn't do it."

"No." Marius frowned. "Right."

"So, when you going then?"

"I hadn't really thought about that."

"No time like the present." Gerd sat back and clapped his hands. "Don't bother about telling your mum and the woman you love. I'll let them know you've gone."

"Hang on…"

"We'll sort something out, I expect. Maybe we can elect a parleement."

"What, a parliament of what? The dead?"

"Sure, why not? No need to concern yourself. We'll give it a go."

"Wait a tick. I never absolutely said…"

Gerd stopped, opening his hands. "Then you're not here for my permission, are you?"

Marius stared down at the table. "Bollocks."

Gerd smiled. "Good. So let's get on to it, then." He stood and extricated himself from the bench. "I'll go and get Granny. Your Majesty."

"Bloody hell." Marius dragged himself upright. "Bloody fucking hell."

TWENTY

The door to his mother's room was closed. Marius knew they were waiting beyond it. All he had to do was turn around and walk away. He could be in a basket before they knew anything was amiss, at the top of the cliff before they worked out he wasn't coming back, and hiding under the bed in a bordello in the cheapest, nastiest part of Borgho City before they decided to do this thing without him and got themselves all senselessly slaughtered...

He opened the door.

The group of conspirators looked up. Gerd and Granny sidled past him and went to stand next to them.

"All right. But I'm not doing this alone."

"You never had to." His five allies stood as one. Marius eyed them.

"We're going to need an army."

Drenthe smiled. "We already have one."

The halls at the base of the nunnery were enormous, great caverns carved by hand out of the rock in ancient times. Marius and Drenthe stood with their backs to the giant wooden doors that dominated one wall of the largest hall, and watched as hundreds of dead were put through their paces by a cadre of muscled corpses.

In unison they raised shields, drove wooden swords forward, stepped, retreated, stepped again, raised shields, repeated. It was all performed in silence. Not a word was spoken, nor a command issued. To the nuns it must have seemed eerie. To Marius and Drenthe, former military men who could hear the tumult of projected voices inside their heads, it was a training ground no different to any other. Marius made out familiar faces amongst the trainees.

"From V'Ellos?"

Drenthe nodded. "The same. While you were faffing about on the water we came directly by land. I'd been drilling them in the warehouses, but now we have a team of fighters to instruct them."

"The tubmen."

"One every quarter for the last two years." Brys appeared at their elbow. "Recruited from the finest docksides, taverns, and whorehouses the north can provide."

"And what's in it for you?"

Brys favoured him with a look of hurt. "Helles. You doubt me." She smiled. "Money, of course. Lots of money."

"Good." Marius performed a mental head count. "You'll have plenty to spend, then."

"On what?"

"Men." He waved his hand at the practising troops. "These aren't enough. We need more. Mercenaries, muggers, thieves, murderers, policemen. I want as many bastards as we can afford, and I want them here as soon as you can fetch them."

"But why?"

"Because we're going to war, Brys, against an enemy that already has an army of soldiers and gets more every time they put a knife through someone's armour. We need bodies and we need them already hardened."

Drenthe butted in. "But you can't drill those sorts into a fighting unit, not in the time frame we're talking about. No matter how skilled they are in fighting one on one, they'll go to pieces at the first sight of real battle against organised troops."

"I have no intention of taking them into a battle." He swung the doors wide and stalked up the corridor towards the stairs, Drenthe and Brys in his wake. "I'm going to start a street fight."

"How?"

He stopped a few steps above them and looked down at their confused faces. "You really think I don't know how?"

Brys grinned. "I think you could start a fight in a nunnery."

Marius grinned back. "What makes you think that?" He turned back to his climb. "And hammers. Equip them all with hammers."

"Why?"

"Because swords create dead people." He made a short chopping motion with his fist, like something blunt crushing a skull. "Hammers destroy them."

TWENTY-ONE

Not for the first time in its fifteen hundred year history, nor even the tenth, the library of the nunnery was home to a council of war. Admittedly, never before had the council contained four dead people, a dancing girl, and a smuggler, but it can't be warrior kings and shiny armour all the time. Marius stared at each of them in turn. Finally, when it seemed like silence had overtaken him completely, he spoke.

"Scorbus is a thousand years old," he said. "His tactics are a thousand years old. He knows nothing of the modern world, of modern cities. He's lain in a box for a millennium without any sort of outside influence–"

"He's had the other kings to talk to."

Marius shot Gerd an annoyed look. "Twenty or so different voices, all arguing against each other, each one with a differing idea of what a King should be. And only two of them fought any real war of conquest. Even one of those was against a tribe in the mountains, not established fortifications on the plains." He shook his head. "No. He'll resort to what he knows best, what's worked for him before."

"He's already taken the main approaches to Scorby," Drenthe interrupted. "If we wait too much longer he'll control the whole of the coastal plain. Helles, we must–"

"No he won't." Again, a shake of the head to silence dissent. "And you know it otherwise we wouldn't have taken so long to get where we are now. No. It's something I realised while you two were eating your soup." He pointed at Gerd and Granny. "Scorbus has been dead for a dozen lifetimes or more, but does he *think* like a dead person?"

The group exchanged doubtful glances.

"Oh, for all the gods in the sky!" Marius rolled his eyes towards the ceiling, then back at them. "Look at what he's done. Gathered troops amongst his own people, concentrated them into one vast army at the start point of his invasion. Rolled across the landscape in a great big, noisy column, waving flags and blowing trumpets more than likely. Slapped down the odd town here and there and winkled out traitors and bendable politicians so he can claim easy victories and keep marching in a nice straight line towards... where?"

"Well, Scorby City, of course. I don't see–"

"Exactly. Straight at the biggest city on the continent, where he can form up all his troops in nice straight lines and nice square blocks and meet his enemy on the field of combat like a good old-fashioned king. And then everyone can look his opponent in the eye, and men on horses can ride up and down giving stirring speeches, and it will all be nice and honourable and formal, and he can rely on human nature to cock everything up so he can wait at the back and pick up the spoils after all the real fighters have killed each other and come over to his side."

"Just like before."

"Just like every bloody battle ever fought by a living army fighting another living army."

"But–"

"Drenthe."

"Yes?"

"How would *you* get into Scorby City?"

Drenthe shrugged. "Travel the tunnels, come up in a back alley somewhere near where I was headed."

"So why didn't you tell Scorbus to do it when you were weaselling your way up his chain of command?"

"Well..." The dead man looked around at the faces that were suddenly looking at him in intense interest. "I only wanted to find out what he was planning. I don't want him to win."

"Why not?"

"Because..." He looked back at Marius. "Helles, you *know* why."

"Actually, I think I do." Drenthe looked relieved by this, as Marius continued: "So, the question remains. Why do it your way not Scorbus'?"

"Well, it's the easiest way, isn't it?"

"Because you're *dead*."

"Well, yes."

"Ohhh," Gerd gasped, and pressed his fists against his temples.

"Yes?"

"His whole army is dead."

"Yes!" Marius threw his hands up. "Now you get it!"

"A dead army shouldn't have to fight a battle." Gerd leaned forward, hands shaking as the implications of his reasoning struck home. "It should be able to run straight to the place it wants to be, then just come up and take it."

"More than that." Marius rolled his hands around each other, expanding the thought. "He shouldn't even need an *army*."

"Well... no... he'd have to... okay, I'm not seeing that."

"Kill the King, what happens?"

"You have a dead king?"

"No." It was Keth who matched Marius stare for stare. "Kill the King, and he becomes your ally. Kill the parliament, and you own the laws. Kill the generals, and you own the army. The army kills the people, and you have the kingdom. The kingdom kills its neighbours, and you own the world."

"Spot on."

"You don't need to have an army. You don't need to march anywhere. You don't need to kill everybody. Just one person. Kill the right person, and people will do all your work for you."

Marius smiled. "That's how a dead person thinks."

"Thank you. I think."

"All well and good," Brys folded her arms, and stared around the group, "but who do *we* need to kill?"

Marius smiled. "Nobody. All the right people are dead already. We just have to collect them. Brys." He turned to the smuggler. "Your tubmen. Where do you get them from?"

She shrugged. "Here and there. Ports, mostly."

"Underneath the ports, yes?"

"Yeah. They drag a body out every now and then."

"Good. Take your tubmen. Send them under the water. Get them recruiting. I want the nastiest pieces of shit you can find, and I want them armed." His attention switched to Drenthe. "Now you. Whatever deal you cut with my father, change it. I want hammers, maces, flails, coshes, truncheons, knobkerries, bits of pipe, chair legs, thigh bones… whatever you can buy that crushes and breaks. Cutting instruments are no good. I want ten thousand of them, and I want to be holding one inside a week."

"And what are we supposed to pay with?"

Marius turned towards his mother. "That's where you come in."

TWENTY-TWO

The room was full of bones. A thousand, ten thousand, a hundred thousand; it was impossible to tell. But they were all the same. Finger bones, each one an inch or so long, white and grey and a dirty sort of brown, piled on one another like a mountain of discarded quill stubs. The group stood at the door and stared in mute shock while Marius bent and scooped up a handful, letting them trickle clackingly down upon their comrades.

"Why don't you tell them what you do with them, Mother?"

She looked at him, then away.

"Indulgences."

"What?" Four heads swivelled towards her.

"Indulgences," she repeated, sighing as she picked a bone up and peered at it. "The dead die so sinful, so full of regret. No matter how noble they are in life, how many times they make the right observances, or attend the masses, nobody dies in a state of grace. They all wish to repent something."

"And the gods keep changing, don't they, Mother?"

Halla said nothing, so Marius pressed home his advantage. "Imagine dying three hundred years ago, knowing in your holy heart of hearts that you're about to take your place in the dining halls of Gnisbrid the

Mighty. Imagine when you discover that Gnisbrid is a false god, and the only true gods are the Spinning Sisters. Or the Ultimate Zzif. Or... What are we worshipping this decade, Mother?"

"We have to survive." She looked up from the finger bone, glanced at the roof above. "We've adapted so many times over the years. We're too small and isolated not to take notice of the world outside."

"No matter the consequences, eh?" Marius kicked at the bones, sending a spray of disconnected fingers across the room. "How long have the dead been coming to your door, Mother? How many have you sent away with these trinkets?"

"They believe." She spat the words out: at Marius, at his companions, at the walls. "At least they believe."

"Fear and desperation. That's your belief." Marius turned to the others. "But it's desperation we can use."

"How?"

"What are the dead following Scorbus for? Absolution. God's attention. Entry to Heaven. With these," he snatched the bone from his mother's grasp and brandished it, "we can give it to them." He turned back to Halla. "Show me where you store the carved ones."

The world is full of sin. More sins than any holy book can list. More than any church can point a disapproving relic at. More than any poverty-stricken yokel out in some forgotten corner of the kingdom can avoid without a travelling priest coming around every couple of years to point out all the ways sin has crept into their tired, misbegotten lives. Because the last thing the church needs is for its subjects to find some small measure of happiness in a life that began, continued, and will undoubtedly end in the shit. It takes a lot of infrastructure to support that amount of sin, more than any church can afford without a lot of gold coming in. But what to do when the majority of followers are exactly those miserable, dirt-grubbing innocents in the forgotten corners? How to persuade them to part with whatever meagre crop of pennies they've dredged up from the dry and unforgiving earth?

Thus: indulgences.

You are a sinner. You can't help but *be* a sinner. And you'll die in sin. *Everyone* does. How much worse, then, to die when the priest is at the other end of the forest reminding some other poor bastard of all the ways in which he is sinning?

But there is a way you can guard against such a circumstance. A scrap of paper, signed by the Holy Father/Mother/Triumvirate/take your pick. Words of absolution. Words of forgiveness. A once in a lifetime, cure-all-ills, one hundred per cent guarantee of divine entry into the afterlife of your choice, backed by the biggest muckity-muck in the denomination of your choice, sin-free and soul as pearly white as the teeth you lost before adolescence, friend. And all it costs you is your belief. And soul. And whatever funds you might have stashed in the back of your hovel beneath the pallet on which you and the missus and all your kids sleep together.

The priest takes a cut. The bishop takes a cut. The church takes a cut. And you get a scrap of parchment guaranteeing you a sinless death. Everybody's happy. Unless, of course, you don't do the decent thing and stay dead.

Then what do you do?

"They've been coming here for two hundred years," Halla said as they climbed the stairs to the main level.

"Two hundred?" Marius frowned. "That can't be right."

His mother glanced at him. "And why is that?"

"Because…" Scorbus has only been King for four, he was about to say. But that was absurd, he realised. The dead had already been waiting for a King long before they dragged Marius down beneath the ground. Some had been waiting for centuries. Of course they wouldn't all stay still. Of course some would seek answers. "And they came to you."

"In dribs and drabs, mostly. One or two a year, wanting to know why God won't take them, why they've been denied their eternal peace."

"And you fob them off."

"What else can we do?" She stopped, turning upon her son. "They were dead, Marius. Walking dead people, begging us to end their suffering. Think what you want of us but we are still nuns. We still believe in God–"

"Any god."

"Whichever god seems most right. And we still care about those who believe, even after death."

"So what do you do?" Granny's voice: respectful, and with so much belief and need it made Marius wince.

"In the beginning the sisters made them comfortable." They continued climbing. "They were ministered to, helped along the way to redemption. Some of them found a sort of peace. Many didn't."

"What happened to them?"

"They left. Went back into the world. Others…"

"Yes?"

"I don't know."

"Yes you do."

Halla made no reply. Instead, she led them along a corridor to a locked door. "In the last three years they've been coming in numbers we'd never dreamed of, all of them seeking absolution. All of them talking about a king who promised them Heaven, and telling them it was where they had wasted their lives all along. And all they want is some way of coming back, something they can hold onto that lets them know it's okay to be here, that they deserve to be in the world."

"So you con them."

"We give them a token, Marius. We give them something to hold onto."

"And what does it cost them, Mother? What do you take from them?"

"They're dead. What more *could* we take?"

She swung the door open and ushered them inside.

The room beyond was not large, but the bustle of activity made it seem even smaller than it was. Twenty nuns sat amongst five benches, with an empty barrel to their left and one the tubmen had delivered to her right. As the group watched, a nearby nun dropped a bone into the left barrel then dipped her hand into the right and removed a clean bone. She placed it in a small vice before her, rolled her shoulders a few times to loosen them up, then picked up a small scratch awl. She leaned forward, frowned in concentration, and began to carve.

"We work six-hour shifts," Halla said, leading the group amongst the tables. "The indulgences are general in nature. We can't get too specific. The range of requests is too great."

"What do they say?" Granny asked, awe in her voice.

"That they are loved by God, that they have the right to walk in his fields, that to die is not a sin but a right." She stopped, bending past a nun to remove a bone just as it was finished. "Would you like one?"

"I…" Granny glanced at Marius. He rolled his eyes and shook his head. "Yes please."

"Here. Take it, with my blessing." Granny accepted the trinket with reverence, then looked defiantly at Marius as she secreted it about herself.

"Feel better, do you?" Marius asked.

"Yes, actually. So stick that in your pipe and go fuck yourself."

Halla blinked. "Yes, well, we aim for perhaps a more forgiving view of those who wrong us."

"Forgive yourself first." Marius brushed past her. "At least she's honest."

"We are honest. We're just…"

"Adaptable?"

"I can see where he gets it from." Keth giggled, and elbowed Gerd. Marius turned. His companions were staring at him, grinning. He frowned.

"You wanted to know what to pay your dead with?" he asked Drenthe and Brys, gesturing at the buckets of carved finger bones. "Gather them up." He faced his mother. "Now," he said, with the nastiest of smiles. "Show me what you do with your dead."

TWENTY-THREE

Marius walked through an arch made up of angelic messengers from a dozen different and largely contradictory gods, and emerged onto a balcony that stood open to the sea. Above him a beatific face stretched twenty feet across the cliff in every direction. Fifty feet below, waves crashed onto rocks like shark's teeth, spitting spray into the air in angry spirals. Wind whipped across the balcony, momentarily staggering him as he stepped out of the shelter of the corridor.

"We give them every honour and respect," Halla shouted over the roar of the waves. "We line the floors with leaves from the plants we grow, and hang tapestries that have been in our possession for hundreds of years. We sing songs that tell of our sister's humility and works, and those of us who have worked with her recount stories of the example she has provided to us all."

"And then you fling her over the edge."

"We send her to her sisters, to rejoin the waters which surround each unborn child within their mother's womb."

"You dump them in the ocean to be bashed to smithereens by the waves." He risked a glance over the edge and stepped back, queasy. "Useless to me. Absolutely useless."

"And what are we supposed to do? Bury them?"

"There are options. There are other ways..." He stopped, looked sidelong at his mother's profile. "Where is your ossuary?"

"No." She shook her head. "No. You don't get to see that. That is sacred space."

"Show me." He stalked towards her, one hand holding his flying hair back from his forehead, the other pointed towards her like the business end of a rapier. "I knew you'd have one, just knew it. Some place you can store your highest and mightiest, somewhere you can stop kidding yourself that we're all equal under the eyes of your little gods, so you can run your fingers through someone's rib bones and send up a little prayer: 'Please, my merciful and wonderful father figure, let little old me be good enough and strong enough–'"

Her slap came out of nowhere, an instinctive movement that caught them both by surprise.

"You don't," she said, "get to say that."

Marius raised a hand to his cheek. The blow hadn't hurt. He was far too dead for that. But in that moment, a hundred memories had spun to the surface, shaken loose by the impact. A hundred moments where he had provoked a similar sting: never physical, never an actual strike, because the wives of ambitious merchants did not stoop so low as to hit their child. But a hundred withering glares; a hundred carefully chosen phrases that belittled or cried disappointment at behaviours he should have known better than to try, but which he had tried anyway just to get the reaction he craved; a hundred dismissals with the knowledge that he was an unworthy child, a failure with no redemption. A hundred times he had set out to disappoint, to upset, to hurt. A hundred successes. And now he was no longer a child, and she was no longer the proper lady wife of a ruthless trader, and there were no more conventions to hide behind.

"You don't get to say that," she repeated. "Those women died doing something noble, not fighting over some grubby back-alley whore or bilking good, honest, hard-working people–"

"Rich people."

"–honest people out of their earnings, like a filthy, common thief. Every woman in here gives themselves over to something higher."

"Every woman?" Marius threw back his head and laughed. "Every woman!" And then his voice was a vicious hiss that left no space for argument. "Not *every* woman. Not the spoiled wife of a money-hungry, hate-filled bastard, not when she had this... priest's hole to duck her head back into any time she couldn't buy herself off with another necklace." He dug into his pockets, emerged with the handful of jewellery he had lifted from his father's house. "There you go. Now you can have both."

She took them from him, eyed them a moment, then whipped her arm outwards and flung them over the edge into the ocean. Marius stared at her.

"Do you know what I had to do to get those for you?"

She laughed. "Oh, so like your father."

"Don't act like you know me."

She pointed to where the baubles had arced out over the water. "You know nothing about *me*."

"I know enough."

"Oh? You know how I met your father?"

"Do I care?"

"My papa was a merchant."

"So, what? You saw a younger version of Daddy?"

"No, it wasn't that." She raised a hand to her hair, tried unsuccessfully to smooth it out. "When I was little, he taught me how to play Kingdom. Penny hands, just for fun, he said. I was terrible at it, always was. We used to joke about how bad I was, how I couldn't see the runs, couldn't pick the balance of play. It was our together time, our daddy-daughter hobby whenever he got a few moments away from the pressure of his life. By the time I was sixteen I was down eighteen thousand riner."

"In pennies!"

She smiled. "I was very bad. Anyway, one day, just after my sixteenth birthday, Papa came home and told me he owed another merchant twenty thousand riner, and if he didn't pay it by the end of the week he'd be ruined."

"Father."

"Your father, yes. So he gave me a case with two thousand riner inside, told me I was married, and that my debt to him was discharged."

"But... how could you marry him?"

She paused for a very long time, until Marius almost believed he had only thought the question and had forgotten to voice it aloud. Then: "He is my husband. I said the words. I held the cord and stood upon the joined rock. Look around you." She pointed back up the corridor, towards the rooms inside the cliff. "I *believe*, Marius. Marriage is a sanctified act in the eyes of God. How can I disobey his rules?"

"How can you...?" Marius fell away from her. He looked into her eyes, saw serenity in her face and a complete disregard for his opinion of her. He saw the complete breaking of whatever bond they had. It had never been about family, or Ygram, or all the ways they had sought to hurt each other. Marius looked into his mother's eyes, and saw God.

"You've got another twenty years of life if you're lucky," he said. "If you ever want to see your god after you die you'll give me everything I ask for. Or you can sit here in your stinking pit and wait for Scorbus to climb down and tell you that this is all you'll ever have." He turned his back on her and stalked back through the archway into the corridor. "And I say I want to see your ossuary, now!"

The others were waiting in the main hallway, half of Brys' tubmen lined up behind them with double-loads of the wooden casks slung over their shoulders. Marius glanced at them as he entered.

"Ready to go?"

"All loaded up." Brys tilted her head at her crew. "Full of salvation for the masses."

"Good. Where's Arnobew?"

The crew glanced at each other, startled by the fierceness of his reaction. "He's down with the troops, drilling them in... well, something he's learned from somewhere, anyway."

"Get him, now."

"Yes." Drenthe moved to obey, thought better of it, and sketched a short bow. "Your Majesty." He left, and Marius stared at the door for long seconds after he shut it behind him.

"He's right, you know." Keth was peering at him as if suddenly she didn't recognise the man she had lain beside for three years. "You've accepted it, haven't you?"

He glowered at her. She didn't get to be right. Not this time, not now. "No," he said. "But it seems like everyone else has." They stared at each other until eventually she dropped her eyes and turned away from him, wrapping her arms around herself as she did so. Halla spared him a glare and moved over to Keth. His mother drew her away from the group, whispering with her in low, murmuring tones. Marius ignored them, keeping his attention on the door until Drenthe returned, Arnobew in his wake.

"Marius!" the cardboard warrior boomed. Arnobew barrelled into the room and enveloped him in a hug that would have expelled the air from his lungs in an instant, if there have been any in them. Marius bore it for a few seconds, then extricated himself. "Is this not a turn-up, lad? They've killed the breath right out of me, and given me an army to boot!"

"So you're happy with it, are you?" Marius looked the bigger man up and down.

"Happy? My boy, I'm exuberantly ecstatic!"

"Yes." Marius leaned in close and smiled up at him. "Mad Warbone."

"Yes, my leader? Hey," Arnobew glanced at Drenthe, then back at Marius, "this decomposing fellow tells me you're the King of things and we're all your subjects now."

"He might be right."

"Capital!" Arnobew dealt him a clap on the arm that staggered the younger man. "Couldn't be happier for you. So." He came to ragged attention and threw an old fashioned Scorban soldier's salute from his chest to the space an inch above his shoulder. "Yes, Your Majesteh!"

"Mad Warbone." Marius smiled, and it was a nasty little thing indeed. "How would you like to command a *real* army?"

TWENTY-FOUR

They marched up the corridor towards the ossuary in regal procession: Marius ahead, Drenthe at his side, Gerd and Arnobew striding behind. Halla and Keth stalked in worried concert at the rear, with only Brys and the tubmen behind them. They stopped a dozen paces from the heavy wooden doors that marked the ossuary entrance. Marius beckoned Gerd forward.

"A thousand years of bones," he said, gesturing to the door. "Separated, counted, categorised, and laid out in perfect order, just waiting for someone to come along and put them all back together."

"Like a Bone Cathedral in reverse."

"Exactly."

Halla scurried forward and placed herself between Marius and the bones within.

"For the last time," she said, arms outstretched as if to block passage. "This is a sacred space. These sisters have earned their rest. Let them be."

"Oh, I have no intention of going in and disturbing them." Marius replied. Halla sagged in sudden relief, and he turned to Gerd once more. "Do you hear it?"

"I do."

Drenthe did too, for he stepped up and stood next to Marius. "Helles?"

"No 'Your Majesty', Drenthe?"

"What is it, Helles?"

Marius smirked. "Wait."

Soon it became apparent to them all. From behind the door came a sound like a billion chittering insects, as if thousands upon thousands of bones were being moved.

"What is it?"

Marius could feel the edges of his grin pulling upwards into madness. "Bones." He laughed, then stopped as he heard how many edges it contained. Because the bones were coming. Clicking, clacking, twisting, pushing, rotating, snapping, dragging, until they came together in a vast, rolling tumult that echoed off the walls and drew the living members of the entourage towards the back of the group in fear, while the dead members moved forward in unconscious sympathy with the deluge of sound.

"You hear it?" Marius shouted. "You hear?"

And they did.

Voices. Hundreds upon hundreds of voices, drawn out of skulls that had been silent too long. Questioning, demanding to know why they had been abandoned for so long, why they had been torn apart and left to find themselves in the dark. Marius planted himself before the door and projected his voice across the uproar.

"Sisters of Tylytene. Warriors. Assassins. Spreaders of lies. I am your King, and I demand your servitude!"

The tubmen fell to one knee. Drenthe joined them, Gerd and Arnobew made to do the same, and were stopped by Marius' glare.

"Not you two."

They stayed upright and faced the door. The noise was growing: feet stomping, voices crying out in anger, bony hands crashing into equally bony breasts. Keth was crying his name. Brys backed against the wall, drew her cutlasses and held them out before her. He ignored them, ignored Halla's cries of "No, no, no," and her babbled prayers to a god in whom only she believed. The invisible feet came together in a single crashing step. Something heavy and angry hit the door: once, twice, a third time. Marius tilted his head.

"Come on, then," he projected quietly.

The door crashed back on his hinges. Marius and his companions stared through it into a hundred feet of blackened catacomb. There, skeletal arms linked, and bodies pushed forward with red hate radiating out from them in waves that staggered even the living members of Marius' entourage. In ranks six wide, a millennia of Tylytene's most venerated nuns faced the world and let out a single, silent roar.

"Mad Warbone," Marius said, laughing. "Meet your army."

They weren't all warriors, of course. The nunnery had been many things throughout its history, and internment had followed the practices of the time. There were plenty of celebrated healers, and whores, and the occasional holy woman. But they were all united by one thing: anger, raging anger at the dissolution of their beings – skulls in this alcove, shoulder blades in another, finger and knucklebones in vast piles in yet more alcoves. Every individual component of their bodies had been bleached and venerated and cast into separate rooms along the sprawling catacombs to lie in isolation, without the will to find themselves again until Marius had called them into action. Now he stood at their head and stared them down: a small man in a female holy space; an intruder in their halls, their minds, and their beliefs, armed only with a sense of purpose that found red reflections in their souls. He glared across their ranks, and spoke clearly to them all.

"I am your King, and you will kneel to me."

A thousand skulls tilted. The first few ranks saw the tubmen, saw Gerd and Arnobew, saw Marius. Slowly, like old trees in the wind, they bent, until a thousand skeletons paid him obeisance. Marius nodded, and turned away.

"Bring the others up from the halls," he told his companions. "It's time we went to war."

They reassembled in the dinner hall, the dead watching the living eat warm gruel; except for Granny, who tucked away three bowls before the others had finished tearing their bread apart, and was only prevented from going back for fourths by the fact that the pot was empty. Once they were all seated, Marius took his place at the head of the table and ran his eyes over them all.

"It's still not enough," he said. The others kept silent. Arnobew made as if to say something, then thought better of it. Marius tapped his front teeth with a finger, smiled to himself, and looked at Gerd. "I know where to get more, though."

Gerd thought about if for several moments. "No."

"Yes."

The swineherd glanced at Keth. "Are you sure about this?"

Marius saw the look, decided to ignore it in the interests of cowardice. "We need bodies," he said. "Armed, organised, and committed to the fight. There are three thousand there, in exactly the shape we want them. We just need to persuade them to fight for our side."

"Persuade *her*, you mean."

"Her who?" Keth leaned forward, frowning. Granny moaned.

"Och, no," she said. "Not the bloody whore."

"Marius?"

Marius aimed a thought of pure poison at Granny, received a mental image of two raised fingers in return. He turned to Keth. "Mistress Fellipan, from Mish. She's recruited three thousand bodies to Scorbus' cause, but we persuaded her to hold them at Cistrion, at least for a while."

"Persuaded."

"Yes." Marius kept his face as still as he dared. "We persuaded."

"I see."

Granny snorted, then glared at Gerd and reached down to rub at her shin. Gerd smiled a bland little smile at Marius and received a mental thank you. Marius turned to him.

"Go to her through the tunnels. Explain everything, and request her assistance."

"Everything?"

Marius risked a quick glance at Keth. As still as his face had been, hers was a statue. "Everything," he said. "Emphasise the bit about me being the real King."

"Just what we need," Granny muttered. "A power-hungry whore and her giant..." Her hands formed two cups. "Distractions."

"Take Granny if you like," Marius told him. "No need to bring her back."

Gerd stood. "That's all right," he said with a smile. "I'll make do without her."

Marius turned his attention to his remaining companions. "Brys, off to the north, as we discussed. Drenthe, to V'Ellos. Get back with those weapons, get them downstairs with the V'Ellosians. Drill them hard. I want them turning as a unit, moving as one body, no matter where I send them. They're going to be our central core, so I want arm-length discipline at all times."

They nodded in unison.

"Arnobew–"

"Warbone, sah!"

He sighed. "Warbone."

"Sah!"

"Your nuns…"

"Fine ladies, sah! Best in the land, sah! Worth a fighting unit to a man… I mean, lady, sah!"

"I'm sure they are." Marius waggled a finger in his ear, as if that might help to clear the echoes out of it. "They'll need to be. They're going to be our shock troops."

"Yes, sah!" Arnobew leaped to his feet. "Kill 'em all and let the god of your choice sort 'em out, sah!"

"No." Marius shook his head. "No on two counts. We're not fighting for any god, and we won't be setting them up to kill."

"Oh," Arnobew looked crestfallen. "The girls won't like that, lad. I believe they're rather in the mood to kill people."

"They'll have to reconcile themselves to my plan instead."

"And what would that be, begging your pardon?"

"Salvation, Warbone." He spread his hands wide, like a carnival barker. "We're going to spread some salvation."

"Oh," Arnobew looked doubtful. "I don't think the nuns will be too happy about that, either."

Keth and Granny sat stony-faced at the end. Marius hooked a thumb at the old woman.

"I want as many indulgences as the nuns can crank

out. Fill the tubs, find more if you need them, don't stop until I tell you."

"Why me? Why not your Mummy?"

"Because I want a vicious unlikeable old crone in charge. Is that okay by you?"

She shrugged. "Fair enough."

"Good. Keth."

In a room full of dead people, Keth appeared the least lively, the most given-in to a withdrawal of the soul. She had not moved since sitting, and now stared at Marius through flat eyes. He felt something twist inside him, and spoke more gently to her than he had since arriving at the nunnery.

"I want you to go with Gerd–"

Her stare intensified. "You want me to meet this woman you... persuaded."

Marius shook his head and leaned forward to let her gaze more fully capture him.

"After you were taken we went to the village. It was destroyed, Keth. Smashed to the ground, everyone gone. I thought Drenthe was responsible, but I don't think so now. I think..." He frowned. "I'm not sure. Just that I want them found, and Fellipan was in the next town, killing recruits for her army." Keth pursed her lips; and Marius tried to read the emotions flashing across her face, but failed. "Keth, you know these people. Even if she's lying, if they're there, you can find them. Please."

She blew her cheeks out, pushed herself back from the table in a sudden spasm of movement. "And if they're not there?"

Marius matched her stare. "Then they're with Scorbus. And I'll have another job for you when we reach him."

"You're that confident I'll still be here."

He blinked. "Well... yes."

She raised a single eyebrow and took her place next to Gerd.

"You'd better be in a talkative mood," she said to the young swineherd. He looked helplessly towards Marius, and he nodded in resigned acceptance.

"Get going, all of you," he said. "I want everyone back here within a fortnight."

TWENTY-FIVE

In the end, it took three weeks. Brys returned from the north with four dozen of the nastiest corpses she could find, and a stream of apologies for not being able to find more. Marius took one look at those she had assembled and dismissed her regret out of hand. He knew at least ten of the dead she brought him, and if the others were equivalent he would rather she hadn't collected them all up in one place at all. He put them to work in one of the lower halls, practising those skills of thuggery and murder that had grown rusty during years at the bottom of waterways, and tried to keep them separated from the rest of the nunnery. Dead and waterlogged they might be, but a building full of women in nun's outfits was more temptation than they needed. For a moment he considered letting them see Arnobew's warriors, then decided against it. They might consider it a challenge; and Arnobew, having worked his charges for a week without need for sleep, might just welcome it. He billeted them as far apart as possible, and set Brys to keep them busy.

She only had to throw one from the balcony before they started doing what they were told. Marius was impressed: he'd banked on at least three.

Gerd and Keth arrived the following morning. Marius met them in the dining hall.

"So?" he said as they entered. Gerd sat down heavily on the bench. Keth ignored them both, went straight to the adjoining kitchens and began to rattle around. Marius stared at Gerd. The younger man kept his gaze averted until Keth returned with a platter full of fruit and a pitcher of water. She thudded down at the opposite end of the table and began to stuff herself, unreadable eyes fixed upon Marius. He waited patiently, matching her stare, while projecting through Gerd's feeble attempt to block him.

"You told her."

The skin at the corner of Gerd's eyes tightened slightly but he made no move to acknowledge Marius' statement. Marius tried again, and again received nothing. Finally, as Keth was swallowing the last of the water in the pitcher, Gerd answered.

"No," he said, his voice as quiet inside Marius' mind as his had been strident. "I didn't have to. She'd already worked it out, not that it was exactly difficult, and it was pretty fucking obvious once they actually met. Thank you so much for putting me in between them."

"And? Did she agree to come?"

"She's outside. Says she wants to talk to you before she commits to 'our little venture'."

Marius snorted. "She's travelled all this way. She's already committed."

"Do you think so?"

Marius decided the higher path involved ignoring Gerd's pathetic sarcasm. He was the bigger man. He would focus on the greater import of the conversation, rather than dragging himself into a tit-for-tat game of snarky comments which would get them nowhere. Marius wouldn't recognise the higher path if a landslide brought it crashing down on his head. He sent Gerd an image that made the younger man choke as if he'd tried to swallow a hedgehog whole, and looked down the table at Keth.

"How did you go?" he asked quietly.

Keth took great care to finish the last piece of fruit before she answered. "I had a lovely time, thank you for asking," she replied, in the sort of sweet voice men throughout history have recognised as the prelude to sleeping in separate rooms. "We saw some tunnels, and an old monastery, and then I got to meet a freakish dead whore with delusions of grandeur."

Marius managed something partway between a wince and a smile. "You didn't get on, then?" he asked, wishing giant metal nails would pin his stupid tongue to his cheek with each word. Keth then shot him a look that suggested she'd like to pin his tongue somewhere far lower than his face.

"No, we did not get on. She is a supercilious, pandering, obscene, murderous, genocidal, social-climbing, filthy slag of the lowest order. And *I* am your lover."

Somewhere, Marius could hear alarms so shrill and urgent that the nuns outside should have been screaming and throwing themselves from the nearest window into the sea below. The alarms were inside his head. Which did nothing to stop *him* wanting to jump from the nearest window. There couldn't be a path worse than the one he was one right now, so he changed it.

"Did you find them? The villagers?"

Keth deflated, her pent-up anger disappearing as quickly as he said the words. "No," she admitted. "They weren't there."

"Fuck." Marius rubbed his face. "They're with Scorbus, then. Damn it!" He slammed a fist onto the table, then blinked as it drove straight through the wood, knocking a fist-sized chunk to the floor. Gerd looked at him askance.

"That's okay, though, isn't it?" he asked. "It means we know where they are. We can find them when we get there."

Marius stared at him for long seconds. "Yes, of course that's what it means," he said. He glanced at Keth, saw understanding in her eyes. Once they were on the battlefield there would be no chance to separate the villagers from the melee. Anyone not with them already would be the enemy. Marius ran a hand through his hair.

"Thank you both," he said. "Keth, I'm sure you must be dying for a bath and a change of dress. Why don't you tell my mother to get you both. Gerd..." he waved his hands in uncertain circles, "just... go somewhere for a while, okay?"

Keth raised an eyebrow. Gerd muttered a surly "Good to see you again, too". But they both stood and made their way through the door. They had hardly left when it swung open once again, and the strained bodice of Mistress Fellipan preceded herself into the room.

"Monastery of Cistrion," she purred, sashaying across the floor and pouring herself into a chair opposite Marius. "You *are* naughty."

"I needed you out of the way." Marius was not looking. He was not. Fellipan leaned forward, and he was most definitely not looking, no sir.

"And now you need me. *In* the way."

"You met my girlfriend." Good. This was safe ground. This was good.

"She seems lovely. We could get on... famously."

"Look." Marius sat back, tapped the table's edge with his fingertips. "Just drop the temptress act, okay? I'm not interested."

"I have a tub of goose grease and two hands that bet otherwise."

"Stop it. Now."

She sat back, eyed him speculatively. "So, it's business then. Actual business business, not…" She arched an exquisite eyebrow, "pleasure business."

"I mean it."

"I have goose grease and two feet that bet you don't."

"I'm not… Feet?"

She smiled. "Hands aren't the only things that grip." Several angels on Marius' shoulders turned up their toes and died. "I don't share *everything* on first dates."

"That's…" He stared into space for several seconds. "That's as may be. But I still mean it."

She sighed. "Okay, so we'll behave this time. Still," she looked around them, "a nunnery. It's been a while." Suddenly she was nothing but serious, pinning Marius with a stare that had nothing of the sex mistress in it. "So why am I here?"

"Because you've tied your flag to the wrong King."

"Oh, honey. I've tied my…" She stopped as Marius held up a finger. "Sorry, force of habit. Now, how about you explain to me why I'm doing such a thing?"

So Marius leaned back in his chair and recounted to her everything he had learned about Scorbus, and the crown of Scorby, and of his own ascension to the throne of the underworld. Fellipan listened with her bone-white face displaying no emotion, until he stopped, laid his hands on the table, and waited for her to respond. She stared at him for long seconds. Her face and the tilt of her body betrayed nothing: the perfect politician, weighing up all angles in inscrutable silence. Finally she nodded, and met his gaze.

"So what do you want from me?"

"Your loyalty. And the three thousand bodies you've been collecting for Scorbus."

She smiled. "They're in the lower hall. Your cute young friend took them down there for me as soon as we arrived. They're already drilling."

Marius goggled. "Then what the hell was all this about?"

"I just wanted to see you, darling. And let you know about the feet thing."

She rose from the chair in one liquid motion and left him staring at the perfect white flesh of her back as she exited. Marius counted to a thousand, very slowly, before he dared stand and follow her.

Then there was nothing left to do but to bring his troops together and lead them up through the carved corridors of the nunnery to the ossuary. The nuns disappeared into doorways as they stomped past: seven thousand dead souls of the most ragged type, in a procession that took more than an hour to wend its way to the top floor. Marius called a halt at the ossuary doors. They were closed, and a single figure in white stood before them.

"Mother."

"Marius." She raised her chin, one small woman in a final act of defiance before an entire army. "Is this how you plan to leave?"

Marius looked about him. "Am I missing someone?"

"You know what I mean."

He shook his head. "What would you like me to say? That I'll be careful? That I'll come back when this is all over? That I love you and wish none of this had ever happened?"

For a moment she looked pierced by his words, but she recovered her composure just as quickly.

"I don't need you to say anything," she said. "I think you've *said* quite enough. But you are setting off to start a war from here, *here* of all places. And you take people whose eternal rest you interrupted with no thought for the consequence to their souls. I want to know that you understand what you are doing to them, Marius. I want to know that you understand what you are taking from them."

Marius stared at her in disbelief. "And you still maintain this charade," he said in wonder. "You still..." He turned to Keth. She stood beside him. Somehow Alno had reappeared from the depths of the nunnery, and now lay asleep in her arms. "We're travelling underground the whole way," he said to her.

"I know."

"A battlefield is no place for a cat." Even a bastard cat like that one.

Her glance went from him, to Alno, to his mother, and back. He held her stare.

"I know what I'm asking," he whispered. "I know what it means."

She passed over the cat silently.

"Thank you." He turned back to his mother. "Here," he said, and gave the cat to her. Alno hissed lazily and swatted at him with as much lethargy as he could manage, leaving him a final, farewell line of white on his forearm. "You want to care about someone's soul, waste it on something living." She took Alno in her arms, and looked past Marius to Keth.

"Are you sure?"

Keth glanced at her lover. "I hate it so much, but he's right," she said. "I will come back, to see him. And you."

Halla smiled a tight, sad smile. "Thank you. And please, look after him." Her eyes lit on Marius for a moment.

"No," Keth replied. "Not anymore." And she turned away. Halla stepped aside, and gestured towards the doors.

"Be on your way."

TWENTY-SIX

An army marched to war. Or rather, it lurched, shuffled, and elbowed about as it tried to push past itself into the cramped confines of an underground corridor to war. Marius strode in front, with Gerd at his side. Behind him, Fellipan and Keth jockeyed side-by-side on twin palanquins dredged up from gods knew where in the nunnery, each refusing to look at the other as their dead mounts tried vainly to fit the into the corridor without jostling each other. Behind them came Fellipan's army: the bedraggled jetsam of Mish, gathered up and forced towards Scorbus, now repatriated under the flag of another king. Then Arnobew, leading his nuns like a cardboard colossus, voice echoing down the tunnel as he sang the dirtiest marching songs he could remember. Any potential objections were quelled, if not by the sight of the skeletons who ringed him with drawn weapons and menace in their every movement, but by the sound, equally raucous, of Granny's laughter as she joined in and urged him on to ever more obscene heights. The nuns kept close to him, finding excuses to run a skeletal finger across his shoulders or bounce a bony hip bone against his, and every now and again the singing would cease as he disappeared from the ranks of marchers with one or more of his loving disciples. Nothing Marius could imagine happening could be anything other than extraordinarily awkward, and just simply damned painful. Yet somehow, the sound of Granny's laughter was still worse. The rest of the army obviously shared his thoughts. To a man they decided early, silently and in unison, to pretend none of it was happening.

And last, in the back, keeping to the shadows: Brys, her tubmen, and the scum. And *nobody* looked at them. Nobody but Marius, who took great pleasure in presenting each and every one of his followers with a new uniform, brought fresh from V'Ellos by a scowling Drenthe: the crest of the family don Hellespont, clean and white on every murderous unbreathing breast under his command. His army. His followers. Marching to war under his banner. Marius occasionally wished he wasn't a small, petty man. But not while he watched Drenthe walk up and down the serried ranks, po-facedly handing out the clothes to be wrapped around the putrid and tattered dead.

Marius marched them for three days, following winding tunnels dug deep through the earth, with only his eyesight and sense of dead reckoning to guide him. He had walked almost every inch of Scorby above ground, whether it was through towns that welcomed or hounded him; ditches that sheltered him; mountain ranges that offered him a thousand escape routes. He could close his eyes and map out a route to anywhere in the kingdom, avoiding danger as if he possessed the senses of a woodland creature. Now he ignored his surroundings and let twenty years of travel guide him. Where tunnels did not exist he called forth minions to make them, watching the dirt disappear backwards along the army's serpentine trail to be deposited, grain by grain, onto the floor across more than a dozen miles, trampled into rock-smoothness by ten thousand tramping feet.

They progressed in this fashion across nearly a hundred miles: a vast caravanserai of the dead travelling towards Scorby City in a straight line with no need to detour around natural formations. At what might have passed for the morning of the fourth day, Drenthe made his way forward and pulled Marius aside.

"Helles–"

"Your Majesty. Say 'Your Majesty'."

"Your Majesty."

"Yes, Drenthe?" Marius' voice was as sweet as sunshine. "May I help you?"

He hid his pleasure as Drenthe performed a slow burn, then refocussed.

"Your Majesty," he said with perfect control. "I need to recommend a diversion in our current course."

"Do you?"

"I do."

Behind him Marius could feel the army grow restless. They had become used to the march, to the rhythm of movement towards the enemy. They were eager to advance, chafing at this unscheduled interruption. Marius focussed on the corpse before him. "And why is that?"

Drenthe pointed to the tunnel. "A mile down there we will come to a cross tunnel. If we travel east we move away from our destination; west and we run towards the Bight of Sharks. I assume we do not wish to break through into that particular body of water, Your Majesty?"

Marius considered for a moment, turning his head to follow the invisible map of the land above him. Drenthe was right, but there was something more, something that nagged at Marius but which he couldn't quite nail down.

"We've been following this tunnel for a while, Drenthe. The bight has been to our left for miles, and I have no intention of moving farther from our quarry than necessary."

"I realise that, Majesty. However–"

"However?"

Drenthe paused, looked down for a moment, then stepped closer. "Look, Helles," he murmured. "I understand that you don't like me, and I understand that you don't want to examine why I had to manipulate you into this. But at least do me the favour of allowing that I might have the best interests of my fellow dead at heart, and that getting you to this battle in the best shape to conduct it *is* in their interest, will you?"

They matched gazes for long moments, until Marius, unable to read anything from the other man's ravaged features, nodded slowly.

"Okay," he said. "So explain to me why we don't just plough straight through and make a passageway of our own, why don't you?"

Drenthe glanced down the tunnel, then seemed to come to a decision.

"There's nothing to be gained from it," he replied. "If we go east for twenty miles we cross a series of corridors that will bring us to the battlefield from a different direction, without the need to work our troops–"

"Our troops?"

"*Your* troops, Hel... Your Majesty." He paused, then continued: "Without the need to work them any harder than we need to."

Marius considered the proposal. It made sense, when presented in that way. Even so, something in Drenthe's attachment to the east chimed wrong. He shook his head.

"Nice try," he said. "But I'm going to stick with my original plan."

"What's that?"

Marius looked him in his ruined eye. "Listen to what Drenthe says and then ignore it." He turned away and signalled to the waiting troops. "Straight ahead," he projected. "Clear me a path."

The army swung into action, relieved to be once more on the move. They covered the remaining mile of tunnel in less than five minutes and barely paused before the first rank of troops began to dig their hands into the earth and claw huge handfuls of it away. They swung their limbs like a row of bone scythes, carving out an indentation that grew to more than a man's height, wide enough for the troops to enter without breaking stride. The army inched forward, those in front passing the excised earth behind. Dribbles of dirt fell with each movement, and were pounded into the floor by the passage of thousands of pairs of feet. Those at the rear were left with little more than a handful, and that was sprinkled back behind them, adding almost nothing to the space. The tunnel floor remained rock hard. Only the tiniest dusting of soil marked their passage as they pushed their way through the unresisting underworld. Marius stared at Drenthe as the first rows began to work. The soldier matched him for several seconds, then smiled and sketched a short bow. Marius turned away from him and followed his soldiers into the breach.

They had proceeded perhaps another mile when the front row suddenly halted. Gerd was with them, and Marius felt his urgent call. He pushed through tightly-packed bodies until he was able to stand shoulder to shoulder with his young friend.

"What is it? Why have we stopped?"

Gerd pointed to the wall. Marius could make out a small break in the flat plane of earth, the slightest variation in the dull grey of the underworld. He sidled in-between two of the diggers, and poked at the wall. His finger met no resistance.

"It's a hole."

"I know. I figured that one out myself."

"Then why call me? It's a cross tunnel."

Gerd leaned forward, and whispered in Marius ear.

"I thought Drenthe said there wasn't anything for miles."

Marius shook his head. "No, he said twenty miles east." He poked again in disgust, widening the hole by a finger length. "Typical of him. Send us that far out of our way to come back a hundred steps later." He kicked the wall, then spent half a minute struggling to drag his foot out of the tiny landslide it caused. "Break us through, then we'll call our friend Drenthe forward and let him lead us for a while where we can watch him."

"Right you are." Gerd tapped the nearest soldier on the shoulder, and as one they smashed through the few remaining inches of earth.

And emerged into the chamber.

TWENTY-SEVEN

The chamber was enormous. Two hundred feet in diameter, roughly circular, with a ceiling that arched thirty feet above them, every surface as smooth as if pounded into place by a multitude of stone hammers, it dwarfed the ragged army that now flowed into the space like an invading virus. A massive stone block had been placed in the exact centre, carved round with geometric designs Marius had not seen since a visit to the Museum of Borgho when he was a child. He stared at it in astonishment.

"What is it?" Gerd was at his shoulder, looking from Marius to the stone and back.

"Gelders."

"What?"

Marius stalked forward and ran his hands across the carvings. "That's what the museum called them, anyway. They're a lost tribe. There are almost no artefacts left, just a couple of funerary mounds and a bunch of cromlechs scattered around some of the more untouched corners of the plains. There's some evidence that they engaged in human sacrifice, from memory. Pots with burned bones inside, some skeletons with cut marks around the hips and upper thighs, as if..."

"They'd been gelded."

"Right."

Gerd frowned. "So why is this here?"

"I don't know." Marius glanced at the ceiling. "We're not near any sites, as far as I can tell."

"No, I mean, why is it *here*?" Gerd gestured around them. "Underground. With us."

Marius turned in a circle. Members of his army were wandering the space to stare in wonder. He tilted his head and frowned momentarily. His followers were beginning to group together, exclaiming while they gestured at points around the circumference of the chamber. He strode towards the nearest one, elbowed his way through the milling crowd, and pulled up short as he saw what they were staring at. Recessed into the dirt wall, with only one face pointing out from the dirt, was a stone column. It reared above him, three feet across and twenty feet tall, its visible face covered in the same geometric carvings as the sacrificial stone in the chamber's centre..

"Oh, good gods."

"What is it?"

"A stone." Marius stared up at it, slow realisation creeping upon him. "It's a standing stone. Dug into the wall."

There was a hollow in the stone at eye height. Sharp lines radiated outwards to the edges left and right of it, with two more running downwards each corner of the base. Marius stared at it, his finger tracing the lines.

"There's something wrong with this."

"It's a body."

"What?"

"A skeleton. Look." Gerd pushed past and ran his index finger along several of the branching lines. "Arms, spine, legs. These would be ribs. Fingers and feet there and there. It's highly stylised, but…" He shrugged. "The hollow would be the skull."

"No." Marius shook his head. "You're right, but no." He looked at his young friend. "The hollow isn't the skull. It *holds* the skull."

"There's another one here!" Fellipan had wandered further down the wall. Now she called Marius over.

"And here." Keth, further on again. Marius ran from stone to stone, his followers gathering behind him as he went. He described a full circle, came back to the first standing stone with his entire army at his heels.

"A cromlech," he said in wonder. "Underground." He stalked back to the centre of the circle and jumped up onto the stone: not fallen, he realised, but laid lengthwise, like a tablet, or…

"A sacrificial stone." He gazed down at it, then turned and took in the immense structure around him. "A dozen pillars. Figures carved… Guardians? Overlooking… defending? What?"

"I don't like it." Granny was at his feet, looking around pensively. "Not one little bit."

"Neither do I." Marius sat down cross-legged and leaned towards her. "Why is that?"

"There's something wrong here. Something ain't right."

"No, it's not." He glanced beneath his feet, tilted his head. "This stone."

"What about it?"

He ran his hand across the surface, cupped the edge in his fingers. "It's smooth."

"Yes?"

"Smooth, as in not weathered. As in new." He jumped down, bent close to the carvings. "These designs. Look at them."

Granny leaned in. Marius was aware of another presence: Fellipan, pushing past him to run gloved fingers along the clean-cut lines.

"No degradation," she said quietly. "They're sharp. Marius, this carving…"

"Wasn't done a thousand years ago."

She shook her head. Marius straightened. "Regroup," he said softly. "Let's get out of here."

The army was shuffling together, forming back into those platoons in which they had started their journey. Keth was already in her litter and, Marius noted, waving to Fellipan to join her. Those troops at the rear were pushing up against those in front as they struggled to see what was going on ahead. Arnobew was striding up and down the lines, bellowing at his troops, shoving them into place. Marius jumped back up onto the stone.

"Drenthe," he shouted. "Find us a passage out of here."

He waited. There was no response. He looked out across the heads of his troops. "Drenthe!"

"I don't see him." Gerd was walking round the stone, staring into as many corners as he could.

"What the hell is he playing at? Drenthe!" Marius projected with as much will as he could muster. He saw those about him reach for their heads, as if staggered by the sudden volume. "Gerd, find him."

Gerd had taken no more than three steps when the dark at the far end of the chamber opened up and the Gelders fell upon them.

They came screaming into the chamber, perhaps five hundred in total: white-fleshed gargoyles with hunched backs and tattered hair, whirling thighbones and maces made from skulls and tree roots. Marius lost several precious seconds to shock, and before he could regather himself they were in amongst the vanguard of his troops. The first line went down under the weight of the attackers. Marius' mind was suddenly awash with screams that broke off jaggedly as bone met bone and crushed the semblance of life into dust. The sound snapped him back into awareness. Before he knew it he had drawn his father's sword and was swinging it around his head like a torch.

"Into them!"

He dove from the altar and smashed an attacker across the bridge of their nose with his first stroke. The Gelder staggered. Marius raised his sword and drove the pommel against his victim's face, again and again, until the flesh split and fell away, and the Gelder stumbled to fall against one of his compatriots. Marius spun. His own troops had closed with the enemy, and organised thought had immediately disappeared. It was nothing more than a melee now, vicious hand-to-hand fighting where only the desire to kill counted: no rules, no fanfare, just brutal, eye-gouging, biting, throat-punching street combat. Marius screamed, an ululation of animal rage. He drove the hilt of his sword into the eye of another enemy, twisting so the quillon plunged point first into the socket and snapped the orbital ridge as he pulled back. A Gelder bone struck him on the shoulder. He stumbled forward and fell to one knee. There was a crunch, and he looked up to see Arnobew, a femur in one hand, throwing away the ragged body of the Gelder who had attacked him.

"Get up, boy!" he shouted, connecting with another assailant as Marius stared at the fallen Gelder for a short moment.

"Alive," he said, then, louder. "They're alive!"

"Not for long!" Arnobew strode past him, bone connecting with another face and crushing it. Marius looked from side to side as he rose. Gelders were falling, their disorganised attacks slowly but surely beaten back by the well-drilled soldiers of Marius' army. The nuns and tubmen were drawing up into lines, allowing Brys' bastards to slip past the end as the elders threw themselves forwards, and wreak havoc and general bastardry upon those at the rear. Marius watched the dead Gelder get back up and slip back towards the entrance at the far end of the chamber, where they disappeared into the corridor beyond. A solitary figure was standing at the entrance, ushering them on as they lurched their broken and lifeless bodies past him.

"Drenthe!"

The soldier turned towards Marius. For a moment, Marius could see the mirth that rocked his shoulders. Then a cry of victory went up around him as the last few Gelders broke and ran back towards the corridor. Marius watched as they reached Drenthe, saw him slip a knife from his belt and slide it into the belly of each remaining attacker as they came to him. Then they ran on. The cheers died out as Marius' army slowly focussed on what he was watching. He leaped from the altar and ran towards Drenthe. His nemesis raised a hand in a mocking salute, then stepped back into the dark.

"After him!"

A dozen nuns broke ranks and flashed past. They disappeared into the corridor in an instant. The army waited. If they'd had any breath to hold, they would have done so. As it was, Marius was aware of Keth's slightness of breath: she alone, of three thousand bodies pressed into the space, made enough noise to be noticed.

Presently the nuns returned, walking past Marius in silence to take their place behind Arnobew. Marius heard him mutter to them at the base of his mind, warm words of support and pride. Then he approached Marius and sketched a sort of bow.

"They lost him, I'm afraid."

Marius nodded, deep in thought.

"Don't be blaming them, lad. They're as good as I could ask for. Mighty gals, each and every one of them. Don't be reflecting on it as a failure–"

"What?" Marius snapped out of his reverie. "Oh, no. No, not at all." He shook himself to full attention. "No, Warbone. You tell your girls good job from me, difficult circumstances and all that. Not disappointed at all. Pats on back all round."

Arnobew smiled. "You're a lying shit. But thank you." He retreated to gee-up his girls and spread the word of their leader's gratitude. Marius fell back into thought. Presently he felt a warm hand on his shoulder. He looked up, into the concerned eyes of Keth.

"Marius?"

"Why, Keth?" he asked. "Why lead us here? Why abandon us? I can't work it out. First he's my enemy, then I find out he's not – he's no friend to me, that's certain, but some sort of ally, and then he's on my side but I'm doing what he wants…" He threw up his hands. "Then this…"

Keth took his hands, drew them back to his sides, held on to them. "It doesn't matter," she said. "It really doesn't."

"But–"

"You never followed him."

"I…" Marius stopped. "No, I did, but only because he made me, and then it was to hunt him."

"You see?" she smiled. "Nothing's changed. If you catch him, it's what you intended all along. Nobody ever swore allegiance to *him*. And everyone here..." She indicated the army around them: silent, patient, waiting to be instructed. "They all wear your colours."

Marius followed her gaze, saw the troops – his troops – looking at him in quiet expectation, and felt a sudden, savage glow of happiness. He squeezed her hands hard enough to make her wince, and laughed.

"Okay." He nodded, raised an arm, and brought it down to point at the tunnel ahead of them. "Come on then, you dead and rotting scum," he shouted. "Let's go and save the world!"

TWENTY-EIGHT

This time there were no diversions, no delays. They made straight for Scorby City at a flat run, carving their way through cross-tunnels and obstructions with barely a moment lost. Within two days Marius could sense the weight of Scorbus' army above them: the anticipation of a hundred thousand dead souls awaiting the command to attack ahead. Marius called a halt and left his troops behind to stalk forward into the dark spaces below the invaders: head tilted, eyes closed, like a bat hunting insects through the dark with no more than the invisible sounds of movement to guide him. He had gone less than a hundred steps when he became aware of a presence at his shoulder – Gerd, watching him with a puzzled expression.

"What are you doing?" he projected.

Marius waved his hands in a shushing motion, then leaned in so that their heads almost touched.

"Voices only," he whispered, pointing above them.

Gerd mouth an "Oh," then held his head in imitation of his friend. "So what *are* we doing?"

"Searching."

"For a sore neck?"

"For Scorbus."

"What are we going to do? Climb up and surprise him?"

Marius shuffled forward, Gerd in his wake. "Something like that." He stopped suddenly, stumbling when Gerd lurched into his back. "Here."

"Here? He's here?"

"Just about."

Gerd eyed the rough dirt above them. "How can you tell?"

Marius wiggled his fingers in a *ta-da* motion. "Magic."

"Oh, I see. Bullshit."

Marius scrunched his face up in mock anger. "No," he said. "Listen." He closed his eyes, and waved for Gerd to do the same. The young swineherd complied. "What do you hear?"

Gerd shrugged. "Granny telling dirty jokes to Keth. Fellipan deliberately ignoring them. Arnobew..." He shuddered. "Eww." Then his face cleared. "Ah."

"Got it?"

"Got it." Gerd pointed around them. "Nothing all around..."

"Foot soldiers, lined up and waiting. No noise because no movement."

"And here."

"Movement."

"Could be a draft animal?"

Marius shook his head. "Remember Fellipan's horses?" He drew a finger across the side of his neck.

"Dead as well."

"Right."

"So..."

"An invading king, expecting action, wondering why the tactics that worked so well before are having no effect now."

"Pacing, consulting with his generals, being busy."

"Making noise." He pointed back towards his own troops, waiting in the same silence as those above. Gerd nodded and they made their way to the vanguard, crammed into the narrow space. He backed them down the tunnel a hundred yards, then set them to work as quietly as possible, clearing a space large enough for troop movements back and forth from the rear to be accomplished without fuss. Gerd pulled him aside as he was supervising the work.

"Won't…" he pointed overhead, "hear?"

Marius shook his head. "He's not listening. And anybody who might hear is standing in line with all their fellow soldiers, commanded not to speak or lose position."

"You hope."

Marius tapped his temple. "I know."

"Oooh. Bullshit!" he mocked, and then let out a cry of "Ow!" as Marius flicked his ear.

"Stop that. It didn't hurt."

Gerd rubbed his ear. "It should."

Marius watched the clearing of earth. "There's nothing more I need to do here. Find Keth and Brys. We need to move on to the next phase."

Gerd raised an eyebrow but did as he was bid. When the four of them were gathered, Marius turned to Brys.

"Finish this off," he said. "Then wait for me to return. I want the troops in the order we discussed earlier, ready to go on my command."

Brys nodded. "How long?"

"As long as it takes."

"By your command." She grinned. "Lover."

Marius grimaced, and turned his attention to Gerd and Keth.

"Now, we–"

"Before we go any further." The look on Keth's face could have boiled water. Marius groaned inwardly.

"Yes, my love?"

"Am I?" She jerked a thumb behind her. "Tell me. Is there anyone in this army you haven't slept with behind my back?"

Marius had never been so innocent. Innocence itself would have looked like a leering, sheep-fondling pervert next to Marius. Marius could have out-innocented an entire orphanage of dewy-eyed moppets.

"Granny," he said. "Arnobew. The nuns, Gerd..."

"There was that one time–" Gerd started, snickering.

"Not helping."

"Well?" Keth wasn't playing any innocent games. Water was in the past – now her expression could boil metal. Marius suddenly knew that anything short of utter honesty would be seen through and held against him in disastrous fashion. He sighed.

"Brys is an old story," he said. "The pages closed on that one years ago."

"How many?"

"What?"

"How many years ago?"

Marius performed innumerable mental calculations in the time it took to blink. He'd first met Keth a dozen years ago, first lied to her a dozen years ago, first bedded her a decade ago, met Brys...even numbers should be divisible. No matter how he tried, he couldn't make them stack up.

"Eight years," he said. Keth nodded.

"And Madam Bignorks?"

Marius stared at her for seconds that stretched out as interminably as a violin lesson. His mind wheeled and flew, desperately seeking freedom. He wanted very much to speak, to comfort his lover, to wave words in front of her like a magician waving his hands, to hide all his falsehoods and prestidigitations and leave her cooing in delight at a bunch of flowers that appeared from nowhere. Instead, his voice, filthy betrayer that it was, spoke three words.

"About five weeks."

"I see." The light in her eyes retreated, to a spot where Marius knew he would never again find it. "Before or after I went missing?"

Before. Say before. As bad as that will be it's nothing compared to the other option. For all that's unholy, he screamed at his tongue, just this once say *before*.

"After."

Somewhere, deep in the back of his mind, his survival instinct climbed into its burrow and pulled the entrance down upon itself. "We thought you were dead," he continued, "We were trying to track Drenthe down…"

But Keth was no longer listening. She was inside her own mind, performing her own calculations, and all Marius could do was lapse into silence and wait until she finished. Gerd was no help, so absorbed in his study of the wall opposite he might be sitting for a doctorate in dirt. Slowly, Keth returned from wherever her inner thoughts had taken her. She looked at Gerd, and the tunnel around them, looked through the earth to the world of corpses stretching underneath the face of the planet: anywhere but at Marius.

"What is it you want me for?" she asked, eventually. Marius felt his shoulders loosen in relief.

"Scorbus is waiting for the city to sally forth. We need to get into the palace and stop them from sending out their troops. But I can't just walk in looking like–"

"No." She held up a hand, stopped him flat. "What do you want *me* for?"

He may have gibbered for a moment. He wasn't sure. But when he realised what she was saying, what she was asking, he found words he should have found a long time before.

"I love you," he said. "Like I've never loved anybody, like I don't love myself. I've loved you since I first saw you dancing in that shitty little tavern, with those grabby sailors flipping ten-penny pieces trying to get them down your top, and you flicking them with the hem of your dress so you could snatch them out of midair, and... I've only ever come back for you, Keth. No matter where I've gone, it's always been *away*, because coming back to you was coming back, even when..." He ran down, and hung his head. It didn't matter. Words were not what she had ever needed. He was too good with words. They cost him too little to give away. "Even when I was failing you."

"Oh, gods." She tilted her head back. Marius could see the twin streaks down her face, tiny rivulets against the grey of her skin. He cursed the dead man's sight that let him see everywhere, but washed the meaning out of everything he saw. "And it would all make sense to you, wouldn't it?" She wiped the heels of her hand across her cheeks, smearing the bright tracks of her tears over her face. "You always make so much sense," she said, sniffing. "I wish I didn't understand you when you did that."

"I'm sorry. I'm so, so sorry."

"I know. I always know." She took a deep breath, held it, then slowly let it out. "I'm not going to forgive you," she said. "I don't want to. It's just... one too many steps, this time."

"I'm sorry."

She nodded, more to herself than him. "Okay," she said. "Now, what do you want me for?"

"Well," Marius nudged Gerd, who made a great show of coming back to the conversation from his advanced doctorate-of-dirt studies. "We need to get into the Radican, into the palace. I have to persuade the King to keep the eastern gate closed, and let us take up the battle with Scorbus. Gerd can get us inside. There are tunnels right up to the base of the royal bedchamber." He smiled. "Some kings aren't as fussy as others when it comes to where they dump their bodies. But once we get in…"

"Yes?"

He shrugged. "The King is a child, Keth. What do you think he's going to do if I come looming up out of the darkness demanding he stand down his army or everyone will diiiiieeeee…?" He gave Keth his best scary-ghost voice, and waved his arms above his head like a father playing bogeyman.

"So you need me to, what? Come looming up out of the darkness and demand he stand down his army or everyone will die, but give him a pretty smile and flash my boobs while I'm at it?"

Gerd almost got a word out. Marius casually drove the heel of his foot down the inside of his young friend's shin, and smiled as he said, "No. I need you to show a young, terrified, overwhelmed kid who has the world crashing down around his shoulders, and a whole lot of angry adults screaming at him every time he turns around, that the scary-looking dead guy in the corner is here to help him. I need you to be the soft voice I bet he wants more than anything in the world right now."

"To con him into following you, then."

"To help him get past this," Marius snapped, stabbing a finger at his face, "and actually listen to me instead of running screaming for his mum the moment I turn up, thus killing the whole fucking city." He stopped, bit back his frustration and self-disgust. Keth watched him for long seconds, then nodded.

"Okay," she said. "Okay." She ran a hand through her hair. "Meet the King, eh?" She smiled wryly. "How do I look?"

"Wonderful." Marius gaze at her: dirt-stained, sweaty, her hair a tangle and her simple dress almost worn through from days of underground travel. "You've always looked wonderful."

"Not enough," she replied, and turned to Gerd. "Shall we go?"

Gerd risked a glance at Marius, and moved towards her. Marius faced away, down the tunnel that ran under the city walls towards the Radican, and led the way, leaving the others to walk behind him so he could feel, just for a moment, alone.

TWENTY-NINE

The palace was shrouded in silence. All light and sound had been extinguished as if those inside hoped to hide beneath some giant blanket until the bogeyman passed them by. Marius and Keth stood in deep shadows in the far corner of the King's bedchamber, and observed him sleeping, swallowed by the vast depths of his richly appointed bed. The King looked frightened and vulnerable. He twitched and murmured, gripping the edge of his sheets with trembling fingers.

"He looks small."

"Of course he looks small. He's a child, Marius."

"He's a king."

"He can be both, you know."

Marius shook his head. "No, he can't. Not right now."

She sighed and left him, moving quietly across the room and crouching next to the sleeping boy. "Your Majesty," she whispered, and when he didn't respond, again, "Your Majesty."

Marius stayed in the shadows and watched as she leaned in close and ran a hand across the young boy's head, smoothing wet hair away from his eyes with a tenderness that made him frown. There was real gentleness in her movements, in her tone of voice. He hissed.

"Quickly."

She shot him an irritated glance, and gave the King a gentle shake. "Your Majesty. You need to wake up."

The King muttered and tried to shake her off. Then realisation dawned, and his eyes shot open. He opened his mouth to scream, but Keth placed her hand over it.

"We are friends, Your Majesty. We're not here to hurt you. We've not harmed you, and we've had half an hour to do so if we wanted." A small lie: they had been in the room for no more than a few minutes, but that would have been time enough. Keth held her touch lightly, and gave the King plenty of time to see her. Marius saw him relax as he took in her tall, willowy frame, her soft skin and long hair. Even after so long spent marching underground, they had an effect on the boy. He relaxed in her grip just as Marius had hoped. "I promise you," she whispered, "we only want to keep you safe."

Slowly, she drew her hand an inch or so from his mouth. The King made no sound, and Marius relaxed slightly.

"How did you get in?" the boy asked. "How did you get past Mother?"

Marius glanced at the floor behind him, where Gerd waited at the bottom of a deep hole. Gillen Goncoy, leader of the Tyrant Triumvirate, had claimed this room during the Kingless Decade. Goncoy's murderous taste in chambermaids had kept him satisfied for seven years, and provided a route straight into the room for Marius and his companion.

"I have a friend," Keth whispered. "He needs to speak with you, and I need you to be unafraid. Can you do that for me?"

The King stared up at her, gave her a quick but uncertain nod.

"Good boy." She smiled, and turned towards the shadows. "Marius?"

Slowly, he emerged from the darkness. He saw the King's eyes widen, and a look of terror cross his features. The boy drew breath to scream and Keth jammed her hand across his mouth once. He struggled, beating at her arm. Keth bore down on him, forcing him back onto the pillow.

"Friend!" he hissed. "He's a friend."

"Billinor?" A raised voice from the next room. "Billinor, my… Majesty? Are you all right?"

The room froze. Marius stood still, arms behind his back, ready to bolt. He and Keth shared shocked glances, before she leaned into the young King.

"One minute, Billinor. That's all we want. Please." She turned his face so their eyes met. "For me?"

He stared at her for long seconds, then, finally, a small nod. Keth gently sat up.

"Billinor?"

He licked his lips. "I'm fine, Mother." Staring into Keth's encouraging smile. "A bad dream."

"Are you… of course, Your Majesty."

Keth exhaled. She and Marius looked at each other.

"Thank you." She took her hands away from the King. For a moment, he looked as if he regretted it. Then he remembered Marius, and turned fearfully towards him, pulling the bedclothes up to his chest.

"Who are you? You're one of…" He looked towards the window at the far end of the room, and seemed to shrink into his bed. "…them. Aren't you?"

Marius knew what he meant. He could feel Scorbus' army waiting outside the city walls as a pressure in the back of his mind, threatening to break through his mental defences and bombard him with their sounds of war.

"They are my people. At least, they should be," he admitted. "My name is Marius don Hellespont. I'm supposed to be their King."

"You don't look like a king."

"And you do?"

To his credit, the boy raised himself up so that he sat upright. He did his best to assume an air of regality. "I am Billinor, son of Tanspar. I am the King of Scorby."

"Tanspar." Marius smiled sadly. "Yes, I've… met your father."

"You have?"

"He was a brave man, even though he was very scared."

"He was? Why was he scared?"

Whatever he had been in life, death had terrified Tanspar. Marius had met him post-death, when he had become a whining slave to fear. It had taken Scorbus, Marius grudgingly recalled, to reinstate any sense of dignity to the man. "He was scared for you, and your family," Marius replied. "He wanted to know you were safe."

The young King stared into his own memories for long seconds. "I don't think we are," he said, softly.

"You can be." Marius came all the way to the bed and perched on the end. "It all depends on what you do."

Billinor looked miserable for a moment. "Mother says to do whatever Denia tells me to."

"And who is Denia?"

"The Chancellor. He's very old." This in a whisper, and a sly smile to Keth. She smiled back.

"I bet he smells of tobacco and old sweat."

The King nodded, and they both giggled.

"Tell me," Marius interrupted. "If you stood on the royal balcony, in your crown and robes, and Denia stood next to you, who would the people acclaim? Who would they believe?"

"I…" Billinor stared at him. "Do you really think…"

"History remembers kings for a reason," Marius replied. "Not advisors. It is the King who makes the decisions. The subjects follow their monarch, not those who would manipulate them." He paused, seeing Drenthe's grinning face loom large in his mind. "Your Majesty."

Billinor stared up at him, eyes wide. "What should I do?"

Marius sighed. For all his bravado, this was a ten year-old child he was dealing with, no matter how he might dress up in finery and sit on a high-backed throne. He was just about to issue orders when Keth leaned forward and took the small hand in hers.

"Billinor, sweetheart." She captured his gaze. "There is an army outside your city walls – no, don't look away, just listen to me. Your people are scared, and panicking. They want you to lead them. You, sweetheart, not your advisor or even your mother. Just you, their King."

"But what do I *do*?"

Marius' *tch* of impatience was loud, and ignored. "You can do two things, Billinor. You can send your armies out to fight–"

"That's what Daddy… what my father did, isn't it?"

"It is, sweetheart, yes."

"And he died."

"I'm sorry, he did. Not all kings fall in battle, Billinor. But if you send them out against the dead, then anybody who goes out there will join them."

"But what else can I do?"

"There is another thing. But you have to be very brave, and make sure your mother and your advisors don't bully you and force you to change your mind. And you have to be strong enough that all your soldiers and all your commanders and all the people who look up to you and believe you – and believe *in* you – will know that what you are telling them is the right thing to do, even though it sounds like the opposite."

"What is it?"

Keth glanced at Marius. He nodded.

"You can't fight this battle," she said. "You can't win it. Stand your troops down, Billinor. Send them back to their homes. Let us fight for you."

"But…" He looked from one face to the other. "What do I tell them?"

"Tell them that friends are here; friends who once lived amongst them, who once held their hands, and soothed their ills, who looked after them when they were sick and dressed them and walked side by side with them through their days. Tell them…" She faltered, and Marius took up the reins.

"Tell them," he said, "that the dead remember. And the dead will defend them."

"But it's the dead who are attacking us."

"Not all," Marius pointed to his own chest. "Not their King."

"But–"

Marius leaned into Billinor's face, and captured the young King's stare. "If your people believe in you because you're their King, if they follow you, if they think they can do anything because *you* tell them they can, who told you it was so?"

"Y… you did."

"And how do you think I know?"

Light dawned behind the child's eyes. He nodded, and smiled. Marius winked. Keth took Marius's hand, and they stood.

"Do you think you can be that strong, Billinor?" she asked. "Can you hold all of those people in your heart, and make them trust you?"

Marius watched the young boy stare into Keth's eyes, and saw him drown in them as he had done on so many occasions. He suddenly knew, with absolute certainty, that Billinor would always remember this as the moment he first fell in love. The King sat up perfectly straight, and Marius caught a glimpse of the monarch he might grow up to be.

"I can."

"Good." Keth smiled. Marius felt a pang of something he didn't think he could identify. "Get dressed while I tell you what we're going to do…"

The routes of a king through his palace are predetermined, mapped, and known to all. But there is no secret passage or shortcut in the world that a ten year-old boy cannot discover half a day after coming into proximity with it. Billinor knew every secret byway the Radican had assembled in the last three hundred years. Marius had broken into the palace on seven occasions over the last two decades, and even he did not recognise many of the corridors the young King led them down. It took them ten minutes to sneak past the sleeping form of the Dowager Mother in the antechamber outside the King's bedchamber, through corridors within the walls that dipped and turned until neither adult could tell if they were coming or going, and down to an exit at street level that Marius had never seen before. From there they climbed the slope of the main avenue towards the square in front of the Bone Cathedral. And stopped.

"Who are *they*?"

The great square at the top of the Radican could easily swallow ten thousand soldiers, but the people gathered below the royal balcony were not soldiers. There were perhaps only five thousand, yet they covered the length and breadth of the open area, clustered together in groups around small fires for comfort and reassurance. Marius eyed them sadly.

"Nobody," he said. "They're nobody. Just normal people."

"What are they doing here?" The King looked up at him in confusion. Marius stared over the fires, watching families huddled under blankets, seeing bindles and trunks at their backs.

"The Radican has always been a refuge of last resort," he said, and then guided the young King away from the safety of the wall, down a short alley on the other side of the main avenue, its end open to the city below. "Look down there."

"It's the city."

"Not quite." Marius pointed to a nearby ring of roads. "See there? The Doge's Walk? See how it follows the shape of the Radican, like a ring?"

"It does." The King jumped up and down. "It does. I can see it!"

"And beyond it, there? The Avenue of Advocates, turning into Silk Alley?"

"It's the same."

"It is. And out again, down there, hidden behind those buildings–"

"The same?"

"Probably, yeah. It's kind of hard to tell from here."

"What are those streets called?"

Marius looked at him askance. "Those are the type of streets that don't have names."

"Why not?"

Marius could have curled up in pain at the innocence in the King's eyes. Instead, he put an arm around his shoulders. "Once you get that close to the outer wall, you're more worried about whether you're going to eat today or not, than whether the silk importer knows where to deliver your order."

"Oh." Billinor looked downcast for a moment, then stared back over his city as if seeing it or the first time. "I really don't know very much about stuff," he said.

"Make it your business to learn. You're King. You're responsible for everything that happens. Don't just accept what your advisors tell you. Find out things for yourself. Don't worry about the big, important, clever stuff. Everyone has an opinion about that, especially if they think you'll pat them on the head for it. Find out about the useless things that nobody else around you cares about, the unimportant things that nobody up here," he jerked a thumb at the buildings behind them, "thinks is worth their time. Then put them all together and make them useful."

"Like you do?"

"Don't do *anything* like I do." He pointed back across the city. "So, your city. Three great rings inside the walls. What does that tell you?"

Billinor concentrated, for long enough that Marius knew before the boy did that he had no idea. He sat down, draping his legs over the edge of the cliff, and the young King followed his example. Marius stared out across the city.

"Three times in the last six hundred years, the walls of Scorby City have been breached by an invading army. Every time, the guard has used these ring roads as fallback positions. The whole city is built around them. You can see the way they step up towards the top of the hill, see?"

"I see them."

"Right. So, what do you do if the walls are breached?"

"Fight?"

"Ah, but you're being overrun. Enemies everywhere, panic in the streets, women, children, fires in buildings, corpses in the gutters. What then? What do you do? Quick!"

"I… I don't know!"

"Good answer."

"What?"

Marius gave him a wry grin. "Half of life's mistakes happen because someone important doesn't know an answer and is too pigheaded to admit it." He glanced at Keth, standing a few feet away from them and most deliberately not paying attention. "Trust me, I know."

"So what do I do?"

He pointed back out across the city. "Fall back to the first rise, use the ring road as a palisade, give the people behind you a chance to move back towards the Radican. Hold position as long as possible, then fall back to the second rise, use the ring road as a palisade there. And so on…" He mapped out invisible warfare with sweeps of his hand, the young boy at his side following the long-forgotten actions across the cityscape. "Two hundred years ago, the invaders weren't repelled until they reached the Doge's Walk. Nobody has *ever* scaled the Radican."

"But…" Billinor frowned. "What happened to all the people? Down there?"

Marius shrugged. "A lot of those streets are named after martyrs."

"But you said the streets out there…" he pointed towards the edge of the city, "don't have any names."

"What does that tell you?" Marius stood, offered his hand to the young King, and hauled him upright. "These people behind us," he said. "They're just getting their retreat in early. No sense in dying for a street without a name."

They walked slowly back down the alley. Keth was waiting for them, leaning on the wall with her arms crossed. She tilted her head to look at Marius as they approached.

"What?"

"You'd have made a wonderful…" She stopped.

"Made a wonderful what?"

She shook her head. "Nothing," she said, turning away. "Nothing." She pointed up the avenue, towards the fires in the square. "So what are we going to do? Can we use a tunnel?"

Marius turned his gaze across the ground of the square. There were surprisingly few grey lines, and none within thirty metres of the Bone Cathedral, as if the presence of that brooding mausoleum was enough death for anybody, even killers. He grimaced. "Nowhere we can come up where we won't be seen. I'd have to be inside the cathedral already before I can see if there are any entry points in there, so…" He shrugged. "That would slightly defeat the purpose."

"Then what?" Keth nodded down at Billinor. "It's not like he won't be recognised. And his pyjamas are hardly handmade."

Marius glanced at the Boy King. His pyjamas probable *were* handmade, he decided. But there was a noticeable difference between hand-tailored imported silk sewn by the finest tailors from the royally-appointed major houses, and patchwork made by stitching together whatever you could afford from Mrs Miggins' rag cart into enough layers to hopefully keep out the cold in place of a fire. He chewed his lip, then stopped. His lip was coming off between his teeth. The dead don't puke, he reminded himself. And brave leaders with nervous ten year-olds looking to them for guidance don't erupt into violent retching fits either

"You're right," he said slowly. "We can't get him across without being noticed."

"So what do we do?"

He looked between them both, and broke out into a grin. "We make sure he's noticed." He ushered them back across the avenue to the spot where he was sure he remembered the secret door opening. "Billinor, how many kitchens does the Radican have?"

"I don't know. I always eat in the dining room."

Marius raised an eyebrow. "You're a ten year-old kid, half-pint. Don't tell me you never sneak out and grab yourself a midnight snack."

Billinor smiled. "Well… I do know where one is."

"That'll do. Lead on, noble Majesty." He turned to the wall and ran his hands across the surface. "Where's the handle for this thing?" Billinor and Keth moved half a dozen feet further down the avenue. They glanced at him as Billinor reached a finger into a small pockmark in the stone, and the secret door swung open before them. Marius nodded. "Ah, yes. Right. There. Lead on there."

Billinor led them through a maze of corridors, deep into the bowels of the palace. They emerged in a small dark kitchen looking out over the cliff that ran alongside the building.

"I can't see anything." Keth hung back as they entered.

"Stay there." Marius could make out the dim grey outlines of all the furniture, and baskets of food waiting to be prepared. Most importantly, he could see all the metal pots, pans, and implements that had been hung about the room, just waiting to be clattered into and sent across the stone floor to bring all the guards within hearing distance running. Billinor, who had obviously visited the room for a million-and-a-half midnight treats, skipped past most of them and started rummaging around in a basket near the doors to a small balcony. He squeaked in victory and began gnawing on something Marius recognised as a Phyllis fruit, a rare crop renowned as the juiciest fruit in the entire six continents. For a moment he wished the dead could slaver. Instead, he snuck across and tapped the young King on the shoulder.

"Bring the lady one of those when we leave," he whispered, "and you'll have a friend for life."

Billinor smiled. Marius could smell the thick line of juice coating the boy's chin, and added Phyllis fruit to the long list of things for which he would revenge himself upon Drenthe. But he reached into the basket and pulled out another one.

"Good lad. Now…" He looked around the kitchen, scanning the shelves. "Any chance you'd know where they store the loaves around here?"

Billinor took his hand, and carefully lead him to a thin door in the corner. Marius indulged him. He couldn't know about his dead sight and besides, this was the first time since they'd met that Marius could sense the young King taking control, revelling in the chance to lead. The door opened into a deep cupboard. Marius felt the cool, dry air within. Perfect. The cupboard was overflowing with bread, enough to feed the boy beside him for months.

"And you eat all this?" he whispered, and saw Billinor shake his head.

"We've got three bakeries, I think. There's a bunch of people working in them. We give a lot of this bread to the staff to take home, and everybody eats breakfast here, you know."

"Well," Marius began to pull loaves from the shelves, "someone's going to have to have Phyllis fruit tomorrow morning." They quickly loaded up two baskets, and Marius deposited them before Keth in the doorway.

"Where did all these come from?"

"The cupboard."

"No, I mean..." She shook her head. "Isn't the city under siege? Are they eating like this in here, while out in the streets–"

"No." Marius shook his head. "Scorbus isn't conducting a siege. He's waiting, just like he did last time. He could ring the city if he wanted, even put soldiers under water at the entrance to the river and sink anything that comes over them; but I'd lay money he's got his entire army in one tight little group at the eastern gate, and he's not even bothered to stop goods coming in and out by the Farmer's Gate or the docks."

"Then what are these for?"

Marius smiled. "Good will. Speaking of which..." He nudged Billinor. The young King stepped forward and shyly held out his hand.

"I got this for... for you."

Keth saw the Phyllis fruit in his hand and smiled. "Oh, thank you, sweetheart." She placed her hand on his cheek. "I'm afraid I don't really like them. But that was such a lovely thought. Why don't you have it for me?"

She hefted a basket and began to sneak down the corridor the way they had come. Marius and Billinor stared after her.

"Doesn't like Phyllis fruit. And I'm supposed to be the one with the dead stomach." Marius picked up the other basket, and they hurried to catch up.

THIRTY

The three figures stood in the shadows at the corner of the avenue and looked across the square at the citizenry huddled around their few small fires. The two taller figures carried baskets piled high with loaves of bread.

"Tell me again," Keth said, "what we're doing?"

Marius watched the dispirited, frightened crowd.

"Did you ever read Hactium's *History of Dek's War Against the North*?"

"I must have forgotten," she replied.

Marius glanced down at the King. "You, young man, should make sure you have a copy."

"Okay," Billinor said, and nodded.

"Dek's army drove into the northern reaches so far that when winter arrived his supply lines were too long. His army was stretched out across almost eight miles of mountain defiles. The northern militiamen wiped out the supply lines. Snow and cold and disease did for most of the rest. Dek retreated in disarray. His army marched almost three hundred miles during one of the worst winters ever recorded, through snow that blackened their toes halfway up to their knees. By the time he crossed the border back into the Scorban Empire, he had lost over eighty per cent of the men he set out with. Nearly sixty thousand dead, all without once engaging the enemy."

"Gods."

"Ten years later, after he had been deposed and exiled, Dek invaded the Scorban Empire in an attempt to reclaim his throne. Every single one of those soldiers who marched with him on that northern campaign rallied to his banner. Do you know why?"

"Serious head injuries?"

"Every night of that ten-week march back through the mountains, no matter where they were or what losses they suffered during the day, Dek visited his men. He threw his tent away, distributed his blankets amongst the troops, even had his own horse cut up and added to the stew pot when the meat began to run out. But most of all…" He brandished a loaf at them. "He sat with them around their little fires, swapping stories and talking. Not as a king to his subjects, or as a commander to his subordinates, but as one soldier to another. When there was bread to break, he broke it with them. When they were down to chewing on their undershirts, he sat with them and chewed his. When it was all lost, and they had nothing else, he was with them. And they loved him for it."

Keth stared across the square. "They think it's all lost."

"Not all." Billinor reached into the basket and withdrew a loaf. Marius nodded to him.

"After you."

Billinor nodded back, wiped his nose on his pyjama sleeve, and stepped out into the square. Keth followed. Marius tucked in behind her, doing his best to look inconspicuous.

They saw him coming. How could they not? He was the only thing moving on the entire plaza. And they would have leaped to their feet, to bow and curtsy and make obeisance to this tiny boy. But Billinor gave them no chance. He closed quickly upon the closest fire, and thrust a loaf clumsily at the big, beefy man who was struggling to rise.

"I'm Billinor," he said. "I'm, um… Who are you?"

The man looked at him. His lips formed the beginning of a word, then another, finally gave up. He tried to bow, take the loaf, and slap his children into obedience all at the same time.

"Guh… Gint, your Maj… Gint Hern. I… Roads…"

Keth stepped forward and laid a gentle hand on his shoulder. "Thank you, Gint," she said softly. "May we join you?"

"J… join?" The man's voice went up an octave. His eyes looked twice their size in the flickering fire light. Marius nudged Billinor.

"Please," said the King. "May we?"

"Y… Of course, Your Majesty." The man made fumbling attempts to divest himself of the blanket he had wrapped around his shoulders. Billinor held up his hand.

"Please don't," he said. "You need it more than me."

Marius winced. It could be worse, he thought. Give the boy a chance.

The King sat and gestured for the others to sit by him. There was an awkward silence.

"So…" Billinor began, and glanced up at Marius with a pained expression. Marius sighed, and leaned forward into the light.

"I know," he said, before the sight of him could register fully upon the others. "I'm horribly disfigured. Don't let it concern you. What His Majesty would like to know is, how far have you come to be here tonight? What have you left behind? How can he help?"

"He wants… to help *us*?"

Finally, Marius saw the penny drop. Billinor took his loaf and broke it in half. Gint had two children, neither one of them older than the young King. He passed each half to one child and smiled at them. "Yes," he said. "I do."

Just like that, the dam was broken. Gint talked, and Billinor listened, and learned, and after a while he thanked the road-repairer and his family for their company and their time and moved on to the next cold, hungry, tired group. Keth and Marius followed him as he slowly drifted across the square, handing him a loaf of bread each time he sat down. They watched in silence as the slip of a boy began to grow into his role as father to the frightened rabble of dockhands, seamstresses, weavers and more, hearing their stories, offering his small moment of friendship and comfort to each of them in turn. And finally, somewhere near the rear edge of the crowd, a child found the temerity to ask him, "Why are you here?"

And Billinor paused, as those around the child froze in sudden fear. He smiled a small, sad smile, and glanced behind them to the forbidding walls of the Bone Cathedral.

"I wanted to talk to my father," he said. In that moment Marius knew the young King had them, as surely as Dek has won his troops, and that forevermore the citizens in the square would think of themselves as Billinor's people, no matter whether they outlived him or otherwise. No matter how many kings they might live through, they would be *his*. The child's father nodded, and stood.

"Thank you for being with us, Your Majesty," he said. Marius heard a sound like the passage of wind through a forest. Five thousand people were standing, facing their King. As Billinor rose, they bowed.

"Um, thank you," he said. "Thank you all." He turned to Marius. "What now?" he whispered.

"Now you proceed," Marius whispered back. "Don't run. Just… proceed."

Billinor sketched a quick nod, and walked towards the cathedral entrance twenty feet away. Keth and Marius fell in behind him, shielding the crowd from the fact that their now-beloved monarch's pyjama trousers were too long for his legs. With five thousand faces at their backs they *proceeded* into the foyer of the Bone Cathedral, and promptly collapsed against the wall.

"This place creeps me out," Marius said. Keth glanced upwards and shuffled closer to him. Marius resisted the temptation to reach out and draw her into a hug. He no longer knew how she'd react, and really didn't want to find out.

"Me too." She reached out and poked the bone-covered wall with a finger. "So many dead." She frowned. "But why does it disturb you? I mean…" She tilted her head in the vague direction of the outer wall, somewhere towards "out there". Marius knew she meant the waiting armies, all those silent, chattering souls who trailed in his wake. He glanced up at the nameless dead, glued together in random abandon.

"That's just it," he whispered. "Look at them." He ran a finger down a nearby femur, followed it onto a scapula and directly onto a floret of patellas. "All this, made from the bones of thousands and thousands of corpses." He looked at her. "And I can't hear a single one."

"What do you mean?"

He stared at the vast walls of the Cathedral, arching overhead towards infinity. "The dead talk."

"Oh, that is so disturbing."

He glanced at her. "No," he said. "It's disturbing when they stop."

She shivered. "Now I see why it makes you uncomfortable."

Up ahead, Billinor was standing in the centre of the main hall, staring at an empty space in the centre of the room.

"I remember standing here," he said. "My daddy... the King... they brought him in on a big bier. I... I remember..." He sketched a salute. "I didn't know any better, really. There was the flag over him, and he'd always taught me... you salute the flag. So I saluted the flag. And then I realised..." He waved in short, jittery arcs. Marius stepped up next to him, and laid a hand on his shoulder.

"He would have been proud."

"How do you know?"

"Would you like to ask him?"

"What?" Billinor looked up at him, eyes wet. Marius nodded.

"Would you like to ask him?" He nodded towards the entrance to the Hall of Kings, at the rear of the main building. "We're here to see him, after all."

"But..."

"Trust me." He held out his hand, and Billinor took it. "I've got you this far, haven't I?"

"Yes. And if my mum finds out I'll get in so much trouble, and you'll be..."

"What? Killed?"

Billinor looked as if he didn't know whether to laugh or feel guilty for something. Marius spared him the problem by pointing towards the Hall of Kings.

"Come on."

They set off across the massive floor, Keth in their wake. Billinor turned his head from side to side as they approached the entrance.

"What's the matter?"

"Why aren't there any guards here? There are supposed to be guards at the entrance all the time."

"They've gone home."

"How do you know?"

Marius gestured to the world outside. "The world's about to end. Where would you rather be at the end of the world, guarding some dead guy or with your family?"

Billinor turned down his mouth. "I'm King. I have to go out and fight and stuff. I don't get to be with my family."

They snuck into the Hall, and Marius looked at the corpse-white crypt at the far end. "And yet, here we are."

Billinor followed his gaze, saw his father's tomb. The grip on Marius's hand tightened. "Yes," he said in a very small voice. "We are."

They snuck across the great space into the tomb space. Despite the emptiness and the lack of other visitors, the Bone Cathedral was simply the sort of place that encouraged sneaking. It didn't seem right, somehow, to go marching across the echoing space with your head held high and a happy, purposeful smile on your face. The cathedral was a place for unconscious guilt, and unworthiness. It was a place to slink, whilst offering silent apologies to someone you couldn't quite identify for things you weren't quite sure you'd done. The three companions made it to the Hall of Kings, and stopped just inside the entrance to draw breath.

"I don't like it here," Billinor whispered, as if revealing a dirty secret. Marius ruffled his hair.

"Nobody does," he replied. "That's what it's for."

They slowly made their way down the line of crypts, each one a lesson in gratuitous artistic sucking up. A thousand years of monarchs lay in state here, those with great reigns arrayed next to the cowards, incompetents and morons in order of chronology rather than worth. Each crypt had been carved into a frieze depicting that king's greatest achievement: if they had all been accurate, Scorby would cover the entire continent and the only people left alive would be the Scorban royal family. Marius winced as they snuck past the line of great coffins. He could hear them, disturbed by his presence, calling out in the dark for information, reassurance. The kings were calling, and it hurt. He steered Billinor to the far end of the line, to a coffin that gleamed whiter than the others, not yet yellowed by age or smoothed by decades of hands reaching through the velvet ropes to connect with a moment of eternity. He heard a sob. Billinor had stopped a few steps behind him, and now stood with his hands over his mouth, tears running down his cheeks. Marius bent down, and rubbed them away.

"It's okay," he said. "It's okay." He glanced back towards Tanspar's tomb. "Look." The front of the crypt showed something that purported to be Tanspar's last battle. The King rode high above his subjects, his profile a mask of glory and righteous anger as the Tallian barbarians fell back under the perfection of the Scorban assault. Marius had seen the aftermath of the battle. It had been the first act in the tragicomedy that his life had become. He remembered no glory, only bodies and corruption and fear. The frieze extended past the corners on both sides: Tanspar's reign had not been a long one. "See there, just at the corner?" A farewell scene. The King, riding out to war, waving goodbye to his adoring family. The young prince ascendant, a golden crown floating an inch above his head. Marius knew the artist was simply getting his sycophancy in early, but it might help the boy. "The most important thing in your father's life," he said. "And you're there with him, now, forever."

Billinor wiped his eyes and stared at the frieze, then at the empty space beyond. "I'll be there one day, won't I?" he said, pointing. Marius blinked. There was a king for you, he thought. Nothing lasts longer than consideration of one's legacy.

"Yes," he replied. "One day. Let's just make sure it's a long while from now, shall we?"

Billinor nodded. Marius turned to the crypt.

"Tanspar?" he projected. "Tanspar of Scorby?"

The flow of conversation around him broke off. Marius shuffled nervously, and asked again. A voice, high-pitched and aristocratic, replied.

"Yes?"

Marius glanced at Billinor. The boy was staring at him, a frown on his face. "Give me a moment," he said. Billinor's frown deepened. "Tanspar of Scorby," he projected once more. "I am Marius don Hellespont."

"And you are?"

"I am..." he paused. "I have brought your son, Billinor. He has inherited a troubled kingdom. He needs your help."

"Billinor?" The voice changed immediately, worry and love displacing the cool reserve. An image of Tanspar appeared in Marius's mind. A father's face, creased in fear. "Is he okay? What troubles him? What is the matter?"

Billinor was staring at him. Marius winked. "We're talking," he said. "Dead people talk within our minds."

The boy looked at Marius with the kind of contempt reserved for small children who suddenly understand that an adult is lying to them. "That's not even a good trick," he said scornfully. "It's just making stuff up."

Marius blinked. Of course, he realised. From the outside, all he can see is me, standing still. He doesn't hear the voices, can't understand what's being said. Any explanation I give him sounds like, well, the sort of lie an adult tells a kid.

"I need something," he projected. "Something only you would know."

"Tell him to trust you," Tanspar replied.

"Trust me."

"Only beggars and diplomats lie."

"Only beggars and diplomats lie."

"Bunnydor."

"What?"

"Say it."

Marius shrugged. "Bunnydor."

For a moment, nothing happened. Then Billinor's hands slowly rose to his mouth.

"How..." He stared at Marius with enormous eyes. "You can't call me that," he whispered. "Only Daddy..."

Marius tilted his head towards the crypt. Billinor swallowed. Marius knelt, and the boy threw his arms around his neck. Marius held him, letting the boy cry against his shoulder. He looked helplessly toward Keth. She stared back, her own tears clear against her cheeks.

"What is happening?" Tanspar's voice in his mind. Marius glanced at the top of the young King's head.

"We've persuaded him," he said sadly. "He just needs a few moments to deal with it."

"Ah."

"Yes."

There were a few silent seconds, punctuated only by the sound of the boy crying. Then Tanspar spoke again, the voice clear in Marius' mind.

"While Billi is... distracted, perhaps you can tell me why you have brought him here to undertake this... form of conversation?"

"There's a war on his doorstep. Scorbus has risen from the underworld." Quickly, he outlined the war waiting outside the walls of the city. "He doesn't know what to do."

"He has advisors. Why does he not consult with them?"

"Because you're his dad. And his hero." Marius dropped his gaze to the clean stone lid under his hand. "He saluted your coffin when it went past him, because it had a flag on it and you'd taught him–"

"To love the flag." Tanspar's voice was deep with sadness. Marius nodded, realised what he was doing, and projected his nod. "So what do you wish me to tell him?"

"I'm sorry?"

"Come now. If we can communicate then I know you are one of us, and if one of us is bringing the King to consult with his dead father then I know why."

Another nod. "Not all the dead rally to Scorbus. We have a plan, but there are few of us, and we need the living to stay out of the way."

"I suspect as much. The question is, my dead friend, why is it *you* are the one to oppose him, and what are you hiding from my son?"

Marius said nothing. Tanspar chuckled.

"Nothing he would be inclined to believe, I think. So you bring him here, to use me as your mouthpiece. I ask you again. What would you have me say?"

"Scorbus has one hundred thousand troops outside the city walls…"

"Gods."

"I want you to…" Marius paused, tried again. "Scorbus wants a battle. He wants the city to send its troops out. If Billinor does that, he's lost before the fight even begins."

"Every soldier killed will become a recruit for the enemy."

"Exactly. And then when it's over, Scorbus comes into the unprotected city and recruits everyone else."

"Slaughter. Genocide."

"Reclaiming what he believes is his. Subjugation by right of conquest. Only in this case…"

"Subjugation involves killing his subjects. But why would Billi not realise this? Surely anyone would advise him not to venture forth."

"Because you rode to war."

"I was killed!"

"You're his hero."

"And what would you have him do instead?"

"Withhold his troops, stay behind the city walls. Let me fight his battle for him. I have troops of my own, dead troops loyal to me. I have a plan that I am convinced will work. I just need Billi… I need the King to keep his people off the battlefield."

"And why would he allow you to do this? You would seem to have more in common with his enemy than with my son."

"Scorbus believes himself the rightful King of the Dead, but he's not. I am."

"And how…" The words were slow to arrive, deliberate, as if the speaker half-suspected the coming answer. "Do you substantiate your claim to this throne, sir?"

Marius winced. He had hoped to avoid this moment, but Tanspar was too canny.

"I was crowned with full ceremony," he said, "and have neither abdicated nor been removed by greater right of succession."

"That is not the full truth, sir."

Marius glanced towards Keth. She had collected Billinor. Now she stood with him and dried his eyes, before directing him back to Marius.

"Please. This is too important."

"You will tell me how you came to your throne."

"Your Majesty, there are greater things at risk than this."

Billinor had turned towards Marius. He took a deep breath, let it out, and took a step.

"Tanspar…"

"You will tell me! Or I shall advise him as I see fit, and damn this city and all within it if it means my boy is safe!"

Marius bent his head. "They found me on a battlefield, hiding underneath a dead soldier. With a crown. So they thought the obvious. By the time they realised, I'd already been proclaimed."

The pause that followed was long enough that Billinor was able to cross the floor and hoist himself up to sit on his father's crypt – ignoring Marius's proffered hands, he noticed – before Tanspar spoke again.

"I was found without my crown. It had been removed from my helm."

"I am not the person I once was," Marius replied.

Again a long pause. Billinor stared at Marius. He shook his head slightly, and the young King frowned.

"And who wears my crown now?"

"Scorbus."

"I see." Marius could feel Tanspar considering, weighing up his options. "Has my son returned?"

"He has."

"You will repeat my words to him, exactly as I say them. And you will recover my crown."

"I… I will."

"You are in my debt, Mister don Hellespont. You will keep my son safe, and recover my crown, and you will still remain always in my debt."

Marius sent him a nod of acquiescence. He looked up at Billinor.

"Ready?"

Billinor nodded. Tanspar began to speak, and Marius relayed his message, exactly word for word. When it was done he stepped back, and Billinor lay down upon his father's cold stone crypt, and spread his hands as wide as his little frame could reach.

"I love you, Daddy," he muttered.

"He loves you."

"I love him, too."

"He loves you too."

"Tell him…" Marius heard Tanspar choke slightly, then continue, stronger. "Tell him to take the passage behind the lower library on his way back. They'll be looking for him, now. Don't go by the kitchen."

"Your father says he'll always love you."

"You promised me, don Hellespont."

"I know." He held his hands out to the young King. Billinor took them, and dropped down off the crypt. Keth had drifted to the back of the room while the conversation had taken place, slipping inside the entrance to the smaller and darker Hall of Queens. Now she returned, and held out her hands to the boy. Marius placed a hand on his shoulder, held him still for a moment.

"I'll see him back safe," Marius told his father. "I promise you. And thank you for helping me try to make it all straight."

Tanspar said nothing. Marius released Billinor and he took off towards Keth at a flat run.

"Wait."

Marius stopped. Billinor, oblivious to the command, threw himself at Keth and buried his face in her chest. She put her arms around him and frowned at Marius in confusion. He gestured her to be patient.

"Yes?"

"One more thing. You came here when I was lying in state. You freed Scorbus."

Marius projected a nod.

"You visited this war upon my son. In every way it was you who brought him to this."

Marius could have made any number of denials, pointed to any number of mitigating factors. Instead, he felt his shoulders slump. "Yes," he replied. "When it all comes down to it."

"Tell me. If whatever plan you have works, if my son survives this action we have advised him to take... will you remain behind, to bring him to talk with me once more?"

"I... No. I don't believe so."

Tanspar's image nodded. "Should I thank you, then, for fetching him here, to inform me of this danger? My ten year-old son, and I shall not know his fate until he is lying here next to me, dead? All I can do is lie here not knowing whether that will be tomorrow, or fifty years. Would you thank a person who delivered you such fear?"

"No. No, I wouldn't."

Tanspar's image flicked off inside his mind. The dead man's voice was bitter in the sudden blackness.

"A pox on you, don Hellespont. I hope you spend whatever eternity you earn in Hell."

Marius looked across at Keth: warm, loving, alive Keth.

"You're about three months too late for that," he said.

They walked back through the Cathedral in silence, pausing at the entrance to stare out at the families still huddled in the Great Square. More refugees had joined them, fleeing the impending doom outside the walls. The great crowd watched in silence as the King and his companions crossed the square. At the corner of the boulevard, Billinor stopped, and turned.

"Billinor?"

He looked up at Marius. "Your Majesty, please."

"I… Your Majesty." Marius bent his head. "What are you doing?"

Billinor bit his lip. He's about to do it, Marius realised. He's talked with his father. He's reconciled to whatever course of action he's going to take. Whatever he does now, he's about to do it himself, alone, for the first time. Billinor straightened, and looked at the older man with eyes suddenly grown cool.

"Behind me if you please, sir."

"Um, yes, of course. Your Majesty." Marius hurried to stand beside Keth as Billinor turned towards the crowd that faced him in silent expectation.

"My friends…" His voice cracked softly. He stopped, and started again. "My friends." This time, there was not a flicker of weakness in it. "I have an announcement to make. I ask you: go into the city, return in a bell with as many as you can find. Tell them… tell them their King has need of them. We have tasks to perform tonight, and not all will agree with us. I leave it to you, my friends, to gather those who will."

A cheer broke out: ragged, thin with cold and fear and something just short of understanding. But it was a cheer, and it was Billinor's. He nodded then, and as lights began to show in windows across the face of the royal apartments, he turned to Marius.

"We need to get back to my rooms. I must dress properly." He glanced up at the building. "Through the passage behind the lower library, I should think."

Marius grinned. "At your service, Your Majesty."

"Yes," Billinor nodded. "Thank you."

They proceeded until the moment they were out of sight of the cheering crowd, then ran like hell for the secret door. Billinor swung it open and glanced up at Marius. "Do you have some really scary and strong dead people who could perhaps stop a whole lot of soldiers and advisors breaking down a door while I made a speech?"

Marius laughed. "I think I can manage that. How do nuns take your fancy?"

"I have no idea," Billinor said as they raced into the hidden maze within the palace. "Are nuns scary?"

THIRTY-ONE

The King stood at the top of the hallway and stared down it towards the glass doors at its far end. Beyond lay the balcony overlooking the giant square. Ten thousand troops could line up beneath it, ready to hear their king's command. Instead, ten thousand peasants, children, labourers and assorted citizenry stood in silence, waiting to see the small boy whose loyalty they longed to reward. The corridor was perhaps twenty feet long, the last twenty feet of privacy the king would have before he stepped outside to change history. To either side of him, short cross corridors ended in thick wooden doors, outside of which stood two dozen of Arnobew's nuns, and as many of the palace guard as hadn't learned that a femur upside the head meant that the King *really* didn't want to be interrupted. Gerd and Keth stood in front, ready to relay any messages that might need to be passed through. Billinor stood at its junction – four and a half feet tall in his slippered feet – and ignored the panicked yelling of his mother, the advisor Denia, and the rest of his inner sanctum. Instead, he stared up at the glowering portrait that hung upon the wall above him: Scorbus the Great, in his pomp, a monster of a man with hooded gaze and massive, monumental presence.

"Is that really him?" the young King asked. Marius cast his thoughts back to the last time he had stood here, when the skeletal Scorbus had stared at this image of him and asked an almost-identical question. He grimaced in sympathy.

"I don't really know," he said. "He didn't look like that."

"I know why it's here." The King looked up at Marius, his smooth, unlined face no longer filled with fear of the dead man before him. Now he was considering something that, to him, was more frightening: making a fool of himself in front of strangers, and adults, and the people he trusted. "It's meant to remind me of what kind of a king I'm supposed to be."

"So I'm told."

"But…" The King bit his lip. "But if that's really him out there…" A wave towards the world outside. "And he's going to kill everyone in the city and kill me and my family and take the crown and make everyone dead…" He stared at the picture, stared and stared until Marius could see the coming question as if it were written in the air itself. "What kind of king am I supposed to be if I'm supposed to be like him?"

Marius gaped at him. Ten years old. When Marius was ten he could barely button his flies without help, and his greatest fear had been accidentally running into the Fish Alley Gang and getting his arse kicked for being out of his parents' street. No matter what this kid did, he realised, someone was going to use it as an excuse to act against him. Children have too many enemies. Ten years old was no age to be a king. He smiled.

"You know something?" he said. "I never liked this portrait." He reached up and pulled it from the wall. Billinor gasped.

"You can't do that!"

"Why not? Who's going to stop me? You?"

Billinor giggled. Marius pointed at the picture.

"Ugly fucker, isn't he?"

The King chortled. "You said fucker," he said, and snorted. "That is *so* rude."

Marius smiled again. That was more like it.

"I'm worse than that." He pointed to a diamond stickpin on the King's chest. "Give me that and I'll teach you something."

Billinor picked it out and handed it to him. Marius held it up.

"See it?"

"Yes?"

Marius waved his fingers. The stickpin disappeared. Billinor rolled his eyes.

"Please," he said, with all the world-weariness of his ten years. "Grandmamma used to do that when I was little." He tilted his head. "Go on, then."

"Go on what?"

"You're supposed to make it come out from behind my ear."

Marius grinned, and raised an eyebrow. "Stupid kid."

The young King stared at him; then slowly, raised a hand and stifled a giggle. Marius poked him gently in the forehead.

"Have we learned something?"

Billinor nodded.

"Good. Now, you know what else?" Marius hefted the portrait. With one quick twist of his wrists he snapped the frame and tore the canvas into two pieces. "It's not important whether or not you act like a dead man." He tossed the broken canvas over his shoulder while the King was still gaping, and leaned down so that he stared the child fully in the face. "You need to be the King that you need to be. Not for him, or the rich people who stand behind your throne and tell you what to do as if you're some kid who doesn't understand. You do it for the people who don't care that you're young, and scared, and probably want to play ring-the-hoop in a park rather than sit in some dusty old throne room and listen to rich adults tell you all the ways you're getting things wrong all day. The people out there who look at you and don't see a kid, but see their King, and who love and trust you because you *are* their King. You're *their* King, as long as you keep your thoughts on *them*. You don't need to worry about what dead people think."

Billinor looked scared again, but he straightened his thin shoulders, wiped his nose with the back of his hand, and nodded at Marius. Not as child to adult, Marius thought, but as monarch to sort-of just-about pretending-to-be-to-get-the-job-done monarch.

"Yes," he replied. "Thank you, Your Majesty."

"You're welcome," Marius replied, then with a grin. "Half-pint."

The King grinned, and began the long walk down the corridor. A mob waited beyond those doors, Marius knew: confused, and terrified, and looking for a reason to panic. Even in the middle of the night, with advisors racing this way and that up and down corridors, with his mother fluttering from room to room calling his name, with the entire world in chaos, the people in that square waited only for the presence of one person. Their King.

Their King reached the balcony doors, and opened them. A sound like thunder greeted him. He stopped for a moment, as if taken aback by the sheer volume, then gathered himself and stepped out. Marius glimpsed a short set of steps placed hard up against the balcony edge before the doors swung closed. He resisted the temptation to sneak up and place an ear against the glass. He had guided the youngster as best he could. What he said now, what comfort or rage or fear he gave his people, was his alone to give. Marius could only hope it coincided with his needs. He turned from the doors, and made his way back to the apex of the corridor.

"It's done," he said to his companions, opening the secret panel Billinor had used to travel directly from his room to the balcony entrance. "Let's go."

THIRTY-TWO

They slid back out through the tunnels bequeathed to them by Goncoy, emerging at the end of an alley in the Whore's Quarter. Marius waved Gerd and the nuns back underground.

"What are you doing?"

He jerked a thumb towards the far end of the street. "I want to see the enemy from the front. I want to make sure my bearings are correct."

"And what are we supposed to do? Buy a postcard?"

"Go back to the others. Wait for us."

"Us?"

He looked at Keth. "You're coming with me, aren't you?

Keth looked between them. "I…" she nodded. "Okay."

Gerd rolled his eyes, and shut the hole behind him. Marius took Keth's hand, then they made for the nearest street.

They slunk from shadow to shadow down towards the black line of the city walls. The further away from the Radican they got, the more empty the streets became. Marius and Keth walked hand in uncomfortable hand, spooked by the eerie silence. Scorby City was the busiest city in the world: more crowded than Borgho City, more officious than the great palace-state of the Amir of Tal, more conniving and streetwise than the entire nation of the desert caravanserai. And it never, ever stopped. Until now.

Marius could feel the silence working upon Keth, feel her twitch harder at every creak or groan, every hidden sound of the city's settling bones that had previously been buried under the cacophony of life. He felt little better himself. He was a creature of noise and chaos. All his skills depended upon being one unnoticed mote in the whirl of city life. Out in the middle of a vacant street, without a press of bodies behind which to hide, he felt exposed, a mouse in an empty field just waiting for eagle claws to grip the back of his neck. They crept along, two mice on a mission, wishing for long grass to offer them shelter. The world stayed silent, until the cobbles changed shape along with the buildings. The city became rougher, less finished. The colours were muted and dirty, the streets less well-defined, becoming little more than dirt tracks that slipped between ramshackle structures that leaned together as if for warmth. Then even Keth could not escape the inevitable question:

"Where is everyone?"

"Waiting." Marius pointed out closed shutters as they passed. "There's an apocalypse outside the walls, and everyone here knows it'll hit them before it reaches the rich."

Keth made to argue, then thought better of it. They were close to the walls of the city now, two miles from the Radican. Every city is built along similar lines. The wealthy claim the land towards the centre, near the river and up the hills, where the water is clearer and the sun shines for longer in the day. The poor are shunted to where the shadows are longest, and where the water has passed under every privy in the city before it comes up to be drunk. Somewhere up ahead, they could hear someone sobbing in a gap between buildings. They shared a look, and Keth ran ahead of Marius before he could call to her to wait.

A small child, no more than six or seven years old and looking as if he was held together with dust and rags, crouched in the mouth of an alleyway. He rocked back and forth on his heels, arms hugging himself, chin pressed tight into his chest as he cried. Keth was kneeling down before him as Marius caught up with her and stood a foot away, arms crossed.

"Hey, hey." Keth put out a hand and laid it on the boy's shoulder. He flinched, and she made shushing noises. "It's okay. We're not going to hurt you. It's okay."

The child tensed, then relaxed as Keth stroked his arms, making comforting little noises as if to a child crying out in its sleep. Gradually, he relaxed, and Keth cupped his chin in her hand.

"What's the matter, sweetheart? What happened?"

The child hiccupped, found his voice through a multitude of sobs and sniffs.

"The... the dead people... me Mam... She said... she said... She... threw... me... out..." He burst into a fresh round of tears and leaned against Keth, who put her arms around him and hugged him tight.

"There, there. You're safe now. We're not going to let–"

"All right." Marius stepped forward and drove a hand in between them. He grabbed the child by the wrist and hauled him free of Keth's embrace. "Show's over."

"What?" Keth looked up in shock. "Marius? What are you doing?"

Marius shook the child. "Cough it up, squirt." The kid was crying in earnest now, struggling to get back to Keth. She leapt to her feet and grabbed at Marius' arm.

"Stop that. Stop it! What the hell are you doing?"

"Come on, stop buggerising me about."

"Let go."

"Miss… help… Miss…"

"I'm. Not. Fucking. About."

"Marius!"

Marius held him aloft, letting him swing like a street dancer's monkey. The kid kicked at his face, and Marius gave him a short, hard shake, so that he howled in pain.

"You're hurting him."

"Check your wrist."

"What?"

Marius nodded at her arm. "Check your wrist. The bracelet I bought you from that little jewellery-maker. Came through the village last year; the guy with the tiny bellows you thought were so cute."

Keth grabbed at her bare forearm. "It's–"

"With him." Marius shook the kid again, and this time Keth stood with her hands on her hips, giving him her best angry-mum stare. The boy ceased his struggle and dangled from Marius' grip.

"All right, all right," he said finally, not a trace of the frightened child remaining. "Can't blame me for trying, though. Worth a week's meat, that is." He ducked a hand inside his smock, came out with a thin band.

"Wrong one."

"Oopaday. My mistake." This time he held out the correct bracelet. Keth snatched it back and slipped it back on. "Thanks for the hug though, lady. Nicest thing I've had all day."

"Oi." Marius poked him the chest, hard. "You're dealing with me, sunshine."

"All right, don't get your linen twist… Holy bugger, look at you." He stiffened, and for the first time Marius saw genuine fear stain his face. "What are you then, mister? You're not the start of it then, are you? Cause I gotta tell you–'

"Shut." Shake. "Up." Shake.

The kid shut. Marius pressed his advantage, drawing him close so that the two of them stared round child-eyes into dead, filmed-over ones.

"You."

The boy gulped.

"You're going to do a job for me."

Something wet began to drip from the bottom of the child's foot. Keth was beginning to make small noises of sympathy. Marius turned slightly, blocking her view.

"You listening?"

He nodded mutely. Marius grinned, knowing it was scarier than if he kept his face still. The child was almost crying now. Marius felt a pang of guilt, then swept it aside. He needed obedience. If fear was what it took... He caught himself. No. That was too easy, too much like the man on the other side of the wall. He blinked, drew his aura back into himself, let his face settle back into merely dead patterns of flesh.

"Listen," he said, and his voice, still stern, lacked the feral edge that had been creeping into it. "Everyone here, in all these buildings. You're an army, right?"

The kid shook his head, began to press his eyes closed. Marius sighed. He probably had stories, this child, almost certainly knew more than one family whose sons had been rounded up and marched away never to be seen again, all of it starting with a sentence similar to that one.

"Not that type of army," he said. "You get them all together, every one of you, and you're an army for yourselves, right? And you're not fighting for some king up on the hill, only knows you to flesh out the wall between you and the other mob's horses. You get them out of these houses, fighting for all of you, you hear?" He gave the arm a quick wiggle. Eyes popped open, stared into his. A quick nod, then shut again. Marius sighed, and let him down.

"Listen." One arm still imprisoned by his grip, the kid was too damn terrified to try to even break away. "Go house to house, savvy? Anybody with a picture, a dead relative, somebody they lost, you get them out, get them into the nearest square. You understand?" Nothing. "You understand?"

A small nod, eyes closed, wishing it would all go away. Marius clicked his fingers, decided to ignore how brittle and dry it sounded. The boy opened his eyes. Marius rubbed his fingers together, and magically, two riner appeared. Despite his fear, the boy's eyes widened.

"One for now." Marius spun a coin into the air so that it landed in the child's free hand. "One when the job's done." He waggled his fingers and the second coin disappeared. The child's face showed momentary regret, then shrewdness.

"How do I know you're on the up?" he asked, the tiniest bit of bravado creeping back into his voice. Marius smiled.

"Because in a couple of hours the King's going to be marching through here, and he's a personal friend of mine. And I'll be asking him."

"Really?" the kid asked, and Marius remembered how young he actually was.

"Trust me," he said. "I'm the King of the Dead." He nodded towards the street. "G'wan," he said. "Get to it."

"Right." The kid spun on his heel and raced around the corner. Marius shook his head to himself.

"How do you know he'll do it?" Keth asked. Marius held up a finger and pointed to the end of the alley. A small head reappeared.

"Another one when I'm done, right?"

"You get more than a hundred, I'll make it three."

The kid's eyes widened to an impossible degree, and he was gone.

"You know he probably has no idea how much a hundred is, don't you?"

Marius straightened. "It's exactly the amount he says he rounded up, if I ever see him again."

Keth coughed into her hand. "Great big hard King of the Dead."

"Come on." Marius reached for her hand. "I want to stand on top of the wall."

"What for?"

"Time we saw what we were facing."

THIRTY-THREE

They stood on the empty battlement and stared out at the invading army.

Marius had been a soldier, when he couldn't think of any other way to make some money. He'd besieged a city more than once. This was like no besieging army he could remember. There were no fires, no sound of industry as teams came back from surrounding forests dragging trees to turn into siege ladders and ballistae. Tents had not been raised. Voices did not ring out in insult. Swords were not being banged against shields, to distract defending troops and remind them of the sharpened steel that waited outside. Horse-mounted braves did not dart forward to within arrow range, taunting the defenders and daring them to waste precious arrows trying to hit a single, dodging target. The sounds of activity, of building for battle, of consuming the resources that otherwise might have fed and watered the trapped citizens behind the walls, were absent.

Instead, the army stood silent, rank after serried rank pressed together into uncountable walls of rotting flesh, a hundred thousand faces turned implacably towards the walls of the city. Only silence reached Marius and Keth: no shuffling, no coughing, no tramping of mud as a nervous soldier shifted from foot to foot. They

339

stood like meat-and-bone statues in the rising light of morning, and not one of them so much as blinked as the sun rose directly into their faces.

"Good gods, that's creepy."

"It's meant to be." Marius gently loosed the ties on his mind and let his consciousness tiptoe across the space between himself and the first rank, opening his mind to the thoughts of the enemy troops. He received nothing back, just a sense of grim determination and absolute belief in the task ahead. And something else, something that finally confirmed the suspicion he had carried all this time.

"God," he spat. "All of this because they're convinced it was God who told them to do it."

"How do you know?"

Marius looked out across the plains. "This being dead," he said slowly. "It comes with different... abilities, I guess. Skills."

"Like what?"

"Like..." He searched for an analogy, gave up, settled for telling the truth. "I can feel them. All of them. A thousand million consciousnesses, pressing up against the sphere of my thoughts. I can pick them out, if I like, one at a time, dip their pockets, or just slip past them all unnoticed."

"Like in the Cathedral. When you said the dead talk. You weren't just–"

"Exaggerating for effect? No."

"All the gods." She looked at him, and Marius saw a type of fear. He turned his head away, focussed on the ranks outside the walls.

"It's not a magic skill or anything. It's just something natural, you know?" He glanced at her, snorted. "No, of course not. Silly question."

"Can you... feel me?"

"What? No." He shook his head. "You're alive. It's like..." He paused, staring at her. He didn't know, actually. It had never occurred to him to try to feel a living mind. He was so hung up on being dead, on his people and his power and his ability to move amongst them. He'd never for a moment considered that "his people" might include those he *really* thought were his. Keth caught his look, and stepped back.

"No," she said.

"I haven't tried yet."

"Don't." She shook her head. Not a denial, a warning. "If you love me..."

"Why?" Marius frowned. "What will I find?"

"That's the point." She glanced up at him, and he saw a flare of hidden anger. "It doesn't matter what you might find. You shouldn't be able to. Whatever's in here," she tapped the side of her head, "It's mine to give or not as I please. My thoughts belong to me, Marius."

"Okay, okay." He raised his hands. "I won't."

"But you would have. If I hadn't warned you off. You would have tried."

Marius said nothing. Keth turned back to the waiting army. "Is that all?" she asked, her voice a tight little squirt of sound. Marius glanced at her out of the corner of his eye.

"I can see where a body has lain. You've seen me do that. I'm..." Connected, he suddenly understood. In a way I'm not to the living world, not anymore. It didn't matter if he could read Keth's mind. Were he alive, he wouldn't need to. He could know her thoughts as truly as his own, via the myriad of sensual indicators the living shared, the panoply of little signs that living bodies use to communicate. But he was dead, and he realised with a sudden shock that he could no more read her now than he could any other living creature.

They fell into silence. Finally, Keth shivered.

"We should go."

"Yes."

They stepped away from the edge of the wall and made their way down to the street in silence, separated by a foot of space and two worlds of belonging.

Three thousand worried soldiers-turned-mothers were waiting for them when they arrived, all but tapping their toes and waiting to be told exactly what time Marius called this, and where did he think he'd been, and did he not give a thought to how worried they all were? It was Gerd who hurried forward as they exited the tunnel and spread his arms in enquiry.

"What the hell took you so long? We were worried sick."

"I wasn't."

"Shut up, Granny."

Marius brushed past him, making his way to the centre of the cavern they had carved out while he was absent. He took a moment to look around himself, at the ragged collection of victims, discarded souls, and outright bastards he had gathered. I should offer them something, he thought. Some great speech to mark the occasion, some stirring words to drive them on and give them heart for the coming battle. I've been in armies. I've seen it done. I've felt the blood thunder through my head and bring strength to my sword arm.

Instead, he turned to Gerd and offered a simple nod. His young friend stepped forward. Marius pointed to the ceiling above them. Gerd concentrated, then tilted his head back. He raised his arms, placed his palms together above his head, and in one quick movement, swung them apart in wide arcs, finishing at his waist.

Above him, the earth split asunder. The sounds of the world came tumbling in. Marius screamed back at it. He punched the air and his army pushed past him, a stream of silent bodies that roared pure bloody murder inside his mind.

Within seconds they were out of the pit, and visiting seven kinds of shit upon their enemy.

THIRTY FOUR

The nuns came first.

They poured forth like a plague of skeletal cockroaches, a flood of silent bone armatures clad only in wimples – and where the hell had *they* come from? – swinging spare femurs above their heads like hammers, crashing them down on the backs and legs of the stunned invaders who surrounded the hole. Arnobew strode ahead of them, his cardboard robes flapping in the wind, bellowing "Repent! Sinners repent!" fit to raise any dead who weren't already wide awake and wondering just what the holy hell had risen up and engulfed them.

Within seconds they had carved a swathe through the ranks of the enemy, an ever-widening circle of soldiers brought to their knees behind them. And in their wake came the tubmen, with Brys astride the shoulders of the foremost, whooping like a child on her first visit to the city as they reached into the tubs around their necks and scattered handfuls of bones as if feeding corn to chickens.

"Salvation," she screamed, cracking the flat of her twin swords against the skulls of those genuflecting about her. "Salvation!"

And slowly, after the first shock of attack had worn off, the circle of dead began to glance at the offerings on the ground about them. Then stare. And then, as the army began, however slowly, to react to the threat posed by Arnobew's women, they dove forward, to scoop up the indulgences, and to weep with joy and thank their gods.

Beneath them, Marius waited. When the first prayers reached him he signalled to Fellipan. She nodded, and waved to her followers. They surged out of the hole, three thousand bodies in a single stream. As the last one left, she ran a leather-clad hand down the side of Marius' face. Marius snapped a nod towards the hole. She arched an eyebrow at him, then turned and slinked upwards out of his vision. Marius resisted the very great temptation to watch her ascend. He turned to Gerd and Keth. Gerd was examining a particularly interesting stretch of the wall somewhere nearby. Keth was staring straight at him, arms folded, face as closed as he had ever seen it.

"Give them a minute," he said, "and then we follow." He looked past them, to the small coterie of bastards still waiting: the thugs and cutpurses Brys had rescued from the bottom of a dozen docks. She stood at their head, cutlasses drawn, a wild grin distorting her features. "They're ready?"

Brys ran the blades of her sword together. Behind her, a voice crackled, "Ready as a virgin in a whorehouse, sonny."

"You're kidding."

"She insisted," Brys replied, just as Granny stepped out from behind her.

Someone had outfitted her with a bandolier and stuffed it with knives. *Someone* had provided her with a cigar. Now she took it from her mouth and pointed the soggy end at Marius.

"Ready to cut and thrust, Kingy-boy."

"Please." Marius pinched the bridge of his nose. "Never pump your hips like that again."

Granny snickered. Marius turned away, straight into Keth's gaze. He busied himself in listening to the sounds above, very deliberately not looking at her.

"Okay," he said after a few moments. "Let's go."

Up above, all was carnage. The nuns had cleared a space nearly one hundred metres across. They held the line against the nearest ranks of the enemy, who had finally realised what was happening and engaged them. Arnobew ran around the ring like a human whirlwind, bellowing orders to his troops in between imploring those outside to accept salvation. The tubmen strode around the circle, flinging their remaining favours into the crowd beyond. Those soldiers subjugated by the first wave of nun assaults had either joined their new sisters or had laid down their arms and now hailed Marius as their saviour as he clambered past them. Granny pushed into them, Brys at her elbow, and set her troops to clearing a path for him towards the centre.

A dozen feet ahead of them lay a small hillock overlooking the surrounding plain. Marius climbed it, and stopped to wait. Around him the battlefield had resolved itself into something he was comfortable with: the sounds of fierce battle, at a distance; orders lost within the confusion of combat; the cacophony of screams, whether they were of the dying, the injured, or simply those trying to make themselves understood over the din of combat. He caught sight of Keth's confused face beside him and suffered a sudden realisation – it was all inside his head. She saw only the clash of weapons, saw combatants fall silent to the ground or run suddenly from one spot to another with nothing to direct them other than the bellowing voices of Brys and Arnobew. Marius had unleashed them for the sole purpose of sowing disorder, which purpose they were fulfilling splendidly, judging by the way the nuns and tubmen were keeping a hundred thousand directionless enemy at bay.

Then Marius saw it happen, at the far edge of the field, at the point furthest from the gates of the city: a sudden stiffening of the enemy lines, as if those at the back, who had been straining to get forward and at least view the action, were suddenly pulled into order. He pointed. Gerd and Keth followed his finger.

"Uh oh."

Marius smiled, a short, feral twist of his lips. He turned to Keth.

"You need to be somewhere else now."

He saw her jaw firm, and a flash of anger light her eyes. Her gaze flicked downwards, across the battle, then back to Marius. He followed it, saw Fellipan astride two of her largest minions, directing the flow of human traffic from one side of the small circle to the other as she supervised the reinforcement of the lines.

"Do you really need to envy the dead woman right now?" He took her arm and showed her the commotion coming towards them, getting stronger as it approached, as if some great shark was swimming through a shoal of fish who had the sense to get out of its path and let it through. "Or do you want to become one?"

Still she said nothing. Marius gave in. "Please," he said. "Whatever it'll take to make you safe. Just tell me, and then do what I need you to do, this once. Please."

Now she looked directly into his eyes. "Okay," she said. "Are you sorry?"

Gerd projected an image of a hand slapping a forehead. Marius ignored it. Instead he lowered his eyes for a moment.

"Yes."

"Why?"

"What?"

She eyed him from a million miles away. "Why are you sorry? Because you're actually sorry, or just because you want me out of the way?"

He stayed silent. Keth nodded. "I see." She turned away from him. "You don't even think they're separate."

She moved past Gerd and began to climb down into the hole. Marius kept his eyes on the spot where she had been. Gerd coughed.

"Right, then," he said. "She'll just... to the King... like we... Right." He closed the hole behind her, and then stood by Marius' side. "So we're just going to wait right here, yes?"

"Shut up now."

"Shutting up." He fell silent. Ahead of them, the enemy lines were folding back, opening up a channel for something that approached at speed. Marius cleared his mind and felt, rather than heard, the elongated cry of rage that bore down upon them.

"He's coming," he said. Gerd shrugged.

"Gods, I hope so. I'd hate to think who it is if it isn't him."

Everyone on the battlefield could hear it now: the anger of a tyrant challenged in his own den, thundering down to deliver judgement. Marius felt all the voices inside his head dribble away, stuttering into silence at the wall of fury. He smiled, waited until he could sense even his own supporters falter and look towards him for his reaction. Only then did he project an image of a hand, held up for silence. For the tiniest moment it caused the onrushing fury to pause, and in that moment he broadcast.

"Scorbus!"

A break in the projection of hatred, and Scorbus the man came through. "Don Hellespont? Is that you?" Marius saw the thoughts of the enemy ripple in confusion, saw his progress towards the line of nuns momentarily arrested.

"Scorbus the Pretender," he projected, and just for a moment was taken aback by the power in his voice, and by the way it made the entire battlefield pause, turning towards him just for a moment with awe in their minds. "Give me back my fucking crown!"

And then there was no more time to think. Scorbus' roar reverberated across the horizons. Before his own army had time to react he was driving forward towards Marius' lines, crashing through the ranks of his own soldiers at such a pace that they were driven sideways against each other. Chaos broke out as those who were forced aside crashed into those who were not. Discipline was abandoned and fighters simply swung at whomever they collided with, everyone assuming everyone else was an enemy without strong voices to guide them. The invading army shattered as if struck by a hammer.

Marius' troops did not.

As Scorbus closed with the line Arnobew was already there, shouting orders. The nuns held just long enough to provide token resistance then gave way, dragging the point of Scorbus' attacking wedge aside with them so that the formation found itself peeled apart even as it burst through into the empty space beyond. As each nun tangled with a soldier, the tubmen moved in behind, pushing the combatants further away from the breach. They pressed an indulgence upon those the nuns had exposed, and disarmed them either by brute force, or – Marius was gratified to see – by the power of their words alone. And still the majority of Marius' line held. And still Scorbus pushed onwards through the tiny gap. The few soldiers he'd managed to keep with him trickled through in a stream no more than four or five bodies wide, to be picked off and separated by those who were waiting.

Then Scorbus broke into the space beyond. Granny's troops reassembled behind him and went to work on the gap itself, a small band of nastiness that drove into the troops attempting to consolidate the breach. Marius turned his attention away from them. He knew what they were doing: slipping past the first few ranks of enemy troops before turning to smash shins and ankles with the iron bars Marius' father had provided. They would build a wall of immobile suffering dead to plug the gap, then disperse as quickly as they had assembled, sneaking in amongst the nearby troops to smash any exposed limb they could find, sowing discord and confusion, a guerrilla force driving by the sheer, base joy of bastardry; tied to his cause, but only so long as it mattered to them. Faced with such pickings, the chain would be loosed. So be it. It all counted, all added to the chaos Marius needed. And there was Scorbus, exactly where Marius wanted him: isolated, surrounded by enemies, and foaming at his non-existent mouth.

He projected a wolf whistle. Scorbus turned his head towards him. Just for a moment, Marius saw the Scorbus of old superimposed upon the staring skull: a massive, bearded visage; thick brows folded over his eyes in rage, thin lips opened wide as he roared. He even had time to see a solitary, recognisable figure steal out from behind the giant King and dissolve into the madness beyond. Drenthe. Of course, he thought. Both sides finally playing directly opposite the middle. Exactly what the traitorous advisor had wanted. Then Scorbus was surging across the empty space between them. The circle closed, held firm against further invasion. It was just Marius and Scorbus, alone, fenced in by a hundred thousand faces, with nothing left to do but destroy each other.

Except that as fast as Scorbus ascended to the top of the little hill, Marius was no longer there.

Instead he was three feet behind, close enough to smack the enraged King across the back of his head with the flat of his sword.

"Here, stupid!"

But as soon as Scorbus swung around, Marius was gone again. He reappeared a dozen feet away, threw a muddied rock that hit the skeletal King on the knee and dislodged the patella completely. Scorbus staggered, righted himself, charged down the hill with his sword raised. And Marius wasn't there either. He was six feet to the side, charging Scorbus from his blind side to crack his scapula with a single blow. Again the King staggered, roared in frustration, and turned towards his assailant only to find empty air.

Three feet below ground, Marius stopped to listen to the cry of aggravation. Gerd was waiting, and Marius went over to his side.

"It's working."

"And this is what you want, to make a psychotic homicidal giant even more unhinged than he already is?"

Marius smiled, and felt insanity at the edge of his lips. "I wasn't doing anything today, anyway."

Gerd sighed, and opened up another hole above them.

And so it went. Marius drew the King from point to point across the circle of observers, never staying still, never stopping long enough to be engaged. He picked Scorbus apart bit by bit – a slap to the back of the head in front of the tubmen; reaching through a hole to grab his foot and bury his leg past the ankle; taking a chip off the top of his pelvic girdle right in front of those converted soldiers who had once formed the advance of his invasion. And slowly, as the combat continued, and the once-demonised King of the Dead began to look increasingly clumsy, as he continued to swing at fresh air and stumble from one miniscule defeat to the next, something in the atmosphere changed.

Where the battlefield had been charged with violence and desperation, and countless tiny struggles for survival, suddenly all focus was switched to the two single combatants. The opposing lines wavered, and dissolved, as even Arnobew's nuns could no longer escape their curiosity and turned inwards to watch. Arnobew, Brys, and Fellipan continued to circle, but now it was with soft words of friendship. They drew weapons out of the hands of their enemies and shepherded them forward for a better view, providing a running commentary. They drew people together, first in small clumps, then in larger groups. Soon what was once a plain of death began to resemble the site of a well-attended travelling show. Marius heard laughter as Scorbus swung his sword at the space where Marius had been standing and fell over. A few picnic blankets and we could start charging, Marius thought as his latest fleeting appearance brought them back to the top of the hillock where they had begun. He brought the jewelled hilt of his father's sword down across Scorbus' back and watched him fall to one knee. Almost there, he thought, and stopped for the merest moment.

Scorbus shot out a hand and grabbed his trouser leg.

The audience gasped.

Marius tried to pull away. Scorbus tightened his grip and hauled him off-balance. The giant King turned his face towards him.

"Got you," he said, and brought his sword arm over. Marius swung his blade up to block it. They clashed, and he watched as the tip of his blade shattered at the terzo and went spinning away.

"Cheap piece of shit!" He struck forward, grinding the broken tip against Scorbus' radius, but the King had him now, and nothing was loosening his grip. He swung again, and again, battering at Marius' sword until the shock of repeated blows dropped it from his hand. The crowd, sensing some sort of completion, began to find its feet. Arnobew had turned from his diplomatic duties and was beginning to run towards them. Brys was unleashing her twin blades from their scabbards. Marius could feel Gerd beneath him, tensing. He went to hold his breath, realised he had none to hold, and tensed anyway.

"Now," he projected. Around them a maze of holes opened up, blocking any approach, Gerd running from one tiny corridor to another beneath them as fast he could, not bothering to look before he spread and closed his arms with a clapping sound like a broken shingle. Marius sensed the cessation of movement from beyond the hillock. He felt his companions slow and stop at the edge of the circle of holes, slowly sheath their weapons and stand in helpless amazement. He spared a moment to smile towards them. Scorbus was almost to his feet, bringing his sword about in a low, flat arc ready to separate Marius' head from his neck. Marius stopped fighting against the slow drag of his leg towards his enemy. He leaned into it, braced himself for a moment, and leaped towards Scorbus' neck.

And was caught.

As soon as he jumped, Scorbus let go of his trouser leg and swung his hand up to grab Marius' throat. Now he stood to his full height, lifting the smaller man like he was no more than a chicken to be beheaded and plucked. Marius grabbed at his wrist, tugging at the thick bones that pressed against his flesh. An invisible gasp ran around the watching armies. Scorbus raised his hand, and turned to display his prey.

"Observe," he commanded, and a hundred thousand minds obeyed him, a hundred thousand consciousnesses pouring into the little tableau. "Observe what happens to those who betray their King."

Marius felt the attention of every dead soul on the battlefield. He narrowed his focus, and projected the slightest of smiles deep into Scorbus' mind. The great King faltered, just for a moment, and looked down at him.

And Marius played his final trick.

THIRTY-FIVE

Never steal what you can't swallow. It had been Marius'
mantra for as long as he had been a thief. It was a way
to conceal the spoils of his trade, to escape retribution.
Now, for the first time he could remember, he used it not
to hide, but to reveal. He raised his hands to Scorbus'
wrists as if tugging feebly at them, cupped them, and
coughed. And caught the thing he had swallowed, back
when he had lifted it from his mother's grasp. A single
finger bone, carved with indulgences.

Marius had been a thief for more than twenty years.
He had stolen from soldiers while they held him at sword
point. He had stolen from the Caliph's virgin daughter
while she had him tied to her bed. He had even, once,
stolen from a hangman as he adjusted a noose around
Marius' neck. Now he stole from Scorbus, even as the
King raised his hand to deliver the blow that would
destroy Marius for eternity.

It was a small theft, and quickly achieved. Marius
simply gripped the hand that held his throat, found the
second bone of the index finger, and with one quick
movement of his fingers, pushed it out and slipped
the carved bone into its place. Less than a second had
passed. Scorbus began to roar, began to bring his sword
down towards his captive's skull. Marius allowed him

a small projection: himself, grinning. Scorbus paused, momentarily confused. And was defeated.

"Hold!" Marius projected as hard as he dared. "What's this?"

For half a moment, the battle paused. Marius focussed on Scorbus' hand, projected the sight of the indulgence bone nestled halfway along its finger.

"An indulgence?" he cried. Scorbus snatched his hand away from Marius' throat, dropping him to the ground. Marius fell heavily, sat with his legs splayed apart, and stared in triumph as Scorbus held the offending hand up to his blank skull in shock. "Why does your King need an indulgence, if God tells him that this world above ground is Heaven?" Scorbus was shaking his head: visible to the few troops that surrounded them, but unseen by the majority of the battlefield; and, Marius noted gleefully, he was too shocked to offer any sort of denial or counter accusation.

"Why does he hide it?" he broadcast. "Why do so many of you accept indulgences from my troops?" He found his feet, took the risk of turning away from Scorbus to address the surrounding combatants directly. "Unless you know," he said to them. "Unless you know that this man is a usurper, and has betrayed you."

Finally, Scorbus broke free of his shock and propelled himself to action. But it was too late.

"Now!" Marius cried. Directly underneath them, Gerd opened up a hole. Marius and Scorbus dropped into it, and as Marius' feet found solid ground below, Gerd closed the hole up around Scorbus' pelvis, trapping him. The fissures that had separated them from the rest of the battleground shut. All of a sudden, the hundreds of penitents who had crept forward to their edges, clutching their own tiny proofs of their disbelief in Scorbus' vision of Heaven, broke forward with cries of betrayal. Marius barely had time to close his mind to the sounds of their assault before they climbed the little hillock and threw themselves upon the stranded King.

What followed was short, and brutal. Even trapped, with the world against him, Scorbus was a warrior of prodigious strength. He swept up his sword and lashed it against the first bodies to reach him, scattering them back down the hillock in a confusion of limbs. But the dead are not so easily discarded as the living. Those who were repelled found their feet once more, and joined the great angry wave that crested the hill and washed over the solitary figure at its peak. The great King was torn apart in a matter of seconds, his roar of rage lost beneath those of his dead compatriots. In less than a minute his voice was silenced by the crunch of something heavy thundering down upon his skull. Marius closed his eyes for a moment, as the King's voice was cut off inside his head, and the dangling legs that kicked and scrabbled for purchase in front of him became just a ragged collection of bones. Then they were not even that, as the life force that had animated them was borne away on the wind, and they fell in clattering profusion to become just a pile of yellowed sticks on the floor before him. Then the earth above him opened, and he looked up to see a ring of dead faces looking down upon him, a familiar one-eyed visage at their centre.

"Your Majesty," Drenthe said, leaning into the gap to offer Marius his hand. Marius stared at it for long seconds. The battlefield, he realised, was unnaturally quiet. A hundred thousand minds were holding their breath, waiting to see what he would do. His actions now would decide the war, one way or another. He glanced up into Drenthe's face, saw only calm assurance.

"Your Majesty," the dead soldier repeated.

Marius nodded, and took his hand. Drenthe hauled him up, until he stood at the exact centre of a hundred thousand faces.

Someone, somewhere, retrieved the crown. The legions of the dead sheathed their weapons. Drenthe stepped forward, golden circlet in hand.

"Your crown, Your Majesty."

Marius took it from him. He stared down at it: a battered, misshapen circle of dirty metal, with a gap at the front where the largest jewel had been dislodged and lost in the fighting. He hefted it gently. A few ounces of gold, nothing more. Not even a true crown, really. A headband, at best. Wouldn't get more than a couple of hundred riner if he melted it down and sold it to some backroom fence in a barroom in Borgho. Give you maybe fifty for the jewels, as long as they could be recut. Damn thing was trash.

Slowly, he lifted it and settled it on his head.

Beaten out of shape as it was, it still slid down. He adjusted it, tilted it back so the front sat above his brow.

"Thank you, Drenthe."

Drenthe nodded and stepped back. Marius stared at the dead warriors around him; felt, at the back of his mind, the anticipation of the thousands who filled the plain; gazed over their heads at the city walls beyond. Behind them crouched thirty thousand souls, terrified and praying. He refocussed on those nearer to him.

The dead were waiting, he realised. For him. For his first proclamation.

"Stop," he said.

And just like that, the invasion was over.

THIRTY-SIX

And now, at last, the great East Gate of the city opened, and an army poured forth. But not the army Scorbus would have wanted. Not a vast wall of terrified men in armour, looking to equally terrified men on horses to guide them into the horrifying attrition of battle. This was an army of a different sort. Ten thousand strong, they flowed outwards in a disorganised stream, scattering in all directions. They moved in amongst the stony corpses who turned to them, confused and uncertain, half-raising weapons against what *should* have been a threat but was so patently not. An army of the people, their young King at the vanguard, dispersing on foot; each one holding a treasured painting, or locket, or etching. Children with hand-drawn images on scraps of paper. Housewives with cigar box lids. Merchants with framed portraits. Every citizen bore an impression of a loved family member. Fathers, mothers, brothers, sisters, children, grandchildren, they pushed through the astonished dead, calling names, holding their pictures up to rotting and time-destroyed faces and asking, "Uncle Gemis? Do you know him?", "Aunty Lof? Have you seen her?", "Mother?", "Father?", "My baby?"

We miss her. We love him. Have you seen them? Do you know them? Are they here? Can we find them?

Have you met them? Are they here? Are they here?

Slowly, in dribs and drabs, the dead came together with those they had left behind. And slowly, as wives and husbands were reunited, as grandchildren raced through the ranks to throw themselves at dirt-encrusted grandparents, as brothers hugged, as wives and husbands embraced like they had thought never to do again, the dead found their humanity restored. They dropped their weapons. They turned their backs upon their army. They sat, silent, as their families talked and talked and talked, and Marius' mind was full of dead weeping as he watched Billinor approach.

"Your Majesty."

"Your Majesty." The King smiled, and pointed at Marius' bent and battered crown. "It suits you."

Marius glanced up at it, and frowned. Around him the war was dissolving like salt into water. He took a moment to stare at the joyous reunions that had ended it, and sighed.

"We need to talk."

A small marquee was erected on the hillock at the centre of the former battlefield. A table was placed within, with two chairs of equal height at either side. Two kings faced each other, with a phalanx of sidekicks around them.

"So."

"So."

Marius gazed past Billinor to the fields outside. A hundred and fifty thousand people milled about, ranks swollen by city dwellers who came to gawp, and wander, and give themselves a reason to say, years from now, that they were there on the day it happened, that they were a part of it. Marius shook his head.

"The living have become too used to the dead."

"Do you–"

"You have no claim on this land. You must leave immediately." To Billinor's left, a tall and spectacularly moustachioed man leaned in, jabbing an index finger towards Marius. Marius stared at Billinor for several seconds, then allowed his gaze to take in the interloper.

"And who," he drawled in his best street-fighter voice, "the fuck are you?"

The tall man reddened at the insult. "I am Lord Denia. I am the King's Chamberlain. I decide the King's policy when it comes to matters of…" he sneered, "politics."

"Really." Marius jerked a thumb at Granny. "This is *my* chamberlain. She can fart sea shanties."

Granny smiled at Denia. He visibly blanched.

"Granny, why don't you remind Lord Denia who I am?"

"With pleasure." The old woman stalked around the table, until she was close enough to flick the buttons on his jacket.

"You can't do that," Denia spluttered. "This is an outrageous breach of diplomatic…"

"Denia." Billinor was impersonating him, Marius realised with delight. The same drawl, the same nonchalant recline against the chair. I do believe the little bugger's enjoying this, he thought. "Be quiet and let the King's Chamberlain speak."

"But Your–"

"Now, Denia."

"I… I… Your Majesty." Denia, finally, realised that everyone but him had remained very quiet indeed, and that it did not represent any form of support.

"Are you comfortable?" Granny glanced around the wall of advisors. Satisfied with the fear in their eyes, she smiled. "Good." She turned back to Denia. "See the lad, there?" She pointed at Billinor. The Chamberlain nodded. "When he dies – and not too soon, I hope…" She reached back and patted Billinor on the head. Denia looked very much like he'd like to protest but that, for the sake of self-preservation, he might just keep it to himself for the moment. "He's quite cute, for a city boy."

"Thank you, Granny."

"You're welcome, sweetie."

Billinor leaned forward and said to Marius in a stage whisper. "I like her."

You little shit, Marius thought with a smile. You *are* enjoying this. "You can keep her, if you like."

"Oh no," Granny said. "I already have one immature, short-arse king to knock sense into."

Billinor laughed. "She called you a short-arse."

"Can we get back to things, please?"

Billinor snickered. Granny shot him an indulgent smile, and turned back to Denia. "When this lad dies, he's going to the Bone Cathedral, high up on the top of that big hill overlooking the city, to lie in a shiny white crypt in the bosom of his ancestors, where he can spend his eternity in quiet contemplation of his deeds and the love of his people. Won't that be nice?"

"I…"

"You, on the other hand." She flicked a button. "I bet you've got a family crypt somewhere, haven't you, sonny? I bet it's made of imported stone, and it's at the posh end of the graveyard, away from all the common people and their dirty, common graves, isn't it?"

She flicked another button. Denia became very interested in something fascinating way over there, far away from having to look down at Granny's grimy hands all over his freshly-pressed jacket. Granny grabbed a button and tugged it. Denia, faced with bending down or losing a button, opted to bend.

"Doesn't matter where you end up," she said. "In the end, you all come down to us. And when you do…" Quick as a snake, her hand shot out and grabbed Denia's ear. She twisted, and held it, so that he had no choice but to look across the table, straight at Marius. "He'll be your King. For the rest of time."

Marius waggled his fingers in a wave. Granny let go. Denia shot up straight, tottering backwards with the shock of sudden release. Granny walked back down the line of advisors, smiling as each one followed her with their eyes.

"So my advice to you," she said, "would be to shut the fuck up, and try not to piss off the King you've got now *or* the one you'll have for all eternity. Savvy?"

"Thank you, Granny." Marius waved a finger to her. "You can come back now."

Granny sauntered back around the table. As she passed Marius, she winked.

"Savvy?" he asked.

"Brys," Gerd muttered.

"Ah." He returned his gaze to Billinor. "The dead and the living should not coexist."

Billinor looked afraid. Marius smiled sadly. "This world belongs to the living," he said, and the crowd across the table visibly relaxed. He looked past them to the fields beyond. "The living have become too used to the dead."

"They have their loved ones back."

"Not just that." Marius shook his head. "The last three years. It's been seeping into the world. I've been shown." He glanced at Drenthe, who inclined his head in the merest of nods. "People integrating them, using them.

The dead have become your donkeys, your resource to exploit." He thought of his father, of the vast riches of V'Ellos. "Your slaves. People don't fear death the way they did. People *need* to fear death."

There was a rustling in the tent: the brush of cloth on cloth as hands fell to the hilts of swords.

"What do you mean?" Billinor crouched in his seat as if ready to bolt.

Marius held up his hand, turned it this way and that while he looked at it. "Look at me," he said. "How dead do I appear to you?"

"Ah." The young King glanced at his advisors. His advisors were terribly interested in the stitching that held the corners of the tent together. "You look, ah, fresh?"

"I was killed six weeks ago." Another glance at Drenthe. Another nod, as inscrutable as the last. "Do you know what state a body should be in once it's been dead for six weeks?" The King shook his head. Marius glanced at his entourage. "Lord Denia?"

"I…" the Chamberlain blanched, sought his liege's reassurance. Billinor gave him none. The old man swallowed. "Your forgiveness, Majesty, but…" He swallowed again. "The corpse, that is, to say, the deceased… decays, Your Majesty. The flesh swells, then falls back in upon itself, gives itself up to ruin. The eyes, and the soft parts–"

"Thank you, Denia."

"Majesty."

He fell back relieved. Marius saw him glance across the table, saw Granny wink and blow him a kiss. Denia turned pale, and shrank to the back of the group. Marius smiled to himself, and recaptured Billinor's attention. "Look at me. Look at my hand. Do you see any swelling? Have I given myself up to ruin?"

"No."

Marius felt some sympathy for the lad: face to face with the King of the Dead, discussing the ruination of the body. Nobody should converse with a dead man, least of all the boy before him. How could he talk to a dead monarch and not think of his father? Come to that, how could he not look at Marius and see his own future?

Pursing his lips in compassion, Marius pressed on. "The world is not right, Billinor. *We* are not right. We shouldn't be walking around, getting in the way of life."

"Then take them away. Take them back to… your place."

Marius opened his mouth to speak. An image of a blue-stained face interposed itself upon his thoughts: the Gelder. Alive, a part of a living, ongoing culture with a history, and rituals, and places of worship. Underground. He looked up at Drenthe, sharply. The other man stared straight ahead, giving him nothing.

"It's not our place," Marius said. "Not ours alone. We cannot simply occupy it and claim dominion."

"But where else can you go? There are spaces that are set aside for you, that we honour as yours." Billinor pointed outside. "Cemeteries, burial fields, and the like. Can we not declare these sovereign lands, so that you do not have to retreat so far below?"

Marius smiled sadly. "And then what? Mill around, waiting for someone to come along and give them news of the afterlife?" He indicated the battlefield. "We tried that. Didn't go well."

"No."

"No."

"Then what?"

Marius was staring at his hand as if fascinated by it. The skin was beginning to pall, to lose just the slightest edge of colour. He flexed it, watched the skin tighten over yellowing flesh.

"It's a lie," he said, half to himself. "We hang around, waiting for someone to tell us what to do, waiting for someone to tell us that God has a special little field of happiness just for us. And it's a lie. Even after death, they don't stop lying to us."

"Helles…" Drenthe stepped forward. Marius closed his fist.

"No." The room became deathly still. Drenthe stopped. Marius spoke, staring at his clenched fist. "There is no happy little field. There is no afterlife. A man lives, he takes his lot, and then he dies."

"Helles–"

"Your. *Majesty*."

"Mar…" Marius turned his face to Drenthe, and for the first time saw him quaver, and fail. "Your Majesty…"

"There is no God," Marius said. "There is no reason for the dead to stick around, hoping for something that can never, ever happen."

"Your Majesty, I must advise–"

"You have *advised* me for the last time, Drenthe." Marius turned his back upon him once more. "You have advised me to this place, this…" He waved his dead hand. "This unavoidable state of being. You advised the ruin of my home and the murder of my neighbours. You have advised me to death."

"Majesty." Drenthe knelt into the edge of his vision. *Marius. It had to be done. You had to take up your destiny. It was the only way.*

Marius would not shift his head to address him. "You took my life away. *My* life." He risked a glance towards Keth, turned back before the distance between them could sting too hard. "I *had* a destiny."

"I'm sorry, I really am. But you know it had to be done."

"I understand that." Now he did turn to the dead man. "I swore when I saw what you did to the village that I would tear you into little pieces and listen to you die forever. I release us both from that vow." Drenthe looked relieved. Marius held up a finger. "But I will not forgive you."

Drenthe stood, looked from Marius to the little group behind him. Gerd, Keth, Granny, Fellipan: they stared back with one face, cold, unforgiving. He offered the slightest of bows, then returned his gaze to Marius.

"Your Majesty," he said. He swung about on his heel, and left the tent without a backwards glance. Marius remained where he was, staring down at his clenched fist.

"I'm sorry," he said, and wasn't quite sure who he was saying it to any more. "I'm sorry for what I have to do."

"What?" Billinor leaned forward in his chair. His advisors leaned with him, eyes fixed upon the bent figure on the other side of the table. "What do you have to do?"

Marius raised his eyes to the young King. "The mouthpiece of God," he said. "God's representative on earth. Tell me," he smiled, and it was a sad, broken thing. "Do you feel God talking to you, King of Scorby?"

"I…" Billinor glanced at Denia, at the line of stiff-backed gentry surrounding him, at the figure of his mother, ignored at the back of the tent. He lowered his head. "I try," he whispered.

"But you hear nothing, don't you?"

Billinor paused, then, reluctantly, shook his head.

"You know why." Gerd said. "We both do." He reached out, and covered the young King's hands in his.

"I'm sorry."

"Me too."

Marius stood. "I'm sorry, for what I'm going to leave you with, and what I have to ask you to do after we've left. If I might offer some advice…"

"Anything."

Marius looked down at the young boy, all dressed up in the crown and robes of a king. "Take your people back behind the wall. Don't let them see what happens. And when they come back out to clean up the bones, let them grieve."

"Is that all?"

Marius risked a quick glance towards Keth.

"Not all."

Billinor followed his eyes, understood what Marius was asking.

"I will." He stood, and held out his hand. "It has been an honour, King Marius."

Marius took it. "It has, King Billinor. One more word?"

"Certainly."

Marius nodded at Billinor's advisors, then leaned over to whisper in the King's ear.

"Fuck 'em."

Billinor sniggered. "You are *so* rude."

The young King gathered up his retinue. Marius and his friends watched them leave.

"What now?" Keth asked. "What did you apologise to him for?"

"Come on," Marius took her hand, and began to walk down the rise towards the city walls. "It's time to put an end to all this."

THIRTY-SEVEN

Life is nothing more than a slow descent into madness. A child is born, tabula rasa, believing only in its own existence and the warmth of its mother's skin. Slowly it grows, taking on gender, growing into society's expectations. It learns bigotry, it learns the class system, it learns to stop caring. And sooner or later, after repeated exposure, it develops the mental illness known as religion. Perhaps it is caught from a parent, or the master to whom the child is apprenticed; or, if truly unfortunate enough to afford schooling, a teacher. But once contracted, this mental virus burrows deeper and deeper into the victim's psyche until it eats out all other knowledge, all other capacity for human evolution... until nothing remains but the illness itself, supporting and nourishing the host body for its own gain so that it may, in turn, be passed on to others: wives, husbands, family, children.

And then, once it has propagated itself as far as it possibly can, this illness can no longer support its host body, and the child who once was nothing but potential withers and dies. But the illness remains, hot and fetid. The body is buried, but the virus animates it, driving it downwards through the dirt until it finds its new home, underground, in the halls and passages of those it resembles: mania-driven corpses, shuffling about in the dark with no purpose other than to nourish the virus, to give hope to the religious disease, to wait for the call of God. And slowly the body dissolves, as the processes of death eat away at the flesh and the organs and the hair. Yet the disease remains, propping up the disconnected bones in a distant memory of the form they once held. The illusion of perception hangs on long after the spark of real consciousness has gone. The mania that had infected the body in life swells to fit the empty skull that once held a brain, imprinted with the sounds and thoughts and memories that filled that ball of spoiled grey meat. Until, inevitably, the disease has nothing to feed upon but itself. The skeleton slows, becomes still. The body settles down in some dank, dark corner. Centuries after the creature that once surrounded it has died, the armature of disease finally runs down and falls into immobility. The virus has eaten itself, and the body is truly, completely, dead. How long it takes depends on how deep the disease took hold, how bright the fever of religion infected the bones. It can take centuries. It can take a thousand years.

A thousand years after the body dies, the disease of religion can still stand that body before a King and demand final justification of its existence.

Marius don Hellespont, twice-crowned King of the Dead – once by acclaim and once by right of conquest – stood atop the walls of Scorby and stared down at the aftermath of battle. His subjects stood shoulder to shoulder, a carpet of living corpses stretching across the plains towards the mountains. A hundred thousand grey and withered faces, some no more than a few weeks old, some hundreds of years in the waiting, stared up at him. Behind him, the citizens of Scorby waited also, praying inside their silent heads that the promises in which they had trusted were true, and that the small, solitary figure on the wall was here to end their fear. Only the height of the wall separated him from the masses below. That, and the thin circle of gold perched uneasily on his head.

For one long, terrified moment, the world fell silent.

Marius closed his eyes. There were too many: too many eyes staring at him; too many grey slits across the landscape where the dead had fallen; too many minds trying desperately to hush questions and fears and demands and pleas that he could still hear, no matter how hard they all tried. The crown burned, a thin line of heat that burrowed into his skin and would not give him release. So he closed his eyes against them all, and let his dead sight expand backwards into his skull, let it diffuse throughout his body, let the deadness of his vision fill him up until he was merely a vessel for death, a lens through which he could look and find only himself. A pillar of grey light, oblivious to the demands of flesh and the world around him.

And at the centre of his being, where the light shone most fully, his thoughts resolved themselves. He saw a grey circle bearing a single grey stone, smoke-formed twin to the crown around his head. Marius picked it up, and stared into the stone as if into the depths of a mirror. And the truth he saw within its depths caused his eyes to snap open, and allowed the world to flood back in.

"There is only me."

"What?" Gerd was beside him, his open farm boy's face creased with a burden of worry Marius had never seen before. Marius stared at him until recognition dawned, and he reached out to steady himself against his companion's shoulder.

"What did you say? Marius?"

But the moment had passed, and Marius was alone in his head again. He stepped away from his friend and stood between the high points of the battlements so that the ocean of dead faces below him was fully in his view.

He raised his head, and projected. His voice echoed across the ghost plains of his mind, deeper and more resonant than it had ever been in his throat. It was the voice of a king, he realised, the sound of ultimate authority: inviolate, unarguable, to be obeyed without question. The voice of God's representative on Earth.

"It started slowly, at first. A body in the midst of the masses suddenly falling, crashing to the ground like a vessel dropped by arms grown numb. Then another, somewhere else amongst the crowd. Then another, and another, and within moments, the army of the dead was collapsing before him as if struck by an invisible flash of thunder. In less than a minute it was dissolved. Where moments before there had been a vast army, now there was only a sea of bones and rotting flesh, a charnel field of his own making.

Too late, Marius thought of his companions. He swung around, but only one man stood behind him.

"Drenthe?"

The soldier made a strangled sound. He stalked past his King, looked down upon the destruction, wheeled to face Marius.

"You… you… fuck," he managed; and then he, too, was gone. He collapsed from the top down, the leathery sound of his body hitting the ground interrupted only by the sound of something metal striking stone. Marius nudged his corpse over with his toe, saw the hammer that Drenthe had concealed behind his back. He pushed harder, sent the body tumbling over the edge of the wall, listened to it strike stone then land thirty feet below. He tried to find sorrow for the destruction, and discovered only emptiness. The dead below him were now only that: finally, properly, dead.

"Bloody hell." A voice beside him whispered in awe. "What did you do?"

"Gerd?" Marius snapped back to himself in an instant. "How did… I didn't think…" He stopped, frowned. "How did you not…?"

Gerd stared past him at the field of bones. "What happened?"

"I'm their King." Behind him, feet scraped across stone. He and Gerd turned towards it: Granny, clambering up the last few steps to the battlements, pausing only to push the dead over the edge of the steps with her feet, and behind her, the three woman: Brys, Fellipan, and Keth.

"I'm their King," Marius repeated. "I'm their conduit to God. When I speak, it's not me speaking. It *is* God, using my voice. That's what they've been taught, for centuries. That's what they believed."

"But you told them…"

Marius shook his head. "The King told them. The one voice they could not dispute. All that kept them going was the chance to take their place in whatever Kingdom of God they believed in. I took it away."

"They had nothing to live for."

"They had nothing not to stay dead for." He frowned. "But I never thought about you. How did you not…?" He waved a hand below.

Gerd smiled. "Oh, please. I know you. When have you ever been right about anything?"

"But…"

Fellipan raised one exquisitely arched eyebrow. "I don't believe in God."

"You–"

"Death was a career move, remember? I'm in it for the power."

"Right." He turned to Granny.

"You owe me." She stalked forward and poked him in the chest. "Fields of green and God's right hand and peace everlasting. You don't get rid of me until I get it, sonny."

"Didn't you hear what I said?"

Granny hawked, and spat over the edge of the battlements. "Think you'd get out of it with a lie like that? Bollocks to you, boy."

"Oh, for all the gods in the sky." He stopped, suddenly aware of the absurdity of his curse. "Arnobew," he said. "Oh, gods, did anyone see…?"

The others exchanged glances, but said nothing. Marius closed his eyes.

Around them, the city was beginning to come back to its senses. Sounds began to filter up from the streets below: doors scraping open, the awkward shifting of metal and leather as soldiers began to emerge from their hiding places, the low rumble of thirty thousand mouths murmuring one simple question to each other, slowly gaining in volume as the only answer to be had was "Let's go and find out." Marius looked around at his tiny coterie.

"I think it's time I went."

His companions looked at each other.

"I don't want to be here anymore," he said. "I…" He looked at the city, at the field beyond the wall, at the two worlds that had him trapped between them. "I don't want to be anywhere." He nodded at a spot further down the battlements, where several grey lines crisscrossed. "Looks like people died there, and were pulled down below. Gerd, can you open one up, please?"

"Easy." Gerd walked across, and spread his palms open above the nearest line. It opened up smoothly, a wide, dark hole leading down into the underworld.

Fellipan and Granny shared a look.

"Whore."

"Filthy crone."

"Come on, then."

They disappeared down it together. Brys glanced at it, then turned and poked Marius in the chest.

"You shit."

"What?"

She jerked a thumb over the wall. "You killed the best bloody crew I've had in bloody years, you selfish bugger. I'll have to go back to living men again."

"I am consumed with regret."

"Yeah, well," She smiled. "I'm getting mighty tired of breaking up with you, broke, shagged out, and without a man in the world, you bloody bugger."

Gerd coughed. "I might be able to help on that score."

Marius and Brys turned towards him in unison.

"You?" Brys eyed him up and down. "Why, I never knew you were interested."

Gerd completely failed to blush once more. Instead, he jerked his throat back and forth for a few moments, coughed something into his hands, and wiped them down the front of his jerkin.

"Here," he said, holding them out. Brys eyed them suspiciously. There, nestled inside, were the coins he had swallowed in V'Ellos. Brys grinned, and accepted them.

"You are a sweet boy," she said, and planted a kiss on him that would have sucked the air right out of him if he'd been alive. "You make sure to look me up if you get bored, you hear?"

She swung about on a boot heel, tipped a wink to Marius and Keth, and sauntered down the stairs towards the nearest tavern. Gerd coughed.

"Yes. Well. I'll just…" He pointed towards the hole. "When you're… you know… whenever." He scurried over, and faced away from Marius and Keth.

Reluctantly, they turned to each other. Marius looked at her from the side of his eyes.

"Keth?"

Keth hadn't moved since she ascended the stairs. Now she stood alone, arms hugging herself, and stared past Marius at the hole behind him.

"I'm not going," she said, then, as Marius made to move towards her with his arms opened, "Don't."

He stopped, the half dozen feet between them becoming an uncrossable gulf. "Why?"

"Why?" She laughed, as much to herself as at the question. "Look at us, Marius. Look at you."

Marius gazed at his hands, still half-raised in supplication. "You told me it didn't matter."

"Oh, Marius. It does. It so does." She held her own hand up in response. "Look at me, Marius. I'm alive. Don't you understand what that means?"

"Am I that repulsive?"

"No. No." She shook her head angrily. "You still don't get it, do you? It means you've changed, Marius. Whether you feel it or not, you're not alive anymore. You don't think like a living person. You said it yourself. You kill thousands, and hardly notice. You push kings and soldiers about like chess pieces, you raise the dead and send them out to die again, you pull bodies up from below the waves and give them free rein to murder. You don't do what living people do anymore."

"I'm still me. I'm still the man who loves you."

She stared at him so long that he began to be afraid that even his words held the power to kill. Then she bit her lip.

"No," she said. "You've not been that for a long time."

He stared at her, his grey-feeling face losing all life. He saw tears begin to streak the dirt on her cheeks. He would have let his match hers, then, but he had no ability to do so. "You're dead, Marius. The King of the Dead."

"I've just killed off my kingdom."

"It doesn't matter. There will be more. You know that." She turned her exquisite, *alive* hand towards the city behind them. "Even now there are people out there on their knees, thanking God or gods for saving them. What do you think will happen when they die, Marius? Where do you think they'll go?"

"I–"

"You might be right, my love. There might not be a God. But that won't stop people believing." The hand retreated, the arm curled back around her chest. "You'll still have a kingdom. And you'll still be King."

"But…" His hands were shaking. He shook them at her. "Come with me, please. I can't do it by myself."

"Be your Queen?"

"Yes!"

She inhaled, then, a gesture made of equal measures love and pity.

"A living, breathing Queen of the Dead, Marius?"

"I…" And he paused. He remembered that later, and tried to give himself credit. He at least paused, before he gave words to the thought that sprang unbidden. "You could always…"

"No." She held up her hand, and her smile dissolved into grim denial. "You won't ask that of me."

"I'm… I'm sorry."

She nodded. "I know you are." She turned from him and looked back up towards the Radican, sprawled along the mountain like a lazy whore. "When we took Billinor to see his father, I went into the other Hall."

"The Hall of Queens."

"Yes," She looked him in the eye. "The smaller, darker, less important one. Scorbus' Queen is interred there. Do you know her name?"

"What? Uh…" He frowned in concentration. "Ulik… Uliksh."

"Uliksh, yes. Tell me: when you released Scorbus, why didn't you take her as well?"

"The Queen?"

"Yes."

"Well…" He frowned. "We were struggling. We only had time for Scorbus. And besides…"

"Besides?"

"The dead…"

She smiled, and it was the saddest thing Marius had ever seen. "They didn't ask you to. They wanted a king, not a queen. A queen wasn't *necessary*."

After an age, Marius nodded. Just once. Just enough. Keth raised her hand to his face, cupped his jaw for a fleeting moment, then let it drop.

"I want to live, Marius. I want a full, happy life. I want to smell flowers and wash in the river and eat food I grew in my garden. I want a baby, Marius. I want to bring up a child and watch her grow into someone who might change the world. I want to grow old and see my hair turn grey and my teeth fall out." She shook her head. "I won't die for you. Not now. I won't kill myself for you."

"What then?"

She flicked her gaze towards the hole. "I don't know. But I can't do it with you. I love you, Marius. But I don't forgive you anymore."

"I love you."

"I know. Despite everything. Despite all the betrayals. Despite her…" Another flick of the eyes, towards Fellipan, waiting in the dark. "Despite all the others, and everything else. I know."

"I–"

"Go now. Go and be King."

"I–"

"I'll see you one day, Marius. One day."

"Keth…"

She turned, and walked away from him. Marius watched her back, until her golden hair disappeared beneath the stone lip of the battlement.

"Marius."

Gerd stood above the hole, waiting. Marius nodded to nobody in particular.

"I'm coming."

Leaving the sounds of the living world behind, Marius the King descended into his kingdom.

ACKNOWLEDGMENTS

As always, my undying gratitude and love to Luscious Lyn and the kids for giving me the time and space to bash my fists on the keyboard without wondering aloud just how much better their life would be if it included a husband or a dad. Actually, I've just realised that there might be *another* reason why they weren't wondering...

Big thanks to the *Corpse-Rat King* beta crew for letting me kill them off in various unpleasant and downright unsanitary ways this time out. And to everyone who read the acknowledgments of my last book and dropped into the Battersblog to leave me a dirty joke I can only ask:

> *What's worse than having sex with your Granny?*
> *Licking the sweat off her back.*

To *battersblog.blogspot.com*, people – you never know, there might be a third one...

ABOUT THE AUTHOR

Lee Battersby was born in Nottingham, UK, in 1970, departing from a snow-covered city in 1975 directly to a town on the edge of Australia's largest desert. In November. He's only just now beginning to recover from the culture shock.

He is the author of over seventy stories in Australia, the US and Europe, with appearances in the likes *of Year's Best Fantasy & Horror, Year's Best Australian SF & F*, and *Writers of the Future*. He's taught at Clarion South, and won a number of awards including the Aurealis, Australian Shadows and the Ditmar.

He lives in Mandurah, Western Australia, with his wife, the writer Lyn Battersby, and an increasingly weird mob of kids. He is sadly obsessed with Lego, Nottingham Forest football club, dinosaurs, and Daleks. All in all, life is pretty good.

battersblog.blogspot.com

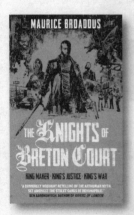

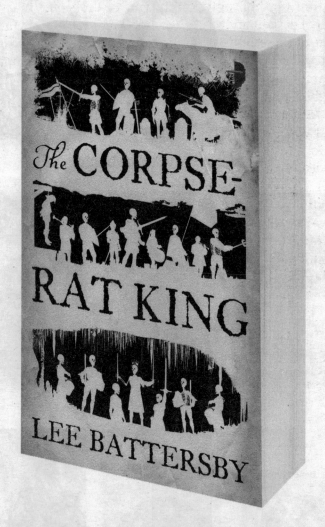

"THE CORPSE-RAT KING IS RUGGED, MUSCULAR
FANTASY, WITH WIT AND STYLE TO BURN."
Karen Miller, author of The Innocent Mage